Stephen's Second Chance: Part II

The Chronicles of Fate Book 4
MM Alpha/Omega Mpreg

Stephen's Second Chance:
Part II

Lucas Lamont

Published By: 4 Horsemen Publications, Inc.

4 Horsemen Publications, Inc.
PO Box 417
Sylva, NC 28779
4horsemenpublications.com
info@4horsemenpublications.com

Typesetting by Autumn Skye
Edited by Tilda M. Cooke

Library of Congress Control Number: 2025936346

Paperback ISBN-13: 979-8-8232-0872-7
Hardcover ISBN-13: 979-8-8232-0873-4
Audiobook ISBN-13: 979-8-8232-0875-8
Ebook ISBN-13: 979-8-8232-0874-1

DEDICATIONS:

This book is dedicated to any artist who finds themselves stuck at the crossroads and needs to decide whether life needs to change or stay the same. Don't give up on your dream, and stay true to who you are. Your story, in whatever medium you choose, is good enough. The world without art is black and white. Let your color shine through and make this a better place.

I especially want to dedicate and say thanks to the following:

> To "J" – for staying by my side during my darkest hour and believing there was still light in this world—even when I couldn't believe it myself.

> To "A" – for giving me time to be a better person so I could show you the best part of me.

> To "M&D" – for unconditional love and always supporting me as your son.

> To "H" – for being the rock I need and changing my life in a way no one else has.

To "M" – for changing my life forever and finding an eternal place in my heart.

To "E&V" – for advocating me, celebrating me, and supporting me in this amazing venture.

To "JMP" – for continuing your dedication and support which has not gone unnoticed or unappreciated.

To "B" – for your patience in putting up with my insanity.

TABLE OF CONTENTS

If you or someone you know is in crisis,
call or text the Suicide & Crisis Lifeline at 988

CAST OF CHARACTERS

Characters	Classification	Age
Robert Daventry (Sur)	Alpha—Type 2	51
Nathan Daventry (Veo)	Omega—Type 3	50
Alexander Daventry	Omega—Type 3	28
Jin Daventry	Alpha—Type 4	24
Kane Matheson (Sur)	Alpha—Type 3	60
Marlon Matheson (Veo)	Omega—Type 3	52
Stephen Matheson	Alpha—Type 4	29
Warren Matheson	Omega—Type 3	D. 16
Carey Hart	Omega—Type 4	27
Daniel Harvey	Omega—Type 2	25
Sean Crenshaw	Alpha—Type 4	32
Eric Dayes	Alpha—Type 3	36

Characters	Classification	Age
Raymond "Rat" Taylor	Beta	37
Bruce Dawson	Beta	40
James Dawson	Beta	38
Dr. Jacob Tyler Erricson	Alpha—Type 5	43
Roman Erricson	Alpha – Type 6	22
Dr. Dustin Cavenbelle	Alpha—Type 4	38
Matthew James Whitmore	Alpha—Type 5	37
Nicholas Hamilton	Alpha – Type 4	46

GLOSSARY

Pre-Wolf Era – the previous existence of humans evolved from primates and also the only existence of the human female gender

Wolf Era – current time, existence of male humans evolved from *Canis lupus* (wolves)

Rank – the biological make-up of a wolf-descendant: Alpha – Beta – Omega

Blood-Type – a categorial gene system to determine purity of the strongest genes ranked 1-5 in Alphas and Omegas

The 6th Blood-Type – an evolutionary anomaly in top tier Type 5 Alphas

Pup – a wolf-descendent child from birth to age 9

Adolescent – a wolf-descendent child from age 10 – 15

Natural Adult – a wolf-descendent man from ages 16 and older

Legal Adult – a male of age 18 and older

Sur – formal title given to an Alpha father

Veo – formal title given to an Omega father

Post Education – beginning of adult and specialized education of 4 Levels in two-year cycles beginning at age 16

Contract – legal requirement to form an official relationship bond including commitment, evaluation of assets, reproduction, and authority

Fated Mate – a highly sought out bond indicated by primal pheromones to connect with one specific mate or "Fate" for care, love, and reproductive purposes

Heat – a 4-month cycle for Omegas at peak fertility where the womb drops for insemination

CHAPTER 01:

EDUCATING THE YOUTH OF THE FUTURE

"And this here, wolf-descendants, is the crown jewel of Tauris Medical Center: our new state-of-the-art laboratory." Dr. Jacob Erricson beamed with pride as he pushed open the large door like he was granting passage into Wolf-God's eternal realm. The vocal response from his captivated audience did everything to affirm the bold comparison.

Every floor tile, metal fixture, counterspace, and piece of medical equipment radiated light like a pure, unblemished diamond sitting under a flawless glass enclosure. Visitors young and old gawked at the grandiose windows which allowed sunbeams to glisten and reflect off beakers, tubes, pipettes, state-of-the-art blood accessioning equipment, and of course, the latest and highest quality computers anyone could hope for. This was to say nothing of what appeared to be an incomparable staff who not only looked the parts of intelligence and success but also acted like it. Tall, educated, statuesque men who wore bright white lab coats effortlessly traveled from place to place, exuding confidence in every completed objective. Now and then, the distinguished employees made eye contact with the tour group and greeted them with respect and gratitude for their rapt interest and support.

One particular employee caught the eye of a petite Beta with ethereal light skin and auburn hair. Taking the risk no one else would notice since he was in the back of the group, he winked at the lab technician and softly smirked when he received one in return.

"Wolf-God, Daniel, can we go anywhere without you hitting on some guy at every inconvenient opportunity?" Alexander whispered while standing next to his incorrigible friend.

The young Beta furrowed his brows and returned a demure glare. "I don't do that all the time," he protested. Daniel saw the employee go to a different section of the lab altogether, but not before he looked back and gave one more flirtatious gesture confirming his interest. The 25-year-old redhead bit his lower lip with intrigue but once again saw his best friend judge his antics. "And what do you mean 'inconvenient'? What makes this place so special that a harmless look bothers you so much?"

As they pressed forward through the large lab, Alexander intentionally kept a generous distance between himself and Daniel to the rest of the tour group so the conversation wouldn't bother those taking in every proud word of the doctor's speech. "I was invited here by Jake as a very kind gesture. There's no reason, other than he's a gracious patron of mine, that he should have let an Omega bartender come in to get a view of this ... remarkable lab. Man, have you ever seen a place like this?!"

Daniel shook his head too, equally overwhelmed. "No, I haven't. It's a really cool place." He switched topics. "And don't you mean, 'Omega bartender and *owner*'?" he corrected.

"Yes..." Alexander replied cautiously, observing anyone for the stare back, affirming they were being inconsiderate to the entire group.

"What was that for?" Daniel inquired.

"What?" Alexander innocently gave back.

"Your tone makes it sound like you're ashamed of your profession."

The Omega tightened his lips but held his patience. "No... not 'ashamed.' It's just... look at these people. Most of them would never even go into South Street Tavern. Hell, most probably don't even know an Omega in this town owns a bar."

Daniel quietly scanned the back of the group and took note of the other guests for the first time since arriving. In the beginning of the tour, he didn't even invoke the attention span to observe the other members, especially to compare visual dispositions. But with Alexander pointing it out, he now realized most of the other tour members were way above any status he or Stephen could even fathom belonging to. Logistical thoughts of benefactors or doctors from other prestigious hospitals filled his mind as he peered at men with flawless haircuts, unblemished suits, and sharp leather shoes. Many were even wearing name tags which were dwarfed by the excessively large tour cards dangling from their necks on lanyards—Alexander and Daniel were no exception.

Then, the Beta looked down at his own attire: sneakers which were new last year, dark blue jeans, and a polo t-shirt. Now he finally understood why Alexander pushed for him to wear something more formal compared to his "everyday clothes" as the Omega aptly put it. But even his friend's efforts of a nicer pair of jeans and button-down shirt failed to stand up to the attire of the rest. Perhaps that's why he kept insisting they stay in the back of the tour group in the first place. "Okay... point taken. But you can't tell me this would be the worst room of critics you ever encountered when it came to your choice of business."

"No... I can't say that." Alexander sighed. A shimmer off a metal lab ruler caught his eye and flashed an unsightly memory in his mind way too fresh to be suppressed at this moment: a sharp knife slicing into his employee's arm. Daniel noticed the change immediately.

"What's wrong?"

Alexander shrugged. "Just thinking about Stephen is all."

"Ohhhh?" Daniel grinned.

"Not like that!" Alexander shook his head. "It's been hard not having him at the bar."

"Weren't you the one who told him not to come in?"

"Half of the guy's arm is held together by stitches and a medical wrap. Yes, I told him to stay away. No one wants a drink made by a person who accidentally gets their stitch pulled or dips their week-old bandage in their shot glass. Besides, I was there when the nurse read his discharge instructions. The doctor said no strenuous activity for up to two weeks due to how close the damage was to a nerve. That basically kills all his barback tasks, and if he can't make a drink, there's no point in him being there."

"Yikes," Daniel commented. "How's he taking your Alpha-like disposition?"

The Omega swayed his head. "I kept in contact with him regularly the first few days, calling him to make sure he was all right. The conversations were fine at the time. But as the days passed, he kept bringing up more and more about how he says he's ready to come back. And every time I told him he couldn't, the more frustrated he was with me."

"How bad is it now?"

"Between the two of us?" Daniel nodded. "We're down to sending one text a day—if that's any indication."

"That's still a lot, if you ask me."

Alexander grew defensive. "Um. Why?"

"Well... I mean..." Daniel paused, wondering if he should even bring the subject up, "there's still the fact he thinks you're his Fated Mate and the run-in he had with Sean before the whole stabbing incident."

It was difficult for Alexander not to visually react. The atmosphere here wasn't the place to be so blatant, but it was also difficult to ignore Daniel's point. However, he wasn't going to be deterred from his own opinion. "Despite the run-in with Stephen, Sean has completely made it a non-issue." The Omega kept a walking pace, now refusing to make eye contact with his friend and trying to give it back to Jake, who was beginning to turn the group back toward the front of the lab. The doctor continued:

"Every day, we get anywhere from two hundred to five hundred samples which need to be collected, labeled, catalogued, separated, analyzed, and reported. On average, fifty percent of those samples come from newborn pups who need their Blood Type identified and approved for their government IDs. And, of course, if you can trace back the six-month period to a holiday or city-wide power blackout, that percentage is much higher," Jake joked. Several patrons were entertained by the comment as he continued.

Daniel used the moment to sneak back in and continue their private conversation. "What? Sean has just let the whole thing about Stephen go?"

"That's the way I'm seeing it. And it's good; I'm hoping it helps create that positive reputation I want my bar to have."

"It's weird."

"Thanks, friend," Alexander criticized.

"If *my* boyfriend of two years started having regular conversations with another guy who claimed he was their Fated Mate, I'd lose my sh—" Alexander's firm hand to Daniel's chest reminded the Beta that his voice was way too loud. He readjusted himself and waited for the next opportunity to come up to finish his train of thought. "You know what I'm saying."

"I do," the Omega confessed. "But I'm also happy to report *that* is also a non-issue."

"The whole 'Stephen says you're his Fated Mate' thing?" Daniel clarified.

"Mmhm."

"How did that happen?"

Alexander put both hands behind his body and linked them as he continued to press on, satisfied with the new turn of events on the subject. "He and I talked in the ER the night he was admitted, and we came to the understanding the subject wouldn't be brought up anymore. He acknowledges my feelings on the whole 'Fate' thing are completely different than his, and they won't change. In addition, he also sees how it affects the professional relationship we have at work, and I'm not about to let that get in the way of anything right now. As long as it stays that way, I don't think we're going to have a problem going forward from now on."

Daniel didn't like the positive attitude his friend had on Stephen or their ambivalent and mysterious connection. The uncomfortable feeling reminded him of another thought. "Hey... was something going on with you that night at the bar when Stephen was stabbed? I heard you were completely out of it to the point where everyone was worried."

Alexander groaned. "Does James tell you everything now, or am I just special?"

Daniel blushed. "What? Why is that a big deal?"

"I'm not sure I like how much time you are spending at Bruce and James's place. I'm not enthusiastic about my best friend shacking up with my employees," the Omega confessed.

"That's 'employee,' *not* 'employees.' Get it right!" Daniel barked.

Alexander laughed. "Wolf-God, I hope so. I don't know what I'd think if you were involved with *both* of them."

"They're brothers!"

"I know that!" the Omega teased.

The Omega scrunched his face. "Ew. Who does it with two brothers?!"

"No one I know." Then, the idea hit Alexander. "Wait... you and James are..." His eyes widened.

Daniel's face turned redder than it was before. "What do you think we do? Play video games all night?"

"You are unbelievable."

The whole group came to a halt as Jake stopped at the front of lab, standing next to an older wolf-descendent who had already captivated his audience without saying one word. All who knew of the Tauris Medical Center's lab knew of the famous doctor, scientist, pioneer, and advocate. This was the moment everyone in the tour group waited for and everyone knew it. "And now, my distinguished guests, I'd like to pass it off to a man who needs no introduction. He is the reason we are standing in this room today; he is the reason we have become the number one city in medical research, and he is the number one reason why we have been able to advance as the unique human species we are. The legend himself: Dr. Paul Birowack."

A delicate yet passionate applause radiated throughout the immaculate lab. All guests and all employees exuded gratitude to the scientist who helped create the modern history of survival by unlocking the capabilities wolf-descendants had—to make sure they didn't meet the tragic extinction which once fell upon primate-descendants years ago. After several seconds, the enthusiasm died to a whisper, waiting on his every whim.

"Thank you, Dr. Erricson, for that marvelous introduction. Please join me in thanking Dr. Erricson for his tour." Another applause rang out in appreciation. "I only wish I had time to partake in these efforts, but as I hope Dr. Erricson impressed upon you, we are a very busy research department in addition to a general identification lab. And, on top of that, I admit he is much better at these than I could ever be. After all, you never want your honored guests to fall asleep in the space you are so proud of. So, I happily leave him in charge of this." The audience approved of the anecdote.

"Let us not forget about our third equal, Dr. Dustin Cavenbelle, who is very much active in policy and procedures. He really is the person who keeps us running at optimal performance every single day," Jake acknowledged.

"Was he not able to join us today?" Dr. Birowack inquired.

"He was originally supposed to be here today instead of me, but I asked to switch with him and sent him off to that conference in Gray City. I'm grateful as it has allowed me to see several familiar faces today." Jake scanned the crowd, acknowledging several acquaintances. Finally, in the back, he smiled at Alexander, who acknowledged him in return.

Dr. Birowack continued, "Ah. That explains it. Now, out of fear of repeating several topics Jake may have already mentioned, I'd just like to open the floor for any specific questions about the lab or services we provide. So, if you have any, please don't hesitate to ask. Mind you, we can't tell you everything, but we will sure try."

Several guests raised their hands as if they had been waiting for this moment for a year. He finally selected an individual who looked very posh in his three-piece suit. "Dr. Birowack, you mentioned being a very busy research lab as well? What research have you done or are you currently working on?" Alexander pinched the bridge of his nose. The question didn't fit the person asking—an obvious plant inside the tour group.

"Yes," Dr. Birowack answered, "we have explored many outcomes in Types mating with those who are gapped from their own—for example, a Type 3 with a Type 5 or a Type 2 with a Type 4. Common misconceptions are that the offspring will fall to an average between the two or favor the same rank of their birth parent. They believe a Type 2 Omega must end up producing another Type 2 if their pup is also Omega. In short, all of this is not true as genetics and DNA don't follow rules of absolutes, and many variables can change any or all outcomes."

Another hand raised. "Have you ever done research on a Type 5 mating with a Type 1?"

Jake chuckled. "It may surprise you, but yes, we have, and more than once." The group responded with their own mixed reaction to the reveal. Although mating with an individual typed one or two levels different was common today, such a gap invoked more questions than answers. The most obvious was the rational consideration of the desirable traits a Type 5 possessed contrasted to the many undesirable traits of a Type 1.

A young doctor-to-be asked the next question. "Paul, I was told your department focused more on genetic anomalies—that your research was fixated on exploiting irregularities to see if they can be useful in society. What do you say to those who believe this is true?"

From the back, Alexander leaned into Daniel's ear. "Damn!" The petite Omega nodded in agreement.

The great Dr. Birowack, however, took the accusation in stride—obviously not his first encounter with controversy. "'Exploit'? Hmm. I don't see it like that at all. Wolf-God has created a world for us to explore and find. Discovering what these hidden secrets are with our own kind is a gift we do not take for granted, nor do we take advantage of it. Everyone was put on this earth for one reason only: to survive. If there are those in the world who have the capabilities to show what our full potential is and are voluntarily working with us, then I don't believe anything we do here at Tauris Medical Center falls within your predetermined notion of 'exploitation.'" Several members of the group clapped their hands and whistled at the seasoned words of wisdom. But the youthful and audacious physician wasn't deterred. He strained his voice above the crowd to make sure his follow-up was heard.

"What about your pet project on Alphas you deem worthy of the moniker 'Type 6'?"

Jake's fist squeezed around the neck of a pen near his side as he closely eyed the brat with disdain. "When you are addressing groundbreaking research which has changed the world as we know it for the better, please make sure you refer to him as 'Dr. Birowack,' especially when you are in the laboratory which was created on it."

"It's all right, Dr. Erricson," Dr. Birowack assured him. He eyed the unknown intern, who was half his age, finally showing some cracks in confidence as he walked toward him, stroking his small gray beard. He took in his neutral scent—another Beta. The courage, or audacity, however one interpreted it, made sense to him now. Then, he cocked his head. "What's your name, son?"

"Desarae. Zayne Desarae, sir."

"You want to be a doctor, one day?" Dr. Birowack asked, already knowing the answer.

"Yes, sir," Zayne replied.

Jake broke his poise again. "That's 'doctor,' not 'sir.'"

The young Beta bowed his head, showing he was giving both Jake and Dr. Birowack their power back. It also read in the pheromone palate coming in subtle waves off his hot neck, which had begun showing small splotches of red streaking out from the tight fabric of his collar. "Yes, doctor."

"I admire you for speaking boldly. No one gets to the top by becoming a follower. It's a great skill to stand up and to stand out, but it is also a burden. My advice to you then is this: in addition to being bold, remember to speak plainly." Zayne began eyeing the floor, a mere fraction of the "Alpha persona" he had portrayed a minute ago. The response made Dr. Birowack think there was a lot more here than what he originally thought. "I don't feel you personally have any ill will toward me, to my colleague, to my department, or even to the rest of the tour group here. But someone in your life does—that I can tell." The lack of response told the masterful scientist he had proven his theory without it even being tested. "To every action in this world, there is a reaction. That is science, that is human nature, and that is fate. I cannot please every wolf-descendant on this earth with what I do or what I say, no matter how much research I have behind it or how many people agree with me. That's the Wolf-God-given right we all have: free will. I used mine to say that there are beings on this earth who possess abilities and powers even I don't understand yet. Some of them can be seen: physical stature and skill, intelligence, social dominance, and gene profile. Others we won't know until years to come: common preferred traits in physical and mental dispositions, procreation patterns in ranks along with types, and finally, pup mortality rate and life expectancy." He eyed Zayne to make sure he was looking at him now: man-to-man. "Some people believe Wolf-God and science are separate or that the two hang in a delicate balance of war and peace. I choose to believe Wolf-God himself created science so that we could understand our changing world and change along with it. We pray to Wolf-God for answers? He sends us messages in science we can see, touch, taste, smell, and hear. If others want to ignore that—then that's their right. I, myself? I will choose to follow that calling until the day I die."

With another subtle reaction from the crowd, Jake stepped in. "I concur. These attitudes that we are doing this for self-gratification or for the purpose of personal gain is wildly inaccurate."

"Isn't that difficult for you to say, Dr. Erricson, since your son Roman is a Type 6 himself?"

Several whispers went throughout the tour group and even spilled into the employees. Alexander noticed the vibe in the room get heavier instantly—including Daniel exchanging stares and winks with the lab tech from earlier. He shoulder-bumped him into paying attention once again.

Jake continued, "It's true: my son is a Type 6, and he does allow us to monitor his progress. With his cooperation, we can compare his data with the data of other Alphas who also share his identification."

Zayne crossed his arms. "So, what is it exactly you hope Type 6 Alphas can do that—let's say—Type 5 Alphas cannot? Or is there anything about this 'Type 6' identification others need to worry about?"

Alexander managed to catch Jake's attention only for a moment. Somewhere, deep behind his eyes, was the truth he sensed in Jake when he was discussing his son with Matthew on two different occasions. With his Omega's connection, he knew Jake was thinking of the same moments he was. Then, instantly, he saw Jake's expression erase its true self and revert back to the charismatic presenter.

The doctor cleared his throat and smiled. "I think that's all the questions we'll take for today. We'll finish up the tour here in the conference room where you are welcome to enjoy some refreshments. Once again, Dr. Birowack, Dr. Cavenbelle, and I thank you all for coming."

<hr>

"The place looks amazing, Jake," Alexander complimented as he and Daniel walked past the lobby on the main floor.

"It's everything we could have asked for. I'm fortunate to work here every day." The doctor beamed with pride.

"Did Matthew Whitmore really pay for *all* of this?" the Omega asked incredulously.

"I know it's hard to believe, but he donated so much to this project that it makes the person directly under him look like he barely pitched in."

Daniel's eyes grew wide as he struggled to keep up with the gait of the other two. "I can't even fathom what that even looks like."

"Me neither," Alexander confessed.

"That's why it's important we count our blessings for what we have in our life and shouldn't take them for granted."

The Omega couldn't believe it; for the second time today, he was thinking about Stephen. Jake's words were ice cold as he wondered if he truly appreciated the Alpha for being there. What impression had he left? He wasn't sure. "Yeah. I suppose we do."

Daniel jumped in, pivoting the conversation completely. "Do your Q&A sessions afterward usually go like that?"

Jake laughed. "Dr. Birowack and I have run into similar situations before. This time was different, however."

"How so?" Alexander furrowed his brow.

"Usually when we receive harsh criticism, we have an idea ahead of time that it's coming. Often, it's another doctor we already know from a competing research center or a visiting news reporter looking for sensationalism or a sound bite. I've never seen it come from an unknown kid before."

"Keeps life interesting, right?!" Daniel slid his tongue out to the side.

"Knock it off!" Alexander whispered back.

"No worries, Alex. Like I said, it wasn't the first, and it won't be the last."

The Omega looked at his phone and sighed. "Thank you for inviting us here. It was breathtaking, and I'm so glad I got the opportunity to meet your boss. He's a very accomplished and eloquent specimen of a man."

"Talking like a scientist now, are ya?" Daniel teased.

"Uh-oh." Alexander laughed.

"You two better get out of here before I make recruits out of you yet."

"Sounds like good advice. Hope to see you soon at the bar!"

"Will do!" Jake waved them off as he returned to the masses waiting for him upstairs.

Right outside the city limits of Tauris City, a home sat one hundred yards off the county road. Broken gravel trailed the long drive up to the two-story house looking worse for wear than it did a decade ago. Marlon Matheson sat at the table, finishing up bills for the month in the quiet kitchen he'd been used to for ten years. Well, *almost* quiet. Across from him, his 29-year-old son Stephen sat experimenting with his pain threshold with his bandages. The occasional grunts eventually made the Omega look up and watch him foolishly play around on his arm, as if he was seeking out landmines. Every so often, he'd find one, and Marlon would wince as he watched his grown pup's pained expression. Finally, after one good hit, he couldn't bear to watch his son do it anymore.

"Why are you doing that?"

Stephen gritted his teeth as he pressed forward. "I'm trying to figure out what I can handle."

"I see that. My question still stands: Why?"

"I need to figure out what I'm going to be able to do when I go back to the bar."

"You still have another week before that happens." Stephen refused to look at his Veo, still scratching at the perimeter of his wound. "Right?" Marlon stressed. "Stephen? Stephen!"

"What?!"

Now Marlon understood. "When have you decided to go back?"

The Alpha hesitated and then spoke softly. "Today." His father threw his pen onto the table in disapproval. "Come on. Staying here has been torture." Based upon the expression, Stephen realized it was a blatant insult. "Not because of you and Sur!" Marlon twitched his lips, not believing the statement. "I swear! It's not the two of you. It's..." He sighed. "Having the bar gave me something to look forward to. I had a job, it was steady, and I was successful at it. For the first time in a long time, I felt like people were getting to know the 'Stephen' I wanted to be versus the 'Stephen' I was."

"And then, there was Alexander," Marlon boldly stated.

The Alpha stared at the table... unsure of how to feel about the tender topic in the moment. "Yeah... it will always be him," he answered deflated.

His Omega father softened his eyes and reached his hand out, remembering what his son last told him about what transpired between the two. "How are you feeling about that?" Stephen shrugged. "You need to figure that out before you go."

"I know."

"Then, are you sure today is the day you want to do this?"

"Do you really think another week is going to magically make me feel any different?"

Marlon relented. "I suppose not. But they say time heals all wounds." After an unwanted reminder of his own loss came through, he readjusted his position. "Or... I guess it at least dulls the pain. 'Heals' might be pushing it."

Stephen looked at his Veo, finally feeling like he could connect with empathy. "I'm right there with you on that one."

The Omega paused before asking the difficult question. "Do you want to talk about it?"

His son fiddled with his bandages once again, lightly gliding the pads of his fingers over the most sensitive areas, imagining that if his Fate was doing it, it would be the most soothing sensation he'd felt in over ten years. But that wasn't a comment he'd ever say out loud. He could barely talk about what *needed* to be said. "Do you... do you think there are others out there?"

"Others like what?"

Stephen gulped. "That have Fates where it ... doesn't work?"

Marlon took off his reading glasses, pondering the thought. "I've *heard* of Fates not working out... but... I don't know any personally. Maybe your Sur has seen it while on the force. In all the domestic calls he's intercepted, I have to believe a Fated couple has been an incident or two."

The Alpha knew what his Omega father was trying to encourage, but right now, he didn't want a life lesson—he just wanted to vent. "I'm getting flashbacks of sitting in therapy sessions. This is totally something Dr. Forrester would talk about." He rubbed his eyes, hoping it would erase the current mindset.

"What would he say?"

Stephen smirked. "He'd ask me, 'What would happen if you accepted that you and Alexander would never be together?'"

Marlon boldly went there. "And?"

The Alpha tightened his lips as he felt his stomach knot. "I don't think I can put my mind in that scenario yet." All at once, his entire body tensed from his neck down to his feet. Even his hand muscles involuntarily went rock solid. Whatever emotional pain was there, it took a back seat to the physical pain once again, as he felt skin which didn't want to stretch in his arm begin to pull. He shut his eyes, forced both arms on the table, and tried to focus his mind elsewhere, another tactic he learned in lockup.

His Omega father saw the whole episode in front of his own eyes and quickly placed both of his hands into Stephen's. "Breathe… breathe…" he soothed. He heard his son grunt in pain and felt his leg bounce up and down under the table as he gritted his teeth. "You're okay… just breathe."

Finally, as if coming up for air for the first time in minutes, Stephen gasped and huffed out of relief, his body melting into the chair. The moment passed. "Thanks." In the deep recesses of his mind, he swore he heard his long-lost brother's voice in his ear whisper back: *You're welcome.* The phenomenon made his head instantly jerk toward the hallway, halfway expecting Warren to actually be there. But instead, his Sur stood there, tall and completely unaware of the previous moment.

"What's going on?" Kane inquired.

Shaking his head ever so slightly, Stephen readjusted himself back to reality and back to masculinity. "Nothing."

Marlon bowed his head, hurt that old relationships still held its grip on his family and that his son still felt the need to hide his vulnerability from his Alpha father. "Just talking about Stephen going back to work."

Kane pulled up and chair and joined his family at the table. "Did you pick a return date?"

Stephen quickly glanced at his Veo. "You could say that." He began tapping his fingers … waiting. His Sur didn't disappoint.

"You're going back today, aren't you?" he assumed, disapproval in his tone.

"Yes, Sur, I am."

"Any point in trying to convince you otherwise?"

"No, Sur, there is not."

Kane nodded. "Fair enough." He analyzed his son up and down. The pheromone palate was mixed—nothing pleasing, to say the least. Physically, at least, he looked strong. "How's your arm?"

Stephen tried his best to save face. "It's good... I'd say 90%." Out of the corner of his eye, he could see Marlon begging to differ; he ignored him.

"You want me to give you a ride in later?" Kane asked.

"No, I'll take Crusher in." The thought of riding on his motorcycle put a smile on his face.

The old Alpha furrowed his brows. "You need your license for that."

An uneasy silence overwhelmed the room. Stephen answered, "I got it a few weeks ago, Dad."

"When?!"

Stephen once again found himself looking at his Veo, completely helpless. Very quickly, he now understood, having "episodes" in this family was genetic. "Before I even found the job at South Street? Veo took me to the DMV."

"Remember, Kane?" Marlon encouraged.

Kane tugged on his suspenders. His eyes froze for several uncomfortable seconds and then darted several times before coming up with. "Ah. Yes." Marlon drew up a contrived look of satisfaction. Stephen squinted his eyes. "Do me a favor—when you come home, try not to park that bike close to the truck. It's bad enough when I try to get it out. I can only imagine how your Veo or your brother handle it."

It was too much. Stephen couldn't handle all the memories running through his mind. And he certainly couldn't handle his father talking about his deceased brother as if he was still here on this earth. He jolted up and began walking down the hallway. He felt his Veo coming down after him as Kane innocently shouted down the hallway, "Something I said?"

"Stephen..." Marlon pleaded.

Reluctantly, the Alpha stopped and turned around. "You're going to get him help at some point, right?!" he criticized.

His Veo crossed his arms. "*You* want to try having that conversation?"

Of course, Stephen thought. No matter how much of his Sur faded, whenever criticized, that's when he'd always be the most cognitive. At some point, he'd ask his Veo just how many times he had that specific conversation; however, now wasn't an option. "Not today." Marlon's shoulders fell. "I'm going to go lay down. Then I'm taking a shower before I go." His Omega father silently nodded. "Are you okay?"

Marlon huffed. "Aren't we all?"

Stephen didn't know how to respond. His foot glided across the carpeted hallway, before he pivoted, returning to the solace of the guest bedroom.

The Alpha crawled onto the bed. Without a doubt, this was the first time since coming home from Brooks Haven Penitentiary that the entire room felt awkward, uninviting, like, dare he think, a prison. He grunted as he thrust his body left and then right, trying to find a position to soothe him.

Frustrated, he snatched his pillow and molded it into a position which allowed him to cradle his head. And then, as if done by some unseen entity, his mind wandered elsewhere...

"*Why won't you tell me? Why won't you tell me anything?*" Warren pouted.

"*I already told you.*" Stephen sighed. "*I'm not your brother.*"

Warren shook his head. His hazel eyes stung, but now was not the time to show any weakness; he knew his older Alpha brother hated that. Like he had done countless times before, he sucked it up with bravado. He hoped he was far enough away so Stephen couldn't scent the hurt. "That worked on me when I was like ten. Can you give me a little credit that since I'm old enough to drive a car, I've gotten wiser since then?"

The Alpha exhaled a cloud of smoke from the final drag of his cigarette and then flicked it into the yard—the remnants smoldering in a lush patch of grass. "Could have fooled me."

The younger Omega felt himself bottling it all up inside. Fading into the background once again, he reached out and put the spotlight on his brother. "What's wrong?"

Stephen glanced at Warren only for a second. "Nothing's wrong. Just quit being annoying." Quickly, he walked around the Omega and back to the front of the garage, where Crusher was set up to be washed. All that was left now was the final touch of polish.

"You only go down this 'I'm not your brother' road when you're having a problem. So, what is it?"

"Hand me that rag." Stephen pointed. As he saw which one Warren attempted at, he scowled. "Not that one! The clean one!" Warren quickly corrected himself and handed him the new one which was still folded. "Idiot," he mumbled as he hunched down to his knees. Gingerly, he squeezed a few drops of polish onto the rag and gently massaged it into the chrome like it was his lover, begging him to caress him. Each swipe soothed him in return. But the moment was short-lived as he still felt his brother's eyes staring at him full of concern. "The brother you once knew is gone, Warren. I suggest you get used to it."

"Oh yeah?" Warren snorted as he recalled several conversations like this before. "What happened this time?"

Stephen's gaze never left his bike as he continued the ominous conversation. "He died this past spring. Consider the man before you brand new and a stranger." He twisted his hips, shoes grinding against the gravel as he held out his hands open to show a warm welcome.

"Nice to meet you, 'Steve.'" he emphasized.

"Don't go there," the Alpha crooned in a warning. Then he smiled as he saw Crusher in a state of perfection.

The young Omega squirmed as he watched his brother meticulously take care of the only thing he loved in the world: his bike. "This doesn't have anything to do with that new 'friend' you hang out with all the time now, does it?"

"What are you talking about?" the Alpha denied.

"You know <u>exactly</u> who I'm talking about. That guy with the little braid going down his back—the one Sur would kill he ever found out? What's his name? 'Rat'?"

Stephen threw down his rag and stood up. Then, he marched over to his naïve brother and pointed his finger straight between the eyes. "You ever tell Sur about him, and you will show up to the next futbol game in crutches! I don't think your team wants their goalie hobbling to block a ball, so I suggest you make the right decision."

"Lay off me!" Warren protested.

"I'm warning you!" Stephen threatened.

"Okay, okay!" the Omega relented. His fingertips flashed with frustration as he pulled at the hem line of his golden t-shirt and then through the sun-kissed blond strands of hair barely staying out of his eyes. "That wasn't the point of why I brought it up. You don't have to get so defensive. I'm just worried is all."

The Alpha removed the bite from his words and lowered his hand. Sensing his brother's submissive pheromones, he realized Warren was being honest in his inquiry. He <u>was</u> concerned. Instead of apologizing, however, he stoically walked back to his bike and zeroed in on his favorite part: the emblem.

A Gunnolf bike, despite its innocent canine origins in name, the company rebranded themselves as the dark alternative to the mainstream rider. Their success since had been based off a "cool cult" status which came with a whole new design and logo. Gone was the wolf with the North Star in the distance. Now, a flaming skull showed the tyranny and rebellious nature of its clientele. Stephen was all too happy to become a part of it. But even his bike was demure compared to the latest trends. Thus, his emblem was small and tame compared to what was available now. Still, he tenderly polished it as if it was the latest design.

"Next week, I'm gonna go in and get this replaced with a Gunnolf Skull that Crusher is worthy of. She'd looking fucking amazing with it on."

"How can you afford that? You don't have your job anymore," Warren interrogated.

The Alpha scratched his throat. "You're right."

"I know I'm right," Warren reaffirmed.

"No, not that. About the 'something.'" The Omega cocked his head and listened intently. "I've just come to the realization that everything here is just a waste of my time. My goal is to get on my bike and get out of Tauris … for good."

Warren couldn't believe his ears. "You're … leaving?!"

"Hell yes, I'm leaving!"

"You think that's smart, bro?"

"Don't patronize me! You're lucky I'm even telling you this." The Omega stood there, emotionless. Stephen reflected on his harsh outburst. Then he sighed. "Sorry. Didn't mean to be like that." Warren gestured with his head that he received his message. "You want my advice? Get out and save yourself."

"Why?" Warren asked in a hushed tone, completely lost.

"There's a world outside of the stupid city, and it's gotta be better than our doorstep."

"You say that now, but what are you going to say when you find your way back home?"

Stephen scoffed. "That's never going to happen."

"What about school?"

"I'm done with Level 2 in school now. I'm not going beyond that. You don't need an education in the real world after Level 2 anyway. It's a good enough time to exit compared to any."

"What does that have to do with leaving Tauris City?"

Stephen took a beat to ponder the question. "Nothing actually."

"Then why are you leaving? The real reason this time."

"Do I really need to explain that to you?"

"STEPHEN!" a voice rang out from the house. It made Stephen growl while Warren jumped nearly a foot into the air.

"Right on cue," Stephen muttered.

Kane burst through the door, ignoring Warren completely. His large feet pummeled the gravel of the driveway until he was mere inches away from his ungrateful excuse for a son. "What the hell am I hearing about you tagging the restaurant?!"

Stephen grinned. "I don't know what you're talking about."

Kane placed his hands on his hips and shook his head. "The hell you don't."

"Oh yeah? What? Did you see something? Is there any proof? Any witnesses?" he sassed. Kane stood there silently. "That's what I thought. Nothing but cowards pointing fingers at me because it's convenient."

"'Convenient' or rightfully placed?" Kane challenged.

The young Alpha pulled out his pack of cigarettes, delicately selected one, reached for his Gunnolf lighter, and enjoyed the familiar taste of burning tobacco once again. "Like I said: if you've got proof, then let's talk. If not, quit wasting my time." Stephen twitched his head toward his brother and then threw the polishing rag at him. Despite not being prepared, Warren still caught it. "Nice catch."

"Where are you going?!" Kane growled.

"Out." Stephen placed his favorite pair of black sunglasses over his eyes and then grabbed his keys from his jacket pocket, heading back toward his bike. But his Sur stepped right in front of it.

"We need to talk."

"Later, pops." The young Alpha waved off.

"No, not later. Now!" Kane pulled Stephen's sunglasses right off his face, pressed them into his chest, and then pointed his muscled finger into his sternum. "You listen here, you disrespectful little—"

Stephen's wolf snarled as he used both arms to push back on his Alpha father's shoulders, ignoring his sunglasses falling to the gravel drive below and his foot coming down on them as he pursued the old man. "Get your hands off me."

Kane's blood boiled as he felt all his muscles tense to solid stone. "I'm gonna teach you—"

"VEO!" Warren called to the house.

Like lightning, the boys' Omega father came rushing out, seeing the all too familiar scene of both his Alphas getting ready to come to blows once again. He slammed his hand into the latch of swing door and ran to his mate and his son. "Hey, hey, hey! Get a grip on yourselves, both of you!" he yelled in his best dominating voice.

"Your son is out of control, Marlon, and I'm sick of it! If this doesn't end now, it's only going to get worse!" Kane argued.

"Worse is where you find out where I'm gonna shove this fist! Right in your—"

"ENOUGH!" Marlon howled. He eyed his mate, the Alpha's dark eyes searing red. "Back up, Kane!" Every ounce of the Omega's phero-mones spewed out to hopefully once again invoke the primal connection he needed to get Kane to surrender his domination. With Wolf-God's help, the father and officer of the law finally retracted and took a moment to concentrate his gaze and focus elsewhere. After Marlon sighed, he faced the other half of the problem. "Stephen, what has gotten into you lately?"

"What are you babbling about?" the young Alpha played off.

"You are just going around and picking fights with anyone who is willing to even look at you, and we've all had it!"

"Yeah, well, the feeling's mutual."

Kane gritted his teeth. "You respect your Veo! As long as you live under this roof, things are going to change around here, and it starts today!"

"Kane!" Marlon's own frustration grew as his mate was beginning to unravel once more.

"I'm not going to be here! I'm not going to be your *problem*, your *problem*, or your *problem* anymore!" The young Alpha pointed to each of his family members—he ended with Kane, emphasizing a hard stare.

"Just where do you plan on living?!" Marlon asked incredulously.

Stephen hiked his shoulders to readjust his attitude and his jacket. "Don't worry. No place any of you will find me. I won't be your 'screw up' that you need to keep tabs on. Doesn't that just excite you?" he crooned sarcastically.

"Whatever your plan is, running away on that damn bike won't make a difference, son," Kane insisted. "They have laws, rules, and cops everywhere else in this world. Why don't you do yourself a favor and straighten up before you learn it the hard way?"

Stephen slowly shook his head and then exhaled deeply. He finally saw his sunglasses, broken into pieces and tattered with rock dust. After picking the pieces up, he pointed to his brother. "This is what I'm talking about." Warren's lips twitched as he saw his brother's hopeless expression. "What a waste." He tossed the remnants in the grass and finally boarded his bike.

Kane, seeing that nothing even remotely got to his son, threw his hands up, gestured his son off, and trekked back into the house, the door slamming behind him.

Marlon crossed his arms, equally giving up on the lecture. "Did you do it?" he asked softly. "Did you vandalize the restaurant?"

Once again, the young Alpha smiled. "Of course, I did it. The fuckers wanna fire me? It's what they deserve."

The Omega's arms fell. "I thought you said you quit?!"

"You say tomato..." he quipped.

Marlon bit his lip. "You're not really thinking of moving out, are you?"

"Let's just say... I have options."

"Where are you going now?"

"I'll be back. I just need to pick something up first. Then, here to start packin.'" For the first time since the argument, Stephen's face faltered, and his pheromones gave off a bitterness: a sign of apprehension and doubt. He hoped his Veo didn't notice it, but he did, like all Omega fathers would.

"Are you in some sort of trouble, Stephen?" Marlon asked, full of hurt.

"What makes you ask that?"

"You're changing, babe. I noticed it, your father noticed it, and Warren noticed it. We're worried."

Stephen gave one quick glance at his younger Omega brother who refused to look him in the eye. Then, he went back to his Veo. A wall instantly went back up, and every genuine interest in the conversation faded away. Stephen once again located his key and pushed it into chamber before soullessly staring back at his Omega father. "Aren't we all?"

A hard thrust of his leg and push on the throttle started Crusher up in a second. He wheeled it back before turning it around and beginning his descent down the driveway, only having one goal in mind: to find the last bit of relief he needed before coming back and putting an end to the current chapter of his life as he knew it. Before his muffler became deafening, he heard his Omega father's cries to him.

"Stephen! ... Stephen!"

"Stephen!" The Alpha jolted awake. His eyes examined the bed and surroundings, and it took him a minute to remember where he was. Marlon stood over him, face concerned and soft. "You were moaning and talking in your sleep. Bad dream?"

Stephen rubbed his eyes and exhaled a light yawn, then he nodded. "Yeah."

"What was it?" his Veo inquired with concern.

The Alpha's heart pounded like it was in the middle of a race. But his mind was shot, unprepared to deal with the memories of the past. He shook his head. "I think I'll deal with this one on my own."

Remembering the last conversation he had with his son, Marlon didn't press the issue further. Instead, he put his hands on his hips and protected his emotions. "You said you were going in today, so I figured you didn't want to sleep too long."

Stephen stretched his long body out on the bed and then looked toward the new alarm clock which magically showed up one day right next to his prized cast-iron motorcycle on the bedside table. "Shit," he mumbled in frustration.

"Going to be late?"

The Alpha thought for a moment. "I guess—technically? I don't know how you can be late for a job your boss doesn't want you there for. He's going to take one look at these bandages and want to throw me into a vat of disinfectant." Stephen began to worry as he considered the unavoidable logic. He cursed himself for not thinking about this earlier and searched his mind on a last-minute trip to the drug store. Then he heard his Veo hum to himself in amusement. "What's so funny?"

"What is it about Alpha wolves who feel that licking their own wounds is going to heal everything?"

Stephen scratched the stubble on his neck. "The physical ones or the emotional ones?"

"Both."

"Just in our nature, I guess." He shrugged back.

"Right." Just out of view from Stephen, at the foot of the bed, Marlon pulled up a medium-sized paper bag.

The Alpha narrowed his views. "What's that?"

"I call it 'the nature of an *Omega.*' While you were asleep, I went in and got you some new bandages, ones that will work better for you when you're at the bar. Take your shower, clean off your arm, and then I'll help you with this."

With his dream still front and center, a wave of guilt washed over Stephen. He only imagined the broken state he left his family in that particular morning. And yet, he never imagined that being the last time they *were* all a family. Then, like a cruel joke, the Alpha remembered seeing Marlon's face the first time he saw Alexander unconscious on Stephen's bed. Considering that, he had a pretty good indication of what his Veo looked like after he sped out of the driveway earlier that same day. "What did I do to deserve you as my parent?"

"You're my son. You didn't have to do anything else."

Stephen smirked. "What? I come from your stomach and just get a free pass?"

Marlon shook his head. "You came from my heart."

"I'm adopted?" the Alpha joked.

"Goofball. Go. Hurry up."

Hot water shimmered onto Stephen's head. Droplets turned into rivers as they glided into curves and rivulets around his entire taut body. Billowing steam hugged his skin wherever it could which made the bandage on his arm even more noticeable. Slowly, he unfastened the metal clips and then pulled the tape back which released the snug pressure he had been used to for days. His tight skin instantly relaxed where it could, but beneath layers of medical wrap, he could feel where a foreign entity forced his arm together in the most unnatural way.

As if unwrapping a gift, he felt the anticipation send nerves to his stomach, and he felt his heart pound. Tingling sensations spiked where his injury anticipated sensing outside air and moisture like a traveler lost in a hot desert without water. Finally, Stephen was down to the gauze which covered the several stitches. The hair on his arms yelped as they were pulled from their follicles with each tug on the sticky tape which refused to let go. He grunted until finally his arm became one with his naked body. Protruding from the natural form was an elevated line several inches long, easily spotted by a delicate weave of thread.

The Alpha bit his lip as he carefully ran his other hand across the top of his arm. His body overpowered his brain and told him the feeling was strange like doing it for the first time. It was sensitive and even tickled in some areas. He tried pulling his arm into the water, but the pressure of it stripped all the innocent sensations away and immediately sent off pain receptors. Without even having to think about it, he removed his arm from the pressurized water. "Ah! Fuck!" He exhaled several times. "Stupid!"

Rethinking his game plan, he grabbed the washcloth and soaked it generously under the shower head, then let the saturation fall onto his wound. The sensitive feeling returned once more. He repeated the step several times before finding the soap and lathering it into his free hand. Like before, he glided his fingers over his arm in several places where it needed cleaning, including the sticky debris left from the bandage marks.

The repeated actions and sounds of the shower soothed him, and he closed his eyes. As he continued to carefully clean his wound, his mind drifted to the thoughts of not being in the shower alone and not having to be the one cleaning his injury. Summoning all his imagination, he imagined Alexander behind him, wrapping his arms around in a bear hug and laying his head on his back.

"Was it worth it?" Alexander sighed as he nuzzled his face into the Alpha's strong back.

"If it prevented you from getting hurt, I'd do it all over again," Stephen assured him.

"You can't protect me from everything."

Stephen hung his head forward, allowing the water to beat down on his neck. "Does that mean I should stop trying?"

Alexander hummed to himself, knowing the Alpha was going to respond that way. "No."

"Then what does it mean?" No answer came. The silence made Stephen lift his head up and then turn around. He faced an Alexander who stood there like a stone statue without any expression on his face.

Finally, he answered, "It means you need to forgive yourself when you fail."

Now the Alpha tensed as he felt his wolf set on the defense. "I will not fail."

Once again, the Omega in front of him didn't move nor change his expression. "You already did once; you will again."

Stephen couldn't believe the boldness Alexander had. It was a betrayal to his wolf and his heart. Suddenly, both of his hands folded into fists. But as they did, sparks of pain ran up his arm, up his chest, and straight into his brain. As his body jolted, memories of Eddie thrusting a knife into his body flashed before his eyes. Soon after, the memory of Warren's lifeless body on his bed staring back at him became front and center. The power of both mental images folded the Alpha at his knees as he slid down the wall and onto the floor of the shower. Once again, all he could hear was his Veo hauntingly screaming at him.

"Stephen! Stephen!"

"Stephen!" his Veo cried out.

The Alpha heard it that time, clear as day. "Yeah?" he huffed.

"Are you alright? I heard you yelp!"

Catching his breath, Stephen finally centered himself back to reality and considered the moment a foolish daydream gone bad. He laughed uncomfortably to himself. "Yeah, yeah. I'll be out in a minute."

"Okay," Marlon replied cautiously.

Grateful his Veo accepted the response, he gave one more deep sigh of relief—mental breakdown disaster averted. With one final moment of bravery, he examined his arm. The opening now had its own heartbeat and appeared redder than it did before. As he squinted, he could see little drops of clear fluid bubble from a cross-hatch. He wondered if he was pushing himself too far. But if the recognition came with the penalty of not seeing Alexander today, he wasn't going to have any part of it. He shut his eyes tightly and shook his head violently, erasing any memory of the past few minutes. The Alpha carefully stood tall and proud once again and shut off the water.

CHAPTER 02:

EXPOSING THE WORLD
AS OTHERS SEE IT

"South Street Tavern. ... ... Hello? ... Hello?" Alexander checked the phone to make sure the call was still active. Considering the bar only had a few customers in it, there was no excuse for him not to hear the voice on the other line. Still, the call was quiet. But not too quiet; someone was on the other line. Listening. Waiting. "Hello?!"

"Is this the owner?" The voice spoke plainly.

"Yes. And who is this?" No answer. "Hello? I'm going to hang up now."

"Your new Alpha employee is a problem."

Now Alexander understood. He played along, throwing out attitude. "What new Alpha employee?"

The voice stayed calm and collected—unaffected by the Omega's shift in tone. "You know who I'm talking about. Everyone does. He's a problem," the voice reiterated.

Alexander paused, telling himself he should have hung up when he said he would. But the curiosity was too strong. "What kind of problem?" Out of the corner of his eye, he saw Bruce catching wind of the conversation and walking up to him. But right before he could interject, Alexander held up his hand and prevented him from saying a word.

"You *know*. Everyone *knows*. And if you don't get rid of him today, everyone is going to *see* it."

"What do you—" Even before he could finish the line, it cut out to a solid dial tone. Alexander grunted as he slammed the phone down.

"Who was that?" Bruce asked, full of concern.

The Omega dismissed him on the spot, walking right past him.

Ever since the mysterious phone call, Alexander couldn't make time go by fast enough. In the final hour before Stephen was supposed to arrive for the first time since the assault, anxiety and frustration overcame him.

"Hey," James whispered to his Beta brother, "look over there."

On the opposite side of the bar, Alexander was wiping down table after table like he was going for the territorial record. He was a well-oiled machine on the balls of his feet, pulling out a chair, swiping it with a damp rag, and shoving it back in just as fast. Unfortunately, his efficiency was waning. His fingers betrayed him as they fumbled with delicate sets of napkins, coasters, and the occasional salt and pepper shaker. Sometimes, the mess took longer to clean up than wiping down the table itself.

"My, Wolf-God," Bruce breathed back, "he's losin' it!"

"Yeah, but who does he remind you of?" James probed.

"Hmmm." Bruce connected it right away. "Polar opposites—"

"Yet the exact same person," James finished.

That was when Alexander caught a glimpse of the two entertained Betas staring at him. "Something wrong?!"

"Nope," both answered simultaneously, instantly going back to mundane tasks as if they never noticed anything in the first place.

The Omega fiddled with his phone. "Stephen should be here by now."

Bruce glanced at his watch. "He's still got two minutes."

"Thank you, timekeeper." He groaned.

James gave a pained expression. He turned his back to his boss and whispered into his brother's ear. "I think that's our cue to mind our own business." Bruce agreed. Luckily, they were granted mercy as they heard melodic roars and backfires of a rider who they hoped was the one they were waiting for.

Alexander heard the noise too. His heart thumped and his stomach hitched as he waited in anticipation. After reflecting on what he must look like from his mental disarray, he regained control and returned to the safety behind the bar. He picked up several glasses which had been air drying near the sink and stacked them in their rightful place as if he'd been doing it the entire time.

After what seemed like another entire day of just waiting, the Omega's inner wolf sensed the Alpha enter the bar. Whatever he could interpret from the intuition was put on hold as both Bruce and James joyously welcomed back their partner in crime.

"There he is!" Bruce boomed, walking toward the Alpha with open arms.

"There's a double sight for sore eyes!" Stephen smiled. "How the hell are you two?" He embraced Bruce in a side hug to help avoid his injury. Luckily, James observed it enough to extend the same attentiveness when he welcomed the Alpha back as well.

"The good-lookin' wolf has nine lives like a cat!" James joked.

Stephen boosted his bravado as he pointed to his brand-new bandage—courtesy of his Veo. "What? This thing? Just a scratch," he blew off. "Nothing to worry about here, practically good as new."

"Is that right? Let's test it!" Bruce said enthusiastically as he revved up his arm, eyeing the center of the injury like a delicious target.

The Alpha's expression changed immediately. "Whoa, whoa! Not necessary. Still tender in one area." He cleared his throat. As the group basked in the moment, Stephen's gaze fell upon the object of his affection. "And there's another sight," he mumbled out loud. With perfect timing, the Omega turned around and stared back. Cautiously, Stephen walked up to the bar and sat down on the stool directly in front of him.

For Alexander, seeing the Alpha was a blessing and a curse. He was forever thankful he was back and in good health. But as he scanned his dark hair, beautiful eyes, and broad shoulders in his tight t-shirt, he saw the curse plain as day. There, on his right arm, wrapped a wound which sent him back to that very night—wondering how differently it could have gone. Refusing to dwell on the matter, he focused. "How is it?" He nodded to the bandage.

"Healing as it should be."

Alexander nodded casually. "How long before you're coming back to work?"

Stephen's face furrowed with confusion. "I'm here now. I expected to work today."

The Omega put his hands on his hips. "Is that what the doctor said?"

"It's what *I* said," Stephen clarified.

"You're not working tonight." Alexander pressed a towel onto the bar and wiped up various marks, leaving a spotless shine.

"And why not?"

"Because I'm not going to be able to live with myself if something happens while you're working." Alexander gave Stephen the stare down which didn't appear to deter the Alpha's original mindset. "The last thing I need is to hear you've popped a stitch which would set you back farther than where you were in the first place."

"There's nothing wrong with me," Stephen tried. "I'll just be a little slower than normal and won't be hoisting patrons up and throwing them out the door like I do every other night." He shrugged, proud of his comment.

"Very funny." Mistakenly, Alexander thought the conversation was over. But Stephen sat there, still with the same expression and pheromone palate which meant it wasn't. "Stephen, come on. Don't do this," he begged.

"What?" he asked innocently.

"Don't put me in the position to be the bad guy."

The Alpha shrugged. "Let me work tonight, and you won't have to be."

Alexander matched Stephen in a staring standoff. Two wolves in the wild leaned back on their hind legs as their eyes shimmered in the yellow lights hanging down from the ceiling, mimicking a golden harvest moon. No noise, no breaths were heard, and the world around them faded to nothing. In the primal state, it was a waiting game to see who would concede. Here, it was no different.

The Omega tried to hold his concentration as hard as he could, but his own inner wolf whimpered and whined, knowing he didn't want the standoff nor the ultimatum. As he broke, he felt his body shrink while Stephen's upper chest lifted in victory, revealing his sharp smile. "I'm serious: the minute I see you wince out of pain, you're outta here!"

"Yes, Alpha," Stephen playfully patronized.

"And don't you forget it!"

***

Hours into a heavy shift, Stephen was on cloud nine. It was as if he had never left or the assault in the bar never happened. *Almost.* Because every time a new customer came in, Tom, the resident bar patron, intentionally went out of his way to find them and point out that the Alpha was back. That, in itself, wasn't a problem; after all, everyone with eyes who walked in could see Stephen for themselves.

But the drunken soul felt the need to explain the whole story over and over again. Every time he did, the story changed, becoming more colorful with each rendition.

"Then..." Tom had to pause as the other bar patrons laughed at his obviously inaccurate story and classic stupor. "Then... where was I?"

Stephen laid his head on the bar. It was nice not to have to look at the inebriated fool for a second, and the counter felt cool on his skin. But the hard surface reminded him it was still out of misery. "Then Eddie pulled out the knife!" The words came out automatically, like a teacher desperately trying jog the memories of a classroom of incompetent students, hoping it would stick this time.

"Yeah, yeah, yeah! That's what happened. Eddie pulled out a huge butcher knife—"

"Pocket knife—"

"Out of his pocket and thrust it into Stephen's chest—"

"Or arm, maybe?" The Alpha hopelessly pointed to his bandage, as if he needed to.

"Yikes!" a bar patron gasped. "That's quite the story."

Stephen shook his head. "When he first came in and started telling it, he told everyone Eddie castrated my balls. And that's when he was *sober*!"

The patron laughed. "Tom was sober?!"

Stephen raspberried. "Right?"

"And finally," Tom stood up in his grand finale, holding one last manly gulp in his fourth glass of beer, "Stephen maneuvered like a ninja, wrestled away the knife, and then stabbed Eddie right in his dick!" An applause from the small crowd Tom had garnered rang out as he drank the final contents in the mug and bowed, almost falling to the floor before grabbing the counter for stability.

"Sit your ass down before you fall down!" Bruce scolded.

"I didn't stab anyone, Tom. Quit making up shit which didn't happen. You're just going to get me into trouble," Stephen criticized.

"That's how I remember it!" Tom defended.

"You weren't even here!" James replied.

Tom waved the notion off. "Of course, I was. You just didn't see me."

"Oh, believe me," James laughed, "we all know when you're here, Tom."

The drunk old man centered himself in front of the Beta. "When are you going to go out on a date with me?"

Even before James could answer, his older brother stepped in. "He's already taken."

Stephen's head jerked. "What? Who? When?"

"Yeah," Tom mumbled. "Who? Where? How?"

"Daniel." James smiled.

"Who?" Tom croaked.

"Daniel!" James grunted. "Never mind."

"Daniel as in 'I'm Alex's best friend, Daniel'?" Stephen asked surprised. The Beta nodded proudly. "Boy... gone for a week and the whole world changes." Remembering that Daniel wasn't there tonight, he also noticed someone else missing. "Where is Alex?"

Bruce answered, "Working on the inventory in the back."

Once again, images of his previous encounter with Alexander in the bar rushed to his thoughts: a highly hormonal and emotional Omega lost in a sea of confusion, hurt, and frustration. His first thought was to go in the back and check on him. But instead, he calmed and prevented wild worries from entering. *He's fine, Stephen. All is well. No need to worry,* he said silently to himself.

"What are you mumbling over here?" James asked.

"Just focusing is all."

"What a first night back, am I right?!" The Beta cheered in victory.

Stephen held his enthusiasm. "It's not over yet."

"How's the arm?" Bruce followed.

"Let's just say I'm being very choosey on what I'm doing."

"Oh, I've noticed. You might wanna work on that poker face more," Bruce warned.

"Shit."

"You want something for it?" James offered, pulling the red med bag out.

"As long as it's just over-the-counter stuff," Stephen clarified.

"There's a couple different ones in there. Help yourself to which-ever one you want."

Stephen unzipped the bag, peered in, and sorted through sev-eral medical supplies: bandages, antibiotic cream, tape, ice pack, and finally, three different bottles. Two were over-the-counter pain killers he'd already been used to, which arguably dulled pain. The third was a prescription bottle bearing the name "Alexander Daventry." Once again, the medication was a complete mystery to him, but the description indicated its use for "hormone regu-lation." Stephen gripped the bottle tightly as he spaced out in per-sonal thoughts on how these affected the Omega. But soon after, a familiar voice cut through his own distraction.

"Tempting... isn't it?"

The sound pierced Stephen to his core and immediately jolted him to the Beta, sitting at the bar, with a satisfied grin all over his face. "What the..." The Alpha couldn't believe who he was seeing in front of him. Frantically, he searched the entire bar to see if they saw who he saw. But everyone around him acted as if he wasn't there or as if he was a regular run-of-the-mill customer; however, Stephen knew better.

Raymond lifted himself and peered over at the prescription bottle in the Alpha's hand. Then he grimaced. "Ew. I wouldn't touch those."

"Why? What do *you* know about them?" Stephen criticized.

"Lose the attitude, asshole," Raymond replied. "I may not have a Ph. D. in pharmacy, but I know more than the average wolf. So quit looking at me like I'm ignorant." Stephen gulped down his pride as his nerves began rising. "A lot of Omegas on the street use that—at least when they can get it." After another quick glance at the bottle, he whistled. "Damn. That thing is jammed full. You'd make more in a day than you would here in an entire week selling that ala carte."

The revelation shocked Stephen as he glanced at the bottle again. But after a quick glance at the dosing instructions, he highly doubted Raymond's claim and assumed he was just puffing for the sake of it. "It says 'take two pills twice a day.' You can't make *that* much."

"Four pills a day?!" Raymond exclaimed.

After a confused look, Stephen confirmed on the bottle once again. "Yeah. Is that a lot or something?"

"I've only seen guys take one—two if they're in need... Sounds like trouble to me."

The Alpha's heart pounded in his chest as he read the sincerity all over Raymond's face. His instinct calmed him down as he rationally considered who he was dealing with. "'Trouble'? I should believe that when it's coming from you?"

"Considering I actually know shit, you should believe it, *especially* when it comes from me."

Stephen was at a loss for words over the subject. Having his former drug dealer sitting there like it was normal spooked his inner wolf like no other. The Alpha tried staying confident in his presence, but there was still no way Raymond couldn't sense the panic deep within. The only conclusion from this was an inevitable collision of his past life into his current one—that wasn't even considering Alexander. What would his Fate think once he found out the hustler was here and sitting right in front of him? What would he do? Stephen wasn't about to have him stick around long enough to find out. He set the pill bottle down on the bar and leaned in. "I don't know what you're doing here, but—"

"Hey, Stephen, aren't you going to introduce me to your friend?" Bruce walked up enthusiastically. Dismissing Stephen's 'caught' look, he took the honor himself and pushed out his muscled arm in a greeting. "Bruce Dawson."

Raymond opened and joyously received the greeting. "Ray Taylor."

"You two former classmates or something?" Bruce asked innocently. He took one deep inhale and then studied his fellow Beta rank. He was entertained by the man's slicked back hair and cargo jacket.

The Beta grinned as he marveled at Bruce's ignorance. He pushed his lips together and held out his finger for emphasis. "That is *exactly* what it is." To add to the dramatics, he shook his head. "You just clocked that like a detective. You're good." He saw Bruce stand taller—taking in the false compliment like an innocent child. Then, he glanced toward Stephen, who now had no choice but to play along. What was his alternative? "My, my, Stephen, your friends are very inquisitive. It's like they're trying to protect you from something. Or someone."

Even before Stephen could comment, Bruce took the initiative. "Our latest employee was just brutally attacked by a former customer of ours. Guess you could say we're just looking out for him. Right, buddy?" He slapped his large hand on Stephen's back. Normally, the Alpha's build would withstand the brute force, but he saw Stephen's body quickly push with it as his expression amplified. "Something wrong? You look like you've seen a ghost."

The words to Stephen were ironic. "You could say that."

Bruce observed the two holding their contributions back as they eyed one another in a peculiar way. "I mean, I get it. You haven't seen each other in what, ten years? It's overwhelming, right?"

"Sometimes, there just aren't the right words." The Alpha felt caught between a rock and a hard place. He officially was placed in the position of a submissive Omega as he waited on Raymond's every word. He now held the Alpha's fate in his hands. And in more ways than one. But the more he saw the hustler's satisfied expression plastered on his face, the more he wanted to strike it off. That consideration alone sent a rush of frustration pheromones throughout his body which made his muscles tighten up in his neck and shoulders, and then, down both arms. That was when he felt a foreign sensation hit in his arm. It vibrated beneath his new bandage. His wolf wanted him to tear it off and lick the healing wound to soothe it. That's when he realized a stitch must have popped. Once again, Stephen struggled to keep his expressions and emotions from coming to light. All he could focus on was the conversation between the two men before him.

"I'm glad I got to meet someone from your past. A friend of Stephen is a friend of mine," Bruce declared. "What will it be?"

"Hmm," Ray rubbed his chin, "I've heard that Trailblazer #4 is good."

"A fine choice!" Bruce affirmed. "It's one of our most popular. I'll be back."

As Bruce sauntered off to make Raymond his drink, Stephen let his true colors show. "What the fuck do you think you're doing?"

Raymond played it off cool. "Having a drink at a bar while talking to my former classmate?" He smirked, enjoying the joke at his "classmate's" expense.

"I'm almost a decade younger than you!"

The Beta raspberried. "It's not my fault he's blind." He twitched his neck. "Either that or jail didn't do anything good for your complexion. Damn. You *do* look like shit."

Falling into the trap, Stephen rubbed his face and breathed in and out, trying to keep himself together. Ever since this morning, his mind had been completely rewired to a mental state he had completely forgotten about. He surmised it had drained his energy, causing his complexion to fall with it. "How did you know I was here?"

The Beta shrugged. "People talk."

Stephen narrowed in. "Which people?"

Bruce interjected, "Here you are. Trailblazer #4 as requested. Cash or card?"

"Cash," Raymond replied, flopping a bill onto the bar. "Keep the change."

"Appreciate it." Bruce nodded, taking the tip like he had a million times before, and then turned to another customer who beckoned to him.

Once again, it left Stephen alone with his former partner in crime. "You didn't answer my question."

Raymond eyed his drink glass, picked it up, and took his first sip. "Ahhh. That *is* good. I'll have to thank who recommended it to me."

Stephen hated the Beta enjoying every second of it. "Who was it?!"

"Take it easy, Alpha," Raymond patronized. "You're fine. There's no fire; quit alarming everyone." He adjusted himself. "You're killing the vibe."

"The only vibe I want is the vibration of your footsteps out that door," Stephen whispered harshly.

"Sure! No problem! Will do it in a heartbeat," Raymond said smoothly.

The Alpha squinted. Raymond's actions were never that simple. "If?"

"If you tell them the *real* reason why you want me to leave." He gave a satisfied expression as he saw Stephen once again show a hint of fear. "And trust me, if you're not honest with your answer, *I* will be."

Stephen gulped. "That's ... not a problem..." He cautiously walked through the scenario in his head. "They'll understand completely, and then it will return to normal as if you weren't here."

"Pffft! Please!" Raymond took another drink and whispered out his sarcasm. "'Hey, everyone, meet the guy who used to sell me W.S. when it was still in its experimental phase. It may have been part of the reason I was put in jail for ten years, but I'm happy just to see the guy!'" He laughed and shook his head in disbelief. "You and I

42

both know that's not how it's gonna happen. But... you keep telling yourself that."

"What makes you so confident?" Stephen bit back.

"Do you really think you're the first 'reformed' customer I've ever dealt with?"

Stephen's stomach turned. "You go after your former customers, even after they've become sober?!" Raymond's expression didn't change. "What kind of monster are you?"

"They don't call me 'Rat' for nothin.'"

"What's it going to take you to leave? What do you want?"

"I already told what I want. What I want is: you."

"Thanks, but I'm already devoted to my Fated Mate."

Raymond rolled his eyes. "You're cute." Then, he remembered himself. "Oh, that's right. You look like shit. So, you're not 'cute.' You're just a fool."

"If you don't tell me right now, Ray, I swear I'm gonna—"

"I want you to realize that yes, there are people out there who *do* reform, and I never see them again. Then, there are people like you and me, Stephen. You and I are cut from the exact same cloth: fathers who wish we were never born, a society that wishes we were anything except what we are, and mates who want nothing to do with us. We. Don't. Change."

The final sentiment stood the hair up on Stephen's arm. "What do you know of *my* mate?"

"I know what you've told me: it's 'complicated.' And if that's how you described it with your *Fated* Mate, I can only imagine what it's like. I feel bad for you when it comes to that. When I found out you worked *here* of all places, naturally, I had to find out what it was all about. Now that I have, it's not hard to figure it out. The only reason a Type 4 Alpha of your stature works under the most prolific bar owner in the city, who is an *Omega*, is because *he's* the 'complicated' Fated Mate... isn't he?" Stephen bowed his head. "That's what I thought."

"He's not 'complicated.'"

"That title must be for you, then?"

The Alpha scratched his wounded arm, feeling the lowest ever since he got back. "No... that title isn't for me, either. I'm just a waste of a human being, destroying Alexander's life."

The comment caught Raymond off-guard. "Damn, man..."

Stephen broke out of his momentary trance of self-pity and returned to his former aggravation. "I want to know who told you I was here!"

"It's not gonna happen," Raymond stated plainly.

"Why?!"

"You know the work I do; it's a code. I don't give names—I only take them. I tell you who my informant is, and my career is over. Besides, there are hundreds of people out there who know who you are now and where you work. Does it matter? It could have been one person; it could have been twenty. You put yourself out there. Now you must pay the consequences."

"I'll ask again: what do I have to do to get you out of here *now*?" Raymond started to speak, but he cut him off. "Without any confrontation or explanation."

"Hmm..." Raymond thought strategically. Instead of giving a reply, all he did was turn his gaze toward a lonely orange bottle with a white label taped to the side of it. Then, slowly, he saw Stephen's eyes follow his trail.

"You're out of your fucking mind!"

"You asked. That's my price."

"Suppressants can be bought at any store. Why do you need *these*?"

"*Those* are controlled and by prescription only. They're highly sought after—and I want them. Or rather, I have a customer base that does."

"There are cameras in here now, Ray. If I put my hands on them, if you put your hands on them, it's going to get traced back to us in five minutes. There's no way it can happen."

"These cameras you speak of, I don't suppose you know where the controls are?"

Stephen shook his head. "Eric, the manager, controls them remotely on his phone. The software here is on the register's computer. It will message Eric, and he'll know I messed with it."

"Then... I guess there just might be a power outage?" Raymond put his elbows on the table and waited patiently.

"Please don't ask me to do this."

"I'm not asking you to do anything. I'm not telling you to do anything. I'm saying: I'm a paying customer in a bar. The wad of cash I have in my pocket can keep me here all night. And if I keep tipping Bruce this way, he isn't going to want me gone anytime soon. But, as you know, I can get candid after my third beer or so... it's why I don't drink. However, I'm here tonight willing to make that exception to celebrate my long-lost friend who I haven't seen since my school days back at Adams."

Stephen couldn't believe what was happening. What hurt worse was the memory of several people telling him not to go into the bar today: his Sur, his Veo, and even his mate Alexander. Maybe, Wolf-God was talking through them all and warning him it would turn out like this. Or, maybe, this was always going to happen. After all, whoever Raymond's informant was really wanted the hustler to show up at the bar and create a living nightmare for him. Mission accomplished. "I didn't go to Adams. I went to Burton."

"Burton? That place was a snooze fest," Raymond dismissed. "So, do you want me to go up to that karaoke machine and hear me 'sing'... or... do you need to go to the 'bathroom'?"

"Really? The bathroom? That's the lamest excuse in the book. Talk about pointing a finger to someone who is obviously guilty."

"Oh, I think you have a reason—a good reason."

"What's that?" Stephen highly doubted.

"You're bleeding."

"What?!" The Alpha quickly looked at his bandaged arm and saw a fresh blotch of red seep through the bright white cloth. "Damn it." He pressed his hand against it, hating myself for every moment he breathed in.

"My offer is getting cold, Stephen. What's it gonna be?"

The Alpha closed his eyes and imagined himself elsewhere: an abandoned road with the wind blowing dust up into the sky, a forest with red and yellow leaves gently falling to the grass below, and a foggy lake with a reflection staring back at him like glass. But none of those places existed here, and Dr. Forrester wasn't in the bar to help him. He wanted his wolf to growl and snarl, telling him to attack the hustler and take his last breath. But all he did was cower to the ground and whimper like a hurt dog, acknowledging that his damaged arm left him completely vulnerable. And if this was what the physical loss felt like, he couldn't imagine the emotional loss after losing Alexander. With a deep sigh, he let go of his Alpha wolf and submitted to the Beta in front of him. "Bruce," he said loudly, getting his co-worker's attention. After he turned around, Stephen pointed to his bandage, and then the bathroom. After Bruce followed and understood his nonverbal communication, he gave Raymond, the dirty rat before him, one last glance. "I'll be right back."

"Okay, what do I do next?" Alexander waited on Eric's every instruction through the phone. "I already did that. Don't yell at me. Just tell me what to do! No, you don't need to come in. What's next?" The Omega stood at the register, hitting every command in his partner's orders, grunting as every third one seemed to either not work or must have been the wrong move. "Let me try this..." Alexander went rogue and punched in a combination himself. Suddenly, on the screen shot up four different displays from cameras raining down on the bar. "Finally!" he huffed. "We're on. Can you see us?" he asked Eric. "How about this?" He happily displayed a middle finger straight into the camera in the corner of the main shelf which held several prominent name brands of liquor. Then, he stuck his tongue out for good measure. "Ha ha. Very funny. I'll call you if anything happens. ... ... No, I'm not worried about that. James blocked the back hallway, Bruce manned the register, and Stephen monitored the front door. No one was in and no one was out. Nothing to worry about. Bye." He looked at the crowd, cheering on the development of the power being back on. "Party on!" he announced to his patrons.

"Can I come out now?" James asked from the back.

"Yes," Alexander sang back. "How were things up here, Bruce?"

"Things were good. Doesn't sound like anyone turned on each other. As a matter of fact, I think that couple over there in the corner just made a pup. If they come back pregnant in a month, you should get naming rights."

"Yeah, right," Alexander dismissed. "Stephen." He beckoned to the Alpha to meet him up at the bar. "I heard about your arm. How is it?" Quietly, Stephen lifted his arm, so the bar lights shined down on his injury. "Aw, man. Do you need to go in?" The Alpha shook his head. "Do you need anything? A cream? An ointment? A pill?" He saw Stephen cringe at the list. "Are you okay?"

"I'll be fine. Just mad at myself." Stephen sulked.

"I told you if you pushed it, this could happen. And this isn't what I wanted."

"This isn't what I wanted to happen either," the Alpha replied.

Alexander observed the darkness which had overcome his employee. He saw it eating Stephen alive and treaded lightly. "Do you ... want to leave? Take it easy the rest of the night?"

For the first time today, Stephen decided to listen to the wisdom of his Fated Omega, the Omega he just betrayed. "I think that's best right now." He couldn't even look Alexander in the eye. "Is there anything you need me to do before I go?"

"The only thing I can think of is a quick trash run, but I don't want you to do any labor which could make your arm worse."

"No. No, I can do that. Easy."

"Hey, I think we dodged a bullet tonight. Customers sitting in the dark in a bar for three minutes with no one dead? We did good. *You* did good. So don't be so down on yourself. Okay?" Stephen nodded. He watched the Alpha go to nearest bin and pull the bag out with a heavy grunt before throwing it over his shoulder. In a gloom, he walked out of the bar and to the back.

"And here's the man of the hour!" Raymond announced to the small brood around him, waving a bat in his right hand.

Stephen couldn't believe the scene before his eyes. Riff raff of all kinds scattered around the alleyway behind the bar like vermin investigating rotten food. Only *these* creatures of the night weren't looking for rotten food; they were looking for hard substances to cure their insatiable appetites. Men, young and old, who died years ago, moaned and laughed as whatever journeys they were on commenced. "What... What are you doing here?"

"I got bored waiting for the lights to come on. So, I texted a bunch of my clients and wanted to know if they were interested in my new find. Boy, I knew I'd create a buzz, but I didn't anticipate this! Look at this!"

Suddenly, two more unknowns showed up, cash in hand. Raymond happily displayed the bottle and shook it. The heavy sound made the waiting customers gasp in awe. Both pushed their dollar bills onto the street hustler as he delicately rationed out a few pills to each.

The sight made Stephen sick to his stomach. *This* is what he sold his soul for? *This* is what his life was like? The experience was familiar and yet so strange to him. He wanted nothing to do with it, especially when he caught a whiff of the two customers happily giggling to themselves after taking the pills Raymond sold them. Both Omegas were in heat. The scent was intoxicating but for all the wrong reasons. It sickened Stephen to think that ten years ago, he would have brazenly tried to court one, if not both, to see if they were willing to let him "play" with them. After all, the feeling of an Omega orgasming in heat was one of the hottest things Stephen could think of. But right now, the thought of doing it made him want to hurl. The only interest he had was in Alexander. And even now, he knew he wasn't even worthy of that.

But that was when the thought hit him. *Oh no.* Quickly, he turned toward the building and scanned for the camera he knew Eric installed to monitor the dumpsters.

"Don't worry about it; I took care of it," Raymond assured him.

"What did you do?! If you damaged it, Eric is going to be out here faster than lightning. He's gonna have every cop on your ass."

"Don't listen to him, guys. We're good for another twenty minutes. Then, we'll clear out," Raymond announced to his clients. Then, he turned back to Stephen. "Tell this 'Eric' that he shouldn't put his camera on a swivel." He used the bat as a stick to point directly to it.

Stephen looked up and saw the lone camera angled in a way which missed the entire back alley. "Great. Now the first person who is going to get questioned is me. Thanks a lot, 'friend.'" His temperature started rising as he felt his lungs contract, almost as if they couldn't register whether he was getting oxygen.

"Not my problem, I'm afraid."

Stephen was about to rip Raymond a new one when he saw one his customers start to approach Crusher. "Hey! Get away from that!"

"Whoa, Stephen... take it easy. He's just looking," Raymond defended.

"If you don't tell him to get away from my bike, I will use that bat on his sternum," Stephen warned.

Raymond smirked but heeded the Alpha's words. "Stay away from the bike, friends. It's off-limits." Several grumbles came in return, but all heeded the Beta's command. "Happy now?"

"I'll be happier when all of you are far away from here as possible."

"I told you, in less than twenty minutes, we'll be gone."

"Well, I won't be here to find out." Stephen grabbed the trash bag below him and brought it to the dumpster. There against it sat another customer, skin and bones, wearing a ripped blue t-shirt and jeans which would have been more suited to be shorts at this point with the amount of skin exposed. "Move!" Stephen growled. The poor soul scrambled upon hearing the wolf's bark and scattered elsewhere.

"Ease up on the tone, Alpha. We're not hurting anybody."

Stephen scoffed. "You're wrong. You just haven't met the person you're hurting."

"Who? Alex? Man, he'll be fine. He'll get another prescription, and it will be as if this never happened."

"It *did* happen. And I'll *never* forget it. I betrayed him in the worst way. I just broke the trust of my Fated Mate—that's a sacred oath, Ray!"

"Sorry, buddy, I'm a Beta. I can't relate. But... I can help you forget."

"What are you talking about now?"

"Here." Raymond tossed Stephen a bottle, and it landed perfectly in his hands.

The nameless bottle gave no hint. "What is it?"

"Open it and find out."

Stephen grunted but humored the Beta. He wished he hadn't. Immediately, the strong sweet scent hit his nostrils and sent several synapses off in his mind. The wolf inside him split in two: one half snarled in anger—hating the familiar substance, but the other half purred in excitement, like seeing an old friend. "Wolf Spit." Ironically, instead of the sweet hint of his former substance, his whole tongue went dry as a metallic taste layered his sense of taste and smell.

"Not quite. Here's the latest formula. Meet its son: Wolf Spit II."

"What's so special about it?" The Alpha's voice quivered.

"It removes culpability. It completely blacks you out, and you don't remember the last 24 hours. Some buddies of mine have even passed the scent test from an Omega and even a lie detector test with this stuff. It's perfect."

"It's not 'perfect'!" Stephen chucked the bottle back at Raymond.

The Beta tried to catch it, but it tipped off his fingers. "Are you crazy?!" He ran after it and grabbed the bottle before one of his clients could get ahold of it. "You need to be careful with this stuff! You know what it can do!"

"And that's why I don't want it. It destroyed my life and everyone around me. What makes you think I want to partake in this?! In any of this?!"

"You're looking at it from the outside, my friend. You've just forgotten is all."

"I haven't forgotten anything. Everyday I'm reminded of how my life fell apart."

"Then do yourself a favor and remind yourself of why you needed it in the first place."

Stephen's voice hitched as a trance overcame him and the visuals in front of him faded away entirely.

"Stephen!" the Beta welcomed. "Your urgency has me freaked out. What trouble did you get into now? Do I need to be worried about who followed you here?" A younger Raymond walked out of the abandoned garage and scanned the roads connecting the back alley and

the few in the distance he could see between the worn-down buildings. Unfortunately, a Beta's wolf sense never intensified to the strength of an Omega's nor an Alpha's. Therefore, he had to rely significantly on his human senses instead. He closed his eyes and listened for police sirens—none came through. After that, he waited for the sounds of any approaching vehicle: motor vibrations and crunching pavement underneath rolling tires, sounds he had conditioned himself to listen for over the years. His nerves settled after confirming no such threat nor investigation was upon them. To ease himself down the rest of the way, he used fingers to rub the base of his rat's tail. The sensation was like no other and soothed his inner wolf.

"I'm not in trouble and no one followed me here, Rat. Now, listen. I'm leaving the city and want to take some W.S. with me. You're the only one I trust to get the formula right." Adrenaline rushed through the Alpha's body. His arms and hands trembled as he wanted this transaction to happen quickly.

Raymond's expression fell. "Leaving? Forever?" Stephen nodded. "No, no, buddy! Come on!"

The affection the Beta showed caught Stephen by surprise. "Why does that bother <u>you</u> so much?"

"That hits me in the heart, man." Raymond placed his hand over his chest for good measure. "One of my star associates and best buds wants to abandon me, and you think it doesn't hurt? Guess I know where I stand."

Stephen looked away and huffed, hiding his guilt. "I don't have time for this. Are you gonna help me or not?"

"Sure, I mean, if you got what I need." The Alpha grunted as he pulled out several bills and handed them over. "That'll do." He grinned. "Though, if you ask me, if you're planning to escape to Wolf-God knows where, shouldn't you be saving up this money?"

"I got enough until I get a job somewhere."

Raymond laughed. "Right, because the last one worked out so well." "Shut up."

The hustler pulled out a bottle of Stephen's prize, held it up to the light, and squinted as he shook it. After he confirmed what he thought was the amount Stephen earned, he tossed the bottle to him. "That's all I got right now. I'm running low from my supplier. He won't be back until next week. You sure you don't want to wait until then?"

The Alpha counted out the pills, not happy about the number he was given. But he was going to have to deal with what he got. "No. If I don't get out now, I never will. Thanks." He waved Raymond off and began to make his exit.

"You've talked about getting out of here a lot more lately than you used to. So, what finally made you do it?"

Stephen stopped and thought about all the reasons why: countless. But to actually describe it? That was difficult. "I think one of my former co-workers ratted me out on spray painting the restaurant. My Sur's on my back."

"Child's play? Why can't you handle that? Your Sur's always on your back."

"Yeah, and I can't take it anymore!"

Raymond grabbed a cigarette out from his pocket and lit it up. "He'll bail you out; he always does."

Stephen shook his head. "Not this time. I think I've used all my 'second chances.'"

The hustler breathed out a puff of smoke. "So? When you get to court, it will be a minor offense, and you'll be deemed as a 'crucial part of society' because of your Type 4 Status. And life will get back to normal."

"And once that happens, everyone will have a concrete reason not to touch me. They already think of me as a screw up who gets preferential treatment. The last thing I need is for them to say 'Now here's proof!'"

"Think you're blowing this out of proportion, my friend." He flicked a few ashes down and took another heavy drag.

Stephen hummed to himself "Maybe. But I'm done carrying the weight of this expectation that I need to be Warren's keeper while setting a good example for him and the entire world because I should 'know better' just because my dad's an officer of the law. The only thing my Sur cares about is his reputation and that I'm tarnishing it every time I take a breath." The Alpha's frustration grew as he saw his father's face clear as day in his mind's eye. "If I had just gathered up the courage to strike him once, he'd know better than to mess with me."

"Then why didn't you?"

Stephen rubbed his eyebrow. "I don't know. Maybe it's because I don't want to see Warren's or my Veo's reaction to doing it. Maybe I'm just a pussy since I know my Sur won't let me get away with doing that."

"He let you get away with roughing up Scott awhile back," Raymond pointed out.

"That was different; Scott and I had an all-out brawl, and my Sur convinced him an assault charge would show up equally for him too. If he dropped it, we'd both be in the clear since my Sur said he'd go after him otherwise."

The Beta laughed. "But between the two of you, Scott looked like he got into a fight with solid concrete and lost."

"Guess he did."

"What else is bothering you?"

Stephen kicked a few rogue rocks off the garage floor and back out into the street. "Remember last week when you had me do a few runs for you?"

"Yeah?"

"I went to this one client who insisted I sit there and listen to his life's story."

"It happens. Some rejects are lonely and just want someone else to hear their voice. That's building a relationship with a customer."

"I'm not looking to build a relationship with anyone!" the Alpha barked back. After the explosion, he regained himself. "He went on this monologue about how years ago, his life was made on the red carpet of his High-Type Status. Can't remember if he said Type 4 or 5 though. But no one ever asked what he wanted for himself." He glanced at

Raymond who was listening intently now, seemingly taking it in as serious. "When all these expectations were handed to him so he could 'make something of himself' and 'do what he was supposed to do,' it became one criticism after another about how he wasn't meeting the goals or achieving that success. And every mistake showed up on his body like a tattoo that people could just look at and go: 'He's not Alpha enough,' 'He's not smart enough,' 'He's not worth of the Status he was given,' 'He's acting like a worthless Low-Type,' 'He's ungrateful.'"

"That's because High-Types live in this world of perfection. It's nothing but lies. Do you have any idea how many clients I have had who are High-Types? Every story is the same: they were dealt an unfair hand, everyone is expecting too much of them, and people forget they're human and think of them as just the Type number they were assigned at birth. They come to me in tears, and I offer them a way to deal with it all that society refuses to see the benefits of. If they saw it our way, the stuff I sell could be mainstreamed and the whole world would chill the fuck out."

"That would put you out of a job."

"Does it matter? It's not as if it's ever going to happen. Thus, my career only gets better and better."

"Until one day you get caught and everything, including your freedom, disappears."

Raymond tossed the end of the cigarette on the ground. "And I suppose you're the one now who woke up and saw the light? Is this some speech that's supposed to make me see the error of my ways so you can save me too?"

"Obviously not." Stephen patted his breast pocket—the Wolf Spit excitedly rattling inside.

The hustler crossed his arms. "I can't convince you to stay?" Stephen shook his head. "Then, it was nice knowing you. Whatever you're looking for, my friend, I hope you find it."

The Alpha refused to say anything more. He turned on his heels and went back to his bike. There was only one thing left to do: pack and get out.

CHAPTER 03:

CRASHING THE PAST INTO THE PRESENT

Stephen woke up to the unbearable sound of what must have been a thousand birds having a quorum in the tree outside his window. Alone, he was sure he could have blocked it out of his mind and fallen back to sleep, but uncomfortable warm air rushed into his room and wrapped around his already heated body. For good measure, a blinding light hit his eyes and forced him to deal with the day. That was when he realized how high the sun was in the sky. Glancing over at his alarm clock, he saw it was way past however long he expected to sleep since he got to bed at... at... the time eluded him.

He sat up and massaged his head. Oddly enough, he felt like he had a hangover, and yet, he didn't remember drinking more than a few complimentary shots given to him from customers welcoming him back. But here it was, a feeling like he had gone too far... way too far. He sauntered into the bathroom to see the damage on his face. He recognized he was still out of it; whether his complexion improved compared to what Raymond described it as last night, he wasn't sure.

The Alpha splashed a handful of cold water on his face and let the streams of water run down his warm neck and chest. Any hotter and he swore the drops would have sizzled off his skin. That was when he took a moment to try and figure out what the hell happened last night. Unfortunately, every attempt came up blank. If his mind was a computer, all the images were pixelated beyond recognition, and he didn't know how to solve the error.

"Come on, Stephen... Think!" he said out loud to himself.

Just then, his Sur walked in. "You're up!"

The Alpha jumped. "Ah! I thought I told you not to do that!"

"Sorry," Kane apologized.

"It's okay."

"Are you going to eat with us before going in?"

Stephen's heart sank as he only imagined what was waiting for him once he walked back into South Street. The Alpha confirmed and followed his Sur into the kitchen.

———

All Stephen did at the table was reflect and try to put the pieces of the puzzle back together. *Ray came in... He was introduced to Bruce... We talked about Alexander's meds... My arm bled... The power went out... I took the trash out...*

"Are you going to eat?" Kane finally said.

The comment broke the Alpha's concentration as he noticed his fork hovering over his plate in his hand. He looked at it and wondered how it was there. "Sorry."

Kane studied his son. The pheromones he was giving off were of frustration and of panic. They consumed him. The old Alpha feared what his son was dealing with. But instead of asking him point blank, he decided to focus on his attire... or rather, his lack of it. "Isn't it usually customary to wear a shirt when you eat a meal?"

Stephen looked at himself, only then noticing how he wasn't put together. "I... I guess I didn't think about it. I can go get one."

Kane chuckled. "Not much point in it now, is there? You're not even eating."

Marlon stepped in. "Did something happen last night? Your arm doesn't look like it survived your shift. Is that why you came home early?"

The Alpha's eyes shifted. "Yeah." Not an outright lie, but it was enough. Looking out the window, he saw his bike sitting in the middle of the driveway. "Dad, did you move my bike?"

Kane peered out. With his expression unchanged, he took a bite and then swallowed. "Looks like the exact place you left it from last night."

Stephen instantly doubted it. "I don't leave my bike right in the middle of the driveway like that. Someone must have moved it."

"I didn't. Did you, babe?" Kane glanced at his mate, who shook his head "No." The old Alpha shrugged back.

"Well, *somebody* must have moved it."

"If anyone came onto this property, they wouldn't have moved it twenty feet away from the garage in plain sight of the window. If they wanted to move it, they would have taken it. That's where you left it. It was like that this morning when I got up, and I was up before dawn."

"I told you it was too early," Marlon interrupted.

"Huh?" Stephen asked.

"Your arm."

Stephen creased his lips and gave an annoyed expression, like any pup would after getting criticized by his parents. "A stitch just popped, that's all."

"What are you going to do now?" Marlon asked.

"I plan on going in, if that's what you're asking."

Marlon put down his fork. "Don't you think you need to slow down? Isn't this a sign that you're pushing yourself too hard?"

"I agree," Kane added before his son could comment.

Stephen himself found it harder and harder to combat his parents' view. With not being able to remember what happened last night in the alley, he wasn't confident what compromising position he put himself into. But being weak for Alexander, or worse, not being there at all, wasn't an option. "Look, I appreciate both of your concerns, but I'm going in. If Alex doesn't want me there, then I'll have to follow his wishes. But unless I'm missing a limb or on my deathbed with a high fever, I'm not resting now."

"You keep doing that with your arm in that condition, you'll go septic, and then you *will* be on your deathbed," Kane countered.

"Cute."

"I'm not kidding," his Sur criticized. "I've been on plenty of first responder calls to where injuries like this all of sudden turn deadly. One minute they think everything is fine, and then the next..." In that moment, Kane's words stalled, and his expression faded until it was blank.

"Kane?" Marlon leaned in.

"Dad?" Stephen followed.

The old Alpha cleared his throat and then set his napkin on the table. "I'm going to the backyard. There's a tree I need to finish pruning."

"You want me to get it?" Stephen rushed, completely forgetting his condition.

Kane gently put his hand out to stop anyone's attempt to dissuade him. "No, no. It's something I've been wanting to fix for a while. No sense in waiting any longer." With that, the Alpha excused himself from present company and walked off toward the back of the house.

Stephen was shocked. "What the hell was that?!"

"I... I don't know." Marlon sat there, equally concerned.

"Did he have some sort of attack?!"

His Veo disagreed. "No. He looked fine."

"He looked like he saw Death!" Stephen observed his Veo's pheromone palate fall, as if a thought occurred. "What?" he encouraged softly.

Marlon pushed his plate away. He didn't want to continue another conversation down a past which hurt so much, and yet, here he was, doing it again. "It reminded me of how he used to act," he admitted.

"Act when? I don't remember him doing that."

"That's because you weren't here," Marlon stated firmly. "By the time I recognized it myself, you were already in Brooks Haven."

Stephen waited. "Are you going to let me in on it?"

"There were times..." Marlon struggled as he dealt with his own emotions bubbling up. "I could just see it in his face. The whole thing with Warren from being up there in your bedroom, the hospital, dealing with the precinct, all the way to your arraignment. It's as if the whole thing flashed by him in a matter of seconds. Everything else just stopped: he didn't speak, he didn't blink, he didn't move, damn it, he didn't even breathe. He was just gone." Now the tears came into his eyes, and he couldn't bear to look at his son anymore. "Sometimes, I worried he was having a stroke or something. I'd talk to him, touch his hand. Sometimes, I'd even shake his shoulder, and he wouldn't react. Eventually though, every single time, he'd come out of it a few seconds later and pretend it never happened."

"What about the last part? Did he just walk out and leave you here every time, too?"

Marlon paused. "Yes, but the answer was always the same. There was always 'something to do.' Trees, bushes, the lawn, the roof, tuning up the truck, or whatever new-fangled project he stowed in that garage. I always found it peculiar."

"Why?"

"I guess... I guess I just imagined him taking a walk down the driveway, speeding away in his truck, sitting on the back patio with a beer, going to the bedroom to read, or calling up one of his buddies from the precinct."

Stephen grunted. "You mean the same ones who don't call him?"

"Stop," Marlon breathed.

"Sorry." Stephen once again studied the condition of his arm, connecting the moments back to Warren's passing, wondering if it was all somehow related. "Dr. Forrester said everyone deals with grief in a different way. Some things are obvious: sadness, anger, depression, and any actions which directly come from them. Others can manifest in ways which aren't obvious. Normal, everyday activities can become its own sort of therapy. But they're so acceptable that no one knows it's actually the problem."

Marlon was surprised. "You learned all that?"

The Alpha shrugged his shoulders. "Dr. Forrester was one of the few from the outside world. It was easy to want to absorb everything he had to say. The sessions with him were what I looked forward to. An hour went by so fast; I remember hoping a few times during our sessions that he'd think our time was so precious or that conversations were so monumental that he'd extend a session an extra ten or twenty minutes. But, like clockwork, the session started at 10 AM and ended at 11 AM." Stephen shook his head.

"Have you been able to get in touch with Dr. Forrester since you got out?"

The Alpha became annoyed. "It's not like I was offered an insurance package. I know he works outside of Brooks Haven, but there's no way I can afford him. I can't afford any doctor not covered by the state."

Marlon hummed to himself. "I might be able to help you with that."

Stephen was apprehensive but humored his Veo anyway. "Really? How?"

"Let's just say there are some nice perks the city is willing to give an officer they know they've screwed over too many times."

The Alpha couldn't believe what his Veo was saying. "You really think you can use dad's former position to get me in touch with Dr. Forrester... and it be covered?"

"No promises, but I'm willing to try anything. Are you able to wait here?"

Stephen bit his lip. "I would but I kind of have to go. Keep me updated?"

Marlon sighed. "Oh, I suppose."

The Alpha got up and hugged his father the same way he did when he first came home after ten years of being locked away. "Thank you."

Marlon kissed his son's cheek. "I love you," he whispered.

"I love you, too." Stephen began his own exit to his bike out in the front. But he was still in earshot to hear his Veo call out.

"Be careful! If you damage your arm again, I'll put you out of your misery myself!"

"Please do!" he yelled back.

Stephen spent way too much time, once again, reflecting on last night's events. It unsettled him that he couldn't control his brain in the way he wanted; in his life, he already had so many who deserted him or forgot about him. He didn't think his own mind would betray him. As he rolled up to the tavern on Crusher, nerves fluttered around his entire body as he thought about his *own* betrayal: Alexander.

The Alpha pondered a million different ways on how it would go as soon as he entered the bar: Bruce and James standing there with the pool sticks, ready to smash him to pieces, Alexander seeing him at first sight and relentlessly screaming at him with all kinds of curse words and wolf slurs, or even more dramatic, cops standing there, waiting to take him in and put him right back in where he came from. A part of him even imagined not being able to step foot into the bar, a mob running out the door and tackling him to the ground while the law read him his rights. Finally, he shook off all the creative fears from his imagination and called upon his wolf to give him strength. He was going to have to face this moment sooner or later; the time had come now.

One scenario he *didn't* imagine when he walked in sat right there at the center of the bar, seemingly waiting for him to enter. That much was obvious; with his sleek hair and slick suit, he eyed Stephen with a confidence and seniority like he owned the place. Truth be told, he wasn't sure if the Alpha *did* own any of the tavern, but Alexander never made a comment as such. But today wasn't the day to ask such an intriguing question, nor was it a day to believe in coincidences neither. The Alpha was here for a reason; Stephen's wolf could sense it. He stopped dead in his tracks upon seeing the confident jerk, not sure how to press forward.

Quickly, he scanned for any sign of solace with those he wanted to see. Alexander was behind the bar, observing him. Bruce and James were on opposites sides but didn't choose to greet the Alpha as they had done the day before. Stephen, for better or worse, knew how to navigate tense situations like this: he didn't give information; he didn't ask for information. He let everyone else come to him. With that, he did as he would have any other day. "Sean," he greeted neutrally.

"Stephen," he replied in his professional manner.

The walk up to the bar was agony, especially with all eyes on him continuously until he sat right in front of his boss. "Hey, Alexander. How's it going?" he asked nervously.

The Omega nodded his head as he prepped garnishes and filled the box near the register. "It's going. And yourself?"

"I can't complain." Once again, the Alpha couldn't help but look at everyone else. Bruce and James still eyed him from opposite ends of the room. At this point, they might as well have stopped working and just stood behind him instead. And then, there was Sean, sitting there, pleased with himself. Finally, Stephen had to address the elephant in the room. "How are you, Sean?"

"Couldn't be better. I took the day off from work and decided to spend it here with my mate." He gestured to the Alpha with his glass.

The words were smooth and suave and completely intentional. Stephen nodded. "Happy to hear it." After the comment, he noticed Sean glance at Alexander; it was an obvious signal.

Alexander looked up and read the signs all over Sean's face; it was time. He edged in slowly. "How's your arm?"

Stephen had no problems showing it off like it was a painless tattoo. "No problems here. Good as new."

Sean took in every word and slowly nodded, not surprised at the Alpha's comment. Once again, he looked at his Omega mate, signaling him again to continue.

Alexander sighed, hating every minute of what was about to come. "Stephen, we need to talk."

The nerves... they boiled inside Stephen once again. Here it was—the obvious conclusion. "What about?" he asked innocently as best as he could, knowing full well where it was going.

"Last night," Alexander began, "I sent you home on purpose. I did it out of courtesy at first, but then..." he eyed Sean, who was waiting on every word, "I realized later it was the right thing to do. I can't have you work here right now."

Stephen's heart thumped in his throat. What hurt the most was Alexander there, now acting like his mate's puppet. Deep inside, Stephen's wolf was combating two trains of thought: continue with ignorance or confess and apologize with damage control. Out of fear, he continued his open-ended questions. "Why?"

"You're injured," Alexander finally said. "It's bad enough Eddie attacked you in this place, but I can't have you working shifts here if it's further damaging you."

There was no way Stephen ever thought *this* was the conversation that was going to happen. His demeanor warped and tried to adjust to the completely different topic he had catastrophized earlier. "No, it's not a problem. I swear. It was an accident; truth be told, I don't even know what did it."

"And that's the problem." The Omega sighed. "If it's anything that happens to you here, I won't be able to forgive myself." Suddenly, Sean cleared his throat and eyed his mate harder. "And it's not just your safety I'm worried about at that point, it's my own as well."

The Alpha shook his head in confusion. "I don't understand."

Sean, now grateful the hard part was over, had no problem taking the conversation over. "You want to play gladiator and risk your condition on your own time? Go ahead. But the minute you do that on the clock, you are putting Alexander and the entire business at risk for liability."

"I would never do that; I'd never hold you responsible for what some psycho did to me."

"That sounds great and all, but there's no guarantee of that." Sean looked at the Alpha as if he was needing to explain to a child that fire was hot and could be dangerous. "Any employee holding a large tray of drinks could trip and have glasses and various liquids splash up and soak through that bandage. Worse yet, an inebriated guest could run into you and put their entire weight on your arm and undo all the healing." He shook his head, disappointed Stephen didn't already see it this way. "You may act all even-keeled and levelheaded now, but no one would blame you after an incident like that happened if you turned on a dime and invoked your right to sue the bar for your medical bills. Or more."

Stephen stared back at Sean with a desire to crush his larynx just to get him to stop talking. Now, the set-up was clear. Alexander had talked to Sean about his return to the bar yesterday and no doubt discussed what happened with his arm. That caused the Alpha to step in and make sure today ended like this. Stephen only wondered what else he ended up telling him concerning the "serendipitous" power outage. He was still holding back every urge to ask about it, but right now, he was fighting for his right to stay period. "What can I do or say to make you believe that I wouldn't do that?"

Alexander rubbed his temples, struggling with his own decisions, not wanting to make this situation worse than it already was. "I told you I didn't want to be put into the position to be 'the bad guy.' I said you were coming back too early. You ignored me. I was right there when you got your discharge papers from the hospital; the instructions were clear, and you ignored them. You getting hurt is the last thing I want for you." That got a look from all the employees, but none of them compared to the look his own mate gave him. "Getting *injured* is the last thing I want for you," he clarified.

"I can still get hurt," Stephen followed up.

Sean cleared his throat. "Look. The law is clear on how this liability works. It's even clearer that your boss has firmly stated you are not in any condition to work and that you do not have *permission* to work until your doctor's orders have passed. Now, I've heard you possess a stubborn disposition, one that all Alphas have." He noticed Stephen give another hurt look at Alexander. The ties which bound were slowly becoming undone. "So, hopefully, with me here to help defend my mate, you won't defy him this time and go against an Alpha witnessing an Omega's common-sense request *and* the open ears of two Betas who are your fellow employees." Sean grinned broadly at both Bruce and James, knowing the two Betas were taking in every word.

All Stephen could think about was how the world he slowly built this past month was vanishing before his very eyes. And now, here was Sean, finally able to squeeze himself into a scenario the Alpha couldn't fight him on. However, there was *one* last loophole Sean couldn't interfere with. Without even thinking about it, Stephen grabbed his wallet, pulled out a large bill, and slapped it on the counter.

Alexander saw the look in Stephen's eye. It was the same yesterday. "What are you doing?"

"I want a double Red Wild, a Wanderer for both Bruce and James, a double whiskey shot for you, and a beer for Sean." The Alpha's breath heaved as he finished the order.

Sean smirked. "Oh, this is pathetic."

"I'm in!" James walked over to the bar, standing on Stephen's side.

Bruce followed, ending up on the other side of Sean. "Me too!"

Alexander pinched the bridge of his nose. "You two aren't helping."

"What do you mean?" James asked innocently. "He's a suspended employee here now as a customer. He walked in with the injury existing. We all know it. The liability is now all on him."

Stephen wasn't a fan of the word "suspended" when it came to describing his mandatory break, but he couldn't have felt better in this moment, having two co-workers standing behind him. Not just co-workers—friends.

Sean wasn't giving up this easily. "Wow. And now, I finally have proof of what I've been hearing. It's happening right before my very eyes."

"What are you talking about?" Stephen dismissed.

"You really are the most selfish Alpha I've ever seen in my life," the Alpha stressed.

"What do you mean?"

Sean sat taller and leaned in. "You contributed to a bar fight, slimed your way into getting hired, got yourself into another bar fight which could have claimed the lives of anyone here, including Alex, and now, you have the audacity to defy your boss when all he's doing is trying to protect you and protect himself. That's letting go of the fact that I ended up with a lap full of beer. As far as *that* goes, I'm being mature and taking the high road. With you, now sitting here with that pompous Alpha disposition, can you say the same thing?"

The small victory Stephen had shriveled up in seconds. The glimmer in his eye and gentle smile on his face fell to nothing. Suddenly, he had a rotten feeling in his stomach. Without considering it, Stephen saw a mirror in front of the one person he didn't see as the common pattern in all of it: himself. The situations, individually, he felt his responsibility was minimal or that he himself was a victim of circumstance. But a pattern was forming... and Stephen was the only common thread in the entire pattern. His wolf whimpered.

Alexander's face dimmed with it and his heartstrings tugged. "That was out of line."

Sean stared back completely puzzled. "Alex—"

"He's right," the once proud Alpha confessed. "Doing this *is* selfish of me. I think I've been viewing myself as a constant victim, and it's blinded me to what's reality." He caught Alexander and held himself there. "I didn't ask for Eddie to shove a knife into me; I know that for certain." Sean rolled his eyes, ignoring the comment. "If I look deep down inside, I did exacerbate the problem with Eddie which got him to that point. Even if you don't agree with that, I have, on more than one occasion, not honored your wishes as not only my boss... but also my friend."

Both Alexander and Sean looked at the Alpha with completely different expressions. Alexander welcomed the revelation, feeling a mutual reciprocity he hadn't had with Stephen since the fundraiser for Jesse Minh. Sean looked like could have crushed the glass in his hand with the amount of force he was putting on it. But Stephen didn't care what he thought. He only cared about Alexander. "You are trying to protect me and you're protecting yourself as you should. That *is* selfish of me. And I'm sorry. I don't want to hurt you ... in any way."

Bruce laid on his hand on Stephen's shoulder, affirming the Alpha made the right decision. "You are a good man, Stephen. You may have had some tough luck, but we like you here."

James continued, "Yeah. You've grown to be a part of this place like the rest of us. You're part of the South Street Tavern family here."

"I agree," Alexander added.

Stephen's wolf purred in excitement at hearing Alexander saying something so confident. However his boss, no, *Fated Mate*, was going to consider him family, he'd take it. To keep that moment sacred, that meant he needed to play nice with Sean. With an Alpha's respect, he turned to him with an honest sincerity. "Would you still accept me buying you a beer if I took a shot before I hit the road?"

Sean glanced at his phone, considered the offer, looked at his mate, and then smiled. "I'm happy to oblige, but that's up to the bar owner."

Alexander was shocked at the sudden turn of authority, but he quickly took on the role. "I'm good with that. And Stephen... thank you."

The Alpha smiled and then pulled himself up from the bar. "Before I go, I better pee. Otherwise, my bladder is going to be cursing me all the way home."

"The only place you're going to be peeing in is a cup, Mr. Matheson," a voice commanded from the entrance.

All at once, everyone turned to see two officers, fully uniformed and fully armed staring back at the Alpha like he was the confirmed vigilante they've been looking for.

"I'm sorry. What?" Stephen stood there, completely clueless as to what was going on.

Alexander was clueless. "Officers, can I help you?"

"I'm Officer Davis, and this is my partner, Officer Gutierrez." Officer Davis grabbed his belt which was snug around his waist with both hands, sizing up the Alpha in question.

"You two make a great couple," James blurted. The first hit came from Bruce up against the side of his head; the next one hit his arm as Alexander reached over and gave him a second hit for good measure. "Ow! I'm just kidding." He shook them off.

"Is there something wrong?" Alexander spoke cautiously.

Gutierrez stepped forward. "We received an anonymous tip that this place was being used as an illegal drug dispensary and that *you*," he pointed to Stephen with a full police baton, ready for any threatening response the Alpha could return, "are the ringleader and prominent user."

Stephen froze and, in an instant, was taken back to a place he never wanted to be. He was petrified the moment he realized Warren was dead, and it was all because of him; now, his fate was being sealed by his own actions again. *Dealing drugs?* The words were foreign at first, but then he realized last night's encounter with Rat technically did fall under an identified statute, and even though all he could fess up to was theft, he knew they were going to try and nail him for more. And that's when the realization came cracking down. *Wolf Spit II. It removes culpability because it blacks out your memory.* That's what Rat had said last night. But what it didn't remove was a trace. *Damn it!* Stephen thought. The hustler led the Alpha straight into a trap and he fell for it. Rat wanted his way. He wanted Stephen back, and when he didn't get everything, he betrayed Stephen and turned him in. There was no other explanation. Stephen couldn't remember last night... because he took the new W.S. formula, and it removed his memory.

The Alpha's voice trembled as he struggled to get back any memory at all which could help put back the events of last night, hoping for any sign that this new revelation wasn't true. "Officers, I think you have the wrong guy. I haven't used any drugs in over ten years."

"You're Stephen Matheson, aren't you?" Officer Davis asked firmly.

"Yes?"

"Then, you're the right guy. But man, I do have to say, you don't look anything like you used to."

"No kidding," Officer Gutierrez commented, evaluating Stephen's build.

"What do you mean like he 'used to'?" Alexander asked, not liking where this conversation was going.

"You may not remember it. Officer Gutierrez and myself just started on the Tauris Police Force when you were getting into trouble. We were brought in to help with your brother's case."

"Something tells me you're not here for a happy reunion," Stephen surmised easily.

"We both have a lot of respect for Kane, son. So, we'll cut to the chase and try to do this as painlessly as possible. Do you want to do this the easy way or the hard way?"

"What are my options?" Stephen asked out of curiosity, but he already knew.

Officer Davis breathed in. "We can evaluate you here and clear you—"

"*If* you do get cleared," Officer Gutierrez clarified.

"Or we can take you downtown now and do it there," Officer Davis finished.

"Wait," Alexander jumped in, "on what grounds? An anonymous tip? *That's* your probable cause?"

"Unfortunately, with Stephen being a convicted felon, we don't need much. That being said, we received some very detailed information, including what you've allegedly been selling and using and where you allegedly keep your stash."

The final piece caught Stephen completely off-guard. "My 'stash'?" *Rat not only wants me punished, but he also wants me to pay with my life!*

"Protonitazene Complex," Officer Davis announced.

Bruce didn't understand the reference, nor did anyone else by the looks of it. "In layman's terms?"

"Wolf Spit or it's shortened name: W.S. These days, the dangerous drug is getting mixed with other O.T.C. medications which are altering its effects, including high doses of sleep aids."

"And I suppose that just so happens to be the one you're looking for on me?" Stephen guessed, sarcastically.

"It is," Officer Gutierrez confirmed.

"This is ridiculous!" Alexander's patience with the whole situation ran out. "This is a complete smear campaign and nothing more."

"Alex, let the officer do his job," Sean insisted.

Stephen eyed Sean from across the room. How convenient this all was for him. But was it a coincidence? Did *he* set this whole thing up? Was the 'intervention' to send Stephen home really a sting operation? The more Stephen thought about it, the more it didn't hold water. There were only a few people who knew which drug the Alpha was even using back in the day, and he certainly didn't tell anyone here. Rat was at the center of it, that he knew for sure. Finally, he honed in on the officer's request. "I'll respect Alexander's wishes. If he doesn't want this to happen here, I'll voluntarily go with you downtown."

"I think that's a good idea, myself," Sean added.

"No," Alexander quickly replied. He ran out from behind the bar and walked straight up to Stephen, conjuring up every Omega's wolf intuition he had. "Please, please tell me you didn't bring or use any drugs here," he whispered softly.

All Stephen wanted to do was wrap his arms around the Omega and hold him. Unfortunately, his focus wasn't on the suspected drug use or even this mysterious place the officers claimed he stowed away. All he could think about was handing over Alexander's prescription to Rat. By no surprise, it was left out of the anonymous report, even though it would have sealed the deal on Stephen's actions. But Rat wasn't about to let this get connected back to him. The only thing Stephen could do now was answer Alexander's question. In his mind, he believed the answers to be true. "I didn't bring drugs in here, and I didn't use anything. I promise." He in turn relented his pheromones to Alexander which stirred his wolf to investigate. It hurt even more when he still felt it, his wolf's connection to his Fate. What was he going to do about it now?

"Do it here." Alexander walked back to the bar.

"Babe, that's not a good move. Think of what customers will do when they see this!" Sean insisted.

Alexander looked at the wall clock and then to the officers. "I have customers who are going to be here in less than an hour right when I open. Can this be done by then?"

Officer Davis nodded. "The sooner we get our process done, the sooner we can leave. I can administer the drug test, and Gutierrez can do the search. We double-team this, and it can be done in 45 minutes."

The Omega looked at everyone in the bar. Sean was sitting on his last bit of patience. Bruce and James were besides themselves. Deep inside, Alexander didn't want this to be true. He couldn't ignore this entire time of all the warnings he had that this could be the outcome. It was all so surreal. The only thing he had left to hold onto was finding out the truth and hope nothing showed. "Get it done."

"You really need to think about this," Sean warned.

"I want it done, I want it over with, and I want to know the answer now! I'm not waiting for this." He nodded toward Officer Davis.

Officer Gutierrez walked toward the door. "I'll call for the dog."

***

"The dog is nice," Stephen said, hoping to cut into the awkward silence.

"Scooter? Yeah, he's our buddy. He's got a great sniffer on him," Officer Davis commented.

"I'm going to hold you to that, considering he didn't tear me apart."

"He wouldn't have done that unless he thought there was danger. So, that's a good sign to start with."

"That looks new," Stephen commented on the rather high-tech labels which were now being placed on the plastic containers. His voice echoed in the large bathroom hallway.

Officer Davis still focused on the form, filling it out near the dual bathroom sinks as he spoke, adjusting his grip with his rubber gloves. "I guess with you being in lockup, your tests looked a lot different. These ones are pretty handy when we're on the road. They say their sensitivity are within 2-3% of those which get the full run in the labs, and it can pick up traces of over a dozen substances—most of which are controlled drugs including what we're looking for."

"Oh good," Stephen mocked.

Officer Davis looked up and smiled. "Be real with me for a second. Are we going to find anything today?"

The answer was still hard in this throat, but Stephen stuck to his conviction. "No."

"Good." After a beat, Officer Davis continued letting his guard down. "I really am sorry what happened to your brother."

Stephen stared at the floor and nodded in acknowledgement. "There isn't a day that goes by that I don't think about him. That's the reason I don't do it anymore."

"You have more than just him, I'm sure," Davis pointed out. "You have your Sur and your Veo and your co-workers here are standing behind you 100% from what I can tell."

"They are. And that's not all." Stephen looked out into the hallway, as if he had X-ray vision, wondering what Alexander was thinking now, especially since he wasn't right there in front of him.

Officer Davis squinted. "Oh? Oh, I see."

"Don't get too excited. It's all unrequited." Stephen scoffed.

"Sorry about that. Hopefully, if we get the news we're looking for, that can get back to where it needs to be."

"Here's hoping," the Alpha replied.

"Okay. You ready?" Stephen nodded. "Is this your name and is it spelled correctly?" Stephen agreed. "Is this today's date?" Stephen answered. "And is this why we are here, and is this what you are consenting to?" Once again, Stephen replied, "Yes." "Hand me your I.D. and Type Card, and then, please sign your name here." The Alpha complied and began reaching for the cup.

"No! Don't touch that," Officer Davis commanded. "You didn't wash your hands."

"Oh. Sorry. I knew that." Stephen felt embarrassed, knowing that's how it worked. "Then, I just take it in there, right?"

"Not quite," Officer Davis started. Stephen's eyebrows furrowed. "It's happening right here."

"Excuse me?"

"Nothing in this bar is regulated. And I don't know if there's some fake wall where you stored warm piss bags or a decoy who's gonna do the test for you."

"I can't believe I'm hearing this."

"You want to avoid all this downtown and have us out of here before you open the bar? Drop 'em," Officer Davis commanded.

"Boy, if my daddy could see me now."

Officer Davis laughed. "Any doubt that he'd hesitate to do this?"

"Ten years ago, if it was to finally nail me so he could teach me a lesson? He'd probably hold the cup *and* my dick to make sure I didn't do anything wrong." Stephen paused. "You don't have to do that part, do you?"

Officer Davis laughed again. "No, thank Wolf-God. But I do have to observe it. Believe me, I've done a lot worse than this."

"I'll trust you on that," Stephen insisted. Clearing his mind of everything else, Stephen opened the lid and carefully set it on the counter. Afterward, he undid his buckle and pulled his pants down just enough to get access to his briefs and pull out his member for all the world to see. Stephen didn't consider himself shy, but of course, being in this situation, his mind refused to let him pee with the same ease he would any other time. Irrationally, the Alpha swore it took him an extra minute to finally gain control of himself until finally the relief came, and he filled it to the required line. He carefully set the cup back down, and Officer Davis swooped in with the cap and sealed the container instantly. "Mind if I—" He pointed to the bathroom. After getting permission, he went into the toilet and shut the door.

Stephen grunted to himself as he swore life couldn't get any lower than this. "Wolf-God, please, if you're out there..." The last time he prayed to Wolf-God, it was to end his life, right before he rushed his bike into the bog behind his yard. Instantly, another strange feeling took over Stephen. *The bog.*

TWO WEEKS AGO...

[Kane] "...Once you got out of the visibility from the property, you obviously had no idea where you were going. The headlight of your bike was still busted out. An hour later, you came limping up the driveway soaking wet and muddy, telling us you crashed the bike in the bog."

An uneasy feeling overcame Stephen in the moment. He swallowed hard as his eyes shifted and struggled to find any recollection of it happening. Nothing came. "I... I don't remember that."

"I *do* remember," Stephen said out loud. Before he could reminisce further, a loud knock commenced on the wooden door.

"Hey!" Officer Davis yelled. "You might want to come and see this."

Stephen closed his eyes. *That can't be good.* With an Alpha's fervor, he walked out the door, waiting for Officer Davis's inevitable news.

"We're clear!" he rang out, snapping off his rubber gloves.

"What?" Stephen broke.

"You sound surprised," Officer Davis noted as he finalized the paperwork.

"Everything about today is surprising me."

"Can't say I blame ya there." He handed Stephen back his I.D. and Type Card and then the pen for the last time. "Sign your name here, and then go tell that Omega out there the good news." He winked.

Somehow, Stephen was able to smile back as he rushed back out to the bar. Everyone out there was waiting for him, including Eric, who must have come in while he was getting the test administered. "It's clear."

"What?!" Sean exclaimed.

Everyone else ignored the sudden comment and instead gave a sigh of sigh of relief while Bruce and James cheered him on as they ran to his side. Before Stephen knew it, Alexander had wrapped himself around Stephen in an unexpected embrace. The Alpha froze instantly as he felt the strength of the Omega's arms warp around him, the warmth of the Omega's body rushing into him, and the strongest scent of the Omega's pheromones consuming every part of his being. Inside, Stephen's wolf sang in a way it never had before. After a moment or two, he finally came to his senses and slowly wrapped his strong arms around the Omega, for the first time ever. He closed his eyes and savored the moment, hoping it never had to end. He couldn't let this be the end.

"Thank Wolf-God," Alexander whispered.

Stephen's body held still, but the wolf inside started to stir, wondering how to take the exasperated statement. "What do you mean?" he tested.

Alexander slowly let go, revealing two eyes heavy with moisture, refusing to let go a single drop. "Oh, it's nothing." He sniffled.

"What? What's nothing?" Stephen pressed.

"Some asshole called me on the phone yesterday trying to scare me. Said that if I didn't let you go, everyone was going to find out who you really were."

The Alpha's heart sank and stomach hitched. "Who?"

"That's just it. I have no clue. They blocked the call and had no intention of identifying themselves. A coward—that's who it was."

Stephen's moment of tranquility stopped instantly and was replaced by strenuous movements rushing throughout his body. He knew there was no coincidence in the anonymous call. "When you say 'find out' about me? Find out about what?"

The Omega crossed his arms and pushed his hip out as he contemplated how to word the information carefully. "At the time of the call, I didn't know what specifically. I thought initially maybe it was just the fact you were incarcerated. But today, when I came in..." he paused as he looked toward Sean once more, hating every second of making the reveal, "I discovered my medication missing. It was in the red emergency med kit behind the bar. Eric and I looked at the footage of the bar last night. The bottle was placed on the bar after you looked at it. It appeared you were caught up in talking to a customer last night, and it was all left unattended. So, of course, when the lights went out, someone grabbed it. Asshole."

Bruce stepped in. "I was going to ask you today if you happened to know more about the guy you were talking to last night. Maybe he was the one who took them. Ray—was that his name?"

An uncomfortable sensation began to engulf Stephen. He eyed everyone in the room, including the two cops who were still there, taking in every word. "Ray Taylor and I haven't maintained a friendship in ten years. Ten years ago, I knew him. Now? He could be a completely different person."

Officer Davis used the opportunity to bring the question forward. "Did you see him take the prescription bottle?" Stephen mustered up all his pheromones and stone-walled his emotions as he shook his head. "Did you see anything before you left your shift last night?"

"Before I left the shift, I did have the med bag out. I was looking for a painkiller on purpose, so I wouldn't have any chance of getting into trouble. When Ray walked into the bar, I got distracted. I didn't put the bottle back, and I didn't put the medication bag away. But I didn't take them. I went to the bathroom, cleaned up my arm, and then I was relieved of my shift." Stephen's voice was firm and constant, but inside, he was screaming. "If I could have done it all again, I wish I had never touched the med bag, or at least had the wits about me to get your prescription back in that bag and where it belongs. Anything that happened to them afterward, I consider my fault. And I'm sorry, Alex."

The Omega nodded as he took in the seriousness of Stephen's words.

Gutierrez piped in, "Don't take all the responsibility. Your boss also needs to take responsibility on the location of where he puts such medications. Any customer could have reached into a First-Aid kit and pulled that out. If they were an irresponsible or drunk person and consumed something they were allergic to or in too high of quantity for an overdose, there's no doubt you'd see a lawsuit on your hands."

Eric threw up his hands and pointed straight at the Omega. "I've told you that time and time again! The way I see it, Alex, you should consider yourself lucky they were stolen. Whoever has them are probably miles away from this place and good riddance. But if they were dead on this floor today, we'd be having an entirely different conversation, and there'd be blood on your hands."

In any other situation, Stephen was convinced he'd have attacked Eric for reaming his Omega in such a way. However, his fellow Alpha rank worded his criticism which opened old wounds once again in a way he knew Eric didn't realize. While staying silent, it allowed Stephen to think of more immediate concerns. That's when it hit. "Wait. There was an anonymous call yesterday warning you to fire me? When?"

"Before you came in," Alexander stated.

The Alpha's pheromones released and revealed his true, raw emotion: anger. "And you didn't think to tell me?!"

"I... I didn't want to worry you," the Omega defended.

"And then, the next day, two cops show up and launch an investigation on me being a drug dealer and user on coincidentally the exact same drug I was put away ten years for?!" Stephen's voice rang out loud and clear in the way which made everyone's wheels turn. "This was a set-up!"

"Sounds like it to me," James said as he nodded at his Beta brother.

"I agree." Alexander stood firm.

Sean looked around the room at everyone who mentally rushed to Stephen's side, including two cops who began to change their attitude. "Just because you don't have any drugs in your system or on you at the moment doesn't mean you aren't organizing yourself as a side business."

Stephen grimaced. "*A side business?*"

"Your reputation precedes you."

"A reputation you've taken a microscopic look at, I've noticed. The only one in this room who knows as much as I do is *you*." The Alpha eyed the elite businessman like a target.

Sean scoffed. "Oh, please. Just because I'm the only smart one in the room who has decided to do his homework does not make me a bad person. As soon as I heard you got hired, you bet your ass I spent hours trying to figure out whether you were putting my mate's livelihood or his life in danger! The fact we are all standing here, waiting for results to find out if you are guilty of bringing this nightmare on us is a full-circle moment if there ever was one."

"As far as we can tell, we're clear here. There's no positive drug test. No substances in his system, on his person, in the bar, or on his bike. And unless someone here wants to tell me otherwise, there are no witnesses or accounts from anyone here he as even committed foul play." Everyone in the room scanned faces, waiting for someone to say something to the contrary. But after a few moments of silence, Officer Davis was satisfied with the investigation. "Then we're done here." Officer Gutierrez walked out first. Before he followed, he turned to Stephen one last time. "If someone does have it out for you, son, this won't be the last time we get a call. Continue to stay out of trouble, and you'll be cleared. So, I suggest you keep on doing whatever you're doing to stay that way." He glanced back at Alexander, remembering the conversation from earlier about the Alpha's relationship challenges. "If you happen to track down who you believe is responsible for the call to the bar and the report to the police, let us know. Same for the missing medication."

"Yes, sir," Stephen promised. An uncomfortable silence blanketed the bar after the officers left. The Alpha's conscience was heavy with knowing he put the entire bar through this mess. That wasn't even addressing his role in betraying the last person he ever thought he would. "I-I think I better head out."

Alexander nodded. "It's just a week. I want you back here on Friday; it's going to be busier than normal."

Sean's eyes grew wide. "Alex—"

"What's going on Friday?" Stephen asked.

"That's what I wanted to tell you before the cops showed up. Believe it or not, there was a silver lining to last night's power outage!"

The Alpha furrowed his brows. "And that was?"

"A rep from W.K.E.B. Radio just so happened to be in the bar that night. I don't know if he was scoping the place out or here for his personal enjoyment, but it seems he was thoroughly impressed with our security efforts and control on the crowd when we were trying to get the power back on. He said if that had happened with the previous owner, all hell would have broken loose. He was relieved we moved past the old reputation."

"Okay..."

"T's Bar normally hosts the Singles' Night event sponsored by the radio station, but the bar's water pipes sprung a leak, and they're cleaning up flood damage. He asked if we'd be willing to host a last-minute relocation! Isn't that great?!" Alexander's expression brightened.

Somehow, Stephen himself managed a smile. "Alex, that's great!"

"Now you have to quit being a stubborn Alpha and get that damn arm healed so I can have you back." That statement had more than one pair of eyes looking at him in shock. The Omega blushed. "At work... back at work."

Sean shoved his phone in his shirt pocket and stood up. "I am so sick of this."

Alexander creased his lips and closed his eyes as he realized where this was going. The Alpha's pheromone palate said it all. "Sean—"

"No. I don't want to hear it, Alex." He grabbed his suit jacket and put it on with disappointment and frustration plastered all over his face. "Every time he causes drama, you ignore it. Every time he causes trouble, you find some way to justify it. And every time I try to look out for you, my mate, by telling you he's a problem, I get nowhere."

"It's not like that," the Omega pleaded.

"See? You're doing it right now!" Alexander tensed at the harsh criticism. "If the cops showing up at the place where you claim people think South Street has moved on from that 'reputation' you talked about isn't enough for you to see it, then you don't want to see it." The Alpha didn't get a response. He shook his head, unable to believe this was what his mate was choosing. "Call me when you've come to your senses."

The Alpha left in a huff but not before giving Stephen one last glare. His pheromones were bright fiery flames wanting to engulf and suffocate the pitiful excuse of a man. But he knew this wasn't the time nor the place, especially the heels of two officers of the law still within whistling distance. "You haven't seen the last of me." He turned on his feet and walked out.

"Sean!" Alexander tried. The Omega lifted his arms and held his head. "I don't believe this."

Stephen gulped down his nerves. "Alex, I—"

"I'll see you in a week, Stephen."

"Let me just say—"

"I said: I'll see you in a week."

Stephen stood there unsure of what to say. But he knew what he had to do. Like Sean before him, he left, scenting his Omega's ever-changing scent once again.

CHAPTER 04:

WONDERING IF IT WAS
ALL MEANT TO BE

"Dr. Forrester," a man's deep voice said through the phone. "Hi, Dr. Forrester. It's Stephen Matheson."

"Well, well," the doctor replied joyfully, "I had to look twice when my secretary wrote your name down on my schedule. How are you?"

Stephen sighed as he pinched his nose. He couldn't believe he even had to say it. "Not well. Isn't that why people need doctors?"

"I ask open-ended questions to assess you. I make no assumptions on your condition nor status," Dr. Forrester replied plainly.

The Alpha smirked. "I have a feeling I know your next 'open-ended' question."

"How have things been since you were released?"

"Oh, hell. Where do I begin?"

Sometime later, Stephen's monologue finally ended. He could only imagine what the doctor thought of him now.

"Stephen," he gasped, "you have certainly been busy."

"You're telling me!" The Alpha laughed, taking a moment to find the humor in the craziness.

"How have you been handling all that?"

"Horribly. That's why I've needed your support. I miss having you there."

Dr. Forrester acknowledged the compliment. "I miss our sessions as well. Not all my patients have been open or utilized services like you did. That goes for those in Brooks Haven and out."

Stephen's mood fell. "Don't count me as a success story yet."

"What's going on?" Dr. Forrester inquired.

"I think... I think I'm having some sort of mental breakdown."

"A breakdown? Do you feel safe? Do you require immediate attention?"

The words stung harder than the Alpha anticipated. Images of sitting right across from the Ph. D. came flooding back, halting the natural flow of the conversation. He started speaking slower. "I'm not ... in any immediate danger." Thoughts of the past couple days reminded him otherwise. But that's not what he was here to talk about. "Something has started to happen. Memories of my brother are creeping into my consciousness. It's like everything I do is reminding me of my past, *our* past. It's flashing right there in front of my eyes, and I'm transported there. Or ... in some instances ... it's transported here. I'm failing to keep it at bay."

The doctor took a beat before answering. "You shouldn't look at it as a failure. Blocking memories does not make a wolf stronger. And remembering them doesn't make him weaker. Know that."

"Thanks."

"You mentioned this just started. Why do you think it's happening now?"

Admitting further failure sent his Alpha status even lower. "I think it's because I feel I'm losing control of everything. My past is haunting my present at a time when the present alone is hard enough to deal with. My former dealer is looking to destroy my life, my Sur's memory is shot to hell, my job at the bar is becoming nothing but drama, and I've betrayed my Fated Mate."

"This is the same Fated Mate you mentioned who doesn't feel the signature connection?" Stephen confirmed. "And this is about betraying him by allowing your dealer to take his medication?"

"Yeah. It is. And... something else." The Alpha paused, gathering his thoughts. "After I left that night, I encountered my dealer happily exploiting his new victory right behind the bar. He tried his hardest to get me to take a new enhanced version of W.S.—the drug I used to take. The drug that..."

"The drug which claimed Warren's life."

Stephen shut his eyes and bit his lip. He wasn't going to cry. He wasn't going to allow it. "Ray said there was a new enhanced version which completely fucks with your memory. He claims the advantage is it allows the user to deny any involvement because—well—he wouldn't remember it."

"And... did you take it?"

The Alpha grimaced. "That's just it! I don't remember. And it's not only that; I don't remember *anything* after that point. The next day, I tried to piece it all together, and I couldn't come up with one scrap to help trigger even the slightest moment of the night after he offered it to me."

Dr. Forrester now realized where this was going. "And your conclusion is: because memory loss is the enhanced drug's signature, that must mean you did indeed take it."

"Exactly."

"I assume you didn't get a drug test to find out for sure."

"Heh. Believe it or not, I had it performed the very next day. Less than 24 hours in fact."

"You did?!" The doctor took in the information, completely shocked. "What was its result?"

"Negative."

"Negative?!"

"Yes, sir."

"I'm fascinated by it all—honestly," Dr. Forrester confessed.

"Great." Stephen rubbed his face.

"How are you feeling after all that?"

Now the Alpha *had* to get real. "Scared."

"Why?"

"Because I don't know why I don't remember."

"Hmm. Let's start here." The doctor cleared his throat. "What *is* the last thing you remember?"

Nerves began to overtake the Alpha. It was a place he didn't want to go back to. He considered himself foolish for thinking it would go anywhere but here. But he couldn't back down now. "Seeing the pills right there in my hand? Smelling them? Teetering on the fact it could have gone either way. I was just gone. It was like I was floating in thin air. Warren was the first thought, and I was sure I was going to go down memory lane once more. But... something happened."

"Go on..."

Stephen's breath became shallower... faster. "My stomach and chest became sensitive, like sparks were running throughout. My mind told my lungs I wasn't breathing, even though I was. And then, there was this taste of blood."

"'Taste of blood'?" Dr. Forrester inquired.

"Well, I mean, there *wasn't* blood. But it felt like it. I could smell a metallic scent through my nostrils, and I could taste it on my tongue. And it wasn't just for a second. It just... lingered there. And then... I... I don't remember anything after that. The next thing I can recall is waking up in my bed. I mean, Wolf-God, I don't even remember getting home. My bike was in the driveway in a place I've *never* parked it before, and I woke up on edge like I witnessed... witnessed..."

"A death?" Stephen huffed in reply. "Simple explanation," Dr. Forrester concluded.

The Alpha couldn't believe his ears. "What? Really?"

"Of course. You have P.T.S.D., Stephen. We diagnosed you with that already. What you had here was an attack—an anxiety attack more specifically."

The explanation was too simple for Stephen. "An anxiety attack? I haven't had one in years! And *now* I get one?! That doesn't seem logical."

"But it is," Dr. Forrester disagreed.

"How?"

"They call it being 'locked up' for a reason. For ten years, you were confined to a space that separated from the world you knew: the good, the bad, and the ugly. That includes facing anyone and anything which reminds of you of what happened to Warren. You may have been trapped in a cell, but that cell also protected you."

Hearing the justification made the Alpha's mind roll in circles. "Oh, come on. I saw so many inmates who had these episodes during lock-up. I didn't have this happen the entire time."

"Everyone is different, Stephen. And let's not forget, our sessions avoided talking about your past for the most part. We focused on the here and now and your ability to cope with not using drugs, not expressing your anger in negative ways, and considering how you were going to deal with the broken relationships of your past. Warren's death, on the other hand? And the fallout before and after? That was something I rarely pushed and was certainly something you rarely offered."

The cold hard truth was tough. However, everything in the past month or so put it all into perspective. "I guess I didn't talk about that enough."

"Are you ready to talk about it now?" Dr. Forrester pressed.

Stephen held his breath. "I think... I think I need more time."

The doctor's tone was soft. "Are you safe?"

"I'm safe." The Alpha spoke confidently.

"I'm always here, Stephen. When you're ready, you call me. We'll schedule a time for you to come in face-to-face."

"Thank you, Dr. Forrester."

"It was great to hear from you. And I look forward to it again."

***

Stephen decided the off week from work needed to be spent honoring his Sur's set objectives since he got back from Brooks Haven. He didn't think his Sur would offer any help. If his arm wasn't healing, he wasn't sure it would have happened. But it did, and Kane took control and monitored his Alpha son about every thirty minutes whether Stephen wanted it or not. Therefore, the young Alpha took up a hammer and nails and fixed the few damaged boards on the siding of the house. Afterward, he spot-treated several areas which needed a touch-up of paint. After getting in touch with Joe, one of the neighbors, about adding additional gravel to the driveway, he gladly helped Stephen and Kane add a new top layer of shingles to the roof.

The results took Stephen aback. From the driveway, the house didn't even remotely give off the same essence it did when he first walked up after being gone for ten years. Like his own turnaround, the house had new life. After the finishing touches of a few branches and bushes being trimmed down to size, the property might as well have been new.

Through it all, the Alpha sensed an overwhelming amount of frustration being carried away through his sweat glands. It made the time go by faster, especially with being able to avoid thinking about Sean, Ray, Eddie, and even Alexander to a certain extent.

Surprisingly, this time around, Bruce and James kept tabs on him and vicariously communicated updates to his Fated Omega. It was disappointing but understandable as to why Alexander chose not to keep in contact. He only imagined what the Omega had to deal with after the ordeal with Sean. He guessed the two needed repair—and as much as Stephen hated thinking it was happening—it wasn't any of his business.

Of all the things happening during his Fix-It week, one thing he didn't count on was how sore his body was. His sutured arm survived and healed nicely; his muscles throughout his body, however? Not so much. The Alpha couldn't believe the work completely exhausted him to the point he wasn't sure he could walk on Wednesday. That's why he called it quits the second half of that day and was bound and determined to use all of Thursday to recoup, knowing he was going back to the bar on Friday. Before falling asleep Thursday night, he was grateful when he woke up—the day was going to be upon him.

What he *wasn't* grateful for was the way in which he was awakened. Loud taps hit the window late in the morning. The Alpha stretched and moaned as his body reminded him he wasn't fully recovered yet from the workouts he subjected himself to. None of that compared to the pain going through his mind as he feared who was at his window now. "Ray. You bastard," he mumbled. His eyes were hazy and his muscles still had him moving at a snail's pace to start, but he only had one objective at this point: get the Beta the fuck off the property and hope his Sur and Veo never knew he was ever there.

However, once his vision cleared and his senses focused, he realized it wasn't Ray at all. The interloper didn't surprise him any less. "Daniel?!" The Alpha grunted as he forced the window up, seeing the young sprite with his small frame and red hair glistening in the morning sun. "What the hell are you doing here?"

"Hey! I wanted to see you," he quickly answered.

Stephen couldn't believe it. "What the fuck is wrong with people?! Does no one use the front door anymore? Did I not get the memo that the new way to get someone's attention is by banging on their bedroom window?!"

Daniel showed his teeth and threw his head back in an unexpected pile of nerves, never anticipating this greeting back. "Yikes! And to think I missed you!"

Stephen removed his bark and relaxed his posture. "Sorry. I didn't mean that. I missed you too." Just then, he saw Daniel use all his might to hop up and fling his body up onto the windowsill to crawl inside the bedroom. "What the—what are you doing?!"

The young Beta grunted. "Are you just gonna stare at me, or are you gonna help me?"

"Wolf-God! Here." Stephen offered the fool the assistance he needed to finally accomplish his goal. Considering the Alpha remembered *his* attempt at doing the same not too long ago, he had to applaud Daniel's tenacity. With recovered strength, he managed to get Daniel in safely without him becoming a mop on the floor first.

"Thanks." Daniel exhaled. He examined Stephen standing there in nothing but his boxers, muscles protruding in a way he hadn't seen before. "Damn. Lookin' good, Alpha." He blushed as he caught glimpses of a little *too* much.

Stephen looked down at his lack of attire, rolled his eyes, and crossed his arms, as if it was to help gain any modesty. "You caught me when I was sleeping. What am I supposed to look like?"

"Dressed head-to-toe like you live in a monastery?" Daniel joked.

"Funny," the Alpha replied sarcastically. Not wanting to perpetuate it further, Stephen found a pair of sweatpants and put them on before returning to the comfort of his bed. "Considering you're with James who could have easily given you my number, am I to believe this is something more than a casual visit?" An uneasy feeling suddenly struck the Alpha. "Is Alex all right?"

Daniel intercepted the panic immediately. "No, no. He's okay... sort of."

"Sort of?"

The young Beta fiddled with his hands. "He's ... stressing out." Stephen waited for the details. "You remember when Alex was having some sort of meltdown the night you were stabbed?"

Stephen scratched his head. "You mean the night you weren't even there? Yeah..."

"It's like that again. Or at least, that's what Bruce and James are saying."

The Alpha couldn't believe his ears. "And *that's* your version of 'Okay'?" He saw the Beta give an uneasy smile back. "Wow, Daniel. I suggest you rethink your definition."

Daniel groaned. "Why is it every time I have a conversation with you, we get into some sort of argument? Do our astrological signs hate each other or something?"

That made Stephen smile. "It wouldn't be the first-time fate has screwed me over." That's when the Beta's expression fell. "What's wrong?"

Daniel hesitated and finally blurted, "I don't want Alex with Sean. I want him with you."

The Alpha had to process it twice—no, three times, before replying. "I... um... Okay... Any particular reason?"

Unable to calm his nerves, Daniel finally found a spot next to Stephen on the edge of the Alpha's bed. "I can't explain it. Sean was always a dick, but it was in that 'mosquito buzzing in your ear' sort of way. But ever since you came into the picture—"

"Oh, *that* makes me feel good."

"No, I'm serious!" The Beta demanded Stephen's attention. "Ever since you came into the picture, Sean has become darker and darker, a person I don't trust."

"He's not hurting Alex, is he? Because Wolf-God if he is..." Stephen was about to lose his mind.

"He's not hurting him. At least, not physically. But the mental stress he's been putting Alex under is getting hard to ignore."

Stephen bowed his head. "As much as I want to beat his ass for it, Daniel, I can't ignore that if *I* was in Sean's position, I would go crazy too. Therefore, it's hard to believe this isn't because of me—it's my fault. And I've worried time and time again that I'm just causing Alex misery."

The Beta shook his head. "But that's just it. You're not. In fact, every single time he's talked about you, texted about you, or hell, even when I can tell he's *thinking* about you, he changes as a person, and it's for the better. And yeah, if I can see it, then I suppose Sean sees it too. It makes logical sense that it caused him to become over-protective. Especially since right before you were hired, Sean asked Alex to contract with him."

Stephen's ears perked up, and his inner wolf began to pace back and forth. "He... *what?!*"

Daniel's eyes widened. "You... You didn't know?"

"Fuck." The Alpha rubbed his eyes, wishing this moment to be a dream. But when he stopped, all he saw was the Beta's regrettable expression. "You're telling me I walked in and confessed to Alex I was his Fate only days after Sean proposed to him?!"

"Yes?" Daniel squeaked.

"Ugh! Shit. No wonder why Sean's wanted my head from day one. He was getting ready to claim Alex for life, and I came in like a homewrecker." At this point, the Alpha felt like the stupidest man on earth. "Well, that settles it. Tonight, I'm going to go in, apologize to Alex. Hell, I'll even apologize to Sean if he's there. Then, I'll give my notice and leave them the fuck alone."

Daniel couldn't believe his ears. "Wait... *what*? Why... why would you do that?"

"Because I didn't know Alex was already set to make a life with him. I can't say for sure if I had known that since moment one if I wouldn't have at least tried. But I've been there a month now, and Alex doesn't want me. He wants Sean, and I can't change that."

"Yes, you can," Daniel insisted.

"How do you know that?"

"Because Alex didn't say 'Yes.'"

The moment hit Stephen like an epiphany. "He ... said 'No'?"

"Well... not really."

Stephen rolled his eyes. "Daniel... come on!" Now he got up, followed his inner wolf, and began pacing on his bedroom floor. The wood creaked beneath his feet when he hit just the right places.

"Alexander point blank told me he can't see a viable future with him. I think he's scared of telling Sean 'No' because he doesn't know who is going to be there by his side if he leaves."

"*I* would be by his side!" the Alpha insisted loudly.

"I know that," Daniel confirmed.

"Then why doesn't Alex..." Stephen sighed and lowered his voice. "I know why... It's because I scared the shit out of him. I'm a wild card, and I'm unpredictable. With so much riding against him, he's a strong-willed Omega, owns a bar, and has criticism about his career *and* his rank... He's protecting himself from me. It's been there all along, and I didn't want to see it." He leaned against his dresser as he continued to reflect. "And look at all the baggage I carry. My arrest record is just the tip of the iceberg. I was an angry son-of-a-bitch looking to make anyone just as miserable as I was. I lashed out, picked fights, pushed everyone who cared about me away, and filled that void with fake, hollow people and drugs. And it cost my brother his life."

Daniel took in the Alpha's low pheromones, truly feeling the hurt he felt. "I heard about the whole drug test at the bar. And to think Sean was there on top of it all; I'm surprised he didn't lunge at you for a brawl after the incident with the beer glass."

"Agreed."

"I was also told he made some comment about your brother that day?"

Stephen nodded slowly. "He did. That's when I lost it. I have a lot of demons to face. I need to admit that. But no man should have to deal with what Sean said to me. I'm not going to repeat it though."

"I'm fine with that," Daniel confirmed. "But... what are the demons you are talking about?"

Stephen looked up at the innocent Beta on his bed. He genuinely cared; that's why he was there. With everything he knew, he was still there, championing him. He wasn't Dr. Forrester, but he might as well have been. Stephen took a seat next to Daniel on the bed and decided to come clean.

"I dealt with being locked up for ten years better than I should have. And it wasn't until recently that I discovered why." He eyed Daniel, making sure he still wanted to hear it. He continued, "I blocked out all the memories I didn't want to face. I mean, I didn't even want to face the memories I *did* remember. Let's face it: you don't forget what your brother looks like when he's lying on your bed... not blinking... not breathing. Then, there's your Sur shouting out commands, thinking the louder he yells, the more successful they'll be. And finally, your Veo... in absolute hysterics... sobbing, wailing, feeling completely helpless." One look at Daniel confirmed what he expected to see: tears welling up in his eyes. The Alpha forced himself to look away but started going down what he refused to admit ... to anyone. "Warren was pronounced dead at the hospital an hour later. I practically ran out of the E.R., found my bike, and sped home faster than I ever dared to in downtown Tauris. At that point, I didn't care what happened to me."

"Where did you go?" Daniel asked, wiping away a tear.

"Home." Stephen chuckled. "The one place I never wanted to see again; that's the only place I could think of going." He paused. "But it wasn't to seek comfort."

"What was it for?"

The Alpha took one deep breath and admitted. "To die... I went home to kill myself. When I got back home, I took off my helmet, revved my engine at the bottom of the driveway, and drove straight into the damn light pole. I was hoping I'd fly off and crack my head open on the solid wood."

"That didn't happen?"

"No. Right before I hit the pole, I lost control of the bike in the grass. I fell off to the side, and the bike hit the pole sideways and busted out the front light. I was so pissed it didn't work. But the adrenaline had left me at that point, and I didn't have the will to do it again. At least, not that way."

Daniel turned his body and looked at the Alpha head-on. "What did you do?"

"I knew my days were numbered. I endured them until the night before I was supposed to go in for my sentencing while I was out on bail. I got the drunkest I had ever been and then went back to my bike. This time, I drove it down the backyard, into the woods, and headed toward the river to drown myself... and then," Stephen stressed, "I missed it completely."

"Missed it?"

"Mmhm. Between being drunk and not having a headlight, I had no clue where I was going. I thought doing it by memory was enough, but I went toward the bog instead and hit a sand pit. I was flown off my bike onto this little island as if I was stranded in the middle of an ocean. The moonlight wasn't enough to find Crusher, so I considered her a loss. I came hobbling up the driveway... told my Sur... and then went to bed. The next day was day one of my incarceration." A whirlwind of thoughts and emotions went through the Alpha's mind. Chains were bursting at every possible link and gave him the clarity he had been missing, avoiding, for over ten years.

"Wolf-God, Stephen. I had no idea." Daniel sniffled.

"You know... the funny thing is... nether did I. At least, not for the longest time."

The Beta's wheels began turning in his head. "Don't read into this too much, but why did you feel crashing your bike into a pole or in the river was the way to do it?"

Stephen hiked his eyebrows. "Fair question." He rubbed his chin, feeling the tough hairs scratch along his fingers. "It would have been easy to overdose the same way Warren did or find a gun I suppose. But I think I felt I deserved something more painful and long-lasting. I guess I felt I owed my brother that. I didn't crash my bike into oncoming traffic because I figured I had hurt enough people. An accident was one thing, but I wasn't going to do it on purpose."

Daniel lightly put his hand on Stephen's shoulders. "I'm glad you didn't."

Stephen looked back with heavy eyes. "Thank you."

"And I know several other people who are glad you didn't either. And one of them is the most important person you're going to have in your life."

The Alpha rolled his eyes. "Fate has made it clear, Daniel. It's not going to happen."

"Wolf-God gives Alphas and Omegas a Fate to have a chance. What *we* do with it is what creates our destiny. It's the fate *we* choose. If you want Alex to *be* your Fate, you can't give up. Giving up is the only way you make sure it doesn't happen."

Stephen looked at Daniel as if he was Wolf-God himself, channeling himself through an Omega he never thought in a million years he'd know, let alone entertain. But here he was... giving an Alpha a cold, hard truth. The ball was in Stephen's court now. His next move was going to determine everything.

Stephen rode Crusher into the city against the backdrop of gray clouds covering the blue sky. No doubt there was rain moving in. His first thoughts were of Alexander and his Singles Night event and how it might affect the attendance. But then his right mind took over and settled on the idea it wouldn't do much since the event was indoors and the fact single Wolf-Descendants, especially young ones, wouldn't be deterred by something so trivial. Either way, all he wanted was his Fated Mate happy. In fact, that's all he could think about on the way in. The conversation that morning with Daniel breathed new life into the Alpha. He swore he even felt his inner wolf growl at him for even *thinking* about giving up. He wasn't going to do that again.

The Alpha pulled into the back alley of the bar, another place he didn't want to remember at the time. Luckily, he saw Eric coming out of the bar with a ladder and a wrench getting ready to do some sort of job. He parked Crusher and hoisted himself off, showing off a cerulean blue dress shirt, black pants, and shined-up shoes. Stephen hoped he'd elicit some sort of compliment from his boss but that's when he saw Eric put all his focus at lining up the ladder perfectly toward the security camera above the door.

"What's going on?" Stephen inquired slowly.

Eric grunted as he took every step up the ladder like he was running his hands across the legs of several large spiders or shoving his hand into a snake burrow. "I thought I fixed this last time. Didn't pull it tight enough."

Stephen eyed the camera, only then noticing the swivel had moved once again. "Someone came back?"

"I guess so." He put the wrench between his teeth and slowly moved the swivel back to its rightful position, aimed directly at Stephen's head. Then, he pulled the wrench out from between his lips and used every single ounce of strength he had to make sure the nut and bolt wouldn't move again without someone directly tampering with it while balancing on their own ladder—therefore directly putting their cowardly face directly into the camera lens.

"Did the bar get hit? Did they vandalize the place?"

Eric stopped his progress instantly. He held the rung and turned slowly. "I'm sorry, Stephen," he muttered.

The Alpha gazed back in confusion. That's when he followed Eric's gaze right to his foot. Underneath his black shoe was a white sheet of paper with professional print all over it. His peripheral caught several copies of the same paper casually blowing off the rugged asphalt. Slowly, Stephen picked up one and gazed at its damning information. His eyes grew wide. "Oh, no."

Black lettering in the traditional form of a newspaper article brought back the memory of an incident over ten years ago: **POLICE CAPT'S SON SENTENCED IN BROTHER'S DEATH.** Below the title sat a crystal-clear picture of Stephen standing next to his lawyer, presumably hearing the judge's terms of his punishment. He barely recognized his body or his soulless expression. As much as he hoped no one else could make the visual connection, it was a fool's hope. Below it, the article gave every piece of information one could need.

Stephen finally looked up with a somber face back at Eric, who was waiting for the inevitable. "Does Alexander know?"

"Kinda hard for him not to. These were plastered all over the front entrance of the bar. We tried cleaning up every single one, but we didn't realize just how many there were. After looking at the footage, there's no hint as to who it was. He was covered from head to toe and did this at about 4 A.M. this morning. We contacted the police and turned—"

The Alpha walked toward the sidewalk, not wanting to hear any more of it. With Eric still blocking the back door with his ladder, he walked around the side of the bar, picking up another stray sheet of paper on his way to the front. An anxious feeling covered him as he pushed the door open. There in the center, he found Alexander behind the bar, both elbows on the rail, hands beneath his jaw-line. In the center, a large stack of white papers sat below him. His gaze was transfixed on the article. Stephen shut his eyes but realized there was nothing else he could do. Therefore, he continued his slow journey up to the bar and sat on a stool right in front of him. The Omega didn't flinch, didn't acknowledge him, and didn't say anything. Seconds ticked by like hours. Until...

"You know... I sometimes completely forget it was your brother who died," Alexander stated quietly. Stephen looked back, half-offended at the comment. "I don't mean it in a bad way. Everything negative in your past has always been focused around the drug use and felony charge. It's easy to forget real people were affected by this... including you." Stephen relaxed his pheromones and understood where this was going. "I don't think I could ever imagine what it was like for you and your family to lose him. Ten years, every single day, constantly being reminded of why you were in prison... *I'd* go insane. How did *you* survive that?"

The Alpha simply shrugged. "There were only two choices I had: survive it or end it all. I don't know where the strength came from to *not* end it all. Wolf-God knows at the time I was entirely in the right frame of mind to do it. But I guess..." he looked straight into Alexander's eyes, "I wanted something more."

Alexander stared back with a wet gloss covering both eyes. A few beats later, he shook out of his trance and sighed. "Man, I gotta stop this." He grabbed the pile of papers and threw them all away in the nearest bin. "I've been in a whirlwind of emotions the last couple of days. It's like I'm to the point where I could cry over spilled milk or something."

Stephen got up from the bar and walked over, full of concern. "Did something happen?"

"Oh, I'm sure it has something to do those meds I take. I'm not getting along with my Sur right now, so I've avoided him completely. He's the one who prescribes them, but I haven't found the nerve to tell him I was irresponsible enough to lose them. The bastard doesn't need another reason to point out I'm a failure in every part of my life."

"*That's* what he says to you?" Stephen's inner wolf began showing his teeth, unsure of how he would react if he saw the Omega's Sur right now in person.

"My Alpha father is very old school and fully embraces the rhetoric of yesteryear on how to view and treat Omegas. If he had any say in how I spent my grandfather's inheritance, I wouldn't be here in this bar right now. There's no doubt about that."

How he found the courage, Stephen wasn't sure. But he did and chose to ask. "Why are you taking those? I've asked casually and even saw the bottle once. Is it just a suppressant?"

Alexander twitched his lips. "It's not something I usually tell people but... what the hell." He folded his arms. "When I started showing signs of beginning my first heat, I was 14 years old. Like any Omega, my dad scheduled me a physical with a doctor to get my first prescription. Funny enough, it was the nicest thing he had done for me in my life up to that point. He didn't even hesitate." The Omega paused as he prepared himself for the second part. "After the appointment, my dad said the doctor discovered that I had a rare condition."

"What condition?"

"My glands would produce hormones and pheromones normally like any Omega would expect for his heat... at first. But even the early signs detected that my body wasn't following through with what it was supposed to be doing. My womb wasn't swelling, and it wasn't dropping. The effects of that drives your glands to produce more and more, hoping to get my reproductive organs working as they should. But since they weren't reacting—"

"You'd never be able to get your heat sated. And you'd be stuck in a heat until you took the suppressants... or... or..." The worst-case scenario flooded his mind.

"Yeah ...exactly." Alexander's face dimmed.

The news rocked Stephen to his core. It explained so much and yet, not enough. "And yet you think this is the smartest decision? To just wait until your pride subsides to get more?!"

"Don't worry," Alexander stressed, "I have another two weeks at least before anything is going to happen. By then, my prescription will be due for a refill, and it will be as if it never happened."

"Have you ever stopped taking it before?"

The Omega thought for a second. "I mean, I've missed an occasional dose or two. If it coincidentally hit near a natural cycle, I noticed it a lot more. But going right back on the meds takes care of it quickly. Other than that, there was only one time I got lazy and didn't take them for almost a week. Since I wasn't on the brink of a natural cycle, it didn't even register that I was completely out of whack because of it."

Stephen eyed Alexander closely and took in his pheromones. There *was* a scent change, and it *was* stronger. Whatever ignorance the Omega had cloaked himself into, he wasn't realizing just how effective it was. That was when Stephen dared to wonder if there was any coincidence the same night Eddie attacked him. "When was the time you experimented with that? Not taking them for that long?"

"There's the man of the hour!" a voice rang out, barging into the place with an entourage following him.

"Oh, good! They're here! Stephen, this is Kort. He's one of the announcers at the radio station."

A suave Alpha greeted them both as if he owned the place. His blond hair, blue eyes, and extremely white teeth glistened as they caught the lights from above. "Kortney Byers, it's great to meet you both." He turned and viewed his surroundings and then pointed to the obvious area where a stage set-up was supposed to be. "Right there, boys!" A few stagehands got to work right away, bringing in a large table, speaker sets, audio and radio equipment, and two large banners to advertise the night's events. "I never thought in a million years I'd be here. What a trip!"

Alexander tried his best to keep a pleasant face. A quick glance at Stephen showed he was less capable. The Omega laughed uncomfortably. "I suppose it is. Anyway, we're thankful for this opportunity. To have this right after Jesse Minh's fundraiser? This is absolutely amazing."

"Make sure to give Matthew Whitmore a shoutout. No doubt he's the reason we're here."

It took every ounce of control Stephen had to not tell the radio personality off, or worse, completely deck him.

Once again, Alexander laughed nervously. "I... I sure will." He prayed to Wolf-God the whole night wasn't going to go like this. Otherwise, he'd trade places with an attendee in a second.

Just then, Eric walked back in with an Omega enthusiastically coming in right in front of him. "Look who I found."

Kortney whipped around and studied the petite Omega. "Ah! Perfect! I got a runner boy for the evening!" He pulled out his wallet and handed the boy a $50 bill. "My crew isn't about to start with a cocktail this early. So, if you wouldn't mind doing a coffee run, we'd appreciate it. And actually..." The Alpha pulled out a piece of paper with a bunch of notes scribbled all over it. "This is what we normally get. If this works out, I'll give you my business line so we can keep in touch for the rest of the evening."

Daniel stood there like a statue, wide-eyed and completely at a loss for words. "Er... um... I... *What*?" He looked helplessly at Alexander and Eric, hoping for some sort of clarity.

Alexander came to the rescue. "Oh, I'm sorry, Kort. Daniel is actually here as a barback for tonight's event. He's not a runner."

Kortney's expression fell to a state of confusion. "Oh." He looked around the place awkwardly, hoping to see another body he could appoint. "Is he coming in later or?"

"*He*? Who exactly?" Alexander inquired.

"My runner. You *did* assign me a runner, right?"

"What makes you think I did that?"

Kortney crossed his arms and gave a condescending stare. "Because it was listed in the contract as one of my requirements." All eyes fell to the Omega who looked completely blindsided.

Alexander's hands shook as he desperately grabbed his phone to find the stipulations the radio station had listed in the contract. Once he found the email, he reviewed all of demands which included dedicated parking, free drinks, and a required radio interview to be posted this afternoon. And finally, there at the bottom, in plain letters, was the indicator of a runner to complete tasks while the crew was dedicated to the event. The Omega gulped and cursed to himself. "Shit." Then, he looked at Daniel with a face which showed his desperation.

Daniel eased his head forward, wondering if he was interpreting the look right. After scanning everyone else in the room, he realized he did. "Ohhh, you are going to owe me big time. You have no idea. Just wait until James finds out about this. He's going to give you hell."

"I know." Alexander deflated.

"The tips tonight better flow in, I swear..."

"Hey, no worries, little guy," Kortney dismissed. "You can start early. Keep the change from the coffee order." He then whispered, "I get reimbursed from the station anyway."

"'*Little guy?*'" The Omega stressed. He then gripped the dollar bill in his fist just as tight as he gritted his teeth as he began walking out for his first task of the night. "Sean: Part Two," he grumbled.

After Daniel left, Kortney turned back to the rest of the staff, completely oblivious to the drama he caused. Then he clapped his hands together. "Okay. So. After my crew sets up, Eric and I will sit down for an interview so we can have that on the radio by 5. That way, most listeners can hear about it or be reminded during rush hour."

Stephen gestured, completely confused. "*Eric?* Don't you want Alexander in the interview since... I don't know... *he* owns the place?"

The tall radio rep pursed his lips and cleared his throat. "I guess that makes sense."

Stephen had enough of this guy. He decided to walk to the back, desperate to find something to do so he didn't say anything he'd regret.

———

With the night in full swing, Alexander somehow found a moment to track down Stephen who was running around like mad. "Hey! How's it going?"

"Busy. That's good, right?"

"Beyond good. I even recognize some of our new regulars who originated from the Whitmore event. It's so surreal." He looked back at the Alpha. "How's the arm doing?"

Stephen lifted it up proudly. "No worries here. It survived a week of doing projects back at the house. This is nothing compared to that."

Alexander put his hands on his hips. "You did—" He sighed. "Of course you did. Stubborn wolf." The Alpha winked at him. "I wanted to thank you for standing up for me earlier."

"When?"

"When Kort decided to cut me out of the interview. In the moment, I wasn't too happy, but now that I've had time to think, I'm glad you did it."

That made Stephen's wolf prance. "I'm not ashamed of you, Alex. And if he is, he shouldn't be here in the first place." Alexander nodded. "Has Daniel marked you for dead yet?"

"Pfft. He'll get over it." He winced. "James, on the other hand..."

The Alpha glanced over, having a clear view of James at the bar. Perfectly timed was his nasty stare back at his boss. "Yeesh. He's not playing."

"I know he's not." Alexander dimmed. "It's not like James gets very many opportunities to work here with Daniel. I know he was all excited about it. Then to find out Daniel got commandeered *and* that I threw him under the bus? I'm lucky he didn't just take Daniel with him, leaving me high and dry. Wolf-God knows I deserved it."

Stephen tapped his foot in thought. "What are you doing to do about that?"

"I gotta talk to him." The Omega surrendered. "I can't have him like this the entire night. Otherwise, his misery is only going to permeate. I don't want that for tonight, especially if it was because of something *I* did."

The bravery forced Stephen to think about his own transgression. Granted, between the two incidents, *his* was way more serious than Alexander's innocent mistake. He had to come clean. "Alex, I—"

"Hold that thought for later. I need to talk to James."

Not wanting to push his boss into a corner, he silently nodded and went on his way, picking up empty glasses and hauling them back to the bar.

✦

The Omega attempted to make a straight shot to the bar, but another man stepped in front of him, dressed as if he was a model planted into the event for exposure. "Sean?! You're here!"

The Alpha gave a concerned expression. "Um, of course, I'm here."

Alexander sighed. "Sorry. I meant I just didn't expect you here so soon." He walked up and embraced him, taking in his proud, dominating scent. Then, he kissed him as if it was automatically programmed into him to do so.

Sean glanced at his phone. "It's almost 9 o'clock."

Finding it unfathomable, the Omega checked his own phone. "Damn. I can't believe that." He shook his head while tracing his hand over his forehead.

"Things going okay? You're not having any issues are you?"

"No..." Alexander stressed.

"Did Stephen come back?" the Alpha mumbled.

"Yes..."

Sean scanned the room, trying to locate the one he deemed the *lesser* Alpha, hoping for a reason, any reason, he could spring into action and force his mate to close the book on the unwelcome chapter in their life. "Is he causing any trouble?"

"Sean, he's not causing any trouble. And I'd really, really appreciate it if you didn't either."

"Alex," his mate commented in disappointment.

"Don't play innocent with me. If you two just avoid each other, it would make my night that much better. Can you do that for me? Please?" the Omega begged.

Sean's inner wolf growled as he "kicked the proverbial rock away" in guilt. "I will behave, 'Alpha.'" he patronized.

"Thank you." Alexander sighed before giving him one last kiss. "I, unfortunately, need to have a conversation with James that I'm not looking forward to."

"Oh?" The Alpha's face showed concern. "Do you need my help?"

"No, it's nothing like that. Wish me luck, though?"

"Good luck, babe," Sean announced as his mate finished his journey to the bar. Afterward, the Alpha couldn't help himself and scanned the crowded room once more. There, on the opposite side, was Stephen, hastily gathering several empty glasses while talking with a couple customers. As if he sensed it, Stephen caught his line of sight. He gestured with his head in acknowledgement; Sean replied the same, plastering on a face of contentment. As soon as Stephen preoccupied himself once again, he pulled out his phone, sent a text, and then smiled to himself. All he had left to do was wait.

"James?" Alexander spoke over the rail. At first, there was no answer, a clear sign of how the Beta still felt. "James?"

Finally, the Omega looked up, dramatically pretending it was the first time he heard his boss. "What can I do you for?"

Alexander read right through his scorned employee. "Can we please settle on a truce? If not permanently, at least for tonight?"

James focused all his attention on a bar towel and folded neatly, as if he wasn't going to use it a minute later. "I know with you being Daniel's best friend and being my boss, I don't have the right to tell you what to do. But I do have the right to say it really hurts me that you did that to not only me but also my boyfriend."

Alexander nodded. "I fully hear you and fully accept that. Just please know it wasn't what I intended. But it's what I needed for tonight to be a success."

"Is that what it's always going to be about?" James inquired.

"What do you mean?"

A couple of guests came up and interrupted the conversation. They ordered drinks and James immediately filled the order. He was thankful for it as it allowed him to collect his thoughts. "When Bruce and I first got here, you beat it into our heads that customer service and building a relationship with them was our highest priority. And we've lived by that because we saw *you* live by that. Personally, I saw you continue that all the way up to the day Stephen showed up. You rightfully kicked Eddie and his posse out for the betterment of everyone else, and I thought it was one of your shining moments."

Alexander wasn't enjoying his Beta employee finding this newfound nerve. But he reluctantly let James continue. "And?"

"But ever since that fundraiser, you've been forgetting about your customers and forgetting about us. Everything has been about 'What does Eric want,' 'What does Whitmore want,' 'What does Minh want,' 'What does Kort want.' When do we get the old you back?"

The Omega was flabbergasted. "I haven't gone anywhere!"

"The hell you haven't."

"Wanna give me any evidence to back that up?"

"Sure." James slapped the bar towel on the rail and leaned in. "We never see you up here at the bar anymore. You're always in the back room messing with inventory, cleaning bathrooms, on the phone, and carrying this aura as if this isn't even fun for you anymore."

Now Alexander was beginning to feel the Beta losing his place and stepping out of line. "First off: All those things are what's needed to be done. The last time I trusted you and Bruce to do that, I got a beautiful $500 fine from the city slapped across my face. Or did you forget that?"

"No," James huffed.

"And second: there's a reason they call it 'work,' James. Sometimes that's just the bitch of it."

"That doesn't mean you can't find joy in it."

The Omega wasn't having it. "Since when could you crawl into my brain and see what I feel or think?"

"I can't," James flung back.

"Then stop acting as if you can! I can't believe you. The number of times you and Bruce have messed up in this place that I've had to clean up is more than any other boss would take, that I can assure you. You've got balls talking like this to me now."

"No. *This* is having balls: after tonight, consider this my last shift." With that, he turned and walked to the other side of the bar, seeking out anyone who needed their next drink.

***

The conversation sent Alexander into a tailspin. His body temperature rose, his head pulsed, and he began to lose his center. Before anyone could notice the state he was in, he rushed to the bathroom corridor and flooded his face with cold water, completely ignoring the odd looks and stares from two patrons wondering whether they should hit on him or get help. In the large mirror, he just glanced back with a gentle smile to indicate he was okay but didn't need to be bothered. That was when he saw the two patrons whisper to each other. One giggled in the other's ear before they both trailed off into the main room.

Alexander cocked his head in a strange expression, wondering what on earth they could be snickering about. He checked his outfit front and back, checked his face, and checked his shoes. Nothing appeared out of the ordinary. That was when he noticed his hands shaking once more. "Get it together, Alex." He rubbed his neck. "What is going on? When was the last time I ate?" As he continued his massage, a sudden thought hit him. An unnerving thought. "When *was* the last time I ate?" He looked back in the mirror and studied himself once more. "No. No. No! Wolf-God, this can't be happening. Not now. Not this early."

In a panic, Alexander only had one thought: to get outside, get water, and run down to nearest store to buy a scent cover-up. As he left the bathroom corridor, he tried making a straight shot out the front door to get to his car. But he caught the eye of Kortney who had another idea.

"There he is!" Kortney announced on the microphone for all to hear. "Let's get our host up here to say a few words who saved the event and let us have another successful Singles' Night!"

"Not now. Not now," the Omega mumbled.

"Alex?" Kortney said once again.

A plastered smile fell over Alexander as he went up toward the stage and looked out over everyone. All eyes looked back including Bruce, Daniel, Eric, James, Stephen, and... Sean. The Omega huffed out a breath as he struggled to gain composure. His hand shook with the microphone being forced upon him. "Well... I... I just want to thank each and every one of you for not only believing in the event but also believing in South Street Tavern. We hope to... we hope to have many of you back in the future. And please..." he wiped his forehead, feeling a trail of sweat coming down, "please make sure to tip the staff whenever you notice them doing a great job. I couldn't do it without them. Without *any* of them." He pushed the microphone back onto Kortney as he quickly strutted off to the side.

The radio announcer laughed as he saw the flustered Omega walk off. "Guess *he* found a hot date," he joked to his audience. He got a full response before he continued announcing advertisers and door prizes to the captive crowd.

Alexander ignored the comment at his expense. Instead, he tried desperately to get to the back. But Sean stopped him before he could exit.

"Hey! Where you headed off to?" Sean gave a concerned look while trying stay upbeat with the crowd.

The Omega fanned himself. "I just... I just need to step out for a bit. I'll be back."

Sean gasped. "Leave? This is *your* event! You've got prime advertising sitting in the bar right now! You can't just leave!"

"Sean, I'm not kidding." Alexander huffed.

Then, Sean's wolf instincts perked up as a sweet scented wafted into the air. With every increasing nerve spewing out of Alexander's pheromone palate, the stronger it became. "Alex... you're.... you're..."

"I don't want to hear it," the Omega lamented.

The utter shock made Sean almost forget his instincts. He wrapped himself around his mate and began to inhale near the pheromone gland in his neck. The strong Alpha's goal now was to get what he had always desired: to mark his mate. But before he could coax the gland to surface in order to claim him, he felt Alexander push off him.

"Stop," Alexander exhaled.

"What? Why?!" Sean exclaimed.

"Because I don't want to do this!"

Sean thought for a moment. "You're right. This isn't the place. Let's go to my car, and we'll head to my place, babe."

The Omega grunted. "No. I mean, I don't want to do this... period!" An uneasy feeling settled in the air. Alexander feared an unraveling was about to take place.

"I'm your *mate*, Alex. What do you mean you 'don't want to do this'?" Sean narrowed in as his wolf instincts heightened. "Did something happen?" His mate shook his head. "Are you sure?" Once again, the Omega nonverbally tried to reaffirm him he was okay. But it was to no avail. Sean stepped out in front of him and examined him once more. "Whoa... you don't look right." He saw his mate roll his eyes and his frustration grew. "Did someone in the bar accost you?" The Alpha started walking up, reaching out to stroke the Omega's soft hair.

Alexander instantly flinched while crossing his arms. "No one did anything, I promise." Automatically, his eyes went up to the bar. Somehow, Wolf-God perfectly placed Stephen centered in the big glass window having a conversation with Daniel. The two were lost in some sort of discussion which intrigued him more than it should have, especially when Sean's gaze followed his and caught the line of sight.

"*He* didn't hurt you, did he?" Sean growled.

"No! Sean, he didn't do that. He would *never* do that."

The Alpha balled up his fist. "But what *would* he do?"

Something in the Alpha's tone startled Alexander. "What are you saying?"

"I'm saying I'm done being the ignorant mate who stands idly by watching his Omega get sniffed out by a wild wolf on the prowl!"

Alexander's eyes widened and his skin flushed. "That's... that's not what's happening."

"Why do you *want* him here?!" Sean demanded as he walked over and gritted his teeth.

"Sean, stop!"

The Alpha walked slowly, following Alexander's every move backward. "Not until I get out of your head what in Wolf-God's name you are thinking by keeping him here! Ever since *he* came into the picture, you have lost sight of 'us' and I am this close to staging an all-out territory war!"

At last, the Omega had nowhere else to go, completely backed against his own car, hearing the anger of Sean's voice and his brute Alpha scent getting stronger and stronger. "'*Territory*'? I am *not* your 'territory.' I am your boyfriend, damn it!"

The Alpha stared back in disbelief. "'Boyfriend'? '*Boyfriend*'?!" Sean roared as his fist went flying straight past Alexander's head and straight into the side mirror of the truck beside him completely taking it off with a crash. "Fuck!"

Alexander shuddered from practically feeling the impact of his mate's fist, only to realize the truck took the hit. But the reaction was almost no different. "Are you crazy?!"

"He's gotten to you, hasn't he?!"

"Who?"

"Don't play me for a fool, Alex!" Sean's finger pointed straight at his mate and then to the object of his hatred in the bar. "Every time I see you in person, and every time I hear your voice on the phone, you are getting farther and farther away from me and closer to his grasp. Stephen has somehow warped you into thinking he's a good guy, that he's worth something, that he can love you, care for you, protect you. And it's nothing but lies! If you choose this path, you will be nothing but miserable and alone for the rest of your life. Fate or not, this man will destroy you!"

Alexander's pent-up fear dissipated as he caught the last statement. It wasn't a coincidence. "What did you just say?"

"You heard me," Sean spat pack. He eyed Alexander as he received an anxious look back. "Yeah, I know your dirty little secret. Your fairytale Fate showed up in the form of an outcast who has no prestige, no following, no money, no status, and no fame." The Alpha smirked. "Well, not the right kind of fame."

The monologue did little for Sean's point or his character. The Omega was only interested in one thing. "Who told you—"

"Hey!" a voice cried out, breaking the heated exchange between the two. Then, the man set his sights on both Alexander and Sean. "Is there a problem here?"

"Stephen." Alexander tensed.

Sean carried the opposite reaction—seeing his mate completely elated over his presence. "Stay out of this!" the Alpha commanded. "This is none of your business."

Alexander spoke softly. "Sean and I need to talk. I'll be back to join you in a minute."

All the Alpha had to do was read both their profiles and pheromone palates to discern otherwise. He confidently shook his head. "I'm not going anywhere." Then he pointed straight between Sean's eyes. "*You*, on the other hand, I think you should go somewhere else to cool off out of respect for Alexander and the bar."

"Who the hell do you think you are saying that to me?!" Sean growled. "'Respect'?! You don't even know the *meaning* of the word! Alex is *my mate*. I'm here to support him, care for him, protect him, and love him until the day I *die*." Sean walked up to the statuesque Alpha who looked equally capable, but he wasn't backing down. He narrowed his gaze straight into his soul. "And I don't plan on doing that anytime soon."

Stephen didn't blink and he didn't waver. After catching a glimpse of Alexander appearing unimpressed with Sean's territorial stance, he said the first thing which came to mind. "Things change."

There was no way Sean heard him correctly. No Alpha, especially one like Stephen, challenged another for his mate. He cocked his head and deepened his voice. "You wanna say that again to my face?"

"Gladly—"

"Stephen! Don't!" Daniel rushed out of the bar with Eric right behind him. Fearing the Alpha was about to make a move worth regretting, Daniel hoped to be the voice of reason. Unfortunately, the Omega had the right idea, but the wrong Alpha.

As Stephen turned around, he saw a fist swipe across his jaw all too late. The impact forced him to grab his face as he staggered to the side.

"No!" Alexander shouted as he rushed up to assess Stephen. He grabbed onto his shoulders and centered his face. "Are you okay?"

"Yeah..." he groaned, "that'll hurt tomorrow."

"Time's up, Alex. It's him... or me." Sean's ultimatum hung in the air.

Alexander stared once more at Stephen and relaxed his body in defeat.

"So... you've chosen then?" Stephen muttered.

Alexander felt a heavy pit in his stomach. The response from his head didn't match the response from his heart. With so many instances of being put to the test of where his loyalties were, he felt this moment was the one in which he did need to decide. And so, he did. Stephen's face winced as he prepared himself to hear the last goodbye and refused to look to look at him. "I'm sorry, Sean."

Stephen's head jerked up and caught the Omega looking not at his mate, but at him. "You... you mean it?"

The Omega found himself overwhelmed the moment even transpired, but after catching his breath, he found himself nodding. "I do."

"Yes!" Daniel hissed as he pumped his fist down by his side.

Looking back into the Omega's eyes, Stephen didn't know what to think. Was this real? Was this a dream? Was this a set-up? "But... why... why now?"

Alexander's stomach became a ball of nerves. "I'm honestly not sure why, but there's something in me that says..." All he could do to finish the statement was smile.

Sean stood there motionless. His wolf snarled as he felt instantly outcast, and he didn't know who deserved his wrath more: his former mate or his former mate's new conquest. "You are the most pathetic Omega I have ever known in my life!" Sean spat.

The Omega's eyes widened as he witnessed his now ex-mate turn into a man he didn't recognize at all. His stance changed, his face soured, and his pheromone palate spewed a threatening aura which began to scare him. "Sean..."

"No!" the Alpha replied, refusing to hear anything more Alexander had to say. He approached the Omega with a purpose but was quickly cut off when Stephen pulled Alexander back and blocked his view. Not wanting to test the Alpha's true strength, he readjusted his disheveled shirt and tie and then smiled. "You're a fool, Alex. This place is a ticking time bomb. South Street Tavern is never going to prosper under your name. I've spent the last couple of years entertaining your sorry ass and waiting in the wings for you, but I'm done. Now, all I have to do is watch you fall and take possession of this place after you."

Alexander crossed his arms and dared to ask. "What?"

Sean smirked. "Do you *really* think I've stuck around this long while tucking my tail on your disrespectful attitude toward the rank of Alpha, lack of consideration, lack of intimacy, and lack of attention toward me and our relationship just because I *loved* you?"

Both Alexander and Stephen glanced at each other in confusion. Then, the Omega concluded what he was truly trying to say. "Wait... are you trying to tell me you only stuck around because of South Street?"

The Alpha laughed. "Wolf-God, no! This place was dead on arrival. I only entertained your pathetic dream because you had funds to keep Territory One Bank happy and that the land was worth more than the whole damn establishment."

"No... that can't be true. The appraisal was lower than what the last owner bought it for," Alexander pointed out.

"I knew what the Tauris Medical Center was capable of once the details of their research center came to pass. But the city can't double an appraisal based on speculation. And once you held the title, it was going to take half a century before the city saw the property taxes it wanted." He grinned and then sang, "But all that would change if the poor Omega owner couldn't drum up enough business and have to sell it all off to someone else who actually knew what they were doing or, even better, knew what to do with it."

Alexander scoffed. "There was no one around begging me to sell the place who actually had a number worthy of giving the place up for nor a plan to tell me what the place should be turned into."

"Alex... he's not talking about just anyone," Stephen concluded. Behind them, another member of the bar approached, listening to every word.

The Omega turned around. "Eric? It was you?"

Eric furrowed his eyebrows. "What are you talking about?"

"It was you, all along?! You were just waiting in the wings to take South Street Tavern from me?! I can't believe this! We were a team! I trusted you."

Eric stood there in disbelief. "The fact you can even say that to me is crazy! I'd never do that to you!"

"No..." Stephen corrected, "not Eric."

Once again, Alexander found himself staring at his ex-mate, completely dumbfounded. "Sean?"

"You're smarter than I give you credit for, Stephen."

"Let's say, I'm a good judge of character," the Alpha replied.

Alexander's eyes began to swell. "This whole time?"

"Oh, don't be getting gushy over me *now*. Yes, that was the goal. It's not like you had a charm about you." Alexander huffed at the assessment. "Securing your loan meant that I had a bird's eye view of your business. But being your mate? That meant I had a view front row and center. Either way, I was biding my time. But no matter what issue kept coming your way, your stubborn nature refused to let this place go. Desperate times called for desperate measures."

Alexander leaned his head in. "You've got to be kidding me."

"What? What's he saying?" Stephen asked.

"That's why you wanted me to contract with you so bad. It wasn't to be with me at all. It was so you could get ownership of South Street." Sean smiled as Alexander finally understood what it was all about. "You bastard."

Stephen saw the Omega lunge forward and stopped his attempt from charging Sean outright. "Let it go, Alex. It's over."

"You need to get off our property, Sean." Eric stood next Stephen, creating a line which showed his time had come to an end.

"No..." Alexander interjected, "I still want to know who told you that Stephen was my Fate."

"Do you really think you deserve to know?" Sean asked, entertained by the request.

Alexander spoke boldly. "What's it matter to you now? I already know who you really are and what you're about. You're standing there, proud of it all, and of how much it hurts me. Think you have enough Wolf-Devil inside you to do it again?"

"Despite what you may think, my goal was never to hurt you. Should anything had come to pass, you simply would have been a casualty." Then, Sean turned his attention to Stephen. "But *you*, on the other hand, I have absolutely no problem watching being destroyed piece by piece." No one in the parking lot had any clue as to what Sean was referring to. They all waited in anticipation of his next move. "Are you ready to show yourself?" Sean spoke down the sidewalk to his left into the dark abyss the streetlight couldn't reach. On cue, a man sauntered into its light and revealed himself for all his worth.

"Who is that?" Alexander asked, completely lost on his identity.

"*Ray?*" Stephen stood there in disbelief as his old partner in crime displayed himself under the streetlamp.

"Stephen. How's the night?" he marveled. The Beta stood there in his oversized sweatshirt, grinning as if he'd revealed himself as a serial killer in a horror movie, his yellow teeth sparkling in the light.

The Alpha gulped. "I have a feeling I'm about to find out."

Alexander stood there in utter confusion. "Stephen, who is this guy?"

A sharp pain entered Stephen's heart as he felt the truth slowly unravel. He sighed. "This is Ray. He's my former drug dealer."

The Omega looked back in shock. "*What*?!"

"*Former*? Stephen, don't be so modest," Ray insisted as he lit up a cigarette.

The Alpha growled. "I haven't taken anything from you in ten years and you know it!"

"Hmph," Ray mumbled back.

Alexander looked up, deep in thought. "But wait... if that's how *you* know him... then that must mean..."

Sean rolled his eyes. "Let me guess: this is another surprise for you?"

The Omega held his head as his pheromones from his frustration and his heat began mixing. "This can't be happening." Stephen walked up, ready to hold him and comfort him, but instantly, he repelled him, leaving Stephen there, frozen. "What does this have to do with Stephen, Sean?! I want to know now!"

"Fate works in mysterious ways, doesn't it?" Sean amused himself by looking at Raymond once again, and then began his story. "Ray and I had already been... well... let's just say 'working' together for years. When he kept talking about how one of his best buddies was getting out of lock-up, I just ignored it. But he was just so incessant on telling me the day was approaching, I finally asked him who the poor bastard was. 'Stephen Matheson' wasn't a name on *my* personal radar, but all that changed one day when who should walk into Territory One Bank to open up a new bank account but the Wolf-Devil himself."

Stephen's stomach wrenched as he was instantly brought back to the day his Veo dropped him off downtown. "Wait... I remember that day. You weren't there!"

"Obviously, I was," Sean corrected. "Knowing who you already were at that point, it only took me a second to recognize you as you walked by my office on the sidewalk. Before you reached the door, I had already coded you to the greeter. Your fate was sealed before you even took your first step inside. Stupid me thought, 'Well, that's the last time I'll ever encounter Stephen Matheson.' Yet then, a couple days later, my mate tells me the bastard had somehow snaked his way into South Street Tavern and got himself a job, no thanks to his stupid business partner." The Alpha eyed Eric with a disdain but then continued, "Naturally, I intervened as best as I could. But all I got was a lapful of beer and laughed at. Once that failed, I decided to invoke the help of someone who I knew could get results." Once again, he turned his attention to Raymond.

Stephen couldn't accept it. "Ray doesn't do that. He has a loyalty he doesn't break." Not sure he could even trust his own words, he found himself staring at his friend who himself was becoming a stranger to Stephen right before his very eyes.

"Everyone has a price," Raymond replied.

"You motherfucker!" Stephen growled.

"Actually, the name is '*Rat*.'" The Beta licked his teeth in satisfaction.

Sean continued, "I didn't know how Ray was going to react to me making an enemy of one of his best friends; I was surprised when he went along with it so easily."

"You should have taken me up on rekindling our friendship when I offered it, Stephen. It would have made the decision that much harder," Raymond insisted.

Stephen scoffed. "Would it have changed anything?"

Raymond danced with the possibility in his head. "Hmm. No."

"Ray got things done quicker than I anticipated. I guess you had already made an enemy at this place on day one."

Another flash rushed through Stephen's mind. "Eddie?!"

"*You* orchestrated Eddie's assault the night Stephen got stabbed?" Eric asked.

Raymond casually inspected his fingernails. "To be fair, I didn't tell Eddie to do that. I simply said 'Scare him enough to leave the joint.' Eddie took it upon himself to knife you. You must have *really* pissed him off."

Sean grimaced while staring down Raymond. "Had I *known* at that point the 'Fate' Stephen was referring to was Alex, I would have known the tactic with Eddie wasn't going to change anything!"

"Hey!! I didn't know the 'complicated Fate' was the bar owner! For all I knew, it could have been pipsqueak over here!" Raymond gestured to Daniel.

"'Pipsqueak?!'" Daniel huffed while fiddling with his phone.

"You came into the bar after that, Ray," Stephen lamented. "You came in, sat with me, talked with me, and confided in me. Why?"

Raymond crossed his arms and twitched his lips. "I was 'on the line' by then. I was assessing whether you could even be ousted. At that point, you were innocent with no easy way to bring you down. Until..." The Beta grinned and winked back at Stephen.

"Until what?" Alexander asked.

Stephen's voice hitched. "Alex... I..."

"The locals thank you for donating your prescription bottle. You did them a much-needed service," Raymond finished and winked at Alexander.

The Omega looked back at Stephen who looked just as broken as he did. "Stephen? No.... no... Tell me that isn't true."

"I'm sorry, Alex. I never wanted to hurt you."

Alexander placed his hand over his mouth as he realized how the night played out. "The lights going out... The cameras in the back lot being moved... That was you?! How could you?!"

"I was worried you'd completely reject me if you thought I was involved with Ray once you found out who he was. He caught me in a moment where I thought if I made this quick decision, it would all go away. I hated every moment of doing it, and I hated every moment after. Please, you have to believe me!"

"Fuck... fuck... fuck!" Alexander found a random car and laid his head on the back passenger window. He scented Stephen upon him and then his hand on his back. "Get off me!"

"Alex..." Stephen tried.

"If you had just listened to me from the start, babe, none of this would have happened," Sean condescended. "I tried warning you every step of the way of what he was like and what he would do, and you ignored me. Boy, I bet you regret leaving me now. I mean, it's one thing for a mate to betray you, but your *Fated* Mate? I can't imagine."

Alexander growled. "I'll never regret leaving you!" Then he faced Stephen once again. "And you? Have you been doing drugs this entire time?"

Stephen shook his head. "Not even once."

"What about that day when the cops came in to do the drug test?" After Alexander asked, once again, all attention went back to Sean.

"Asshole," Stephen quipped.

Sean stood firmly. "Hey, I'm allowed to call the cops anytime I fear someone is using drugs, especially if it's in my mate's establishment."

"*Former* mate," Daniel pointed out.

"But they didn't find anything," Stephen defended.

Sean carried an annoyed expression. "Yes, indeed. I was very, very surprised." As he focused back on Raymond, the Beta began whistling.

"Doo-dee-doo-dee.... what?!" Raymond asked innocently.

"You want to explain to me how the cops didn't find anything?!" Sean demanded.

"I don't admit to nothin'. And I'm not about to now! Let's just say I'm equally surprised." Raymond grimaced.

"Then he has them," Sean concluded.

"No, I don't!" Stephen replied.

Eric stepped in. "I've had enough of this. Sean, I want you and your hoodlum friend off my property now. If either of you are seen back here, I'm calling the cops and giving them a detailed report of your actions."

Sean laughed. "Oh, please. A couple of Low-Type bar owners, an ex-con, and a pitiful Omega tying me and Ray to a slew of crimes with circumstantial evidence? No one is going to believe your words."

"Eh-hem..." Daniel interjected. "They won't have to. They can believe *your* words." The Omega then decided to turn up his phone volume to the max. *"...A couple of Low-Type bar owners, an ex-con, and a pitiful Omega tying me and Ray to a slew of crimes with circumstantial evidence? No one is going to believe your words."*

"And that's just the ending. If you want me to start it eight minutes ago, we can listen it again."

Raymond spit on the sidewalk as he tossed his cigarette. "Fuck! I told you, Sean! This is why I don't do confrontations in public venues! I'm gettin' out of here," Raymond declared as he started walking down the sidewalk.

Sean stared back in disbelief. "Ray! The kid's probably bluffing!"

"I'm not sticking around to find out. Too many witnesses as it were. Besides, you have a lot more to lose than I do. Good luck to you!"

"He's right, you know," Daniel added.

"Shut up, Omega. The police aren't going to do anything. They don't have the evidence nor time to care," Sean spat.

"That may be true," Stephen commented, "but I'm sure Territory One Bank would love to know about all your 'dealings' as well as intentionally approving a business loan on their behalf while betting on it to fail. How much evidence do you think they require before they quietly demote you and then just get rid of you all together as if you weren't ever there?"

"Especially since," Daniel whispered, "I'm still recording."

Sean stared back at an audience who wasn't there to play his game anymore. The hairline on his head began shimmering with sweat starting to bead down his face. He swallowed hard and then slowly took a step backward. "It's been nice knowing you all. Have a good evening." One final moment was given to his former mate of two years. "Goodbye, Alex. It was fun."

The Alpha hustled to his car, took one last look at South Street Tavern, one last look at Alexander, one last look at Stephen, and then entered the safety of his car. Finally, his car revved and drove off into the night.

CHAPTER 05:

TAKING A CHANCE ON FATE

Several patrons had gathered near the scene by the time Sean's car was heard going down the street, its racing cams giving away his location down every city block. None of the employees knew what to say nor how to proceed. Eyes went back and forth, waiting for someone else to break the silence. Finally, Bruce pushed through the crowd huddled near the door to find out himself what the issue was all about.

"Alex? Eric? Is everything okay?" the Beta asked cautiously.

Eric was the first to come alive again. "We're good. Get back inside. We'll be there in a minute."

"Eric," Alexander pleaded as he solemnly walked up to the Alpha, "I... I'm sorry." The Omega read his expression all over his face. Condemning his business partner and admitting the lack of trust he had wasn't going to slide without consequences. Eric's face confirmed it. All he did was nod slowly in return. "I know there isn't a lot I can say right now to convince you otherwise, but I didn't mean it. I panicked."

The Alpha's dark skin shone off the yellow city light as he inhaled deeply, controlling his discontent. "How long have you been harboring this fear about me? That I was only in this, biding my time, to eventually usurp everything we created here?"

"I never thought that about you."

"Yeah, right," Eric dismissed.

"I'm being honest! The only times I have ever thought about it is when my confidence gets shot to hell, and I feel my world is crumbling all around me. And it has nothing to do with you—it's 100% me. That's what happened tonight. I put it all on you in that moment. Please, all I'm asking you to do is give me the benefit of a doubt." Alexander gave all his words and all his submissive pheromones to Eric in that moment.

The Alpha noticed the sincerity immediately; however, his expression changed very little. But the Omega had known Eric for several years by this point. If he didn't make a decision immediately, it communicated the conversation at hand sufficed. That's what Alexander had to live with once again. "We'll talk. Just not now."

The Omega exhaled and accepted the response as a truce, knowing he was only in the beginning steps of repairing the trust. Then, his attention went to Daniel, who was standing near the building like a lost puppy. "Daniel," he beckoned, "did you really record all that?"

The Omega grinned. "Nah. Just the last part." He went to the recording on his phone and backed it up as far as he could. Unfortunately, it missed most of the good stuff needed to condemn Sean and Ray for their conduct.

"Damn," Eric replied. "It would have been nice to have it in our back pocket should we need it."

"I guess we'll just have to rely on convincing them we do. Hopefully, the fear it will keep both at bay," Alexander concluded.

"Let's hope." Eric gave Daniel a firm tap on his shoulder. "Thanks, man. You may have saved the night."

"Anytime!" Daniel smiled as Eric hustled himself inside. Once there, he disbursed the on-lookers and refocused the bar on its festivities. "Are *you* doing okay?" He honed in on his best friend.

Alexander shook his head. "I don't know even know the definition of the word right now. My boyfriend—correction—ex-boyfriend, just admitted to me he was fed up with our relationship a long time ago and that he was only in it for the business, one of my employees allowed his drug dealer to steal my meds and then lied to me about it, and then the drug dealer proudly reveals he's been in cahoots with my boyfriend the entire time to sabotage and practically kill Stephen, and then I put my foot in my mouth by accusing Eric of betraying me, the only person who hasn't forsaken me." Daniel gave an offended expression. "*And* you!" He rubbed his temples and growled to himself. "And Bruce.... and..." He paused.

Daniel couldn't understand the hesitation. "James?"

"Sort of."

"What do you mean?"

"Before I tell you, I want to say I'm sorry that I put you in the position I did earlier. You're no one's 'errand boy.' You're my best friend, and you're here because you are an amazing person. I didn't mean to take advantage of you, and I didn't mean to take you for granted."

"I suppose I can forgive you." Daniel smiled back. "But what does that have to do with James?"

Alexander's face fell. "In defending you, James felt I was dismissing him as well. I antagonized him for no reason other than the fact I'm stressed out and made him a target. So, I'm sure to get back at me, he told me he's quitting after tonight."

The young Omega gasped. "What?!"

"He didn't tell you?"

"No! I mean, I've been pretty busy being this 'errand boy.'" He rolled his eyes and then chuckled to himself. "What happened after that?"

Alexander shrugged. "Nothing really. It wasn't too much after that all *this* went down, so... I haven't been able to talk to him again. And right now..." The Omega looked back to a lonely Stephen, propping himself up on a large tire of a pick-up truck, staring down into the asphalt.

"...you have other pressing matters to attend to," Daniel finished. Guilt showed all over Alexander's face which he thoroughly picked up on. "You want me to talk to him?"

"It would mean the world to me if you did," Alexander replied. "I will."

"Thank you." He gave Daniel a deep embrace which already began the healing process. "Tell him I will also talk to him once the event is over tonight."

"Will do. Sounds like we're all going to need a drinking party ourselves when this is done."

"Shit." Alexander laughed.

Just then, Kortney stuck his entitled head outside. "Daniel? We need another round. We're damn near parched!"

The spritely Omega clenched his fists and teeth as he watched Alexander try everything he could not to laugh. Daniel then melted into the submissive form Kortney expected of him. "I'm right on top of it, Kort," he sang. Once Kortney was out of sight, he scowled at Alexander. "*Extra* tips. I mean, huge!"

"Your pile will be bigger than the rest of ours!" Alexander affirmed. Daniel waved it off as he resumed his role.

As Daniel walked back in, a couple patrons exited the tavern. The first quickly walked by with a purpose. The second walked casually as he pulled out a cigarette and a lighter. His concentration blocked every opportunity to dodge Alexander; instead, he bumped right into him. "Oh, damn. Sorry!"

"No, no. It's okay," Alexander reassured. But before the man continued his journey away, the Omega stopped him. "Wait, I remember you. You were the guy who came in here with his buddies after Matthew Whitmore announced the fundraiser rally. Siro, right?"

The Alpha rolled his eyes yet smiled at the good-looking Omega. "I feel like my fate is always going to be tied to that man."

Alexander winced. "Sorry. Forgot it wasn't a positive thing."

Siro blew out a cloud of smoke from his first inhale. "At least you got my name right. You're the Omega bar owner, right? Alex?"

He nodded. "Mind if I take advantage of you and bum a cigarette?"

Siro effortlessly reached into his pocket, pulled the pack out, and assisted the Omega in lighting it as he had done endless times before for many others. "*You* can take advantage of me anytime you want." He winked.

Alexander smiled. "I'm not keeping you from your date?" He casually gestured to the other patron who had finally noticed Siro's absence and was patiently waiting about a half block up.

Siro glanced over. "Who? Him? That's not my date. He's my friend. We came together."

"Both of you are leaving empty-handed?"

"It wasn't my goal to find my 'happily ever after' in there. Getting sucked off in the bathroom stall was enough."

Alexander choked. "Oh. I see."

"Siro?!" the lone friend called out.

"One sec!" Siro replied before turning his attention back to Alexander. "*He*, on the other hand, was hoping to find his Fated Mate."

"Damn. No pressure." The Omega flicked the ash to the sidewalk.

"All I hear from Roman is how that's all he'll accept. He fully believes Wolf-God has put him on this earth to only be with his Fated Mate. 'It's the gift bestowed to all of us, and we shouldn't accept anything less. Thus, we should be grateful when we find him and take it as a blessing.' At least, that's what he says."

Alexander felt his insides react to the whole proverb. It was as if he could feel Wolf-God lay his head in the crook of his neck and confirm everything Siro spoke of. "And... what do you say?"

"Me? I say *we* make our fate. You see what's in front of you. You decide. Fate doesn't happen until you do something about it. If it feels right, why ignore it?" The Alpha grinned and then gave another nonverbal gesture to Roman, whose patience was running thin.

"Makes sense."

Siro, feeling bold, decided to push his own fate. "What about you? Think fate has put us together in this moment? Are *we* the next thing that's 'right'?"

Alexander took in the moment in stride and bit his lip. "I thank you for the offer, but no. I'm afraid that's *not* our destiny."

"What are you going to do about your heat then?"

The Omega gulped. "You noticed?"

"Take it from me: any Alpha with an operational mating gland knows you're in need."

"Fair enough," Alexander replied. "To answer your question... I think I have someone else who is taking care of that responsibility." The words being said aloud made his own mind go into hyperdrive. With the sentiment, he couldn't help but look toward Stephen who hadn't moved. Siro caught the line of sight.

"That guy over there? What makes him so special?" The inquiry was out of curiosity. Siro was more interested in watching the Omega squirm versus spewing jealousy hormones.

"Well, he says he's *my* Fate," Alexander stated smoothly.

"Hmph. And what do you say?"

"I guess I need to find out."

Suddenly, Roman walked up to the conversation. "Are we leaving together, or should I leave you two alone?"

"Damn, Alpha. Chill out. Pay your respects to the bar owner," Siro insisted.

"Oh, sorry," Roman apologized. "Hi. I'm Roman. And I guess you've already met this knucklehead."

"You're a great wingman, Alpha," Siro condescended.

"He's fine. It was nice to meet you both, but I have some things to attend to," Alexander insisted.

"Sounds like it." Siro bit his tongue flirtatiously.

As the trio parted their separate ways, Alexander had a flash of a memory which stunned him. *Roman? Jake? Jake Erricson? Does that mean Roman is...* But as he turned around to try, both Alphas were already up the block, lost in their own conversation.

Stephen, finally feeling the moment was safe, approached the Omega. "Who were they?"

Still lost in the haze, wondering if his intuition was right, Alexander's voice slowed. "Nothing... Someone I... It's nothing." He shook it off.

The air grew still as the Alpha tried to figure out what to say. He figured his safest option was to give Alexander a way out. "Do you ... want me to leave?"

"Leave? Why?" Alexander crossed his arms and waited.

Stephen took notice of the posture immediately. "I don't deserve to be here. And I don't deserve you either. I think... I guess I only hope you'll let me explain?" Alexander nodded slowly but gave no indication either way on how he felt. "Please believe me when I say as soon as I made the decision to let Ray take your prescription, I regretted it immediately. I was coerced and then I let it happen. As an Alpha, I should have been stronger than that."

"Can we drop the whole 'rank' defense? This isn't the night I want to hear a run-down of toxic Alpha-ism."

"Sorry." Stephen gulped. "What else can I say?"

"That 'Ray' guy. You told me and the cops you hadn't done any-thing with that guy in ten years!"

"And that's still true. He came by my parents' property and tried to pick up where we left off, and I wasn't having any of it. I didn't lie to you or the cops about how any of it went down."

Alexander scoffed. "No. But you worded it just right, didn't you? To make yourself look all innocent?"

"It's a hazard of growing up as the son of a cop. For nearly twenty years, I heard stories about how my dad was able to find the perfect piece of information or slip of the tongue to incriminate someone. Every kid growing up imagines having to try and come up with stories to hide their conduct from their parents at some point, but if someone had even told me what was coming down the road for me and my family, I would have run so far in the opposite direction." A long pause set in as he played so many times throughout his life all his decisions could have been wiped cleaned or come out a different way than they did. "Do you hate me?"

The Omega considered the question. "Sometimes I want to. And yet, I can't."

"Do you regret saying what you did earlier?"

"About?"

Stephen gulped. "Choosing me over Sean."

Alexander scratched his chin and drew in a deep breath. "No."

The Alpha's face lit up. "Really?"

"When you look at it all objectively, Sean is right. If a relationship is measured by what you put into it, I wasn't doing my fair share. I think, in any normal situation, I would have equally been bothered by how much Sean was doing—or wasn't doing to be more accurate. But, at the end of the day, we just grew apart, and I was content with that." The Omega huffed. "Well, that was before I realized it was all a ruse and some part of a long-term scheme."

Stephen's nerve got the better of him. "And when it comes to me?"

Alexander sighed. "I know where this is going."

"You can't tell me you broke it off with Sean in front of a half-dozen people, chose me in the moment, and yet still say I'm not your Fate."

The Omega cleared his throat. "I can honestly tell you I don't know."

Stephen pushed. "Then how do we find out?"

"Hey!" Eric interrupted while poking his head out of front door of the tavern. "I know you two have a lot to talk about, but we still have an event in full swing inside here. Can you figure out your love life later?"

Alexander blushed.

"You heard the man," Stephen commented.

"I, myself, am in the position of being on my best behavior, so... can we talk about this after the event?" Alexander offered.

Stephen approached the Omega slowly. "Are you going to be able to hold out tonight? Or are you going to have to bow out early?"

The Omega laughed nervously, knowing *exactly* to what the Alpha was referring to. "I... I think I can hold out." He took in the Alpha's scent and swallowed hard. "I guess if I need to leave or have to fight someone else off me, I know who to turn to help me?"

The heart in Stephen's chest thumped hard like a drum. He stared into the Omega's eyes, hoping the sincerity was there—that Alexander's submission was real—that he could interpret *his* role as Alpha as true. "Always." Alexander smiled back.

"Hey!" Eric came out again.

"We're coming, Eric!" Stephen announced as Alexander led the way back in.

"What did you say, Alpha?!" Eric played.

Stephen took the hint. "I mean, we're coming 'boss.'"

"That's right. I should put you on another week's probation," he half-joked.

"He's good, Eric," Alexander reassured. "Any issues now are between him and me."

Eric hummed to himself. "I've had to climb that damn ladder twice to fix that camera in the back due to the shenanigans he was involved with. I'm not letting that slide."

Stephen surrendered. "Consider me your 'bitch' for the next week then."

Alexander gasped and grinned. "You have no idea what you just agreed to."

"Ohhh, I'm going to enjoy this," Eric marveled.

"All right," Alexander announced. "Ready? One... two... three..."

"South Street!" the staff shouted before knocking back a drink in honor of the night's success.

"We made it!" Daniel announced gleefully while pulling James into a hug and giving him a peck on the lips.

Alexander moaned. "Just barely."

Eric put his hand on the Omega's shoulder. "Hey, no one died, and no one got hurt. That's what matters." Stephen cleared his throat while pointing to his jaw in full disagreement of the statement. "Oh. Sorry. Almost no one." The bar laughed as they saw Stephen shake his head, taking it in stride. "Fucking Sean."

"Had I known working for you was going to involve receiving several assaults, I would have demanded hazard pay," the Alpha joked.

Alexander ran his hand through his hair, reflecting on Stephen's comment, feeling a wave of guilt wash over him. "Maybe you should have."

Stephen noticed the mood drop instantly. "I'm kidding. It's worth it."

The Omega looked back dumbfounded. "How? Why?"

A smile crept on Stephen's face. "Because you're here. That's why all of us are here." All eyes fell to the Omega in agreement.

Alexander scanned the room, feeling the proud pheromones exude from each one of them. His last look however, fell on James, to whom he hadn't spoken to since their last argument. "I think... I'm also the reason why someone is leaving?"

The attention all switched to James who knew exactly what his boss was referring to. He looked away and sighed. Then, he took one more look at Daniel who smirked back. "Look, I'm sorry for what I said. I was out of line."

"No," Alexander disagreed, "you made some good points. I shouldn't have lashed out at you."

"Be that as it may, I should have said it a different way, and I shouldn't have stuck my nose where it didn't belong. Daniel is your best friend, and he was here tonight for you. Whatever arrangement or disagreement you have is between you two. I should have just butted out."

Alexander sighed as he gazed upon his best friend. "What's it like, Daniel, to have a handsome man defending your honor?"

The short Omega giggled to himself. "It's an amazing feeling. It's not as if you don't know it. You have one here too."

Alexander blushed as he glanced back toward Stephen. Then he cleared his throat. "I do."

"Any development on that?" Bruce boldly asked.

Alexander hummed to himself while he looked at Eric. "Hmm. Well, Eric and I talked about it... and..."

Stephen caught the silence. "And..."

"You can pick up your last check next Friday," Eric boomed.

Stephen's heart dropped. "Wait... what?!"

"Just kidding!" Alexander finished.

The Alpha scrunched his face and smiled back at an audience who enjoyed returning the tease at his expense. "You got me."

"You're not off the hook," Alexander clarified. "We're going to have a very long and detailed discussion about what actually happened and how it's going to be here from now on." In unison, every other member "Ooo'd" and "Aww'd" like a live sitcom audience. "Not like that!" he protested.

"Uh-huh," Daniel crooned, then yawned. "I am exhausted."

"Did Kortney ride you hard?" Eric asked.

"I'm spent!" the Omega replied. "No wonder the guy isn't mated. He's as high maintenance as they come."

"Did he ask you to wipe him too?" Bruce laughed.

Daniel shut his eyes in disgust as the visual went through his mind. "No, thank Wolf-God. But funny you should say that because he did ask what toilet paper you had in the bathrooms."

Alexander cocked his head. "He did not."

"He did!" Daniel insisted.

"And what did you say?" the Omega followed up.

"I just said I didn't think it was anything special. Just regular toilet paper," Daniel commented.

James bit his lip as he recalled all the other eccentricities the prolific radio host had. "And how did that go over?"

Daniel imitated the queen. "'Oh,'" he deflated, "'I don't suppose there is a high-end supermarket open at this hour? No? Shoot. I guess I'll just hold it in and make a diamond and sell it to loyal fans.'" The bar erupted in laughter.

"He did not say that!" Alexander condescended.

"Okay, maybe not that last part. But the first part is true," Daniel pointed out. "I got the impression he never went back to the bathrooms after that."

"Where the hell did he go then?! He was slamming down those free drinks at a pretty good rate," James pointed out.

"Maybe he went out back and pissed in the alley way," Bruce thought offhand.

"Ew," Alexander quipped. "I hope not. It's not the best-looking alley as it is. The last thing I need is for it to be smelling like piss this summer." Then he looked at Stephen. "Besides, that's where you park your bike. I can't imagine you want every Alpha who walks by pissing on your rear tire."

All were entertained by the comment, but not Stephen. A dark cloud fell upon his face as he considered the comment. "Right..."

Alexander took notice of it first. "Stephen?"

The Alpha's stomach knotted as he dared to think anyone messed with it from the event. But he wasn't worried about just "anyone." He had one person in mind specifically. With a determined agenda, the Alpha darted to the back of the bar, hoping and praying his worst fears hadn't come true. As the door flew open and he stepped out, he saw everything that was supposed to be there... except one. "Fuck... fuck... FUCK!" An emotional downpour radiated from the Alpha as he held his head. Quickly, he went to each side of the alleyway and then tucked his head out to the side of the bar, but there was no sign of it anywhere. Crusher was gone. Lost in his own angry thoughts, he didn't even notice the rest of the staff file out, watching his every move as he cursed the day he ever met Raymond in the first place.

"Stephen?" Alexander tried cautiously.

"WHAT?!" the Alpha growled back.

The entire crowd winced at the reaction, knowing this wasn't going to end well.

Daniel asked the obvious question, "Where's your bike?!"

"It's gone!" the Alpha shouted again as he paced back and forth, kicking every broken chunk of asphalt away that his foot could find. "Damn it!"

"How?!" Alexander asked.

"Ray has connections. He probably called someone and had it towed. It could be anywhere by now."

"Are you sure it was Ray? What good is a bike to him?" Bruce asked.

"He's a bottom feeder. Odds are, he'll know a guy who wants it for parts. He sucks up every dollar he finds. He'd sell the whole thing for fifty bucks if the cash was there, ready for the taking." Stephen groaned in heartache. "Why is this happening to me?!" To himself, the question was rhetorical. He knew why. He betrayed his Fated Mate; that didn't go without consequence. Wolf-God himself took that bike and reminded Stephen what he almost gave up in protecting a lie that should have never been there to begin with.

Right there, in the alleyway, Stephen fell to his knees, failing to hold back tears. He closed his eyes, not wanting to be there or have anyone else there. But, instead, he heard the footfalls of someone approach him and come down to his level. Without even looking, he took in the scent: a deep well-aged pomegranate. His mate. Two hands grasped his shoulders, which only made him tremble more.

"Hey," Alexander whispered, "we're going to fix this. We're going to find your bike."

Stephen finally opened his eyes and saw the Omega reciprocate the softest pheromones yet. He didn't necessarily believe his words, but the care he showed was enough. "And how do you propose going about that?"

"A police report for starters," Alexander replied. Then, he looked at Daniel, who got the hint immediately.

"Already on it!" Daniel lifted his phone from his pocket and immediately called for help.

"James, Eric," Bruce called out, "follow me around the block. We'll see if maybe some joy-rider took it and parked it somewhere else." Without hesitation, all three men began their search for the lost bike.

That left Alexander and Stephen alone in the otherwise quiet night. "See? I told you," the Omega reassured.

The Alpha murmured, "She's all I could count on for the last couple years of my life before I was incarcerated. That bike is all I have."

Alexander huffed. "That's not all you have in your life. You have three friends banding together at 2:30 A.M. looking in the darkest corners of downtown Tauris City for your bike for Wolf-God's sake, another one on the phone with the police, and me."

Stephen looked up once again and honed in the last comment. "*Do* I have you?"

The Omega rubbed his hair as he thought about how to respond. He looked deep into the Alpha's dark eyes, still wet with moisture. A magnetism pulled him toward Stephen, and before he could register what his body was doing, he felt his lips press gingerly into Stephen's.

A flood of emotion raced through the Alpha, and the wolf deep inside him perked up, as if he sensed his long-lost mate in the wilderness during a dark winter. Whatever heat he felt from being full of anger and despair, multiplied again to a sensation he'd never felt before. As the kiss dissipated, all he could do was stare back in awe. "I... I don't know to say."

"Me neither," the Omega replied.

"Does this mean you believe?" Another stray drop of moisture ran down the Alpha's face.

Alexander felt his own emotions get the better of him. He wiped away Stephen's tear with his thumb. "What I do know... I like it when I'm near you. I like it when I'm with you." He paused. "I know deep in my heart I can trust you. And when you're not around, I don't feel like myself anymore."

Stephen's face shone and his heart fluttered at the comment. But it was short-lived as he began thinking of the logistics. "I don't know how much I'm going to be around with my bike gone."

"We're going to find it."

The Alpha stood up. "I have to get the police report out of the way and then get a taxi home. Maybe you'll forgive me if I'm late tomorrow?"

Alexander walked over to him and shook his head. "Don't worry about it. I'll give you a ride home."

"I'm not having you drive twenty miles out of the city to drop me off and then drive back home at this hour," Stephen rebutted.

The Omega paused, contemplating, and then proceeded slowly. "I don't live far from here. What if you just came back ... to my place ... with me?"

Stephen stared back and gulped. "Are you sure?" After a moment, Alexander nodded. "But you're in heat. I mean, I'm not an untamed animal, but this situation isn't normal. You're my Fate,

Alex. Hell, I haven't even marked you. That alone has tested all the willpower I have. Can you imagine what I'm going to want to do if I spend the night at your place?" The words came out all at once. Immediately, he wanted to hit himself for being so candid. But every move Alexander was making tonight was throwing him off-guard. He wasn't prepared for any of it. And he definitely wasn't prepared for Alexander's response.

Alexander's eyes fell to his feet as he spoke. "I think I have a very good idea of what you are wanting to do. And... I'm okay with that." He looked up, once again, locking onto the Alpha's gaze. His own heart began pumping, but that wasn't the response he was focused on. It was the biological need deep within him becoming stronger, like a constant beat of a drum that had his full attention. Acknowledging it only made it stronger.

Stephen was about to reply when Daniel back from his phone call. "Cops are on their way. Said they'll be here in ten minutes."

The Alpha broke from his trance only for a moment. "Think they can get here in five?"

Daniel furrowed his brows, having no idea what the question meant. Alexander, on the other hand, couldn't face the comment with a straight face. All he could do was listen to the strong beats of his heart and listen to his inner wolf prance in a way it hadn't in a very long time.

"Don't be so negative. It will turn up," Alexander encouraged as he stepped into his downtown apartment.

Stephen walked in behind him, trying to keep himself in check. "I have no doubt it will turn up. It's the *condition* it will turn up in that frightens me. Fate has this pattern of making sure I experience every possible ounce of retribution and misery ever since I was released."

The Omega laid his keys on the countertop. "It hasn't all been bad, has it?"

Stephen smiled gently. "No. It hasn't." He scanned the apartment. Although the building was visibly older from the outside, the inside had been modernized extensively. With all the stress and worry Alexander carried for the past month or so, he wondered what allowed him to live comfortably in such a place; but right now, that wasn't his main concern. "Wow, this is really nice."

"Thanks." The Omega ascended into the living room, admiring it himself. "It's been a work in progress turning it into a home, but I like it." After a deep sigh, he laid himself on the couch and noticed Stephen standing in the kitchen. "Are you going to come in?"

The Alpha fidgeted but didn't advance. He laughed nervously. "You know, I imagined being here with you countless times in my mind. But..."

Alexander sat up straight. "But...?"

"I never imagined it would be like this. I thought I'd walk in here like a dominating Alpha or a dashing prince. But here I am, not even sure how to approach you." His face fell as he worried about what his Omega thought of him—if he was even worthy of his Status.

"I've already had a 'dominating' Alpha in my life—several actually: family members, friends, business partners and associates, customers, and yes, even relationships. I'm not looking for someone to sweep me off my feet and carry me off into the sunset. I'm looking for my other half, the one who completes me." The words were heavy and prophetic.

Stephen, upon hearing the words, used them as his signal to advance and sit next to him on the couch. He could scent the Omega's anxiousness all over him. There was no doubt they were thinking the same thing. Slowly, the Alpha's own scent began to change as butterflies hit his stomach. He finally gathered the courage and began to slowly press in.

Alexander inhaled and then pressed his arms against the Alpha's shoulders. "Wait." The moment came to a halt.

"What? Did I do something wrong?"

The Omega found the ignorance entertaining. "Did you forget the fact you let your former drug dealer walk away with my prescription and the fact you hid it all from me?!"

Stephen's wolf whimpered as he relaxed. "What can I say to make this better? I'm sorry, Alex. I really am."

Alexander paused and shook his head. "How were you okay with doing that? What did you expect would happen? Did you really think nothing would ever come of it?"

"It's ignorant but yes. I drew a line in the sand that night with Ray and told him I wanted nothing to do with him. I never even saw him again after that." Alexander crossed his arms at the reply. "Losing you was my biggest worry, but I know now the decision I made equally put me in jeopardy, maybe even more so."

"This wasn't a hundred dollar bill, Stephen. It was my medication. You knowingly put me in danger over that decision and it hurts. A lot." A stinging sensation hit Alexander's eyes as his wolf felt betrayed. "How do I trust you not to do that to me again?"

Stephen readjusted himself, hoping to show a strong conviction. "Ray was the only ghost in my past big enough to sabotage everything I had worked hard to move beyond. When he showed up at my parents' place completely unannounced, I was ... flabbergasted. He wanted me back then and there, and I beat him at his antics." He sighed. "I just didn't have the power to do it twice."

Alexander narrowed his eyes. "When?!"

Another dark memory came to light. "The same night I was stabbed in the bar."

The Omega eased up on his criticism as his eyes trailed down to Stephen's arm. "Oh." A wave of guilt fell upon him as he himself reflected on decisions he wasn't proud of. He cautiously reached out and glided his hand over the Alpha's muscled arm. He sensed

Stephen struggle between staying calm and bracing himself. It wasn't until he brushed up against the protruding scar that he realized why.

"Ah." The Alpha flinched then gritted his teeth.

The Omega quickly retracted. "It still hurts?"

"Scar tissue is sensitive." As the pain subsided, Stephen followed Alexander's hand all the way down to his. He took it in his own and squeezed gently. "I can sense from your pheromones what you're thinking. And it's not your fault." The Omega's head bowed in shame. "We've both done things we regret. I just want to move on and start my life with you... my Fate." Alexander looked away. "You're still not there, are you?" The question came out more like a disappointing statement.

Alexander set his sights outside on the crescent moon completely unbothered by the clouds passing by. He studied a silver line which made the formation pop against the blackened sky. There wasn't a lot of time left, however. Dawn was less than two hours away from painting itself across the horizon. Inside, he could feel his wolf, planted in the middle of an endless field, with nothing standing in its way but itself. Waiting for life to happen was over. "There's only one way to find out," he whispered.

Stephen studied the Omega, evaluating his sincerity. But when he took in Alexander's pheromones again, the wall that had been built vanished. That made his inner wolf stand to attention, as the strongest scent began permeating out. His heat was simmering and beginning to bleed through, stronger with every passing moment. A magnetic force pulled him forward until his lips were right on the cusp of meeting Alexander's. No longer sensing any hesitation, he finished the act, feeling the heat between them rise and grow more intense.

Alexander's chest heaved as excitement and nerves rushed throughout his entire body, all the way to his feet and his trembling fingertips. He grabbed ahold of the Alpha's shoulders as he felt a strong hand on the back of his neck, insisting his body close the space between them.

The Alpha's lips parted, and he felt a warm soft tongue glide against his. A low growl erupted in pleasure as he welcomed the sensation and encouraged the act of exploration to continue. But as much as he wanted these slow, subtle movements to continue, the patience he had held ever since he first scented his mate was dissipating exponentially. It didn't help that he felt Alexander's skin become even warmer and flush red. The Omega was no longer resisting his heat as he had earlier in the night. If Alexander had any hesitation, he was going to have to intervene now. Letting their passion continue was going to bring about a point of no return.

That was when Stephen slid his hand from the back of Alexander's head to the side. There, in the crook between his neck and shoulder, was the soft tissue of his mating gland. Only, it wasn't soft. It was swelling and began thumping in sync with his heartbeat. Alexander must have felt the change at the same time he did because his body rose and then disconnected.

"Aw, fuck." The Omega panicked as he stood and began pacing between the living room and kitchen, his breaths becoming stronger, faster.

"What? What's wrong?" Stephen replied, as he stood and watched the panic set in.

"It's happening..." Alexander swallowed hard.

"It's just your mating gland," the Alpha tried to reassure him.

The Omega grunted. "Very aware."

"I ... don't understand the problem. You knew it was going to happen. You knew what it was going to force us to do, right?" Stephen began to unwind, worried Alexander *did* have second thoughts and was going to force his wild wolf to heel at the last second.

"I know that, Stephen! That's not the problem." Alexander grimaced.

"Then what is?"

Sweat began to form on his forehead. He foolishly thought merely wishing his mating gland to calm down would stop its onslaught. But he knew, as he was always told, once it was activated, there was no stopping it. That was the eternal consequence all Omegas subjected themselves to once they allowed their heat to advance. "I've never been claimed before," he blurted.

The words were inconceivable. There was no possible way this was true. "How?!" Stephen asked in pure disbelief.

"My first heat showed up as an adolescent, and I haven't had one since. I've never had a hormone load big enough to trigger it." The Omega gritted his teeth. "Is it supposed to hurt like this?!"

Stephen rushed up and held onto Alexander who was beginning to unravel. "Let me do my job; it will all be over." Selfishly, the urgency was coming from deep inside as his own need was beginning to take control of him. When Alexander wiggled his way free, he became a moving target, and his Alpha's wolf didn't like it. A dominating aura overtook him, and he chased after, cornering him up against a wall. "Come on, Alex. This doesn't get any better until we do this. You know it. I know it."

Even though the Omega knew the Alpha's words were true, he stayed defensive. "You've been wanting to claim me from day one. Do you really think I expected you to say anything less?" The Omega once again gritted his teeth as another prominent contraction in his neck took ahold of him. "Damn it!" He tightened his hand around the gland, hoping it would soothe. It was all in vain.

"You're right. I've been going insane, watching from a distance as Alphas and Betas looked you up and down, licked their lips, and claimed you with their eyes. You're mine, Alex. My only hope is that once I claim you, maybe you'll finally see what I see. But this isn't just for me, babe. You deny this now, and your need is going to push you to a point of desperation to where you aren't going to care who claims you. Now is the time to tell me once and for all: do you want me?" Stephen didn't anticipate the question to throw his confidence into jeopardy. However, upon uttering the ultimatum, his heart was doing a somersault, worried to death where it was going to land.

Alexander shut his eyes in pain, and not just in physical, but emotional pain as well. "I'm just ... so ... scared. Where are you going to go after you claim me?"

Stephen took one step closer. "Nowhere. Once this happens, I'm bound to you until the day I die."

A large watery drop fell from the Omega's eyes. Several seconds later, he removed the hand covering his gland and let it fall to his side. His voice hitched. "Claim me."

Delicate fabric covered Alexander's neck, preventing Stephen from getting unfettered access to his prize. With a tight grip, he gripped both sides of his shirt and hoisted it up until his entire upper chest was fully exposed. The cream-colored skin on his chest was completely smooth minus a focused area of hair naturally growing in the center. Stephen etched the image into his mind as he could practically see the man's heart vibrating beneath his breastbone. The Alpha couldn't believe it. The words he had been waiting to hear forever had finally been said. They were magic. He wanted to hear them again. "Are you sure?"

Alexander nodded his head. "Claim me. Please... Alpha..."

Immediately upon the submission, Stephen flicked his tongue against Alexander's earlobe and then trailed down his neck. The Omega's body spasmed and then grabbed onto him for dear life. Stephen nudged his head against him, opening the space to his neck, leaving it completely open and exposed. Once again, he attached his mouth to his hot, smooth skin and began sucking on the area, gingerly at first, and then harder. He made his way to Alexander's mating gland and teased it incessantly.

The Omega squirmed against him. "Why are you doing that?"

"I'm waiting for the next contraction. When it happens, I'll do it."

"You're going to wait until I'm in pain?!" Alexander whined.

"The harder your gland is, the easier it's going to be to puncture. You'll thank me later."

The Omega snarled, "Doubt it." A moment later—he felt it—a pressure getting ready to force itself to the surface, the strongest one yet. "Stephen... it's happening... it's—" Before he could even finish the sentence, he felt a strong sharp pain radiate from his neck, down across his body. An uncontrollable yelp pierced the unsuspecting night as he desperately grabbed Stephen and clung to him for dear life. The excruciating pain frightened Alexander as he feared it would never cease. But only a moment later did it all fade away. Like a rushing ocean wave overtaking the sand, a soothing ease washed over him. Pleasure instantly melted his body back against the wall as he felt his knees become weak.

Even more so, Alexander began feeling primal reactions he thought he'd never experience in his life ever again. He began sensing his loins going into hyperdrive. His cock, finally being allowed to give into its natural urges, began pulsing inside his jeans. And not just pulsing but begging for release. It embarrassed and excited him at the same time. However, it was when he felt Stephen's arms slowly glide down to the small in his back that he noticed his insides pulsing and producing slick in a way he didn't think he was capable of. He didn't know what to do as drops leaked out of his now contracting hole. Was he supposed to say something? Was he supposed to excuse himself? Instantly, he snapped back to the present, very aware of the Alpha still sucking on his mating gland.

"Wait..." he panted.

Slowly, the Alpha retracted his teeth and then his lips, but not before licking the site of his visible puncture marks still showing hints of mating gland fluid emanating out. "Are you hurt?"

"No," Alexander reassured him, then chuckled out of embarrassment, "I couldn't be farther from it." He blushed, as he saw Stephen stand a little taller at the indirect compliment. "There's just a lot happening I'm not used to."

The Alpha took one deep breath and knew exactly what he was speaking of. "Your slick." It was all Stephen could focus on now that a spotlight had been put onto it. A moment ago, Stephen was consumed by a well-aged, deep pomegranate scent, Alexander's signature scent, one that would be with him for the rest of his life. Now that he claimed him, his mind and body would remember the scent like any other familiar scent which triggered profound memories never forgotten.

The mere enjoyment of it, however, was short-lived, as another visual change had taken place. Stephen gasped. "Your eyes."

"My eyes?!" Alexander quickly walked over to the nearest mirror, fearing he had blown a blood vessel or was suffering from swelling. Neither were the case.

"You're dilating..." Stephen pointed out. "You're giving me permission to..."

The Omega closed his eyes and was instantly transported into the spirit body of his wolf. Back in the desolate field with a dark blue sky and golden wheat, its ears perked up as it heard the call of its other half. Relying on its instinct, it chose a direction and began racing through, bending and snapping every delicate long grain as if it was nothing. The wolf yipped as a scent began cutting through the wind: a smoked cherrywood still hot from the fiery flames which consumed it. Never once did the intoxicating scent feel foreign or misplaced. It belonged to the Omega wolf. It belonged to Alexander.

When he finally opened his eyes again, Alexander saw Stephen's eyes go through the same change. The Alpha's dark brown eyes transitioned even darker until they finally matched his own. "And you're giving me permission to..."

Stephen threw his own head back as a hard thumping sensation instantly hit his neck with a sharp electrifying pain. "Ah, Wolf-God! Fuck!" His hand instantly went to his own mating gland, and he backed away, hoping the moment was just that—a moment. Instead, it only became stronger. His muscled body fell under his weak legs back to the couch as he foolishly tried to overcome the primal need on his own—hoping that merely wishing it to calm down would do the trick.

"Stephen! It's just your mating gland. It's okay," Alexander attempted.

"I know!" the Alpha growled in pain as he hated the fact the whole scene from a moment ago was now playing in reverse.

"Then what—"

"Confession time..." Stephen gritted his teeth. "I ... haven't been claimed before either."

Alexander couldn't comprehend it. It had to be a joke. "You... *what?!*"

"Please don't Alpha-shame me. Now isn't the time," he begged.

The Omega still couldn't get passed the declaration. "There is no way you've never claimed an Omega."

"I've claimed *them* before, yes. But I've never let them claim *me!*"

"How is that even possible?!" Alexander asked, as he continued to watch the Alpha battling his own pain.

Stephen's hand pushed down even harder on his mating gland while the other gripped the couch cushion for dear life. Neither move relieved any sensation. For a brief second, the Alpha finally realized what it was like being an Omega, completely powerless to a heat. "I was never interested in them, only the fact they were in a heat. There was nothing to reciprocate... ugh! Damn it."

Alexander shook his head. "I still can't believe this. You were in prison for ten years. Didn't an Alpha ever want to 'pull rank' and claim you as his bit—" Stephen growled at the notion his mate ever thought he'd sexually submit to another Alpha—the ultimate humiliation when used as such. His black eyes targeted him back like two raging bullets piercing a target. "Sorry! Sorry! Point taken!"

Once again, Stephen found himself enslaved to his primal needs. "This would really be great if we could talk about this some other time!" he yelped.

"Shit. Sorry!" Alexander remembered himself. He sat on top of the debilitated Alpha and instantly started undoing the buttons on the majestic blue silk shirt. More and more heated skin was exposed with each unbuttoning. He grabbed Stephen's large hand covering the source of the pain. Unfortunately, a weakness hit him, and he went in for a deep kiss instead and then laid his forehead against the Alpha's. "I don't know if I can do this," he whispered.

"Yes, you can," Stephen assured him as he wrapped his hand around the Omega's back. "Just let your wolf guide you. Just bite down—hard—and let him do the rest. The worst thing you can do is hesitate or stop too early. You got it?" Alexander's lip quivered as he slowly nodded. "I trust you."

Once again, the Omega found himself relying on his wolf instincts in the most desperate way. The journey of running was finally over. Stephen's wolf was now there in front of him in all his glory. Its fur beckoned to the breeze, its eyes sparkled in the sunlight, and its desire danced all around him. All Alexander's wolf had to do was meet him halfway—and finally—it did.

Some involuntary action must have physically moved Alexander toward Stephen's mating gland, because before he knew it, he found himself attached to it, hypnotized by it. Behind the serenity, he could hear Stephen cry out in pain, but for his wolf, it was just a whimper. A natural metallic taste glided onto Alexander's tongue, but soon after, it was replaced by the essence of a man that completed him in a way he had never experienced before. Stephen's scent was now his. *Stephen* was now his—and it wasn't just sexual.

An overwhelming sensation overcame the Omega, tearing him completely down the middle. Half of him never wanted to stop taking in Stephen's mating gland, but the other half couldn't synthesize the message his wolf was trying to communicate back, the message the Alpha had claimed since day one. Finally, it was too much bear, and he retracted his mouth from Stephen's mating gland and then off his body completely. Moisture instantly began welling up into his eyes which were beginning to refocus back to normal. "Wolf-God..." he whimpered.

Stephen found himself abruptly awakened from a trance-like state. In one moment, he had gone from an excruciating amount of pain to the ultimate pleasure, to finally, his mate backing away slowly with his hand covering his mouth in utter emotional disbelief. "Alex?"

"It's you..." Alexander blurted out. "It was always you..."

Deep inside, Stephen's wolf howled in victory as it finally received the validation it wanted for so long. He knew. Finally, he knew. Alexander was his Fated Mate. And, for the first time, Stephen was Alexander's. The revelation had Stephen wiping away his own stray tear, completely catching him off-guard. But even more so was Alexander's response. Disbelief and feeling overwhelmed was expected, but something else was flowing to the surface: anger. "Why are you upset?"

Alexander's tone went dark. "I can't believe this." On his heels, he turned and aimed himself toward the bedroom, leaving Stephen completely behind.

"Alex! Wait!" Just as quickly as Stephen's wolf celebrated in the connection, it once again found itself racing to find its other half like a runaway damsel in a fairy tale. Luckily, the bedroom wasn't that far, nor was the door slammed in his face. Still, just the same, there was the Omega, standing in the corner of his room near the window facing away. All he could hear now was the sound of raindrops hitting the glass and his lungs trying to recover from what he thought was the purest moment in his life. "We're Fates, Alex." The Omega refused to turn and look at him, struggling to center his emotions. "Doesn't that give you comfort? Doesn't that give you clarity? You said it yourself: you always thought there was something about me that made us connect in a way you couldn't explain. Here it is! We were always meant to be together. Doesn't that make you happy?"

"Happy? *Happy?!*" Now, Alexander turned, facing an Alpha with an utterly lost expression. "I'm furious! I'm pissed-off! I damn near have every right to *hate* you!"

Stephen's wolf whined. "Why?!"

Alexander grabbed his hair, nearing the edge of insanity. "I'm a 26 year-old Omega who just found his Fated Mate..."

"There are some Fates who wait longer than that. Some don't ever find—"

"My Fated Mate is an ex-con who went to prison for ten years for drugs..."

Stephen furrowed his brows. "That didn't seem to stop you from bringing me home with you... so, why—"

"Meanwhile, in those ten years, I dealt with an Alpha father who treated my younger Alpha half-brother like wolf-child from the heavens while I was treated like a dull piece of property..."

"What do you—"

"Had an Omega father who bent to the emotional abuse even more than I did, not to mention the physical abuse..."

"He did what?!" Stephen's mind was reeling from the candid monologue but didn't know what to do or what to say.

"Then I spent the next ten years criticizing every Omega who even dared to remind me that the submissive rhetoric still existed, shutting out every Alpha and Beta who even gave me the slightest impression they were out to ridicule me, control me, or make me submit to them, and then completely going insane by finding myself in one of the most dogmatic professions which perpetuates every-thing I stand against..."

Stephen shook his head. "You won that battle when you got the bar—"

"And then hopped from bad relationship to bad relationship thinking every time I must have been the problem in each one because I wasn't the cookie cutter Omega all Alphas are told to expect from their mates. The punchline to it all is, I thought I had finally found a great guy, one *any* Omega would have been lucky to have: handsome, successful, a High-Type, and accepting of Omegas as equals. And then, I found out, tonight, Sean was nothing more than another fucking Alpha who was there to do nothing more than fuck with my mind and break the last bit of hope I had that there was any happiness out there for me!"

The Alpha's throat went dry. "I ... don't understand. What does that have to do with me?"

"YOU WEREN'T THERE!" Alexander sobbed as he stood there completely helpless.

Stephen felt as if he had been hit by truck. The Omega's pheromones slammed into him and radiated throughout his body as his heart ached in a way it never had before. With it came clarity. He finally understood why Alexander was who he was, and he finally understood the relationship they had for the past couple of months.

In his teen years, the Alpha went down a path, a selfish one. Once drugs became his focus, perhaps Stephen's legal troubles were inevitable. But the day Warren overdosed didn't just cost Warren his life; it also cost Alexander his. For ten years, there was a zero chance either of them was going to find each other. If Stephen had stayed the straight and narrow, did that automatically mean the two were going find each other sooner? No. But Stephen single-handedly made sure it didn't. That was Alexander's message.

Automatically, Stephen went up to the shattered Omega and wrapped his arms completely around him. It comforted him that Alexander didn't resist, but the relief was short-lived. In his arms, he held his Omega who was completely beside himself, crying against his chest, his heated body vibrating. He kissed his forehead and sighed. "I'm sorry. I should have been there for you."

"I was so alone," Alexander mumbled.

"I know that now. But you're not going to be anymore," Stephen declared. "You're my Fate. And I love you."

The Omega's chest heaved as he finally felt his wolf slow down. Behind it, Stephen's wolf was right there, as if they never parted from their Fating encounter. After wiping his tears away, he gazed into his mate's eyes and kissed him deeply once more.

CHAPTER 06:

MAKING CHOICES WHERE NO ONE WINS

Alexander and Stephen stood there in his bedroom, completely transformed from their kiss. Both of their half-naked bodies pressed up against one another, matching their heartbeats as one. The sounds of their labored breaths only fueled their passion as they continued their maiden exploration.

Stephen's wolf purred as he noticed his mate take initiative to move his hands up and down his back and then glide to the front of his pants. Not wanting the Omega to take control yet, he hoisted the Omega up, locked his legs around his waist, and maneuvered him to the bed. The landing was soft as he laid Alexander's back onto the comforter. Once again, he felt eager hands pull at his waistline. This time he let the trembling hands grasp the metal clip and pull it open. The fabric glided down his legs as he kicked them the rest of the way off. But Alexander wasn't going to have his way... not unless Stephen had his way first.

In sly move, Stephen found both of Alexander's hands and squeezed them tightly in his. Then, he hoisted both of his hands above the Omega's head and held them there. The look Stephen initially received back was in confusion as Alexander jolted in response.

All the Alpha did was smile gently and then press his lips against his one more time. But afterward, he glided his tongue down past the Omega's chin, down his neck and to his collar bone. The first stop was to his soft unsuspecting armpit which he vigorously licked up and down, waiting to see what kind of response he'd receive. It didn't disappoint.

Beneath him, Alexander squirmed from the overwhelming sensation. Stephen decided to try the other in an attempt to see which side was more sensitive. It was instantly clear the latter armpit was the more sensitive one as he heard the Omega gasp and felt his hips push upward. The Alpha chuckled to himself as he took his tongue once more across his armpit, gliding across its soft hair, back up his neck, and to his lips. Alexander mistook this as a sign to try and wiggle himself free of his grip. Stephen shook his head. "No. Not yet. I'm going to make sure every last bit of you has my scent."

Alexander moaned in response—half in pleasure, half in frustration. The irony of being dominated by his Alpha wasn't lost on him. No other Alpha even hinting at the idea would have gotten as far—and they didn't. But yet, here Stephen was, having his way and owning him for as long as he wanted. The Omega's face flushed red as he dared to admit to himself that he liked it. He liked it a lot. It reminded him of just moments ago when he begged his Alpha to claim him. Feeling brave, he said it again. "Alpha, I want you inside me. I want you to claim me."

Alexander heard the Alpha growl and moan in approval. However, Stephen showed no sign of instantly giving him what he wanted. He instead began flicking his tongue against his taut nipples which were obviously heightened in their sensitivity due to his heat. The response was wired deep into his loins which once again reminded him of the state he was in. Slick once again started producing in a way that was preparing him for the ultimate physical exchange. Unlike earlier, Alexander decided it wasn't a burden or issue. If anything, it was driving Stephen's wolf to go further. And he was about to find out just how far.

The Alpha did indeed scent the Omega's hot slick, preparing his body for penetration. Stephen had nearly forgotten just how strong the call was. It was nature's siren's song, an incessant beating drum which needed to be quelled. That temptation alone was what drove Stephen to finally set Alexander's arms free so he could instantly rush to the Omega's pants and equally shed them. The Alpha didn't give any modesty back as he completely stripped Alexander of every piece of clothing left on him.

Stephen studied his mate in awe. He had a subtle build with legs hairier than he anticipated which seemingly melted away to nothing once they met his torso. Protruding straight up and at attention was the Omega's full-sized erection glistening in the yellow light of his bedroom floor lamp. Stephen bowed his head low and took in Alexander's scent as he kissed and bit his inner thighs. He wasted no time after that, consuming the full length of his member, making it disappear down his throat. Once again, he felt the Omega's body twitch in reaction. As best as he could, Stephen held his waist down as he let his throat do all the manual labor hands free. The moans and gasps emanating only fueled the Alpha to go further, knowing he was driving Alexander insane. The truth was, however, the Omega had no idea just how much Stephen was equally tormented, his own member straining against the now soaked fabric of his underwear. It tormented him and demanded attention—demanded worship. Unable to ignore it any longer, he stood up and peeled off the tight fabric in one quick motion.

Alexander immediately took notice of his Alpha's cock, rock hard and precumming like a leaking fountain. His own sexual arousal caused him to immediately take advantage of the moment and thrust his body upward until his face was mere inches away from Stephen's hips. The Omega lifted his face and glanced up, waiting to see what the Alpha would do. Stephen stood there and didn't move.

Slowly, Alexander used both hands to grab the waistband of his underwear and slowly pull them off, revealing a throbbing member long-since waiting to please his mate.

With a firm grip, the Omega grabbed the base of Stephen's cock and stroked the large shaft, initiating even more fluid to gush from its opening. He heard the Alpha growl above him, his muscles trembling in anticipation. Alexander's hunger grew to the point to where he himself couldn't wait any longer. He swallowed Stephen's cock with a wolf's fervor, savoring every drop he could. Every time he heard Stephen's low growl develop into a full moan, he tried every technique to illicit the sound from him again and again. He used his tongue to circle the cockhead while he massaged the hot heavy sack below begging for release.

Stephen couldn't believe what was happening to him. Weeks of sexual frustration had his mind reeling; nothing created in the most detailed fantasies prepared the Alpha for what was actually happening. He absolutely envisioned himself pleasing Alexander, making him moan in ecstasy from the pleasure. But to have the Omega equally servicing him while he stood over him? That was a dream. But at the same time, Alexander's wet throat was causing him to become overly sensitive. If he didn't stop him, the dream was going to be over faster than he wanted.

The Alpha pulled his cock from the Omega's throat and lifted him up to standing. He grinned, which silently gave his mate a compliment for his work. Then, he felt Alexander lean in and press his tongue into his mouth, giving Stephen a full taste of his accomplishment. It was a flavor he wasn't used to. All it did was urge him to reach the destination he wanted to get full used to the flavor he hadn't even tried yet.

He smoothly turned Alexander around which gave him full view of his long torso, large ass, and prominent legs. Stephen bear hugged and pulled him in tight until their bodies were flush. Once again, he inspected the Omega's mating gland with his mouth: red, tender, fragrant. He explored his hands down the front of Alexander's body, gliding past his nipples, his belly button, all the way down to his own full erect member. He rhythmically began stroking it which involuntarily pushed his hips back harder onto his own cock which was exactly what he wanted.

Alexander's own pleasure weakened him at the knees, and he found himself naturally falling and bending over the bed. Not a moment after, he found Stephen's naked body on top of his, thrusting up and down as he moaned and licked into his ear. "You're driving me crazy!" the Omega managed to blurt.

"You haven't experienced anything yet," Stephen moaned. He pushed off and gave himself a targeted view of his Omega's vulnerable body, waiting in anticipation. The Alpha knelt down on the floor and pulled the Omega's legs apart completely, exposing the entry to his insides. Alexander's entry was naturally red, but it was pulsing, readying itself before Stephen could do it himself. Leaking out was his clear slick, designed to be a natural attractant and lubricant to a primal Alpha, should his physical urges give way to an unapologetic onslaught. But Stephen had no intentions of wolf-handling his Fated Mate that way.

His face dove in and his tongue darted deep inside the soft layers of Alexander's body. The scent and taste were intoxicating alone. But it was his mate's involuntary jolts and whimpers in pleasure which had him completely hypnotized. Every move and every sound told him to go deeper, longer, and more intense. He used his large hands to massage the soft skin of his hips as he continued until he was sure had the Omega completely delirious.

Stephen cleaned his lips with his tongue and fingers before using the natural lube to test two fingers inside Alexander's hole. The Omega arched back as his breath quickened, getting used to the new sensation. Once both knuckles were tucked away deep inside, the Alpha pulled them out slowly and then shoved them back in. The heated inner walls spasmed and pulsed until finally they relaxed.

Alexander noticed it as well, as he sat up on all fours, completely out of patience.

"Stephen, please! I want you inside me," the Omega begged as his resolve had left him several minutes ago. His heat had fully consumed him as his body felt like one giant heat source burning him from the inside out, all his reproductive organs letting him know he was alive and operational.

The Alpha stood and massaged his large cock, using the lube from his mate's hole and his own member to slick himself. He lined himself up, ready for entry, and then stopped. And didn't move.

Alexander, sensing Stephen must have wanted him to go the rest of the way, began pushing his hips back into him. But immediately, he felt a muscled hand on his lower back stop him from pushing back farther, effectively stopping any minute sensory of penetration. "What? What's wrong?" the Omega huffed.

"No. I won't do it," Stephen said firmly.

Alexander's head whipped back in disbelief. "What?! What-what do you mean?"

The Alpha stood there like a statue, frozen. Then, he shook his head, standing up and moving away. "Not until you tell me."

"Tell you what?" Alexander's hand went up, completely lost, still feeling the drumbeat of incessant need inside him.

"I want to know when you knew there was something between us—something more than just two strangers who met in a bar."

The Omega couldn't comprehend what was happening. All the passion, all the lust, all the intensity, completely stopped... for this?! "You... you can't be serious about wanting to do this now."

Stephen flexed his muscles. "For a month, I was ridiculed, dismissed, criticized, interrogated, suspended, stabbed, punched, and questioned all over the fact I knew a truth deep inside me no one else would acknowledge. The only person I cared about was you, and you were the only person who could give me the validation I needed. And you cut me off time and time again. But at the same time, you kept me there."

Once again, the Omega was lost in a complete haze due to his heat. "Stephen... I'm sorry... I... didn't mean to..."

"When did you know?!"

The Omega buried his head into the comforter and moaned in agony. "Please don't do this..."

"Tell me!" Stephen commanded.

Alexander froze there, helpless. The biological need was pushing him to the brink of insanity, and his mate knew it. Primal wolves were displaying their true wild instincts. But the Omega didn't have the stamina nor the will to withstand his needs. And he knew his mate was fully aware of it. Tears began escaping the Omega as he finally relented. "Maybe I always knew," he finally confessed emotionally. "There was always a faint aura of something that told me you were the one. In all the things I don't have answers to, I can tell you this: it wasn't like it was supposed to be."

"'Supposed to be'?"

The Omega nodded, out of breath. "The way you said you knew—how your wolf knew—that's how it's supposed to be. I didn't have it. It wasn't there. But the moment I first saw, I sensed it. But it was so quiet, so soft, I dismissed it." Alexander turned around and laid flat on his back.

Stephen closed his eyes and calmed his voice. "When did you notice it getting stronger?"

The Omega stared at the ceiling in thought. "There was a moment at the fundraiser. After Matthew's speech, I was overflowing with joy and pride, and I began thinking of all the people there who were enjoying it with me: Whitmore, Minh, Jake from the Medical Center, Bruce, James, Eric, Daniel... and then I thought of you. And when I did, I immediately looked at you and saw you looking at me. I liked it. I knew then," he hesitated, "I knew then that something was different. When you came back after the suspension, and we had that argument in the bathroom corridor, I think we connected."

Stephen walked up to bed and leaned over, holding his weight with his arms. "You *did* feel it, didn't you?" Alexander nodded slowly. "What do you feel now?"

"The way I'm supposed to," Alexander finished.

The Alpha situated himself between the Omega's legs and pressed his hips into him. Once he was lined up, he gave Alexander one last cautious look. In return, the Omega nodded as his breath quickened in anticipation. Finally, the Alpha's large cockhead pushed open the delicate opening and led the way deep inside into his mate.

Alexander felt inch after inch penetrate him deeper, feeling a sensation like he never had before. Heat pheromones intensified every sensory gland and nerve in his body unlike anytime previous. Once he felt the base of Stephen's cock against his entry, he wrapped his arms and legs around him and kissed him deeply.

The Alpha began gently rocking backing forth, testing the Omega's threshold. No matter how hard, soft, long, or short each thrust was, it only elicited pleasure. That gave Stephen permission to pump himself continuously in and out of Alexander, sending them both writhing in emotional bliss.

The Omega was the first to comment in absolute pleasure. "You feel amazing."

"No," Stephen passionately disagreed, "you do."

Alexander huffed. "I wonder how long it's going to take for my heat to break since my womb won't drop."

Stephen's movements once again slowed to a halt as he began to analyze all the sensations his human and wolf scent were being subjected to. Without saying anything, he pushed Alexander's hips up and found the best position for the deepest penetration possible and slowly guided himself in until... "Are you sure?"

Right before the Alpha said it, Alexander felt the exact same sensation he did. His eyes grew wide. "Oh, Wolf-God..."

Unexpectedly, the base of Stephen's cock began to grow to a generous size larger than the shaft. Both he and his mate began moaning in the abrupt new pleasures and shocking revelations happening at the same time. Alexander's pheromones released a stronger, sweeter sensation which told Stephen's wolf it was time to inseminate his Fate. The call from his natural wolf to do so only initiated once there was contact with a womb—fertile or not. And Stephen's large member had found it and just penetrated it.

Alexander's body sensed the knot and began contracting against it, practically commanding him to thrust back onto his body automatically without his cognitive consideration. The scent coming from Stephen was equally powerful, driving his every move. "I can't believe this is happening."

"Me neither." Stephen panted as they both gave into each thrust and each interval of pleasure.

"I love you," Alexander squeaked out.

The Alpha smiled as his wolf raced to the top of the mountain, arched its back, and howled at a golden moon. "I love you too."

⁓⁓⁓

A strong, warm light beamed in from the large window and heated the bed where two bodies laid, intertwined with a soft white sheet barely covering them both. Alexander stirred as the combined warmth from the sun and his mate's body made it impossible to stay asleep. Discomfort grew as he assessed the moment; it wasn't the heat of Stephen's body locked onto him which bothered him. It was the suns. He knew the feeling. *That* feeling indicated he had slept longer than what he was anticipating.

The Omega came to his senses and tried to untangle his body from his mate's. But immediately, Stephen caught on and latched on even harder, giving away that he was fully awake.

"I need to get up," Alexander announced. Stephen grunted in disagreement. "I need to get my phone."

The Alpha groaned again. "Uh-uh."

"*We* need to get up. I don't think its anywhere near morning anymore and..." he gave his body one final thrust and released himself from Stephen's hold, "I think we're late."

The Alpha's body flopped on the bed from the momentum left of trying to hold onto his mate. He grinned at his failed attempt as he told himself Alexander was lucky he was still incoherent; otherwise, he'd never have gotten away. He relaxed and took the failure in stride, waiting for his mate's inevitable return.

"As I suspected," Alexander sighed, "we were put on a lovely group text wondering if we died. I called, so they know we're going to be late."

"Good. Now you can come back to bed." Stephen smiled.

The Omega rolled his eyes in amusement and then crawled back in. He locked onto his mate's gaze. "What?"

"What color is your natural hair?"

"Brown."

"You should let it grow out," Stephen encouraged.

"Yes, Alpha," Alexander playfully said back. Once again, he noticed his mate staring back at him. "What are you thinking about?"

"I dreamt about this countless times. Just hoping that those were dreams and this isn't."

"It's not." Alexander kissed his mate.

"How are you feeling?"

"Sore." A smirk followed.

Stephen couldn't help but feel it as a badge of pride. "Guessing another round isn't in the cards today?"

"You guessed right."

"Does that mean *everything* is off the table?" The Alpha grinned.

"What on earth could you want to accomplish right now that you didn't last night?"

"Hmm." Stephen playfully thought. He pulled down the sheet until Alexander was exposed all the way to his belly button. Then he glided his fingertips softly up and down his chest. He noticed his Omega twitch in response—a good sign. Even more so when he kissed his slightly defined pec and then tugged at his nipple. His mate's breathing pattern changed. It only told him to go further. Bending over, he eyed Alexander's nipple like a target and began licking it before completely taking it in his mouth. As he did so, the Omega's breathing changed to a heavy inhale until he finally began moaning in a rhythmic pattern. Stephen used his hand to reach over and grab the other nipple, massaging it and gently pulling on it, completely enjoying his mate's euphoria. "Mmm. How's that?"

"Amazing." Alexander huffed.

"Yeah? You enjoy that, my Omega? You enjoy that, boy?"

A sudden drop in pheromones consumed Alexander and hit the pit of his stomach. Unsightly memories made the pleasure stop instantly. He tried to ignore it, to separate the comment as best as he could. But it was to no avail. "Uh. I need to stop." When Stephen put the brakes on, Alexander used the moment to get back out of bed, continuing his breathing, although now it was for a completely different reason.

"What's wrong? Something I did?" The Alpha examined his mate in a complete panic with no clue what just happened. He sat up and continued to watch his mate commence a short pace back and forth.

"I-I just need to refocus and get to work. We should go."

Shock consumed Stephen, still lost on the origin of the one-eighty turn of events. "If I did something I shouldn't have, I'm sorry. I... Can you tell me what I did?"

The Omega ignored the plea as he focused on finding clothes he could immediately jump into, blanketing him back to safety. "Just let me process it; I promise I will explain at some point but not right now. It's not inherently you; it's me. Know that."

Stephen felt a cold sensation wrap around him. After a beat or two, he followed Alexander's lead and began dressing himself. The entire time had him completely lost. He couldn't think of what to do or what to say. What was worse was his mate making him completely powerless. The wolf inside him had no clue how to proceed. After both were presentable, Stephen followed his mate out of his apartment like a lost puppy.

The drive to the bar was even more awkward than in the apartment. Stephen's mouth was completely dry; his tongue was locked and prevented him from saying anything. All the while, he constantly flipped back and forth with staring out the windshield and staring at his mate. The rumblings of the engine and friction of the pavement were the only sounds heard. They became deafening and more noticeable than they should have. "I'm sorry," Stephen managed to squeak out. Alexander turned his head and gave a half-hearted smile in return. Then he took one hand off the wheel and reached across the center console, beckoning for his hand. The Alpha cautiously embraced it. It gave little comfort as he questioned the gesture: was it sincere or a front? He didn't know.

Stephen had hoped pulling into the bar parking lot would have brought some sort of relief. But the car shutting off only created a more awkward silence. Alexander once again turned and finally gave some acknowledgement to the atmosphere. He leaned over and gave him a peck on the lips.

"I know you are. I promise you, this isn't you. I will tell you. Okay?" he said quietly.

Fitting the atmosphere perfectly, Stephen creased his lips into a cautious expression barely feeling comfort or reassurance. They both exited and entered the tavern.

The first thing Alexander noticed was the bar was already open. Initially, he had mistaken the cars in the parking lot as customers from last night avoiding driving while under the influence. But it appeared that wasn't the case. Walking in, he observed Eric collecting and analyzing receipts. It surprised him. "I thought you were taking the day off."

"Yeah, I am," his business partner stated.

"Typically, that means you aren't here when that happens. What time did you get here?"

The Alpha glanced at his phone. "Little over an hour ago."

"So... what are you doing?"

Eric finished a calculation, mouthing them as he wrote down the results on a notepad. "I'm gathering last night's numbers," he said, not even looking.

Alexander furrowed his brow. "Worried I can't do math?" The Alpha ignored the comment completely and finished his work. When Eric turned the pad around, Alexander expected it be pushed his way so he could see it. But at the last second, the Alpha changed course and led it down to the customer to his right. He furrowed his brow as he saw the patron look the report up and down several times.

Alexander waited before saying anything. First, he couldn't understand why a customer was so interested in the numbers. Second, he couldn't believe Eric would freely offer the information up to a complete stranger as if it was any of his business. He began opening his mouth to get answers, but Eric preempted him.

"Alex, this is Nicholas Hamilton. Nicholas, this is Alexander Daventry, co-owner of the bar."

The newly introduced Alpha sat there as a figure of authority. He was completely put together with a suitcoat and shimmering gold watch to accent his cufflinks. He stretched out his hand in a greeting. "Nick will do just fine."

The Omega reached out and commenced the handshake. "Hi," he followed up, unsure of what was happening. "I'm sorry. Do I know you?"

Nicholas understood the vibe. "No, we've never met. And I'm taking it that you haven't heard my name before." Alexander took a moment before slowly shaking his head. "I own a couple bars here in the city: Oasis and Cliffside Bar & Grill."

"Oh, I know those. I've been to Oasis but haven't ventured to Cliffside before—always wanted to."

"Hope you enjoyed Oasis?" Nick inquired.

The Omega nodded. "It was a good experience: great service, nice staff, good vibes all around I'd say."

"I've worked hard on the locations over the years to get them up to the standard I expect."

"I can tell. I mean, owning *two* locations? That doesn't happen without being successful. You're doing something right."

"I appreciate that." The man nodded, never expecting anything less. "Word on the street is this place has seen a complete turn-around of the reputation it once had under the previous owner."

"Like yourself, I found it to be no easy task," Alexander replied. "It's not perfect by any means, but as of late, it has been rewarding. Hopefully we only go up from here." He glanced at Eric; an inhale gave away anxious pheromones. It was obvious he was waiting for something.

The businessman continued, "Regretfully, I couldn't make it to Jesse Minh's rally here a couple weeks ago. And I even heard about the last-minute change you had on hosting the Singles' Night T's Bar usually hosts."

Alexander grew into a smile. "It's been overwhelming but also exciting. On some nights, I swear we've doubled the customer base we had before those events. Even now the number of customers this afternoon wasn't like this even a month or two ago."

Nick turned and observed the respectable crowd present and gave off a satisfied expression. "What an accomplishment. That's great to hear."

"Thank you." Alexander spoke softly. The formalities were losing steam. He gathered up the courage to figure out what was going on. "I don't mean to be forward, but would it be safe to say you didn't come all the way here just to congratulate me?"

By this time, Stephen made his way back up to the bar next to Alexander and leaned over, resting his weight on the counter. The conversation was intriguing to say the least. His mate's expression followed his own, unsure of where this conversation was headed. The presence of such a person was way too much effort for just an introduction and a compliment.

Nick looked down at his water glass and picked it up. After a quick drink, he continued, "I'm curious of your goals here. Do you imagine yourself staying here for the long haul?"

Alexander respectfully considered the thought. "I mean, with business going well, I have no reason not to."

"Any other ambitions outside the bar you've ever considered?"

The Omega snorted. "The process it took to get this place and get to this point? I've only been able to think about the here and now. There was no time to consider anything else. Wouldn't even know where to begin."

"Sounds stressful." The Alpha made a subtle hint at Eric. Their conversation was moving along as it should have.

"Some days even that is an understatement."

Nick smoothly pushed in. "Have you ever thought what it'd be like if you didn't have to carry that much stress? To have the power to relieve yourself of that much responsibility? Be able to take time off, relax, recharge?"

Alexander sighed. "I can't say I haven't thought about it—multiple times in fact. But you know as well as I do, this can only be as successful as the amount of work you put into it."

Another look at Eric gave Nick the signal the matter at hand was finally here. "Alex, I want to give you that opportunity—the ability to not carry the workload and the stress you currently have. What would you say to that?"

The Omega scanned the members of the group, trying to see if there was any hint as to where this was going. "I'd say I'd be intrigued as to your thought process on how that would happen. With you being successful, I'd love to hear tips of the trade or ideas on how to adjust to the 'smarter not harder' philosophy. Is this an investment thing? If so, I don't have the funds right now to cover an expense like that. Maybe a year down the road."

"Not so much an investment," Nick drew out, "more of a sale."

Alexander furrowed his brow. "You mean like a partnership? You want to buy a partial stake in South Street?" Nerves began to rise within him as he saw the successful Alpha adjust himself.

"Not a partial stake but in totality."

The Omega once again looked at his business partner who looked very much like he had waited on this moment from the get-go. "You-you want to *buy* South Street?"

"I must admit this isn't the first time I considered doing so. It was something I also approached the previous owner on, and I considered it again after he lost it. Even at that time, I wasn't sure what potential was left here. You, however, proved this place wasn't a lost cause and did a lot of work to get it there. I don't think there is any reason why you shouldn't be rewarded for those efforts."

"By losing the place?!" The conversation had Alexander completely caught off-guard. He didn't know to react to such a proposition. One look at Stephen at least confirmed he wasn't going crazy; he appeared as equally shocked as he was. But Eric once again showed he was in a completely different headspace. From the moment he and Stephen walked in this morning, it was clear all Eric was waiting for was an answer, and he feared which one.

Nick gestured. "I wouldn't word it as *losing* it. I'd view it as a victory, a show of what your hard work did—paid off in spades."

Alexander rolled his eyes. "With all due respect, this isn't the first time I've been propositioned to give it up; albeit it, you are really the only one who I can say is doing it in a respectful manner versus patronizing me on even going into the venture from the start. I appreciate that. However, every offer which has been thrown out to me indicates that interested parties have a *very* different view on how much my hard work is worth. 'Insulting' is the word I'd use."

The Alpha thought for a moment and then peered at the notepad Eric gave him earlier. He casually flipped it to an empty page and wrote down a number in pen and passed it over. "Would you consider *this* number an insult?"

The Omega took one glance and immediately showed his stunned reaction.

Stephen himself caught the number and couldn't help himself. "Whoa..."

"You... um... wow! There's no way this is a real offer. Do you have any idea how much more this is than any other offer I received?"

Nick sat proud of himself. "I told you: I recognize what this place is and what you've done to change it into what it is. The potential here warrants it, don't you think?"

"*I've* always thought so. I haven't run into another person who thought the same," Alexander confessed. "This is a lot..." the Omega caught himself, "to handle I mean." He rubbed his chin as several thoughts scrambled in his mind. "Please excuse me if I seem out of sorts. I didn't walk in here imagining this would happen today."

"Absolutely. I understand. This would be overwhelming to anyone." There was a silence that followed which indicated a hesitation. Fearing it was losing momentum, the Alpha pushed again. "Would you mind sharing your initial thoughts?"

The Omega took a deep breath in. "Every other time, it was just so easy to walk away. *This,* however? At least I can say it's something worth thinking about." He bit his lip as a gut check set in. "But there's no way I can make this decision now. I don't even know if I could give you an answer in a week."

Nick couldn't hide a look of disappointment. Even if he did, his pheromones gave a read instantly. "What gives you pause?"

"You said it yourself: I put a lot of work into this. From the start, blood, sweat, and tears were sacrificed to this place. Giving all that up in a day? I'd be amazed if anyone could do that. Then, there's even considering what I'd do from there. This was my dream. I said I haven't thought about any other options, and I was serious. And that's just me! I have other employees to consider here. Stephen, Bruce, James... what about them?"

"Oh, don't worry about that. The transition would be smooth, and I'd never cut them loose just because of the acquisition. They're the experts here; they know the routines, know the work, know the customers, and I'm fully aware of that advantage."

Alexander was relieved at the perspective. "I'm sure they'd be grateful for that. But I ... don't know how much you and Eric talked before I came in nor how much he has told you. But it's *not* common knowledge about what role he has here. Everyone knows him as the manager and we're absolutely a team." He smiled at Eric. "And I've been grateful for him every step of the way." He swallowed his nerves. "Eric is actually part owner here. 30%. Therefore, there's no way I could make this unilateral decision on him. Usurping him on the process and telling him he doesn't have a choice in giving up his ownership? That's a whole discussion itself."

Eric observed Nick's solemn look and prepared himself. "Look, Alex, I thoroughly am grateful that is your philosophy. And your comment on being a team and recognizing me means a lot." He swallowed hard. "The offer isn't for *us* to get out of South Street. It's for *you* to get out of South Street."

Alexander leaned forward, completely flabbergasted. He wasn't even sure if he heard Eric right. However, based on the three expressions surrounding him, he understood this was *exactly* what he heard. The Omega's lungs hitched as he began to feel ill. Never before had he felt so uncomfortable in his own business—not even when Stephen walked in on day one and tried to convince him they were Fates. "Eric... we need to talk—alone."

Eric immediately walked toward the outside of the bar, already anticipating this was the next step. He entered the back hallway and waited for Alexander, knowing the immediate reaction he had subjected himself to. "Believe me, I'm totally aware of how you're feeling right now, and I don't blame you."

"You give me one fucking good reason I shouldn't kick your ass out of here and ban you from ever stepping foot back into this place!" the Omega seethed.

The Alpha huffed. "You can't afford to buy me out. That's the obvious answer."

"I don't believe this. I absolutely Do. Not. Believe this!"

Eric cringed. "If you could just lower your voice a little..."

"Don't you *dare* tell me how to act in my bar, Eric. You cannot be doing this to me right now. Do you remember last night when we had the conversation about my irrational fears about you trying to undercut me like this?! I felt like a complete fool. Well, shit. It doesn't appear so irrational now!"

"I understand how this looks." The Alpha tried to do any sort of damage control. However, it was to no avail.

"I'm not convinced you do!"

"Not the best way to go about it, I completely understand. But I refuse to accept this as hypocritical."

Alexander smirked. "Oh, please do explain."

"Do you have *any* idea how much you hurt me last night? Do you?!" Eric lashed out. Alexander turned his head in frustration. "You announced in front of Stephen, you announced in front of Daniel, and even customers, that I was some snake in the ground from the beginning, essentially sticking me in the same category as Sean!"

The Omega sighed in regret. "I *apologized,* and I meant every word. What happened last night was completely insane, and I unraveled. Please don't take that to heart."

Eric shook his head in what he considered a convenient cover-up. "What you said was a clear admission you thought worse of me. Appreciation? Teamwork? You must be joking. If not this, what else would I have had to do to make you feel I was nothing but scum? Would I have had to do anything? Or did I earn that title for simply existing?"

"So, what are you telling me? Have you always thought for two years I was treating you unfairly? Did you think I thought any less of you before last night?"

"Last night opened my eyes to a lot of different situations which have occurred since we went into a partnership that make a lot more sense now—I'll tell you that."

Alexander crossed his arms. "Speaking of last night, what happened to us having a discussion? You said that's what we'd do."

Eric's black skin shadowed in the light as he gave himself one final gut check before uttering his position. "After the whole ordeal last night, I stayed up for hours thinking about all this. I'm not sure what can be repaired. If it is what you said—that it's a 'you' thing—I don't know what I'd have to do for you to feel better. Because my fear is that the perfection you have in your mind about how *I* need to act is unobtainable. And it's not fair."

The Omega was beside himself. A buildup of emotion broke the surface. "What is all this? How did this happen in less than 24 hours?"

Eric once again went into confession mode. "Nick has made a few side comments before. In the beginning, I thought he was just teasing when he talked about his feelings on you 'swooping in' and grabbing it before he could. But the more I saw him, the more he brought up the subject and made random comments. Finally, I point blank asked him if he was truly serious. Turned out he was."

"He came here?! How did I miss that?"

"Alex, come on. I work for the city in the business division. The discussions happened when I had to do rounds at his properties. He has two of them; it created a lot of opportunities for the conversation to come up."

The Omega shifted his weight. "Why is this the first time I'm hearing about this then?"

"Like you said, we've run into this before. You've been so tightly wrapped on proving yourself as of late, there's no way I could have brought him up. I even tested the waters."

"When?!"

"The night you called me in after the protestor broke the window. Don't you remember?"

"I think so?" Alexander squinted as he vaguely recalled the night Jake came into the bar. The two had just finished discussing the incident before Eric rushed in—fuming—and leading him right to this very place to scold *him* for allowing the customer's conduct—as if it was even in his control.

"You completely shut the whole thing down. I considered it a dead subject. With our good fortune the past few weeks, it was easy to put it all on the back burner." He paused. "But last night changed all that."

"You didn't answer my question."

"I texted Nick this morning wondering if he was still serious about buying South Street. He said he was. After explaining to him I had an investment in this place and didn't want to leave, he wasn't bothered. I told him there was no way you'd consider it without a worthwhile offer, and he assured me you'd be very happy with his figure. He was the one who brought up coming in this afternoon. I didn't know what his offer was going to be until right before you came in. And you have to admit Alex, that's one hell of an offer. And that's at 70% of the ownership even."

Alexander massaged his temples, trying to relieve the stress boiling up inside. "That doesn't make sense. If you concluded our partnership was a lost cause, then why didn't you talk to him about selling your share versus mine?"

Eric was taken aback the Omega couldn't figure it out. "Nick wasn't interested in only having 30% of the place. And he wasn't interested in partnering up with... with..."

"An Omega?"

Eric didn't respond. "What happened, Eric? What did I do?" Alexander spoke softly.

"You cut me out, Alex. The number of times Stephen screwed up in the place and the number chances you gave him? That not only had me completely stunned; Bruce and James were equally there too. You single-handedly brought back Eddie, Craig, and the rest of them, after I *specifically* explained to you those weren't the right customers to have here. You even endangered Stephen's life over it!"

"If you had any idea of the guilt I'm *still* carrying from that—"

"I told you not to carry your prescriptions here out of safety; the number of things which could have gone wrong with that are countless. You pissed off James for no other reason than to spout your mouth off. If he had quit, you know Bruce would have followed him immediately. It was hard enough trying to get anyone here in the first place when we advertised the opening before Stephen took it. That alone could have tanked us. And let's be honest, last night, once again, you decided on your own Stephen got another chance."

"That's not true!" Alexander protested.

"Really?" Eric doubted. "If I had said no, would you have honored that?" This time, it was Alexander who fell quiet. "Exactly."

"This is completely unfair."

Eric scoffed. "Welcome to my world." He pivoted. "You have an opportunity here, Alex, that I don't think you're ever going to see again. I'd think about that. In the meantime, I'd appreciate it if you could quit acting like an entitled pup and get over the delusion you've been the kind of partner anyone else would tolerate. Because I'm sick of it." With that, Eric pushed himself passed the Omega, hoping Nick still had the patience and stuck around.

Alexander stood alone in the back hallway. The last time he and Eric were here having a heated discussion, it was all so different. He shut his eyes and tightened his fists as he tried to hold himself together. His stamina was shot to hell, and he felt an overwhelming sensation completely take over. Immediately, he headed to the back door and pushed it open. Harsh and heavy breaths involuntarily spilled out of his lungs as his voice began trembling. He wanted somewhere to go—a haven from this nightmare. But the alley gave nowhere to go to seek such comfort. The last place he had to consider was the other side of the dumpster. He lunged his back flush against the side and slowly felt his knees become weak. After his body reached the torn-up asphalt beneath him, he released himself and began sobbing uncontrollably.

A million thoughts ran through his head. The course of his life changed in such a short amount of time, it hardly seemed real. After the protestor busted one of the front windows, he found himself desperately praying for a turn in good fortune—figuring it would completely go unanswered. Then, Matthew Whitmore gave him an opportunity of a lifetime and gave him hope like he never could have imagined. "Stephen," he said out loud. Wolf-God had a sick idea of how to truly discover he was in fact his Fated Mate, not to mention deciding Stephen was the one for him in the first place. Even though Eric was correct that there were plenty of reasons to let him go and dismiss him all together, he really did have to confess the pull was there, no matter how weak it was. Now that he was claimed, the true intensity of the pull had finally revealed itself. But were the consequences worth it? He wasn't sure. On top of that, there was this morning.

The anger he felt on why it happened enraged him, origins all the way back to childhood. Animosity consumed him as he realized just how much it permeated his life: his mistrust, his paranoia, his attitude, and his jaded philosophy on Alphas. All of it was created and yet *he* himself paid the price—him and everyone else he lashed out on. "You bastard." He crumbled. The solidarity was short lived as he heard footsteps scrape against the alley.

"Alex?" Stephen said as he turned the corner and saw his mate.

Upon seeing his mate, Alexander quickly stood up as if it somehow showed any level of strength. But looking at his mate as a completely broken wolf made him whimper once more.

"Babe..." The Alpha sighed as he quickly reached out and wrapped his body completely around him—holding him.

"I don't want to do this anymore. I can't," Alexander managed as he laid his head on his Fated Mate's shoulder.

Stephen stroked the back of his head and neck. "I'm here; it's okay."

The Omega lifted his head. "No... no it's not." He wiped his fallen tears and settled himself. "I brought this on myself."

"Brought what? The buyout? That was Eric," the Alpha countered.

"And he did that because of me. I've been a complete and utter asshole to every Alpha I've ever met in my life." He sniffled. "At least, it seems that way."

"I don't believe that."

"Really? Last night I think you were pretty clear on telling me I did the same to you. You damn near read me to filth and wouldn't fuck me until you said it."

Stephen creased his lips, acknowledging the way he manipulated his mate's heat in the moment. "I guess... the pent-up frustration of it all finally got to me. I shouldn't have done that."

"No... no, I deserved it. Just like I deserved everything," the Omega concluded. "I just have it so ingrained in me, I feel it's everyone else's problem and not mine." He looked his mate in the eyes. "That's why the instance happened the way it did before we left my apartment."

"Are you ready to tell me?" Stephen asked.

Alexander exhaled and nodded. "Yeah. Yeah, I am." He took his time gathering his courage and gathering his thoughts. "My father, my Sur, completely abandoned me after my brother Jin was born. Not in the physical sense but emotionally, mentally, I just became this useless, inconvenient reminder of the old life he had but obviously didn't want anymore." Stephen didn't move or react. He continued to stand there, patiently listening. "When I got older, I started acting out. I suppose it was for attention." Alexander grew frustrated at the memories. "And I got it; Wolf-God, I got it."

"What do you mean?"

"I got hit. I got hit a lot." He bowed his head as if he deserved to be ashamed of it. "And I think what was even worse than being hit was the fact I still didn't feel like his son. I was his ... 'boy.' His disrespectful, disappointing, and disgusting 'boy.'"

Stephen's heart broke at the revelation. Now the picture was clear. It wasn't that Stephen wasn't there all those years to protect him from being criticized or tormented due to being an Omega; it was the fact he wasn't there to protect him from the monster his father was. "Alex, Wolf-God." Once again, he grabbed his Omega and squeezed him tightly, as if it could protect him now. He kissed his forehead before feeling a rush of dark, hateful pheromones flood his glands. He wanted to invoke the old Stephen he was, find Alexander's Sur, and show him what it was like to mess with an equal opponent. There was no way he'd win a match against him. The wolf inside would fight to the death if he had to. All the Alpha knew now was if he *ever* hurt his mate again or even crossed paths with him, Wolf-God have mercy on him—because Stephen wouldn't.

He centered his mate and made sure he understood every word coming out of his mouth. "You are not responsible for how he treated you, and you never were. Do you understand me?" Alexander couldn't respond. "Do you understand?" His mate finally managed a nod. "I will never let that happen to you again. I will die before the day ever comes. And I don't plan on that happening anytime soon."

"I just... I want to move on. I'm sick of this controlling my life."

"We can get you help; you won't do this alone. I'll be there every step of the way. You're my Fate. That means forever bound. And I plan to show that in every way possible."

Alexander sighed. "This Eric thing... I can't even fathom how he thought he could do this to me. Talk about losing my faith in Alphas," he commented.

"That was unforgivable the way he did that. Watching that happen... I didn't know he was capable of that."

"Giving up South Street? Man." The Omega couldn't comprehend it.

"Would that be so bad?"

Alexander found himself completely confused again. "What?"

"After what he did? Do you really think staying here is the best idea? Look what you'd have to put up with."

No, the Omega heard it right. It was déjà vu. "Why would you say that? Don't you know how much South Street means to me?"

"Of course, I do," Stephen assured him. "I saw it from the moment I walked in. But things are different now. Eric proved that today."

"That means I should just cower? Wave the white flag?"

"As messed up as it may sound, I don't think Nick is wrong. You left a legacy here and the offer he gave proves that. Why subject yourself to all this when you can finally start a life without all the drama of the bar?" He paused. "So, *we* can start a life."

The words did little to give Alexander any comfort. "'We'? You and me?"

Stephen was unsure how it was such a vague concept. "Yes?"

"I just last night had my inner wolf tell me that you are my Fated Mate. And that's after the complete rollercoaster ride I experienced to get to that point. Now, you think that just because you claimed me that we're starting some 'Happily Ever After'?"

Stephen found himself at a loss for words. "I don't understand. We fated each other, consummated our love... What more could you want?"

"How about trust? How about honesty? How about not coming out here to tell me a fucking repeat of what Nick said?"

"It's not as if I'm saying you're weak or incapable or somehow a failure. I'm only saying I recognize all the crap you've had to put up with. Why do you need that in your life? What were you expecting me to say?"

"How about asking my opinion?!" The Omega stared back in disbelief. "How about not offering your advice when I, moments ago, was completely blindsided by two people who practically made the decision before I even came in. Did you see how Nick reacted when I didn't give him a resounding 'Yes'?! It was like I completely disrespected him and was crazy for even thinking anything other than handing it over."

"I'm not trying to belittle you. I'm trying to help you," Stephen attempted.

Alexander curled his lips. "To help me get rid of 'stress'? To give me the only way out to 'relax' and 'recharge'?" Stephen didn't respond. "You know, I wonder how many Alphas get told they should let someone take their business off their hands using that same philosophy: a mercy offering. If I went to Nick and used the same reason to buy his bar, what do you think he'd say?"

Stephen's voice shrank. "I... I don't know."

The Omega slapped his hands against his hips, completely giving up. "Right."

CHAPTER 07:

WITNESSING THE CONSEQUENCES OF ACTIONS

No one blamed Alexander for taking several days after the ambush to distance himself from the bar. The move was ironic considering it was one of the justifications as to why he should sell in the first place. However, that didn't mean the next week was any less vexing. Every one of the staff felt as if someone died or was subjected to a life-altering change. And considering the issue at hand, the latter concept was still a possible outcome.

Stephen was able to arrange his schedule with Eric to use his Sur's truck for transportation for evening shifts. That, unfortunately, was where the comfort stopped. It had been a few days since the proposal and the first shift the Alpha worked with Bruce and James alone. He walked into a decent crowd but a very demure pair of brothers. Both caught sight of him from opposite ends of the place. Neither one gave a resounding welcome; instead, he received a subtle acknowledgement. "Hey, Bruce," he said cautiously.

"Stephen," he replied in monotone.

The mood was set, Stephen surmised. He sat in front of the Beta and tapped his fingers on the bar. "How are things?"

Bruce acknowledged him only for a second before going back to rearranging several beer mugs. "It's going." He shrugged.

"Missed you the last couple days."

"Are you here to work or just to sit there and chat?" Bruce snapped.

Stephen was losing his own patience. "I don't know... Am I welcome to work?"

The Beta eyed him back with disdain. "Seems to me like you're welcome to do anything you want: fight, criticize, lie, consort with dealers, sleep with the boss," he sarcastically listed off before going into a thinking pose, "and... oh yeah, encourage him to sell off the place so James and I lose our jobs."

A customer came up and paid his bill which gave the Alpha a moment to think before he spoke. After he left, he replied, "I don't suppose it's the last one that has you upset the most?"

"What do you think?" he mumbled.

"I think that's a 'yes.'" Stephen sighed. "Nick said if Alex sold it, he'd keep you guys on. So, I don't know why that's such an issue."

Bruce raspberried. "Pfft. Take it from me, Stephen, someone who's been in the workforce for over twenty years, that's not how it works."

"Care to tell me 'how it works' since I'm so inept? I mean, I'm still getting used to human ways since the spacecraft dropped me off only a month ago."

"Don't get smart with me," Bruce warned. "First off, anyone who's acquiring a business can say whatever they want to your face to make it sound good. After the exchange of power, it's *their* world, *their* rules, and they can do whatever the hell they want." The Beta rustled up a couple beers and set them on the bar. James came by to pick them up, only giving another subtle acknowledgement before heading to the customers' table. "You may not know Nick Hamilton, but James and I do."

"What am I missing then?"

"He's got his own staff and his own management. I guarantee you James and I would be on the payroll for a month or two before he started cutting our shifts, replacing it with people from his own pool, until we were forced to quit. *That's* how it works. It's bad enough you turned on Alex, your *Fated Mate*, but here it sounds like you didn't want to consider *anyone's* feelings on the matter."

Stephen held his head in his hands. "Can you two please give me a break?" he pleaded. "I have been in purgatory with Alex ever since that day. If you're worried that I haven't paid the consequences for saying that, let me dispel it right now. The fated bliss lasted about five seconds. I can barely get him to talk to me."

James came up from behind. "Must be tough."

The Alpha turned his head. "You have no idea."

The younger Beta decided to take a moment and sit next to "the enemy" and entertain his presence. "It's true, then? You two really are Fated Mates?"

Stephen couldn't help but feel the conversation should been more enthusiastic than this. "Yeah... we are. Once we claimed each other... I don't know. I finally broke through. The night we had... it was intense. Probably one of the best nights of my life. Maybe even *the* best. Then, the next day, everything just crashed."

"What happened? I mean, besides the obvious," James asked.

Stephen paused. "Has Alex ever talked about his Sur?"

The younger Beta swayed back and forth. "He doesn't bring him up a lot, but whenever he does, it's not complimentary."

"Did you... did you know he was abusive?"

Both brothers looked at each other in confusion. "No..." Bruce replied. "How abusive?"

Stephen immediately regretted bringing up the subject, but he couldn't stop now. "Like 'beating up your kid' abusive," he growled, triggered by the anger of it all over again.

"Wolf-God, no!" James gasped. "He did that to Alex?"

Stephen nodded. "That's what he says. And it completely explains his behavior toward Alphas. Apparently, it all started when his younger brother Jin came into the picture."

Bruce nodded. "Now *that's* something we've heard about before. Alex has always thought his brother was treated like the golden child. But neither of us knew *that* about his Sur. That's outrageous."

"I wish had known it so much sooner." Stephen grunted.

"Why?" James asked.

"You don't see it?" Stephen asked incredulously.

"See what?" Bruce replied.

"That this is why Alex is the way he is. The wall he built, the harsh attitude toward Alphas, and the 'I have to do it all on my own' philosophy. It's all rooted in his childhood." Both Bruce and James looked at each other in awe, carrying the same thought. "What?"

Bruce smirked. "Did you get a degree in psychology when you were in lock-up?"

"Might as well. I had enough therapy myself over ten years, I could have."

James gave his older brother a look before finally initiating a cease-fire and sitting next to his friend. "When did you find all this out?"

"The same day Nick came by. After Eric dropped the bombshell, it sent Alex into a tailspin."

"If that's the case, he hasn't recovered from it," Bruce stated.

That made Stephen's ears perk up and his stomach drop. "Why do you say that?"

"From what Eric has said, he's been ill, held up at home for the past few days."

Stephen shook his head. "Guys, I went to his apartment before coming in He didn't answer."

"No, sorry. He's not at his apartment. His parents' place."

The answer didn't sit well with the Alpha. "What the hell would he go back there for?"

"Admit it," Alexander smiled at his younger half-brother as if he was a wise-old parent witnessing his child learn about the lessons of adulthood, "staying in Tauris City hasn't been that bad."

Jin eyed him back with disdain but relented. "It hasn't been the worst."

Alexander was going to have to let the lackluster attitude suffice. Only a month ago, he recalled his Alpha half-brother practically screaming at the top of his lungs how much he hated being in Tauris City and living with his parents—a sentiment they both shared at one point in time. But unlike Jin, the Omega found moving to an apartment and finding a life outside his childhood home was enough to quell the urge of running a thousand miles away. Jin, on the other hand, was bound and determined to hop a plane and never look back, leaving Alexander completely alone. Now that Jin was content with his current situation, the Omega thanked Wolf-God he didn't push the issue further, forcing Jin completely out of the Territory, which was the opposite of what he wanted. "But I suppose staying with me would have been a death sentence?"

"No way in hell was I ever going to move in with you. You've got enough drama in your life as it is, and I don't want any part of it." Jin was satisfied with his words until he happened to glance over at his brother's reaction. "Sorry."

"Actually, I think you nailed it," Alexander confessed.

"Is that what you wanted to talk to me about?" The Omega nodded. "Then, let's hear it." Jin flipped back his black hair and opened a pack of cigarettes. Instead of lighting one up and offering a partial, he pushed the pack toward Alexander. His brother eyed the shiny package complete with a golden moon and wolf silhouette on the front. After a beat, he waved the offering off.

Alexander stared off into space, remembering their last conversation on the front porch like it was yesterday. Only a couple months ago did he and his brother have a similar conversation right after Stephen entered his life. And here they were again. "Stephen was right."

Jin exhaled out a cloud of smoke. "Stephen? You mean Alpha ex-con?" Alexander shut his eyes, holding in his patience at the unwelcomed moniker. He nodded. "About?"

"He *is* my Fate."

Jin's shaped eyes widened. "Damn. That sucks, bro."

The Omega furrowed his brows. "Excuse me?!"

"No one wants an ex-con for a mate, especially one as rough and unrefined as he is."

"You have no idea what you're talking about, Jin."

The Alpha's expression was completely lost on his younger brother's train of thought. "What the fuck you being defensive for? I'm just basing this all on what you've told me!" No response came in return. For Jin, that came with realization. "He's really gotten to you, hasn't he?"

Alexander gulped. "I guess so."

Jin tried to search for a silver lining in the dark revelation. "I mean, as long as he hasn't claimed you, it shouldn't be hard to dodge him."

The Omega winced. "A little too late for that." Alexander ceremoniously pulled down the neckline of his shirt, exposing the scars from his mate's imprinting.

Jin nearly jumped out of the chair. "Holy shit!"

"What?!" The reaction made Alexander nearly do the same.

"You let this prison freak claim you?! That's for life!"

"It's only for life if I want to be," Alexander defended.

"*Do* you want it to be for life?" Once again, no response came. "Sur is going to kill you." Jin quickly glanced through the open window which irrationally could lead a sound wave through the kitchen, down the hall, and into the bedroom corridors.

"It would be great if Sur didn't find out, if you catch my drift." The Omega shot his brother a stern look.

Jin tossed the butt of his cigarette out to the green grass below the porch. "Good luck! A restraining order and witness protection program wouldn't keep him from finding out."

"How do you figure?"

"You can't be ignorant to how popular you and the bar are now. I still have friends randomly texting me 'I didn't know your brother owned a bar.' Completely silent for two years, then you host a rally for a politician, and now you're Tauris City's next buzzword."

That was the next thing Alexander needed to bring up. An unsettling feeling took over him as he had dreaded for years a conversation like this could happen. The last thing he wanted was for his brother to ever get the upper hand on this one. "About the bar," he huffed. "Eric... he..." Even before the Omega could finish, he observed his younger half-brother flex his hands which sent pulses up his arms and into his neck. "He went behind my back and found Nick Hamilton to try and buy-out South Street from me."

In a flash, Jin shot up from his chair and began walking to his car. "I'm going to kill him. I'm going to tear open his neck—"

"Jin, stop!" Alexander commanded as he chased him down. Finally, he reached him and laid both hands and his shoulders as he centered his eyes upon his. They were damn near blood red with intent.

"I knew he was going to do this to you. I knew it! I told you!"

"And I don't want to hear it! You've been saying it from the beginning and this isn't what it looks like."

Jin stared back in disbelief. "'Not what it looks like'? Are you insane? Do you need to be committed?"

"Not funny, Jin."

"And I'm not kidding! If you think this is anything else other than what I've been saying *or* you think this is okay because you somehow deserve this, then you *do* need to be committed."

Alexander turned up his nose at the thought and spoke softly. "What *if* I deserve it?"

"Why on earth would you say that?"

The Omega let his hands drop in defeat, letting them wave like long branches down by his side as he sulked. "What if I can't handle being an Omega in an 'Alpha World'? What if I can't be that unrelenting, unforgiving, unapologetic 'Alpha' that everyone expects out of a business owner? Because, apparently, when I do it as an Omega, I don't get respect. I just get labeled as a 'nightmare boss' or 'difficult to work with' or worse, just a plain old 'bitch.' And once I try to show any humanity at all, I get even worse labels like 'weak,' 'unprofessional,' or... or..."

"Unworthy?"

Alexander ignored his brother's contribution. "I know I wasn't perfect when dealing with the whole Stephen situation..."

"But..." Jin encouraged.

Alexander walked over and leaned against his own car which was next to his brother's. "I didn't know it would shine a spotlight and become an anecdote for how everyone already thought of me." He glanced at Jin, who gave off the impression he knew what his brother was referring to. "I know I can be a hard ass sometimes. And I know I shut people out, especially Alphas. But when it's always been there—"

"It just becomes natural," Jin finished. "And you don't stop to think that you're contributing to your own demise." Alexander laid his head in his hands. "Hey, bro, it's okay. It's not a 'you' thing. It's not an 'Omega' thing. It's a 'human' thing. And you know what that means?"

"That I'm a horrible human?"

"No." Jin laughed. "It means we're *all* capable of making that mistake. And, in my opinion, it's not a mistake to do it. It's a mistake not to *recognize* that's what's happening. And look at you, being able to call it out all on your own."

The Omega sniffled and managed a smile through a fallen tear. "Well, technically, you helped."

"Ah, you had it. I was just being a dick of an Alpha who wanted it to *seem* like I deserved all the credit." He caught Alexander with another smile. "How'd I do?"

He chuckled. "Flawlessly."

Suddenly, a strong voice from down the hall reached the ears of both young men. "What the hell is going on out there?"

Both Alexander and Jin jumped up, recognizing their Sur's voice immediately. They readjusted themselves with the former yelling back, "Nothing! We're just talking."

Jin refocused himself. "You might want to get out of here before Sur starts asking a bunch of questions. I, myself, need to get out of here before he starts talking to me."

"He doesn't want anything to do with me," Alexander said reassuringly as he remembered what happened the last time Robert, his Alpha father, went poking around in his personal life. He turned the tables on Robert and went in tenfold, uncovering an unsightly affair between him and some random Omega right in his childhood home.

Jin disagreed emphatically, "Oh please, our Sur has always been about keeping his eye on you and you know it, especially as of late—though I don't know why." Alexander refused to look his brother in the eye, fearing it would cause him to reveal what Jin didn't know about the affair. "Next to your public life, he'd love to scrutinize your personal life, *and* the Alpha you tamed."

Tamed, Alexander thought.

The sentiment was beginning to show itself as a running theme. From ruling the bar with an iron fist, his relationship with Sean, the way he treated Eric, all the way to the relationship with Stephen, there was this common thread of him somehow mind-controlling every Alpha around him in order for them to be tolerated. Now, it wasn't what the Omega needed. After a beat, he reached into his shorts, pulled out his sunglasses, and headed for the driver side door.

"Where are you going?" Jin asked.

"Somewhere else. Does it matter?"

Jin was instantly disheartened. "Why?"

"Because I was wrong," Alexander replied. "I thought I could get some support from my brother whom I haven't seen in over a month."

"Don't be so dramatic, Alex," Jin condescended.

"See you tonight." Alexander shut his car door and exhaled as he desperately reached for his phone.

[**Alexander:** Please tell me you are near your phone and are free to hang out. I feel like my life is falling apart and need to get away. I don't suppose you have a remedy in mind to help alleviate stress?]

[**Daniel:** I know just what you need! ☺]

"I tell you my life is falling apart, and your solution is to take me *bowling*?!" Alexander asked incredulously.

"What's wrong with that?" Daniel replied innocently as he casually led his friend to the service counter. "You already work at a bar, my apartment is boring, and bowling is a great way to relieve stress!"

"I'm in Hell. I'm in the seventh circle of Hell," Alexander concluded.

"Hey, I just read that book in The Archive! I didn't know you ventured into Primate-Descendent culture."

"I don't," Alexander replied.

"Then, how—"

"It's called an 'expression,' Daniel."

Daniel's face fell to that of unease as he focused on the gentleman waiting on his command. "Good afternoon..." the Omega squinted as he looked at the name tag, "Bennett. I need a size 7." The Alpha behind the counter smirked and highly doubted the Omega's claim. Daniel could read it all over his face. "And a half! Please," he smarted. Bennett chuckled and quickly retrieved the request. "And this bundle of joy over here needs a size 10."

"Look at you, being a chivalrous knight," Alexander sang.

Bennett took notice of the attitude. "Bad day?" Alexander rolled his eyes. "Here." Alongside the shoes, the Alpha slid a small card toward him. "Hope this helps. And if you need anything, you just let me know." With a large smile, he winked.

"Thanks," the Omega replied flatly as he grabbed the card and his shoes.

Daniel watched his friend leave the counter completely unphased by Bennett's generosity and subtle pass. He studied the attendant who appeared wounded himself and gave an awkward look before chasing after his friend headed to an empty lane. "What the hell was that?!"

Alexander held the card up, signaling for Daniel to take it. "Here, it gets you a BOGO on a specialty drink from the bar."

"Sweet!" Daniel crooned. "Now, let's see, usually there's a service button on one of these monitors..."

"It's right there," the Omega replied solemnly.

Daniel criticized, "Man, you have got to shake out of this funk you are in."

"Wow. Shortest pep talk ever."

"I don't even think a monk would approach you. He'd rather tap the shoulder of an Alpha with four guns on his hips and a knife taped to his chest to ask for directions before asking why your pheromones are all jacked up."

Alexander landed in the lane chair and began to tie his shoes. "They're not jacked up. I just need to destress is all."

"What you need is to get laid," Daniel insisted. He couldn't help but notice the rabid dog content on biting back with every other comment fell silent on this one. "Or not?"

"Let's just say Stephen and I made up for my dry spell."

"Oooo!" Daniel teased. "Details!"

"Absolutely not!" He casually got up and began his journey to find the right weight and grip for his bowling ball—Daniel on his tail.

"Oh, come on," the short Omega pleaded.

"Nope."

"If I have to suffer your attitude through three games of bowling, I should be entitled to something that helps give you a redeeming quality." Daniel lifted several candidates, realizing none were even in the realm of the weight he needed. He scratched his head. "Don't they have an '8-pound section' or something?"

Alexander looked up. "Over there." About halfway down was a cart under a proud neon light that read: *Pup Balls*.

"Really?!" Daniel moaned.

The degrading moment made Alexander smile for the first time since getting in. He leaned over like a condescending parent talking to his young pup. "I'll get it for you. Do you want the pink one or blue one?" He received an angry look back with a strong middle finger aimed right toward his head. "Pink it is." Despite the comment, Alexander decided to be nice while returning with a lime green ball instead and set it in the queue.

"Do you want to go first or second?" Daniel asked.

"Doesn't matter," Alexander replied.

Daniel rolled his eyes and shook his head as he entered in both their names and started the round. "You're up." He watched Alexander line up his first shot and throw the ball down which nailed the sweet spot to collect all the pins. Strike. Daniel twitched his lips. "I guess there won't be a warm-up frame." He pivoted. "So, fine. If you're not going to satisfy my tastes by giving me a play-by-play, you have to tell me something. Obviously, something has you off your game," he glanced at the scoreboard again, "so to speak."

Alexander popped his knuckles out of nerves. Then, he searched around, wondering if anyone was listening in, as if they'd care. "Stephen was right."

"Right about?"

"He *is* my Fated Mate."

Daniel gave a gentle smile back. "That's great."

"You make it sound as if it was old news."

"I knew that since I met him. *You* knew that since you met him. I thought after the Singles' Night event you tossed Sean aside for Stephen *because* he was your Fated Mate?"

Alexander disagreed with the assumption. "No, I did that because I knew Sean wasn't right and that there was something about Stephen I couldn't ignore. Was it my inner wolf trying to tell me Stephen was my Fate? Maybe." Then he noticed several pins staring at him from the opposite end of the alley. "Bowl."

Daniel came out of his trance and found the neon ball Alexander had picked out. The throw was decent and had its course set well in the beginning until it slowly veered to the right. Two pins. "That was... That was less than ideal," the Omega commented.

"It's okay if you knock down more pins on your second throw. You won't get into trouble. I promise." Alexander smirked.

"Feeling better?" Daniel threw back sarcastically. All he received back was a shoulder shrug. With that, Daniel knew he'd get whatever was eating Alexander out of him soon enough, but right now he was worried about his own redemption. A green orb rushed up from the ball return, inviting him to finish out the first frame in a spare. He glided his hand casually over the air vent and then gripped his fingers into the sphere. This time, he readied himself slowly, took a deep breath in, and perfectly hit the marks with his feet as he loaded up his shot and hurled the ball down the open lane. A deep breath hitched in his throat as he relived the unfortunate fate of his previous throw. One pin.

Alexander scrunched his face and then nodded his head. He walked up to his friend and patted him on the back. "The only place for you to go from here is up."

"Don't patronize me!" Daniel huffed back.

"I had a fluke on the first run. Don't get your balls in a knot on the first frame." He stuck out his tongue. "Like you said, we have three games of this," Alexander offered. Daniel crossed his arms and pouted his way back to the score man's chair, giving him a perfect view of his form. It was an effortless, choreographed dance the way Alexander slid himself up to the approach line and released the ball with a sheer force sure to crumble any obstacle in its way. The ball narrowed in on its prey like a black pool of ominous death until it smashed all ten pins down, scattering them helplessly into the back of the deck. The Omega smiled at his own accomplishment and then slowly muted it as he turned to face his friend who cocked his head and his eyebrow in confusion while maintaining his pouty attitude. "Second frame stroke of luck?"

"Uh huh. I see." Daniel shook his head. "You don't even like this game," He muttered.

"I'm starting to think you don't either."

Daniel snorted. "I'm getting there." Nerves creeped up his throwing arm and began growing insecurity as he thought about his approach and what he was doing wrong. He surmised he was turning his wrist as he released the ball, causing it to change its course. The young wolf inside centered himself, but unfortunately, the human outside did not. The ball made an immaculate trajectory down the lane, never wavering from its straight path... about eight inches to the right of where he intended. Three pins.

Alexander scratched his head. "What if next time you—"

"Where's that bar attendant?!" Daniel squawked.

"You rang?" a smooth voice replied.

"You?!" Alexander blurted as he instantly recognized the masculine specimen as the same person who handed them their shoes.

"Yes, sir!" Bennett tossed up a circular platter, balancing it on his finger as if it were a basketball or pizza crust, before tucking it under his arm and finishing off with another signature wink. "So, what can I get you two?"

Daniel shook off his current mental state and blurted the order on Alexander's behalf. "Two Red Wilds, please."

Alexander nearly hurled at the order. His swore he felt his stomach pulse in panic at the thought. "Daniel..."

"Oh, that's right. The more you drink, the better I'll bowl. Better make those doubles."

Alexander's frustration grew. "Daniel."

"Got that card I gave you?" Bennett asked.

"Right here." Daniel smiled as he handed it over.

"I'll have those out to you promptly!" the Alpha said as he walked off.

"Thanks."

"Daniel!" Alexander finally yelled.

"What?" Daniel asked, completely lost.

"I don't want a drink right now!"

"You're really turning me into an Alpha today. Yes, you need a drink. It will relax you," Daniel replied swiftly.

"No... I don't," Alexander confidently stated back.

"Why?"

"Because I *can't* have a drink right now." He stressed, feeling completely vulnerable.

Daniel sat there, tapping his foot as he tried to comprehend a rational reason for the mini meltdown. All the same, the rhythmic sound halted immediately when one, and only one, came to mind. "Alex..." he paused, "are you pregnant?"

Alexander squirmed uncomfortably in his chair as he thought of the right way to answer. "A little."

Daniel leaned in, trying to comprehend the logistics. "What? You want you to take a nap and see if you sleep it off?" he replied sarcastically.

"Don't start," Alexander lamented.

"What does 'a little' mean?!"

"It means, I'm relying on my wolf instincts here. I haven't checked."

"Oh." Daniel sat there, lost in a haze, unsure of how to proceed. "I'm assuming it's Stephen's?" Alexander looked back, ready to smack him. "That's a 'Yes'!" He cleared his throat. "Does he know?"

"Not yet," he replied solemnly.

Daniel nodded. "What are you thinking about?"

Alexander sighed. "I can't get my mind to settle on one damn thought. I think about Stephen, I think about Eric—"

"Eric? Why Eric?"

That's when the Omega realized, he didn't know the latest news on the bar yet. "Eric talked to Nicholas Hamilton." The look on Daniel's face read he had no clue about who the man was. "He's the owner of Cliffside and Oasis. Eric is trying to convince me to sell South Street to him. Or rather, trying to convince me to sell South Street to Nick and *him*." At this point, Alexander wished had Eric's head in his hand, so he could toss it down the bowling lane and knock down twelve various influential Alphas, including Nicholas Hamilton, who believed it was okay, much less, humanitarian to treat an Omega in this manner.

"No way!" Daniel gasped. Alexander nodded in return. "What an asshole! Why the fuck would he do that?"

If it had been right after the reveal, Alexander would have had no problem ripping Eric to shreds over the cowardice move. But, with the amount of time that had passed, it was getting harder to ignore the core of his message and the responsibility. "Am I a good friend?"

Daniel couldn't help himself. "Meh."

"Be real."

Shaking his head, Daniel lifted himself and sat next to his fellow friend and rank. "You are my *best* friend. Does that mean you're perfect? No. Does that mean you're always on my side? No. Does that mean you're always nice to me? Definitely no. That's not what a best friend is. A best friend is someone who cares enough to give a damn about you and accepts who you are as a person. I *know* you do that for me, and I hope you know I do for that for you." Alexander stared back while taking in the assessment. "What does this have to do with Eric?"

"From his perspective, I haven't been the best business partner *or* friend. And... I'm not sure he's wrong. I think he's realized with the success of both events South Street is at a crossroads. He either uses it as a launch pad to turn the bar into what we've always wanted, or we let it pass by and stay in the status quo before Matthew Whitmore ever graced us with his presence." Then the hardest part went through his mind. "And now, it's whether or not I'm going to be a help or hindrance to that success."

"But you *both* made South Street what it was today. You told me Whitmore said the whole reason he booked South Street was *because* of you. Eric can't discredit that."

"True. But that doesn't mean I've made it easy. I think I've let my Alpha inferiority complex take control of me."

"Ohhh." Daniel drew the sound out.

"What was that for?"

"You think I haven't noticed?"

Alexander slumped in his chair. "That obvious to you?"

Daniel snorted. "You could say that. Why don't you just confront the root of your problem?"

A moment later, Bennett returned with two tall drinks. "Two Red Wilds!"

Daniel sat up and cautiously took both drinks. "Say Bennett, it looks like we also need a large lemon lime soda." He looked at his best friend for confirmation he got the order right. Alexander gently smiled back.

"Any vodka in that?" he asked while writing down the note.

"No. Just the soda," Daniel replied.

The Alpha finished writing down the order and then gave the two a very entertained grin. "You got it."

After Bennett was completely out of sight, Alexander continued, "It's on my 'To-Do' list. And I'm happy to say, I'm going to address it right after I talk to Stephen."

That caught Daniel by surprise. "Really?"

"Indeed."

"Who is this Omega before me?!" Daniel teased dramatically and then switched his voice to a prim and proper statesman while holding his hand out in a greeting. "Good afternoon, sir."

Alexander played along. "Salutations. I'm Alexander of Daventry. And you are?"

"I'm Bartholomew. But you can call me—"

"Annoying! That's what I'll call you."

"Bitch," Daniel muttered under his breath.

Once again, Bennet came around. "One virgin lemon-lime soda." He handed the glass to Alexander. "To the virgin."

"Wow..." Alexander replied.

Daniel busted out, "Not even close. If you only knew."

"Just kidding." Bennet winked. Then he gestured with his head. "When you due?"

Alexander nearly choked on his first inhale of bubbly citrus. "I'm sorry?"

"You're pregnant, right?" Bennett asked, still confident he knew the answer.

"Um, yeah? How'd you know?"

"You're not the first Omega to walk in here and have an order corrected. Besides, your pheromones are giving it away. Either that, or you're in heat. But that was highly unlikely considering you decided to come out here with another Omega while shunning every flirtatious pass headed your direction."

Alexander looked the brazen fool up and down. "Well, aren't you just the 'Prince and the Wolf' all rolled into one."

"See? Point made. Congratulations to you and yours."

"Thanks," Alexander replied coldly.

"Yikes. Shouldn't you be happier?" Bennett dared to ask.

"It's a long, complicated story," Daniel answered.

"Hmm. If you're interested, I got an open seat at the bar if you want an ear. Or maybe tomorrow night if you're free?" The Alpha bit his lip, giving himself away in the process.

Daniel chuckled. "Already taken, sir."

Bennett groaned. "I knew I shouldn't have picked up this shift." He wandered off, setting his sights on other unsuspecting customers.

After the willful bartender made it out of sight, Alexander took the opportunity to switch focus. "You and James are really hitting it off, huh?" he commented optimistically.

The young redhead began to blush, successfully turning his face into one bright fireball. "We're just so in-sync. He's a gentleman. I love the way he smiles. He could cure depression with one cheeky grin. His eyes are so kind and hypnotic. He always wants to make sure I'm happy." The reflection made his heart skip a beat. "I've never had anyone like that in my life before—ever!" He paused. "I think... I think I'm in love with him."

Even Alexander's cold heart melted at the sight of Daniel being so open. "Come here, you!" He grabbed Daniel's arm and pulled him into a deep hug. "I'm so happy for you."

"I am happy for you as well," Daniel pointed out as he let go of the embrace. "It may not look like it right now, but Stephen is a great guy. And, in my wolf's soul, I know he *is* meant for you and you for him. It *will* work out," he stated confidently.

Alexander non-verbally agreed, looked up at the score board, and clicked his tongue. "Alright, let's get this show on the road. How about I just close my eyes and throw it."

Even though Daniel knew what his best friend was doing, he reluctantly decided he should keep the game's integrity. "No. Play like you're meant to. Don't waste a shot like that. I'll be fine. Like you said, I can only get better than this."

Ignoring the virtuous approach, Alexander decided to continue with his original idea. "Let's just see what happens." He held the large bowling ball in his hands, centered himself, and visually memorized everything around him: the approach platform, the foul line, the lane arrows, and the gutters. After one deep breath, he shut his eyes and threw the ball down the lane, not caring how far it went before it landed in the gutter. He kept his eyes closed and waited for the sound of it smacking the back deck. But instead, he heard the crash of several pins clashing against one another. The sound pleasantly startled him, and he opened his eyes happily waiting to count the few pins he hit.

His mouth, however, dropped completely open when he couldn't see one single pin left stand. "Oh... my..."

"Turkey!" Daniel criticized.

"That's what it's called!" Alexander said.

"Is that right?! How convenient," Daniel smarted back. He looked at the two bar drinks staring back at him innocently. "If I order a third one of these, does that count as a 'turkey' too?"

Alexander furrowed his brows. "I think that's called 'throwing in the towel.'"

Daniel laid back in the chair and crossed his arms. "Next time, we're doing a painting class."

"He *still* hasn't talked to you?!" Bruce asked Stephen, completely stunned as he wiped down newly washed steins and flutes behind the bar.

Stephen shook his head as he finished up a small order for the crew doing warm-up rounds at the pool tables, readying themselves for the tournament coming up in a couple hours. There, with them, was the Omega in question, acting as if nothing was wrong. "Other than straight business talk? I haven't been able to get much. It's like he's avoiding me."

"And that's just in the bedroom," James joked. The Alpha, on the other hand, didn't find the same humor. "My bad."

"At least I have you two back on my side." Stephen paused. "Or so I think?"

Bruce and James glanced at each other and then smiled, the former taking the lead. "Ah, I guess so." He winked while playfully smacking him in the arm with the wet towel.

Tom, the vintage regular, sat upright, decently sober this Friday afternoon. But the night was young. "You need to surprise him with a dinner. Bring flowers, fancy string music, and uh... uh..."

"A beer?" Stephen finished sarcastically.

"A beer always helps!" Tom assured him. "Speaking of..."

"Already on it." Stephen smiled as he got the Alpha his regular.

James growled. "Tom, move your chair back over where it was, or I'll move it for you." The stern look was a warning shot. The old man took it with sincerity as his wolf whimpered. He carried it back over, out of the Beta's personal bubble, and nodded for an apology.

Bruce decided to encourage the hopeless fool, to keep him from feeling slighted. "When was the last time you were in a relationship, Tom?"

The Alpha scratched his beard. "Well, now... let's see... Who's Pack Alpha of the City these days?"

Bruce bared his teeth in regret, realizing it didn't help his cause. Instead, he quickly grabbed a neon balloon and quickly blew it up to its full size. But instead of tying it off, he came down on it hard and popped it instantly. The whole house reacted, being caught off guard by its sudden burst. "Oops."

"Man, how many of those do you need?" Tom asked, fiddling with his ear, wondering if he'd gone deaf.

James stuck his tongue out as he eyed several gaudy balloons, overdone colorful streamers, and confetti tossed on several tables. "Oh, Alexander is sparing no expense tonight. He wants everything to be perfect."

"What's the occasion?" Tom asked before chugging half his beer.

"Did you even read the sign on the door before you walked in?" James asked incredulously.

"No. What'd it say?"

"It's Eric's birthday!" James replied.

"Who's that?" Tom slurred.

The Omega sighed. "I'm done." At this point, James didn't know if Tom truly was suffering from a memory disorder or if he was just trying to get under his skin for choosing Daniel over him. Either way, he took it in stride and played it off as another idiosyncrasy. Then, he threw a question out to the group. "It's Eric's night off anyway. Who wants to celebrate their birthday at the place they work?"

Stephen gestured with his head. "Why don't you ask him yourself?" The man of the hour walked in looking like royalty. A white dress shirt popped from his black skin, shiny white teeth, and a sparkling watch and cuff links set him off like shiny dollar coin. "Hey there, birthday boy!"

"What is all this?" Eric stressed dramatically as he smiled at all the decorations.

"Just wait until you see the piñata!" James teased. "Hope you brought a stick big enough to break it open."

"Oh, it's big enough." Eric winked. "It just hasn't been used for a while. Hopefully, that changes by the end of the night."

"Loaning it out for others to use? I'll have to alert the customers," James continued.

Tom caught wind of the tongue-in-cheek conversation and perked up, setting his sights on James once again. "I thought you were with Daniel?" he moaned.

"Drink your beer," James commanded.

Stephen stepped in, changing subjects. "The question on everyone's mind is why you decided to celebrate your birthday at work."

Eric looked up from his phone after texting friends he had arrived. "Uh—where else am I going to get free drinks and service all night?"

Bruce smirked. "I don't know—do you plan on tipping?"

The manager pulled out a large bill and teased it out like it was a baited hook. "Does the staff remember my pick of poison?"

The Beta snatched it from his hand. "Permanently burned into my memory." Immediately after, Bruce began working on his order.

"Excellent. Besides, having it coincidentally fall on the pool tournament is fun. Especially, since there is someone on Team Tundra I wouldn't mind getting a phone number from by the end of the night." Eric smiled as he cautiously turned his attention to the right.

"It wouldn't by chance be the one guy Alexander has handcuffed himself to for the past fifteen minutes?" James pointed out while avoiding the ire of Stephen.

"Huh?" Eric himself had to readjust his focus to catch what was *really* there. As several players of the aforementioned team set-up rounds on the outer tables, the captain had somehow captivated the Omega in question to a lesson in the skilled sport. "I see that." He quickly glanced at Stephen and knew where the comment was going. "And no, that's not who I'm referring to. That's Wade. Though, even I have to admit, I could see why Alex would want a lesson from *him*."

"Yeah, Stephen can 'see' too," Bruce pointed out.

"Shut up," the Alpha replied under his breath, hating every moment he watched his Fated Mate move in tandem with Wade.

James caught on. "And we can also see how Alex does a really good job of holding Wade's stick too." Right on cue, Alexander and Wade bent over the large table, guiding a shot to a solid in the corner pocket.

"Look at that nice, long, stroke," Eric egged on.

Bruce smiled as he saw Stephen's face turn red. "What do you think? Did they just meet tonight, or have they been practicing together for a while?"

Stephen was beside himself. "I hate each and every one of you right now."

The entire group laughed at the Alpha's expense. After the moment passed, Eric was the first to speak up. "Why is it such a big deal? They're not doing anything."

James leaned over and said what Eric needed updating on. "Things aren't smoothed over on the home front yet."

"Oh." Eric finally understood. "Wish I could help you, man, but I'm not sure where I stand yet either. I wasn't kidding when I came in here surprised that Alex did all this for my birthday, considering the whole Nick fiasco."

"Actually," Bruce pointed out, "that was me and James for the most part."

The manager's shoulders fell. "Well, that explains it."

Stephen rifled his mind for an explanation he'd be satisfied with. "Maybe the birthday party, the pool tournament, and distraction with Wade is what he needs right now. I mean, he looks ... happy." Once again, all members found themselves glancing over at a completely ignorant pair continuing trick shots with a proud stick and solid balls.

Tom snorted. "Maybe a little too happy."

"You guys could help me out if you would keep your minds out of the gutter!" Stephen snarled.

"'The gutter'? Aww, he told you?" Daniel whined as he entered.

James was the first to catch sight and grabbed his boyfriend after he waved to Alexander in the distance. "Hey, you! You snuck up on me." He firmly planted a kiss on the Omega before bringing him up to the empty seat next to him. "And tell us what?"

"You said 'gutter,' right? Alex and I went bowling yesterday so he could blow off some steam and decompress. Believe me, I'm not doing that again. He kicked my ass three times in a row."

James went the less complicated route. "How bad are we talking? What was the total?"

"The three-game total?" Daniel asked. James nodded. The Omega squinted as he crunched numbers in his head, pretending he didn't already have the numbers regrettably stained into him. "518 to 91."

As the supportive boyfriend, James bit his lip and chose to hold on what would have otherwise been fresh produce for a good heckling. Instead, he rubbed Daniel's back in support. "Bruce, get him a Double Red Wild. And I'm buying Stephen and Eric a drink too." To his right, he saw a lonely Tom give him the puppy dog lip. "And get Tom a beer." He relented.

Stephen only caught one comment from the entire conversation. "What did he want to decompress about?"

Daniel adjusted himself in his seat. "That's Omega-to-Omega information only."

"Fine," Stephen griped.

Bruce patted the Alpha's shoulder, hoping he could get some sort of comfort. The moment, however, was short-lived, as he noticed one of the pool tournament players come up and beckon to him. "Ricky! You my man tonight?"

"That I am. And I'm ready with our first drink order." He handed over a piece of paper with all the players' requests.

Bruce picked it up and scanned the list which held no surprises, except for one. "Hey, I see you snuck Alex on here with a water.

That's a chaser, I assume. Did he say what he was ordering with it or refer to something like 'my usual' when you talked to him?"

Ricky shrugged as he walked away. "No, he just said 'water.'"

The Beta himself took it in stride and handed the list to Stephen. "Your Fated Mate wants a water."

"What?" Stephen doubted casually. He grabbed the list and scanned it to confirm. "Wolf-God, he must be out of it. Pool tournament night, Eric's birthday, *and* a Friday night? And all he wants is water? Who on earth is he?"

"The day he met you, I think he slammed down three shots," James pointed out.

"Thanks for the reminder, friend," Stephen replied as he worked with Bruce to finish out the order.

Daniel found himself squirming in his chair, unable to get comfortable. "Heh. Yeah. What a trip."

His Beta boyfriend was the first to notice. "What's up with you?"

"Nothing," Daniel said nervously. He turned his chair which inconveniently put him head-on to his best friend who had finally ended his one-on-one session but was still lost in a joyful conversation with the team captain of the billiard team. The young Type 2 couldn't help but zing a "W.T.F." look straight toward Alexander who caught the look while casually looking over. What ensued afterward was nothing more than a ridiculous pantomime conversation back and forth where neither understood what the other was trying to convey. Fed up, Daniel finally grabbed his phone and began a frantic text.

Stephen caught Daniel's nerves in his nostrils as his pheromone palate began reading like a panic mode. Considering it was obvious where he was putting all his attention, he couldn't help but question him as he finished up the league's order. "Daniel..."

"What?" The Omega jolted in his chair, completely immersed in his mission.

"Did Alex tell you something?" Stephen interrogated.

"Yes," Daniel replied.

The Alpha gave a deadpan face in return which read the statement gave him no help. "Did Alex tell you something I should know?"

"Maybe," the short Omega drew out.

"Man, this is going nowhere. I can't get a read on any Omega today," Stephen lamented.

Bruce rubbed his chin. "Even the playing field. Get him liquored up."

"I'm fine without being manipulated into handing over information, thank you," Daniel spat back.

"No, not you," Bruce corrected. "Alex."

"A lot of good that is going to do!" Stephen criticized. "He's the bar owner. He already gets free drinks. If a Friday night/billiard tournament/birthday party isn't enough to make him want to drink and his bad attitude doesn't make him want to drink, then, I don't know what the hell would want to make him drink. With how hormonal he was last week, it's almost like the only reason he wouldn't..." A conclusion hit him across the face like the answer to a tough trivia question in the final seconds of a game. Only this conclusion wasn't a tough conclusion to come to and this wasn't a game. Once again, he eyed the petite Omega frantically texting while equally trying to be invisible. "Daniel..." No answer. "Daniel!"

The trembling Omega's hands jumped as his phone shot off the counter and onto the floor behind the bar. "Yes?"

Stephen tightened his lip as he treaded carefully. "Is Alex..."

Immediately, Bruce caught onto the train of thought. "Oh, shit."

Eric stood there in disbelief himself. "No... he couldn't be."

"We just took care of his heat last week. That's *exactly* what he could be!" Stephen snarled. He began pacing back and forth as he practiced his breathing exercises.

"Guess that means you didn't go the protection and suppressant route, eh?" Eric surmised. That got him a look that said *Don't fuck with my mate.* "That's a no!"

"Come on, guys. We don't know that," James challenged.

"Just go up and ask him," Tom suggested.

"No way I'm doing that!" Stephen spoke confidently. "Can you imagine what purgatory I'm going to be in if I'm wrong?"

"You're not wrong," Eric assured him. "Daniel confirmed it for us."

"I did not!" Daniel defended.

Stephen rushed forward, giving an Alpha wolf stare to his mate's best friend. "What did he tell you?!"

Daniel gulped. "He said he wasn't sure."

The Alpha growled and pounded his fist. "Great! What am I supposed to do with that?"

Tom looked at his nearly empty glass and finished it off. "Give him a reason to tell you he is." With that, he pushed the empty glass toward the bartender and winked.

The entire group looked at Tom in awe, wondering how he so easily maneuvered himself into the position of the smartest person in the room.

Stephen took the hint and organized his thoughts. "Okay, we gotta do this right... uh.... I need a drink... something neutral.... uh... a vodka shot!"

"A *vodka shot*?" James soured. "Talk about something easy to say no to."

"Not a shot! Mix it with something. Pink lemonade!" Bruce offered.

"Are we 16? That's so Level 1 boring!" James criticized.

"Spruce it up!" Tom demanded.

Eric snapped his fingers. "Lemon-lime soda. And make it a double!"

Bruce agreed. "*Always* make it a double!"

"Add a lemon slice for garnish!" Tom pointed out.

"A great idea!" Stephen nodded.

"Now you need a name for it," James directed.

"A *name*?" Bruce cocked his head.

"Yeah, a name!" James gave the expression like he could hardly believe his brother found the concept so foreign. "You're trying to impress an Omega with a drink *and* have them drink it? It better have a name."

"Pink Slipper!" Stephen blurted out.

"The fuck?" Eric spat back.

"I don't know. Just go with it. Just go with it!" he gushed. Then, a communal silence. "Now what?"

"Someone has to deliver it," James offered.

All at once, eyes slowly turned to the one person in the group noticeably silent this entire time.

Daniel looked like a deer in the headlights and completely beside himself. "No way!"

"You have to!" Stephen begged.

"Why me?"

James leaned into his lover. "It's going to be easy for Alex to deny a drink from Stephen if he's still mad at him. Getting this from you, he'd have to come up with a damn good reason to say 'No.'"

"What about *me*? *I've* got plenty of reasons to say 'No.' I'd like to keep my head, thank you! Both of them—depending on which one he decides to decapitate!" Daniel looked at each them with a weakened pup face as none of them had a response to his claim. "None of you care if I survive this?"

James came in with the back rub. "You'll be fine, babe, I promise." He cleared his throat and deepened his voice. "We can do that thing you like when we get home tonight."

The Omega's eyes leaped to the ceiling as he comprehended what his lover was referring to. He narrowed his eyes. "Twice," he countered, "and *I* get to be on top," James agreed without hesitation. Daniel looked at the pink innocent drink staring back at him at the table. Its juxtaposition on where it was headed was a horror story. He swallowed his nerves, picked up the glass, and headed toward the lion's den.

That left James as the target for a very intrigued audience. "Don't let your minds go too far off the deep end." He rolled his eyes. "He's talking about playing his favorite racing video game."

Stephen furrowed his brows. "And the 'be on top' comment?"

"He wants to be Player 1 so he can be on the top half of the T.V. screen." James laid out his hands that told his captivated audience the logic made sense. After everyone gave their own subtle reaction, he took a swig of his own drink. "Afterward, we have sex, and he likes to be on top."

"Ugh," Bruce moaned.

"You sleaze," Stephen added for good measure.

"*You* should talk," James clapped back. "How many times with Alex did it take to put you in this predicament?"

The Alpha cleared his throat and said quietly, "Three." He laid his head on the counter and put hands on top for good measure. In his mind, he half-expected to hear back from Daniel now. But the seconds ticked by like hours. He waited. And waited. And waited.

Eric, unable to deal with the silence, decided to ask the very next topic which came to mind. "Any updates on your missing bike?" he asked optimistically.

Stephen flipped his head up. "Why don't you just shoot me?!"

Daniel walked with the frilly drink in hand all the way to the side of the bar with the billiard tables. He had no trouble taking in the sights: Alexander appeared like a statuesque Alpha in his tight red t-shirt. His right shoulder had this unnatural magnetism to Wade's who was sporting an equally tight navy-blue polo, the name "Tundra Titans" as the proud logo—only a slender pool cue separating them. Daniel dramatically cleared his throat. "Ah-hem."

"Hey, Daniel!" Alexander smiled. "Wade, I'm not sure if I introduced you to Daniel. He's my friend."

Wade stood taller, his smooth black hair glistening perfectly. "I'm sure we've been introduced." Even so, he stuck out his hand for a greeting.

"*Best* friend," Daniel clarified.

Alexander bobbed his head in subtle annoyance. "Yes, *best* friend. How could I forget?"

"You come here to watch the tournament tonight?" Wade asked.

"No, not for that." Daniel spoke abruptly without thinking. "Oh, don't get me wrong! I love pool. But I'm here for Eric. It's his birthday." The young Omega turned around and gave a kind gesture back to the crowd. It wouldn't have been such an awkward move had the entire bar of misfits not all waved back at the same time. That left Daniel with a stuck expression on his face, one he was worried his "best friend" would see right through. And he did.

"What's *that* all about?" Alexander turned his head to the side, noticing several guilt-ridden faces poorly execute a recovery.

"Nothing!" Daniel insisted.

Wade ignored the entire exchange and continued his own train of thought. "I've just been giving Alex here a few pointers on how to line up shots on those hard-to-reach angles."

"I could see that," Daniel acknowledged.

Alexander supported the enthusiasm. "My game is okay, but I always get tripped up on the difference between a rail shot and a rail hug. And that's the last thing you want to worry about when you're trying to get the Big 8 in the corner pocket."

Daniel flexed his eyebrows. "Funny. Last I heard you did just fine getting railed with the Big 8 all the way into your corner pocket."

Wade choked on a swig from his beer bottle while Alexander gave back a look that could kill. "That was informative."

"I need to get back to work, Wade." The Omega blushed. "You'll want to get back to your warm-ups anyway. The Keyotes will be here in probably ten minutes or so. I appreciate the tips."

"Anytime, anyplace." Wade gave a nod and conveniently found one of his teammates who was looking for his attention at the adjacent billiard table.

That left plenty of space for Alexander to look at Daniel as if he had committed some dastardly deed in the House of Wolf-God. "What the hell is wrong with you?"

"Getting chummy with mister Wade there?" his friend teased.

"What? Stephen comes into my life, and I'm not allowed to talk to another Alpha?"

"No. I didn't say that," Daniel insisted. "They're playing the Keyotes? What they hell is a 'Keyote' anyway?"

Alexander crossed his arms, losing his patience. "It's a singing Coyote." He pivoted. "You've been acting weird ever since you walked in the door. You barely said 'Hi' to me and then you send me text messages that don't even look like English." The Omega pulled out his phone and rescanned messages which didn't even make a discernable word much less a cohesive sentence. "Did you have a seizure or something?"

"No," Daniel faltered, "was just texting too fast."

"What was so urgent? And what's this strange-looking concoction you have permanently attached to your hand?"

The short Type 2 Omega finally came to his senses and remembered why on earth he even ventured over in the first place. "Oh shit. Um, this is a Pink Slipper!"

"What?" Alexander wasn't enthused in the least. Being an expert on making a drink for years, he didn't know what to make of the glass in front of him.

"A... Pink Slipper?" Daniel's confidence began to wane, and the glass was sweating less than *he* was. "It's for you!" He smiled overdramatically.

"It's supposed to have coconut crème liqueur in it. Gives it that pastel look."

Daniel couldn't believe his ears. "Wait... that's actually a drink?"

"Yeah," Alexander leaned down as he examined the glass further, "and what liquor went into this? It's obviously not rum."

"Vodka."

"Who the hell made this?" Alexander swiped the glass from Daniel's flimsy wrist and gave it the smell test, still wondering what mad scientist created it.

"Stephen did."

"Why the fuck would Stephen make this for *me*?" Then, he whispered, "And why would *you* of all people give me a drink in the bar considering the conversation we had—" The Omega's inner wolf barked and told him to look behind his friend only for a second. There, at the head of the bar, stood a man doing a piss poor job at concealing himself. Much to Daniel's chagrin, he began to walk past him.

"Where are you going?!" he flipped out.

At the last second, Alexander did a one-eighty which placed his back toward the audience he *knew* was watching him—giving the attention back to Daniel. "This was a set-up, wasn't it?" Despite the obvious trap, Alexander took it in stride and smirked as he watched Daniel suffer, his legs dangling above the fire.

"Wha-what do you mean?" He tried holding his composure, but every time he looked up, his gaze slowly trailed from Alexander to a crowd behind him looking like they were ready to signal "abort mission."

"Stephen wants to know if I'm pregnant and used you to get the answer, didn't he?"

Daniel's wolf whimpered. "Maybe?"

"If he sees me take a drink, he's going to assume one answer. If I *don't* take a drink, he's going to assume the other—right?"

"Possibly?"

Alexander stood there, still holding the mysterious pink mixture with his fingers. He closed his eyes and allowed his inner wolf to speak. It shamed him for keeping his mate at a distance for so long.

The Omega acknowledged it was time to come out of the dark and accept fate. "Then, let's not disappointment him." The Omega pivoted once again and made a straight line toward the bar. By now, everyone was staring at him: Stephen, Bruce, James, Eric, and even Tom. Alexander swallowed hard, took one last look at the pink medley, and set it back on the bar, completely untouched. Then, he found Stephen's eyes and locked on them hard and uttered one simple word. "Yes." After a beat, he turned to his business partner, with whom he still hadn't mended fences. "Happy Birthday, Eric."

Bruce choked, James squealed with glee, Eric gave his hundred-dollar smile, and Tom gestured a congratulatory sentiment with his newly filled beer.

Stephen, however, stared back wide-eyed. After the subtle sentiments died down, he spoke up. "Can I see you in the back for a moment?"

Alexander's heart thumped in his chest as he mentally prepared himself for an immeasurable ridicule. The Alpha—no—*his* Alpha damn near looked like he had been hit by a truck or that someone else he knew had. Unsure of what to say back, all he did was nod and lead his mate to the back hallway. Once there, he wrung his hands in worry, trying to come up with a worthy explanation of how this happened and why Stephen was finding out this way. "Before you speak, I just want to say I don't know for sure if I am. I haven't taken a test or gone to the doctor to make sure, but—"

Stephen, in a flash, lunged at the unsuspecting Omega, grabbing his hands and forcing each one flat against the wall. He thrust his hips tight into Alexander's and nuzzled his mouth into the crook of his neck. The Alpha let his inner wolf take over as his lungs exhaled a low growl in his quest.

"What are you doing?!" Alexander blurted, completely lost in fear.

"Don't. Move," the Alpha commanded.

Alexander froze like a helpless pup in the wild, unsure of any thought or action. His fingertips trembled as every single nerve-ending in his body became alert. Whatever response the Omega imagined his mate possessing, it was nowhere near the reaction commencing before him now. What was he going to do? Yell? Hit? Oddly, none of those answers seemed right. But when he felt Stephen's mouth consume his now healed mating gland, forcing it to contract and elevate, he knew the right answer. Claim. Once the realization set in, Alexander gasped in pleasure *and* in worry. "Stephen! We can't do this now!" he uttered in a breathy whisper.

The Alpha ignored his Fated Mate's words and continued his objective. Now that Alexander knew what the goal was, it allowed Stephen to gain access to everything he wanted: his mind, his body, his pheromones, and his slick which began to permeate even more with every moan the Alpha vibrated into his neck. "Mine!" he purred.

Alexander hummed in amusement as his body continued to twitch in the rising pleasure. "You jealous wolf! I was just talking to Wade. It's not as if he was going to take your place and—" A burst of pleasure ran throughout the Omega's entire body as he felt Stephen bear down and break into his mating gland, inhaling every pure scent flooding out. Alexander's hands shot off the wall and quickly wrapped around his mate's arms and shoulders, pulling him closer out of pain and pleasure. "Did you forget my scent?"

Stephen knew the question was nothing more than sarcasm. How could he forget Alexander's scent? The richness of the pomegranate was burned into his memory, and it would never ever leave him. It flooded his senses and made his inner wolf stronger with each intake. However, this wasn't the goal. This wasn't the goal at all. Stephen grasped his mate even tighter and focused his wolf even harder on the mating gland. He was coaxing it into overdrive and wasn't going to stop until he got the answer he was looking for. At one point, he almost thought it a lost cause and contemplated giving up. But, in the last possible moment, his wolf found what it was looking for.

"Stephen?!" Alexander's voice became worried as the intention appeared to have changed instantly.

Once again, Stephen did nothing but answer back in a low growl. His wolf became a detective, like finding a trace of a wondrous object deep within the earth. It wanted to dig—throwing clods of dirt and rock high into the air—giving him unfettered access to his desires. And finally, he found it. In tandem with his mate's heartbeat, Alexander's mating gland was producing fresh secretions from his pheromone palate which weren't stored up. The fresh pomegranate scent intoxicated him but the new, rich, vanilla bean scent coming through locked him up completely. Once he identified it, it was all he could focus on, and it became bolder and stronger.

Not having access to Omegas for ten years in lock-up forced Stephen to remember only what he had heard growing up. That an Omega's scent would change once they were pregnant. Considering he never had a mate nor impregnated one, he wasn't sure if the claim was real or not. Now, there was no doubt, at least in his mind. Alexander's scent *had* changed. The savory vanilla scent *wasn't* his mate's. It was their pup's. Alexander was pregnant with his offspring. "My mate. My pup," he moaned into Alexander's ear and then gave a gentle peck on his neck.

Alexander's emotions overwhelmed him as he fully collapsed into his mate. "I'm sorry I didn't tell you."

"Mine," was all Stephen said back as he held his mate close and closed his eyes.

"I still need to test it," the Omega insisted.

"I already know," Stephen assured him. "What do you need a test for?"

"Maybe it's just the stubborn wolf inside me," Alexander offered as he exhaled into his mate's shoulder.

"I love you," Stephen declared.

"I love you too."

The silence lulled the two in their moment, completely void of anything else other than the intoxicating scent of pheromones wrapped completely around them. Both knew the location and time weren't ideal, but that was life. Life wasn't going to wait for them. And life, shortly thereafter, reminded them it was still there.

Bursting out of the silence came a loud melodic tune, filling every corner of the tavern with the bravado of several men singing a jolly tune—or at least trying to:

Hail the Keyotes—the mightiest of mighties!
We own the prairie—the mountains and the gray seas
Stand against our enemy—we won't go down easy
Say it with me: We can't be beat!
Howl at the moon: 1-2-3!
AWOOO!

Stephen's eyes nearly jumped from their sockets as he took in an entire bar erupting like a pack of wild wolves. Correction: coyotes. "What the hell was that?!"

Alexander raspberried. "One of *many* little chants you will hear from that team tonight."

"Save me," Stephen teased.

"Me first." Alexander smiled back.

Stephen pulled his mate's forehead closer and kissed it. "Always."

CHAPTER 08:

REVEALING THE EMOTIONS OF REALITY

Alexander rushed through the front door, straining to find the hallway bathroom. Once he was in, his hands shook as he opened the delicate cardboard box and slid out the white stick in all its glory. He danced out of nerves as he frantically searched for the directions, trying as best as he could to ignore the occasional strange sounds hitting his ear which permeated through the walls. "Okay," he exhaled, "pass the absorbent tip through the urine for at least ten seconds." He laughed. "I could do a minute at this rate." His voice strained as he carefully set the test on the edge of the toilet and released himself from the tight confines of the shorts which felt like a prison on his pulsing bladder. Finally, he was able to finally release what he was convinced must have been a gallon of soda onto a delicate pad. He closed his eyes in relief, humming to himself as he counted to ten in his head. But, once again, more noises coming from the other side of the wall rattled his concentration. Now, it was to the point to where he couldn't ignore it anymore. "Veo?" No answer. "Sur?" No answer. Immediately afterward, a loud thud was heard which rattled the bathroom lights. "Shit."

Alexander quickly cleaned himself up and tossed the test and the box into the trash before racing down the rest of the hallway to his parents' bedroom. With all the horrors he had in his mind, he didn't have this one. There, scrambling on the floor, was a young man struggling to get his underwear back on who bore no likeness to his Veo whatsoever. On the opposite side of the bedroom was his Sur in an equally compromising state, hastening his every move to become decent once again. "Who the fuck are you?!"

The boy's ice blue eyes pierced Alexander's as he growled back. "Get out!"

"No. *You* get out!" Alexander replied automatically.

"Alex!" Robert yelled. "Don't speak to him that way."

"Him, who? Who the hell is this?"

The young Omega stood up and gulped. "I'm Carey."

Alexander furrowed his brows. "That didn't answer my question."

Robert gathered his own nerves. "He's mine, Alex."

"What? Your concubine?" Alexander smarted as he watched the Omega finish pulling up his pants.

Carey gasped. "The nerve you have to call me that!"

"I'm sorry," Alexander laughed sarcastically, "were you looking for a different title? Because I have a few others in mind."

"Shut your mouth right now! Don't make me do something I'll regret," Robert warned. He found his glasses on the nightstand and stared down his Omega son.

"'*Regret*'? In my entire life, I can't think of one sleazy or Alpha-brooding move you've *ever* regretted." Alexander gestured to Carey who stood there, completely helpless. "And apparently, here's another one."

"I'm not some whore off the street!" Carey crossed his arms as he tried to find his center. "I'm his lover."

Alexander's expression highly doubted the claim. "You *must* be joking."

Robert walked around the bed and wrapped his arm around the trembling soul, looking for validation. "He's not."

The confidence struck Alexander's core. Anger and hurt rose up in him as his pheromones became sharp. "How on earth are you able to stand there and say that?! How can you do this to Veo? What are you going to do when—" Just then, a deep inhale of Carey's own pheromones told him all he needed to know. He looked at the young sprite and swallowed hard. "You're in heat, aren't you?"

Carey looked at Robert whose blank expression gave him permission to continue. "Yes. Yes, I am."

Alexander looked at the two men in awe. Standing there, before him, it didn't make sense. None of it. "You two aren't really trying to..." He couldn't bring himself to finish the rest.

"We are," Carey said confidently. "In fact—"

The front door opening and closing struck everyone in the bedroom with a fear that could turn a face white. Alexander didn't think his heart could fall lower in his chest. "Oh, no." He gave one frightened look to his Sur before racing out to the main hallway.

"We're home!" Nathan rang out. "Jin, did you grab the two grocery bags from the backseat?"

"I got 'em," he grunted, carefully balancing bags on the brink of tearing open if he maneuvered wrong.

Nathan turned around as he heard his eldest son trample down the hallway. "Alex! I'm so glad you're here. We need to talk."

"Talk?!" Alexander blurted nervously. "Talk about what?"

Before Nathan could continue, he heard his mate rush down the hallway. "Robert?"

"Babe!" The Alpha contrived a smile as the heat rose on his face.

Jin found the whole scene utterly suspicious. "What the hell is up with you two?"

"Nothing," Alexander innocently replied.

Suddenly, a loud noise emanated from the bathroom. Nathan took note of it first. "Who's in the bathroom?"

"No one," Robert replied foolishly.

"Robert?!" a voice echoed behind the closed door.

Jin furrowed his brows. "Doesn't sound like 'no one.'"

The bathroom door clicked open, and Carey walked out for all the world to see, his arms innocently tucked behind his back. "Hi." He spoke calmly.

"Hi." Nathan scanned the boy up and down and tried to avoid the worst. "Alex, is this a friend of yours?"

Alexander wished he could do this day over. Instead of heading back to his parents' home, he should have retreated to the safety of his apartment. Now, he was in the middle of a predicament he never imagined possible. Lying was the last thing he wanted to do to his Veo. But telling him the truth hurt even more. He couldn't bear it. So, he slowly shook his head instead.

Naturally, that only led to one conclusion. Nathan slowly shifted his eyes to his life partner, his voice heavy and deep. "Robert?"

The Alpha held his human side tall and statuesque, but his wolf coward in defeat. "This is... is..."

"I'm Carey." The Omega stepped forward and threw out his hand like it was a peace treaty.

Nathan mechanically accepted the non-threatening offer. "I see."

Robert attempted to navigate the conversation. "Nate..."

"Stop!" his mate commanded. A silence set in which felt like hours. No one knew where to focus their attention, not even Nathan. His gaze, at first, went to the front door and the family car sitting in the driveway. Then, it was to the formal living room, barely used except for large family functions and gatherings. Finally, his eyes gazed down the hallway where he could pick out several happier memories than this: birthdays, holidays, celebratory announcements, funny anecdotes, and healing moments. But not this time. Not this time. Nathan's pheromones boiled to the surface as his legs and arms began to shake with adrenaline. He laser-focused on his mate and gritted his teeth. "How am I supposed to maintain any dignity in this house, if you insist on throwing your disgusting behavior right in my face?!" he huffed with hurt and frustration.

Alexander couldn't believe his ears. He cocked his head and stared at his Omega father. "You... you knew?!"

"Don't be a fool, Alex. I've been with your father for almost thirty years. Did you think I was just sitting here, all this time, ignorant of who your father was or what he was doing? Did you not think Jin was a big enough wake-up call that things were never going to change?!" Nathan covered his mouth as he hated every word he uttered. Tears instantly stung his eyes as the past played itself all over again.

The empathy caught Alexander right in the heart and followed suit. "Then, why stay with someone like that? Didn't people around you whisper enough for you to wake up and leave?!"

"We are a family, Alex. That's why we stay together. And I don't know who you think all these people are who came around trying to warn me or give me updates on what was going on with or without my knowledge, but I'll tell you it was almost no one. Wolf-God, I don't suppose *you* would be one of them who knows a lot more about your father than *I* do?" Alexander hung his head in defeat. Nathan gestured sarcastically. "Thank you."

A stray tear fell down Alexander's cheek. "Veo, if you knew what I did—"

"I think I should go?" Carey interrupted.

"I think that's best," Jin answered as he stepped forward, ready to defend his adoptive Veo from another traumatic ordeal if need be.

Carey made nimble movements toward the bedroom. "Just need to grab my bag."

Robert intercepted. "I'll grab it."

"Actually, I was hoping I could talk to you..." The Omega gestured to his lover, hoping to magnetically pull him to the bedroom.

"This isn't the time," Robert insisted.

Carey moved with him, leaning into his ear. "I *really* need to talk to you."

"What's that?" Nathan asked, pointing to an odd object hidden in Carey's hand.

"A thermometer," Carey played off as he tried to push Robert to the bedroom.

Jin knew better. "That's not a thermometer; that's a pregnancy test." All eyes looked back at him with ample curiosity. He cleared his throat. "I mean, I *think* that's what they look like," he played off, hoping to recover himself.

Nathan's heart broke as he finally realized what was happening in his own home. "After all these years, Robert? You'd do this to me, again?!"

"I'd like to go elsewhere for this conversation..." Carey stood there, a ball of nerves.

"It isn't going to happen," Robert insisted. "There isn't going to be a heat sated and there isn't going to a pup. Not without—" he snatched the test from Carey's hand and looked at it with awe, "a miracle."

The old Alpha felt every bone and joint in his body click and creak as he tried to find his center. He never thought two red lines could change his future forever. He stared back at Carey, not with pride, but with annoyance. "How long have you known this? How long have you been keeping this from me?"

"Taste of your own medicine, Sur?" Jin commented.

"Well... I..." Carey searched for how to explain this mysterious pregnancy test but didn't know how to proceed.

"How could you do this, Robert?" Nathan cried.

"I didn't!" the Alpha insisted.

"Why should I believe you when it's right there in front of me!"

Alexander couldn't hold his mouth shut any longer. "Because he's telling you the truth." He shifted his stance and held the moment. "That's not Carey's pregnancy test. It's mine."

"You?!" the crowd sang collectively.

"Whoa..." Jin instantly connected the hesitation. "Ex-con got you pregnant?"

"Jin, you don't have to call him that! He has a name, okay? It's 'Stephen.'"

A moment later, Nathan broke out of his own problems and stepped into this new one. "You know what? I'll grab the bag." Before anyone could even register the change of attitude, he swiftly left the circle of damnation and headed down the hall.

Robert was beside himself. First, his attention went to Carey. "What on earth did you want to talk to me about if you knew this test wasn't yours?!"

Carey took in the Alpha's scent and began to clear his mind of the haze he allowed to be there way too long. "There was no way I was going continue down this path if you had already gotten someone else pregnant—especially your mate. I thought this was something *you* needed to tell *me*."

The old Alpha couldn't believe his ears. "That's ridiculous." Next, he eyed his son with disdain. "And you—you let that low-life impregnate you?!"

Alexander felt verbally pushed back as he couldn't understand his father's comment. He had said almost nothing to either of his parents about who Stephen even was, let alone tell them anything to do with their relationship. But then, the logical explanation set in. He slowly turned to his younger Alpha brother, the traitor in his own blood. "You told them?"

"Alex, I didn't mean to," Jin pleaded as he saw his brother's reaction to the betrayal.

The entire group jumped as they heard a loud door slam. Nathan was back down the hallway, apathetically carrying a bag he had little care to pay attention to. He handed it to Carey and gave a neutral look. "I'm sorry I couldn't meet you under different circumstances, but I think you know where the door is."

Carey stood there in shock, not sure where he fit into the picture at this point. But before he left, Carey walked up to Alexander and reluctantly handed over the pregnancy test. "There was a moment where I was jealous it wasn't me. Now, I'm starting to think I dodged a bullet. Good luck." He gave his distant lover a cautious stare before retreating to the safety of the outside world.

"So, it is true," Robert criticized.

"What's true?" Alexander snarled.

"You abandoned Sean, probably the best chance you had at a successful life, and attached yourself to some no-good vermin for the next 18 years?"

"Oh, please." Jin waved off. "He won't be around that long."

"Excuse you!" Alexander exclaimed.

"What happened to Sean, sweetheart?" Nathan asked.

"'What happened to *Sean*?'" Alexander couldn't understand the man before him. For one moment, he was the hurt partner of a manipulative player for a mate. And now, suddenly, he was the devout parent, hell-bent on being a critical one. "What happened to *you* five minutes ago?"

Nathan ignored the observation. "This is what we wanted to talk to you about. And frankly, the only conversation I can handle right now."

Alexander scanned all three of his family members, standing there like this was an intervention. "Just how much did you tell them, Jin?"

The young Alpha grasped at a defense. "You were talking crazy. You couldn't decide if you were happy or sad. You couldn't decide if it was a good decision or bad decision—"

"So, you made it for me?!" Alexander spat back.

"You turned it all around, got mad, and blamed me! For nothing!"

Alexander crossed his arms. "You acted the same way when you decided to banish yourself from Tauris City forever."

"Yeah, bro, I know. And guess what you did then? Run back to our daddies and told them everything. Why do you think all of sudden you're special?!"

"Stop, you two!" Nathan turned to his Omega son. "What happened to Sean?" he insisted once more.

"He was using me!" Alexander admitted. "He wanted nothing to do with me. He only wanted what I represented and what I could achieve. And if I lost it, he was just going to swoop in and take what he could and then run away with it."

Robert shook his head in shame. "You chased him away."

Alexander growled, "All I had to do was take a page from your book." Quicker than he could register, he felt a slap radiate across his face. Soon after, several childhood memories rushing in after.

"Alex!" Jin gasped.

"Robert! Are you crazy! What the hell are you doing?!" Nathan rushed to his son's side.

Alexander was a cold statue, much like how he used to be. But life was different now. He was older. And he had a life beyond himself to protect. Unafraid, he walked right up to his Sur and stared him down straight in the eye. "You do that to me ever again, and I'll show you what it's like to be on the other side. And that 'other side' I'm referring to isn't where I'm standing, it's where you'll be laying—permanently." The Omega felt his Alpha father's wolf snarl only for a moment, but then, for the first time ever, concede to a whimper, with submissive pheromones perfuming the air: a smoldering fire dying down to dust. With the victory at hand, Alexander pivoted and headed to the door.

"Where are you going?" Nathan pleaded.

"There is nothing else I want here," Alexander insisted.

"What about this Alpha? Stephen?" Robert piped up.

Alexander's voice continued his frustration. "Do you even care?!"

Robert walked over with his interrogation mode on full display. "You're my boy," he flung with attitude.

The Omega's hand pounded the door like a hammer—another memory flash terrorizing his mind's eye. "You bastard," he murmured. "I know you better than you know yourself."

"What's your point?!" Alexander shook with adrenaline, staring outside the front door instead of giving his Sur any visual attention.

Robert assumed his familiar role in a matter of seconds, practically ignoring his Omega son's previous warnings. "In two years, you wouldn't let Sean, a high ranked Type 4 Alpha, with a successful career, great stature, and great profile get you pregnant, but you'll let some wasted human being do it? Why?"

"He's *not* some waste of a human. He's—" In an instant, it struck him that his parents didn't know. His eyes went back to his younger brother, who tried to stand there all innocent himself. "*That's* the one thing you didn't tell them?!"

"Tell us what?" Nathan asked.

Alexander slowly turned and faced his entire family. Considering this *was* going to be the rest of his life, he better get used to saying it. "Stephen Matheson isn't just some guy off the street who walked into my bar. He cares about my feelings whenever I'm frustrated or sad, he stands up to Alphas with egos who think I'm less than a person just because I'm an Omega, he'll protect me from jerks who come into the bar looking to cause trouble, and he sees right through people who are genuine scum. Yes, he has a past. Yes, he's not perfect. Yes, this isn't going to be easy. But nothing in my life has been. But I'm not sure what else in my life I'm waiting for. My inner wolf says it's him. Stephen is my Fated Mate." A glint struck his eye as he smiled for the first time since he first admitted it to Stephen in the bar's parking lot. However, the moment was short lived with his Sur's voice cutting into the serenity.

"No, he's not." The skepticism broke through.

"What do you mean, he's not?"

Robert scoffed at the whole notion and everything with it. "He's not your Fated Mate, and you're not pregnant."

The Omega's head hurt as he tried to comprehend the assurance in his father's voice. "I'm sorry—something you know that I don't?"

"Apparently so," Robert answered back. "Maybe it's the lowly medical profession I have, the pointless twenty-plus years of experience, and the foolish six Levels of school I took to get there that's talking, but you must have forgotten your medical condition that renders you infertile?"

Alexander had waited all day for it. Now, the conversation was upon them. "You mean like how I'm not supposed to be going through heats?"

"Exactly!" Robert replied.

"Well, I did. An excruciating one at that."

"Sure, sure," Robert dismissed.

"How can you deny that so easily? I know what a heat feels like!"

"Says the Omega who has never properly had one. Look, I'm not particularly interested—especially when it involves the ex-con—but just because you got horny one night doesn't mean you had a heat."

Alexander stared helplessly at the test still in his hand. "And what about this? It's positive!"

"It's a hysterical pregnancy. It happens. Have you ever heard of a false negative? Here's a false positive."

Nathan felt for his son. "I'm so sorry, sweetie."

The Omega grunted. "Why is it when something monumental happens in my life, this family always tries to find a reason break me down?!"

Robert had enough of this defensive act. "Because for 28 years, you have been nothing but an ungrateful pup!"

"Robert!" Nathan gasped.

"You have no care for how the real-world works, Alexander. You're not on this earth to make a life above and beyond Alphas, yet you want to go and challenge them at every possible turn you can find. You did it to Sean, you did it to Eric with the bar, you did to the city when you bought that Wolf-God forsaken place, you did it to your friends growing up, and you did it to me. The only time I could ever rein you into place was when you listened to me about your health. Thank Wolf-God you got a prescription to prevent you from getting pregnant. That's the last thing anyone in this world needed—*you* as a parent telling your pup that the conduct you still stand by today is how he should act. If anything, I did you a favor!"

Jin squinted in thought. "You mean prevent him from getting heats—not pregnant."

Nathan chimed in, "That's what he meant."

Alexander's face twitched. "But that's not what he said. And it makes all the more sense."

"Why?" Nathan asked.

"Because the whole reason I am pregnant is because I *did* go through a heat. And the whole reason I went through a heat is because I stopped taking the medication."

Robert had daggers in his eyes for his son. "You did *what*?"

Nathan had the complete opposite reaction. "Alex?! Why would you do that?! Don't you know how dangerous that is? Your condition!"

Alexander was over the game his Sur was playing. "What condition? Had *you* ever heard of it before?" he asked his Veo. Then he eyed Jin. "How about you?" Neither had a response. The condition itself was an anomaly to common sense. No one, however, ever questioned it. Then, he went back to his Sur. "I've missed doses before—sheer laziness on my part. Whenever I've let it go too far, my body always reminded me it was time to take them. Feeling those symptoms," he shook his head, "scared the shit out of me. But when my pills were stol—erm, I mean, lost, I didn't want to talk to you at the time. I didn't want anything to do with you. So, I waited until what I thought was the last possible minute."

"You risked your own health for something stupid like that?" Robert chuckled. "Is there any doubt you aren't in your right frame of mind?"

"Why didn't you tell me my medication was a suppressant?" Alexander asked.

Nathan playfully disagreed. "A suppressant? No, no, no. That medication hasn't been used for that since the dark ages. It doesn't keep up with the system as we age. Doctor Hyatt said when you got older, we'd have to increase your dosage up to three pills a day until your child-bearing years were over and then you'd taper off again. But a suppressant? That would change a lot of things—much more than just your heat symptoms I think."

"I take four, Dad," Alexander corrected.

"Wolf-God! When did Doctor Hyatt tell you to do that?!"

"Veo, I haven't talked to Doctor Hyatt in years. He's not even the name on my prescription bottle anymore."

"Robert?" Nathan asked, fearing his son's worries were no longer a foolish theory made up in desperation.

The Alpha held his own until he was beyond the point of caring. "How has it been operating like 'normal,' Omega?"

"What does that mean?" Alexander wondered with attitude.

"Your personality is hard enough to deal with when you're *not* hormonal. Don't sit there and tell me, you've just been the cherub pup on Wolf-God's cloud in the heavens or the apple of anyone's eye going through all this. Anyone in your life have an opinion of you as of late?"

The coincidence was maddening but even more so, scary. "That is none of your fucking business."

"I had a hard enough time reining you in as a spiteful adolescent. If you didn't think I had nightmares based upon who you would be once you transitioned into your adulthood, you're more ignorant than I thought."

Nathan held his heart as he stood there, another witness to Alpha extremism. "Babe, what are you saying?"

"No Alpha Sur would allow their *Alpha* Son or *Beta* son to free think or talk back the way you did. I was convinced your Veo somehow screwed up the pregnancy while not on my watch with the way you acted. I tried rationalizing everything in my head in how you could be so bold as an *Omega.*" He smirked as if it was all some cruel joke. "Such wasted potential. If it wasn't for your reproductive organs or pheromone palate, I was convinced you could have been an Alpha. Maybe then, I could have had enough respect for you. Perhaps even the world could have. But no, you wanted to be an Omega with an opinion, an Omega with entrepreneurship, an Omega with a business, completely shutting out your Alpha brother, who, in my opinion, should be *owning* a bar before you were even allowed to *serve* a drink in one."

A horrible feeling overtook Alexander as he tried to surmise its natural conclusion. "Sur, did you do this to ... teach me some lesson?"

"I did what I had to do in order to not make you, your brother, your Veo, and me not implode as a family."

"Because what you were doing was enough?" Jin spat back to his Alpha father. Everyone looked back in awe as the Alpha son stood up to his preferred rank. "Is that what I was all about? Was I some failed experiment because *you* couldn't take the responsibility of being a failed parent?"

"Don't you dare talk to me like that!"

"You're done, Robert," Nathan declared, drawing a line in the sand between the rank of Alpha and Omega, and inciting the balance the natural world created. He was calling his mate's bluff. Now, all he had to do was answer. And Robert did. Slowly, he gave up his Alpha posturing and simmered down to an approachable pheromone palate.

Alexander stepped back in. "Is my condition ... even real?"

Robert swung his head, foregoing responsibility once more. "Who is to say? You had an abrupt hormone reaction that surprised everyone. Several conditions regarding sex and procreation exist, including ones that say Alphas have an elevated Status up to Type 6.

I guess it gives them magical powers or something. I don't suppose this Alpha of yours is claiming he's one of those, too?"

"You are a complete and utter coward. You didn't do this for anyone's betterment other than yourself."

"Oh yeah? How do you figure?"

"Because I can't be your 'boy' if another Alpha owns me, especially if he's my Fated Mate." Robert didn't comment on the allegation. He continued to stare his Omega son down like a worthy opponent in an old western shootout. "You didn't want to know what Alpha could 'tame' me if you couldn't do it yourself. Or worse, find out what kind of Alpha I'd find that would drive you even crazier than I was. Or…" Alexander's eyes trailed down to his stomach. He slowly took his hand and glided it over it. A pup was growing inside him—one who hadn't experienced the childhood he did, one who hadn't lived the adolescent years he did, one who wasn't being subjected to the life he had now. But the longer he stayed in that house, he would. "I won't let you do this to my pup. And I won't ever forgive you for this."

Nathan rushed to the door in hopes of saving his Omega son from an eternal decision. "No, wait. Don't leave, yet. Please," he begged in a soft voice, trying everything to connect to another Omega in the way *they* only knew how. It worked as he saw Alexander melt for a moment. But once again, Robert came through, destroying the moment instantly.

"There you go, running off again like an ungrateful pup when life gets too hard or when someone does something you don't like. What you should really be doing is thanking me!"

The sheer utterance barreled over Alexander. "'*Thanking you*'?!"

"Take a look at yourself in the mirror, boy. You're a 28-year-old Omega who is pregnant with the offspring of an ex-convict. You own a bar which can't decide if it's running on the brink of ruin or the brink of success. The only respect you get is through Eric, who miraculously, has held your business up until now, through all your drama. Then, he offers you a new life on a silver platter. Nicholas Hamilton is one of the most successful names out there in the business." Once again, Alexander found himself eyeing his brother in disdain. "And with the offer he gave you, I think you need to reconsider."

That was something Alexander didn't discuss with Jin. "How do you know what Nick offered me?"

"I called him," Robert said proudly. "Had a great chat with him. He's a charmer. If he talked to you the way he talked to me, I'm surprised you didn't take it on the spot. Luckily, I reassured him you'd change your mind and do the right thing." The Alpha silently praised himself for standing at the head of his pack once again, where he rightfully belonged.

"Is there any part of my life in which you don't feel you need to meddle?" Alexander griped.

"I didn't get myself involved with you playing 'doctor' to yourself when you went off the meds and decided to get yourself involved with ex—"

"Stephen!"

"Fine." Robert rolled his eyes. "*Stephen.*"

"My Fated Mate," Alexander stated with confidence.

"And this is a good thing?!" The old Alpha rubbed his head in utter frustration. "Why don't you just admit where you are right now, Alexander Daventry? You have two legacies here, boy, and they can't co-exist. You cannot raise a pup in a bar while running it with an ex-convict who was put away for..." He beckoned to his son.

Alexander gulped. "Drugs and negligent homicide."

"*Negligent?* Oh, that's just perfect," Robert sang sarcastically. "So, when you're not worried about whether or not you're going to get accosted, assaulted, maimed, robbed, or killed at the bar, you're going to be constantly worried about whether or not he even has the brain functionality to watch his own pup breathe."

"That's not true." Alexander crumbled.

"Is that the kind of life you want for a pup? You're running out that door, with the intent of never coming back and wanting to subject yourself to nothing but a complete and utter failure. And all of this is because you have some sort of fogged up view of what you think a Fated Mate is? That's not the life an Omega ever dreams about, Alex, and it is certainly not the life of someone who thinks they can be a parent, be a bar owner, fight the establishment, and do it all on their own."

"I won't be alone," Alexander cried. "I trust him to be my mate, and I trust him to be with our pup."

"I wouldn't trust him to watch the neighbor's kids from across the street with an ambulance at the ready, let alone a poor, defenseless pup." He grabbed his son's shoulders and steadied them, peering into his saturated eyes. "Come on, Alex. You know you don't want this. You don't want to be left alone."

Alexander tried, "Stephen will be there with me."

Robert honed in. "Then why isn't he here now? Is it because *he* doesn't want to be here? Or is it because *you* don't want him here?"

"It's because..." The Omega's voice cracked as his tears began falling freely.

His Alpha Sur pulled him in deep. "There, there. It's okay. This isn't an easy decision. But you *need* to decide."

"I'm so scared," Alexander whispered back, completely falling back into the role he was all too familiar with.

Robert nodded as he once again looked into his submissive son's eyes. Suddenly, it all came back: Robert was the virile Alpha in the family and Alexander was the small, submissive pup, needing to learn a life lesson all over again. "I know. If there's one thing about us that has always been true, it's that the Daventry family is strong and capable of making tough decisions. You have a bar. And you have a pup. You know you can't have both. What do you want to do? What do you *need* to do?"

Stephen strutted into the kitchen, whistling as he aimed for the fresh brewed coffee. "Good morning!"

Both Kane and Marlon turned and stared at their Alpha son. Then they shot a lot look at each other, wondering who just walked in.

Marlon pressed slowly, "Good morning. And how are you?"

"Couldn't be better." Stephen delighted as he took his first swig from mug. "Man, this coffee is good!" He floated to the kitchen table, joining his family. After situating himself, he finally acknowledged the awkward stares he was receiving in return. "What?"

"Good party last night?" Marlon asked.

"Eric's birthday? It was okay. Considering I think his goal was to get laid by the end of the night, I'm sure he was satisfied." Stephen gave a cheeky grin before another generous gulp. Then, he realized where his family must have taken the comment. "Not by me!" he swiftly corrected. "Some billiard player." He decided to keep his mouth shut on how he thought the statement had a double meaning and casually cleared his throat.

Kane readjusted himself in the wood-backed chair. "Anything else?"

Stephen exhaled, knowing he wasn't giving a good poker face. He steadied his coffee mug on the table and centered his thoughts. The Alpha Wolf inside him was damn near giddy! It hopped up on its back legs and yelped with glee, nudging his human form to finally spill the beans. "I have news that I have been wanting to say ever since I first got out of Brooks Haven." Stephen looked up and glanced out the large kitchen window. The lush green grass was full, the wildflowers were bountiful, and large white clouds filled the vast cerulean sky. It was all so inviting. "Alexander is mine."

"*Yours?*" Kane squinted his eye and wore a doubtful expression. A subtle cop persona surfaced as he wondered where on earth the conversation was going. "Did you corner him into a mating contract or something?"

Marlon lightly hit his mate's shoulder while rolling his eyes at the dense comment. "No, of course not!" He locked eyes with his Alpha son, joining him in the show of elation. "Does that mean he's finally…". Stephen nodded his head and even blushed. "Oh, babe!" The Omega jumped up from the table, walked over, and hugged his son as a proud parent. "I'm so happy for you!"

"I missed something," Kane stated as he became the lone family member not in on it—a familiar occurrence from yesteryear.

Stephen chuckled as it amused him his Alpha father couldn't put it together, completely forgetting his Sur's mental condition. "Dad, don't you remember? When I met Alex, I discovered he was my Fated Mate. But he was so adamant that I wasn't…" The Alpha quickly reflected on all the insane moments which brought him to now. "I'm just so glad he finally sees it."

A blank expression covered Kane as he tried to put into place everything his son was telling him. "Right. Okay. Yeah, I remember." The words were mechanical, but he chose not to dwell on them. "How did it happen? What made him finally come around?"

Marlon returned to his seat, equally waiting on their son's every word.

Stephen rubbed the back of his neck as he tried to put it into words. "Alex takes a certain medication. I don't know much about it, but from what little we've discussed, it's almost as if the suppressant he was taking was blocking his wolf's spirit. I mean, I think his inner wolf knew something. That's why Alex was struggling with it so much." His mood fell. "That's why he felt so compelled to keep me around." It was hard to acknowledge once again that with everything he put the Omega through, any "normal" human being would have cut him loose forever ago. Not wanting to focus on such criticisms once again, he continued, "There were a couple of times where, for one reason or another, he wasn't taking the medication. I think I noticed it; hell, I think *everyone* noticed it the night I was stabbed."

"Low-life scum," Kane muttered to himself. "That assault needs to be taken care of. You should be going after the bastard for medical bills. Pain and suffering too."

"Yeah, I know, Dad. But I have other things on my mind which are more important right now."

"Like what?" Kane asked, lost on how the new information warranted him putting the assault on the backburner.

Here it was. The moment Stephen had been waiting for—possibly his entire life. "Alex and I are going to have a pup." The Alpha looked up and waited for his parents' reaction. In the minute amount of time it takes a raindrop to fall from a leaf to the ground, he formalized their responses even before they spoke.

Marlon reached for his chest as it completely burst with emotion. "Stephen... really?" His voice teetered as his excitement gave himself away. Stephen affirmed the news and sent his Veo into a joyous roar—both now standing in celebration. "This is amazing! Congratulations to you both."

Kane remained in the chair deep in thought. "When did you have time to do that?!"

"Oh, stop it, Kane!" Marlon scolded while still holding onto his elation. "This is all just... oh, I'm so happy for you. What a complete turnaround. Who could have imagined this—even just a year go?"

Stephen himself acknowledged how his life appeared set up for something completely different than this. "I... I don't know." Butterflies of emotion sprung from his stomach. "Sometimes, I just wonder what's going to come up and take it all away." Marlon dismissed the notion and gave his son one more deep embrace.

"Who's that?" Kane asked as he leaned to the side to see a vehicle roll up into the driveway.

"Hmm. No one I know," Marlon announced. "Stephen?"

A feeling overcame the Alpha as he watched a brute of a man exit the sleek car and take in the sights of the house. He didn't like it at all. "Wait here."

Without even waiting for his parents to respond, Stephen made a straight shot to the foyer and out the front door, greeting the Alpha on the gravel. "Can I help you?" he said sternly.

The unknown man removed his sunglasses and took in Stephen's Alpha scent which was growing stronger by the second. "You must be Stephen."

"That depends. You are?" Stephen placed his hands on his hips as he took in the stranger's scent. He was an Alpha no doubt. But the scent was oddly familiar. The stranger's older age threw him off as he couldn't place how he knew him. It wasn't from his former life, and he didn't recognize him from lock-up.

"Robert Daventry." The Alpha thrust his hand out in a formal greeting.

The name sent a shiver down Stephen's spine. As if some robot possessed him, he returned the handshake as he concluded now who he was. "You're Alex's Sur."

"Good intuition. I like that in a man." Robert smiled, entertained by his own words. He received nothing in return. "I'm just here to drop off a letter." On cue, he handed over a small envelope which bore the name "Stephen" in a gentle cursive.

The Alpha cautiously accepted it. "A letter? From who?"

"Alex. Who else? Wolf-God knows I'd have no other reason to be here." Once again, Robert looked around, criticizing every sight he could see.

The envelope sat heavy in the Alpha's hand. "What's going on? Why didn't he just call or text? Why didn't he just wait until our next shift together?"

Robert stuck both his hands in his pockets. "Considering the sensitivity of the issue, it was determined this was the best way."

"The '*issue*'?" Stephen was losing his patience. Everything about the Alpha read arrogance and superiority. And even those descriptions were complimentary compared to what Alexander had told him. The thought of the man hurting his mate was beginning to overtake his rational senses. "What do you want?" he seethed.

"It's simple: stay away from Alexander and stay away from South Street. From the sounds of it, you've done nothing good for him or the bar. That Wolf-God forsaken place is enough for him to handle. He doesn't need you and your history causing him anymore drama than what he already deals with," Robert stated firmly.

Stephen refused to back down. Instead, he walked right up to the Alpha and stared him in the eye. "I suppose when it comes to drama in his life, you're enough?"

Robert didn't even flinch at the comment. Instead, he just smirked and cocked his head. "Like I said, you're not Alexander's concern anymore. So, there's no reason for you to stick around." Before Stephen could even comment, he made his way back to the car and pulled his sunglasses out from his breast pocket.

Stephen eyed his every move. "I don't know what Alexander has told you, but he's my Fate!" he yelled across the driveway. "And we have ... things ... going on in our lives which are going to keep us together. I suggest you get used to the idea."

Robert gave one final look to the Alpha and shook his head. "Those *things* you say are also nothing you need to worry about anymore." Watching Stephen's expression drop was the cherry on top of his prophetic announcement. He gleefully turned the engine over and began to reverse out of the driveway. "Have a good day."

The car's wheels squealed and kicked gravel up as it made its way back to the main road, leaving Stephen in a hazy cloud of dust. All that he had left was an ominous white envelope staring at him. He didn't want anything to do with it—didn't want to open it. But he knew he had to. He carefully tore the top off as he slowly walked back toward the house. As he continued to read it in the foyer, the skies darkened. Both parents came out, greeting him in the hallway.

"Stephen? Who was that?" Marlon asked, not liking his son's expression.

It was hard for the Alpha to pull away from the long, convoluted explanation on the letter, but he found himself able to tear himself away only for a moment. "That was ... Alexander's Sur... He came by to drop off his letter from..."

"From?" Marlon pressed.

Stephen gulped. "Alex... He's... He's..." The Alpha's hands began to tremble.

"What's wrong?" Kane sensed the happy celebration they shared only moments earlier coming to a complete halt.

"Alex... He's ... selling the bar?" The words on paper were written in a foreign language he couldn't comprehend.

"Is that such a bad thing?" Kane threw out. "That endeavor couldn't have been easy. Now that he's pregnant, maybe he doesn't want to deal with all that. You know, rearranging his priorities."

As much as Stephen wanted to take in his Sur's optimism—he knew better. "Dad, you don't understand. That bar is Alexander's life. I was there when Nick tried to buy it from him; it was like he was trying to buy our pup. Which ... when it comes to that..." Stephen's expression turned cold.

"Babe?" Marlon pressed, feeling the hurt pheromones consume his son.

Stephen could barely believe the words coming from his mouth. "He's terminating it."

Both Kane and Marlon stood there, not sure how to proceed. Neither of them got the chance to say anything, as Stephen immediately turned on his heels and marched back out to the driveway.

The Alpha's hands started shaking as he crumpled the note in his fist. Fed up with it still being there, he tore it to shreds and threw it on the ground below. He marched harder and faster, past the driveway and into the side yard, staring at trees decades old which never experienced the pain he knew now. Stephen couldn't decide on a path. He started left, down the hill, to the woods and river he was used to. But a sudden memory of Warren flashed before him, and he turned one-eighty and started right, toward the pond. Another memory of a very young Warren standing in the water, completely innocent and unaware came upon him. And then, the thought that he'd never get the chance to see his own pup do the same—whether he was supposed to or not. Once again, the mere thoughts stopped his descent and turned left again, begging his inner wolf to make a decision. All it could do was whimper and howl, mourning a loss it already knew. He stopped, unsure of where to go. In the large green open space, there was nothing to pick up and throw, nothing to destroy.

Footfalls from his Alpha father came from behind which startled Stephen off his lone train of thought. He didn't want to face his Sur, couldn't handle it. Once again, he found himself walking straight out to the property line, beautifully set off by large pines, red oaks, and maples. "There must be some mistake," Stephen said as he held his head. "People don't do that. Fated Mates don't do that."

"Son..." Kane tried as he struggled to get closer to his son.

"I was there in the bar," Stephen said in disbelief, slowing down his pace as the sorrow set in. "When he told me, I claimed him right then and there. I scented him. I scented... He was there! I was there! WE WERE THERE!" Stephen shouted as he collapsed in on himself, falling to knees straight onto the soft grass below. Angry sobs and roars jetted from the Alpha's lungs like he never had before.

"Son, it will be okay," Kane tried as he saw his son sobbing on the earth below him.

Stephen growled as he hiked himself up. "No, it won't! Don't you get it?! This family won't ever be happy. This family isn't *allowed* to be happy. EVER! It's one big fucking joke Wolf-God does when he's bored, sitting up there alone! His Alpha pack abandoned him years ago and so he has nothing better to do than fucking mess with our lives to make us miserable so he can FEEL SOMETHING!"

Kane reached out and pulled his son into the tightest hug he ever experienced. Not even Warren's passing brought on the need to be a strong Alpha father like he was now. At first, Stephen resisted and tried to wiggle his way free, but Kane held on harder, using every bit of strength he had, strength he didn't even know he possessed just to hold on and tame his son's wild emotions.

Finally, Stephen couldn't withstand his father's attempts. It had nothing to do with his physical strength; it was his emotional one. An outpouring of pheromones came out in a way Stephen had nearly forgotten and was convinced his father didn't know how to invoke anymore. The pheromones seeped into Stephen's lungs and made him utterly collapse onto his father's shoulder as he let loose an emotional cry. After its release, Stephen finally gained control of his breath long enough to have the ability to squeak out another cruel truth. "It should have been me."

"What?" Kane asked while looking at his son.

"It should have been me," Stephen said coldly.

"What are you talking about?" Kane feared the worst as he looked at his son's hopeless expression.

"Warren should be here—not me. It should have been *me* upstairs, not responding, not breathing, not able to experience life anymore. IT SHOULD HAVE BEEN ME!"

Kane's inner wolf barked back. "That is not true! Don't ever say that!"

"What? You like that between the two of us it was him?"

"It shouldn't be either of you!" Kane roared. "I never wanted this for him! I never wanted this for you! Wolf-God is not up there in the heavens playing roulette on who should live and who should die, Stephen! That's life and the choices *we* make!"

Stephen shook his head, amused at the claim. "And that's just the second chances we get, right?! Over and over again?! All the near misses in life we refuse to tune into and take heed?! I, myself, can't even take a fucking hint! I get put away for ten years for murdering my brother—"

"Stop. Right. There," Kane warned.

Stephen huffed as he calmed the hysterics. "Doesn't matter anymore."

"Why?" Kane demanded.

"I used, Dad."

"'Used'? When?" The revelation caught Kane off guard.

Stephen winced and shut his eyes as he revealed the shameful confession. "That night—the first night I went back to South Street after the attack—I ran into my old dealer. Or rather, he found me. He'd been bound and determined to get me back under his wing. I wanted nothing to do with him! But ... he wouldn't take no for an answer." Kane stood there, continuing to listen to his son intently. "He cornered me into the position of handing Alexander's suppressants or whatever they were over to him so he could sell them to his clients. I hated every second of it, and in my lost turmoil, I had a weak moment." He slapped his hands against his legs in defeat. "Ten years to learn from my mistake with Warren, and then I go and fuck it all up!"

Kane crossed his arms. "What happened?"

"Wolf Spit. Ray had a new formula he wanted me to try, and I did. He said that there's this new effect that renders you completely mindless, and it erases your memory of what happened. Thus, the next day, when I said I couldn't remember what happened with my bike in the driveway, I was serious when I said I couldn't remember." Kane looked away for a moment but refused to say anything in return. Stephen went on. "I don't know how much he gave me or how much I did, but my mind is completely blank on it. In addition, there was a day where two cops came into the bar, and I had to do a drug test. That stuff must be fast-moving through the system because it didn't show up. Somehow, I passed it. Fooled the cops. Fooled everyone."

"Davis and Gutierrez are fine cops. I promise you—if there were drugs on you or in your system, they would have found it."

The response made Stephen trip. "Davis and Gut—wait, how?"

"They worked for me. Do you think it wasn't going to get back to me that my own son was on the radar?" Kane amused himself in his son's astonished expression.

"Then why didn't you—"

"I was going to bring it up. But then..." This time it was Kane's turn to hold his head in guilt.

"Then..." Stephen pressed.

"You really don't remember coming home that night, do you? Just like the night you crashed your bike?" Kane asked, already knowing the answer. "You don't remember coming home and confessing every little detail you just spewed now?"

That made Stephen's stomach drop. "I did *what*?!"

"The drug dealer coming by the house, coming into your work, lying to Alex about where his prescription bottle went, getting W.S. and bringing it home. You already told me," Kane said smoothly.

"This... this did not happen," Stephen claimed in disbelief.

"You came home drunk and completely out of your f-ing mind!" Kane sang. "I told you that you had left your bike in the middle the driveway because you *did*. Your Veo was worried sick when we didn't hear you come home when we expected you. You open and slam doors and walk like you have boulders on your feet. We know each time you come home from work—even when you act like an idiot and try to come in from the bedroom window. Reliving old memories, were you?"

Stephen blushed red. "I guess I didn't know I was that loud." The Alpha eyed his father like he was an adolescent all over again. "So, what went down? What am I missing?"

"I met you at the door. You were completely hysterical—kind of like now." Kane thought better of his words. "Sorry."

"It's okay."

"I didn't want your Veo to see or hear you in that condition, so I kept you outside and we talked. Well, *you* talked. I listened. By the end of it, you had told me about your old dealer giving you the drugs. You swore up and down you never even touched them. You said you put them in your bike and then went to another bar to get yourself shit-faced. And believe me, you did."

"This... this is incredible." Stephen stood there in disbelief.

"Oh, just wait. There's more. After you went to work the next day, I get a call from Davis saying he and Gutierrez were enroute to a call on suspicion of you using, possessing, and dealing drugs at the bar. If the previous night hadn't happened, I would have driven down to that bar myself and made sure they dissected you and that place to find every little piece of evidence against you." Stephen swallowed hard as his Alpha Sur was beginning to transition to his old self. But then, it faded. "But the previous night *did* happen. I told Davis to administer the drug test; *I* needed the assurance myself. Then I told him that you had confessed to me that you were set-up by some lunatic. I said if the test came back positive that he should take you in and throw the book at you for all of it: the theft, the drug use, the possession. However," he paused, "I said that if there were no signs of drugs in you or on your person and the bar, he could just let it go and let me deal with it. In exchange, I'd hand over the drugs I found on your bike, which I did."

Stephen's lungs hitched as he couldn't believe what his father was saying to him. "You told officers of the law to not pursue their job? To lie?"

"Please. Wouldn't be the first time I asked a cop to do that on your behalf," Kane reminded him.

Stephen hitched his brows. "Point taken." A throbbing sensation hit his head as he tried to take all the information in. Déjà vu was here to stay. "I paid for it in the end. Ray had my bike towed. I'm sure he sold that 'ala carte' too," he gruffed.

"Your bike is behind the garage next to the wood pile."

Stephen threw his head forward. "WHAT?!" Immediately, he found himself running toward the garage and to the large stacks of wood conveniently hidden by a large tarp. He grabbed onto the plastic and tossed it which revealed his old friend. "Crusher!" Tears damn near formed again as he saw his loyal companion, sitting there innocently.

Kane slowly joined him and watched his son's pheromones rise for the first time. "To be honest, I thought you'd have found it before we talked."

"Dad, none of this makes sense! Why is this here? *How* is this here?"

"I told Davis from the get-go that I thought you were a pawn in someone's scheme to destroy you. Davis agreed, considering whoever turned you in had *way* too much information to be an innocent bystander. But they knew you had just gotten out and were under my watch, so I asked them to give you the benefit of the doubt. I figured if anyone was going to take you down again, they were going to do it at the bar. Thus, I had a gut feeling. I told Davis and Gutierrez to move your bike the night you went in. Then, to wait."

"Wait for what?" Stephen asked.

"A call. It was either going to be from you to report your bike missing or from another anonymous caller looking to turn you in. Lo and behold, someone decided to call in and say that you had drugs on your bike and that it was at the bar. Only problem was the story didn't make sense because—"

"Because Davis and Gutierrez already had the bike," Stephen finished. "Sean must have gotten overzealous before it was finished and relied on Ray to get the job done. They wanted me to go down right in front of Alex the night of his heat. If they could have had cops out there that night to point out my bike, it would have ruined me *and* Alex. Damn it!"

"After that, they called me, and I told them to haul it here. It's been here ever since."

Another thought hit Stephen. "Wait. What about the drugs?"

"The drugs? I told you: I turned them over to Davis and Gutierrez."

"No. The day they showed up to the bar, they had a drug dog with them. They used it on the bike. Any trace on the bike, and it should have picked up."

"Did you see the canine inspect the bike?"

"No. I stayed in the bar. Didn't want to see it."

Kane twitched his lips. "Interesting."

"I don't believe this." Stephen shook his head. Soon after, he began to approach the bike.

"Don't touch it!" Kane scolded.

"Why?"

"You said it yourself. There could be drug residue on it."

"Okay... what do I do about that?" Stephen asked, completely lost.

"Like it or not, this is going to be Crusher's home for a while. I used my one free ticket with Davis and Gutierrez, but if anything happens after this, including detecting a trace, you're toast." He sighed. "Everything non-metal needs to be replaced, and we're going to have to strip it."

"What?!" Stephen looked at the bike as if he needed to put it down.

"It's a small price to pay, Stephen. You'll get her back."

Stephen groaned. "Unlike Alex." A sharp feeling rushed through his heart once again thought his lost future.

Kane looked at him in awe. "You still haven't learned, have you?"

"Excuse me?"

"What did I say when you first found out Alexander was your Fated Mate and he refused to believe it?"

Stephen's eyes widened. "You're going to play memory games on *me*, now?"

"I said, 'fight for him.' And damn it, Stephen, you're not fighting!"

"It's over! What am I supposed to do?"

"You said he was 'terminating the pregnancy.' Is that what it said, or had he already done it?" Kane asked.

Stephen's mind reeled as he struggled to remember what was now crumpled and torn bits across the property. "I'm sure it said he was going to."

Kane grabbed his son's shoulders. "Then go out there and save your mate and save your pup! This isn't over until it's over."

"Dad, I—"

"Go!" Kane demanded.

"Alright, alright!" Stephen surrendered. Both men hurried to the front of the garage. Kane scrambled to his pockets and pulled out the keys to the truck, practically throwing them at his son. "Dad, thank you. This means everything. And I'm sorry."

Kane smiled. "I guess I can give you a second chance."

"I love you."

"I love you too, son."

CHAPTER 09:

LISTENING TO THE GREAT GRAY WOLF

The truck's tires squealed to a halt in front of the bar. Stephen had barely put it into park before he rushed out of the vehicle, leaving the driver side door completely open as he rushed inside. Among familiar bar patrons and staff, he searched frantically. "Where is he?!"

"Stephen! You're here!" James said in surprise as he made his way back up to the bar.

"Who are you looking for?" Bruce asked as he looked at Stephen with concern.

"Alex!" the Alpha caught his breath. "He's getting ready to make a big mistake!" Out of the corner of his eye, he saw a customer gawking back at him right in front of Bruce who carried a face like the one he knew way too well: a man with shaped eyes and pitch-black hair. "Who are you?"

"I'm Jin," the Alpha said back. "I'm Alexander's younger brother."

"Stephen. I'm the Fated Mate."

Jin nodded. "I figured as much."

"Where is Alex?"

"Oh, man." Jin turned his jaw in a slight moment of panic. "I don't know if I should tell you."

"If I don't get to Alex now, he's going to do something he regrets."

"It's already done, Stephen. I'm sorry," Jin regretfully stated.

The Alpha steadied himself to the bar and laid his arms on it as he took in the dark information. "I just—I didn't think he'd do it."

"It's for the best, I think," Jin stated as he took a drink of his cocktail.

The wolf inside Stephen growled as he balled up his fists. Unable to withstand it any further, he grabbed Jin by the shirt and stared menacingly back down to the Alpha. "What did you say?!"

"What are you doing?!" Jin croaked as he found himself trying to peel away from Stephen's grasp.

"Stephen!" Bruce yelled as he tried to pull the Alpha off him. It was no avail.

"How could you think that is better?!" Stephen roared.

Another voice from down the hall came rushing up. "Whoa, whoa! Stephen, take it easy!" Stephen instantly recognized the voice as Daniel. The petite Omega now tried squeezing his entire body between the two Alphas as if he was a crowbar. Daniel, himself, instantly regretted it as he found himself now suffocating between two statuesque wolf-descendants. Finally, in Daniel's panicked attempts at air, Stephen felt forced to let go of his iron grip. "You *really* need to work on finding outlets for your anger! Man!"

"What's your problem, anyway?" Jin said as he readjusted himself.

"He was just trying to support you, Stephen," James defended.

"*'Support'*?" The Alpha couldn't believe it.

"That's why Daniel and I are here. To help him since this whole ordeal is really emotional for him," Jin laid out.

"Yeah," Bruce continued, "you were in support of it all along. You knew Alex couldn't handle it, so he took care of it."

"Why would I support Alexander hurting our pup? Or get rid of it?!" Stephen felt his stomach go nauseous and about ready to throw up.

Daniel looked back in shock. "The pup? Alex isn't doing anything to the pup. Is he?!"

The Alpha looked up and scanned the rest of the crew sitting there—staring back at him—wondering if he needed a leash and a time-out kennel. "You... you guys aren't talking about the pup?"

"Hell, no," Bruce answered with confidence. "We're talking about South Street. He's selling part of it to Nicholas Hamilton."

"Oh." Now Stephen looked back at his audience in shame. "I'm sorry, guys. You have no idea where my train of thought is."

"No kidding!" Daniel replied. "I go to take a whiz, and you have his brother in a chokehold!"

"Please, I didn't mean it. I—"

"Don't worry about it," Jin answered, still not sure how to take the new Alpha. "Certainly not the introduction I was expecting. But then again, I've heard a few things."

Stephen fidgeted. "As much as I want to sit here and mend fences, I *really* need to get to Alex. Where is he?"

"He went to meet up with Sean." Daniel took out his phone and sent out a message. "And... yup, he's still there."

Another bad aura overcame the Alpha. "Where?"

"The bank I assume," Daniel surmised.

The Alpha lifted his head to the heavens. "Why is this day going like this?! I gotta go!" Stephen swiftly made his way to the exit.

"Well, wait! What was all that talk about hurting your pup?" Daniel shouted back.

"Not now, Daniel. Later!"

Sean slowly tore off a large document from a printer and laid it in front of Alexander. "Sign here, sign here, and finally, here." He watched his former mate follow each line and smoothly glide his signature over it all. He swallowed and then looked at the Omega like a wolf lying on its back. "Is it bad to say I missed you?"

Alexander looked up and smirked. "Coming from a two-faced son-of-a-bitch who was secretly waiting to take advantage of me and destroy me? Nah. I expected it."

The businessman coughed and then gave a smile back. "I see." Then, his expression relaxed. "It wasn't always like that though."

Alexander stopped his signature on the last line of the document, taking in Sean's words. "No. It wasn't." After thinking on the statement for a moment, he finished off the last signature and handed the large paper back. "You were right though."

The Alpha glanced over the document, scanning each and every pen strike. "About?"

"I did do things in the relationship which drove us apart, and I'm sorry for that. Without the fanfare, without the drama, I don't know if you could tell me if you truly were in a relationship with me only for South Street, and I don't want to know the answer. But I'd like to think it wasn't."

Sean swallowed his pride, very thankful his glass cubicle came with soundproof doors. On the other side, the rest of the immaculate bank worked like a well-oiled machine, completely unaware of the conversation taking place from inside. "It wasn't. I guess, in the end, it was just easy to say it was once... once I saw it falling apart."

Alexander nodded in gratitude. "Thank you."

A moment held both the former mates still. Both looked at each other without contempt or vexation. It was different being in the position where they no longer felt obligated to be civil and kind. Now they were choosing to. Sean was the first to shake off the moment. "Okay." He clicked his tongue and tried to nonchalantly bring up the awkward conversation. "I assume this holds up *my* end of the bargain."

"Not so fast," Alexander slid in. "In addition to playing nice on the business side, you also agreed to stop trying to sabotage me, any of my staff or customers, or the bar itself. And that also means telling 'Ray' to take a hike and find someone else. Stephen is off-limits."

Sean hid his lips while he thought of the high stakes at play both in ego and legal aspects. He cleared his throat. "And in exchange for that..."

"No one will ever say a word about your personal interest in South Street or your conduct with Ray," Alexander stated confidently.

"And the recording on Daniel's phone?" Sean stated delicately.

"He's standing by, waiting for my signal to hit the delete button."

The Alpha tapped his hand on his desk, gauging on whether he got the bad end of the deal. "I still wish you could have just brought him here to do it."

"This is the best I can do, Sean." Alexander crossed his legs and leaned back into his chair. "Regardless of if he was here or not, he could have already sent that voice clip out to fifty people and you'd have never known. Seeing him hit the button here is meaningless if you don't trust him. Or trust me." Sean hummed as he considered the claim. "The fact is we both have information which could destroy each other. If Ray somehow gets ahold of Stephen, I lose my Fated Mate back behind bars. And, I'm sorry, if you think you have the biggest disadvantage in this deal, I have to passionately disagree. We have two options here: we either trust each other here and now, or we spend the rest of our lives looking behind our back. I know which one I want. What about you?"

Sean rolled his pen between his fingers. After rocking back and forth in his executive chair, he stood up and buttoned his suitcoat. Alexander quickly stood to attention himself and waited. The Alpha relaxed his rugged face and stretched out his hand, signaling a truce. In return, Alexander eased his nerves and shook the hand in return.

"May I walk you to the front?" Sean offered his hooked arm as he adjusted his glasses with the other.

"You may," Alexander replied. Together, they both walked out to the open lobby. Large three-story windows illuminated the white marbled floors, the white marbled walls, and all the customers therein. One particular customer stuck out like a sore thumb. "Stephen?!"

"There you are!" Stephen huffed in elation. His wolf whimpered at the sight: his Fated Mate wrapped around the arm of his former mate. Learning his lesson with Jin, the Alpha kept his wolf at bay and approached Alexander exposing his soft belly and rambling, "Look, I know I made a mistake with South Street but please don't terminate the pregnancy and please don't go back to Sean."

The Omega stood there completely dumbfounded and unsure of what to say. "I... er... um... what?!"

"Stephen, nice to see you," Sean said, enjoying the Alpha before him in pieces.

"Wish I could say the same!"

"Stephen!" Alexander hissed above a whisper.

He gave one final look to his former mate. "I need to get back to work so I will leave you two alone."

The Omega wore a gracious expression. "Thank you, Sean."

"Remember, if you need anything, don't hesitate to call. Territory One and I are at your service," Sean stated politely. He gestured to Stephen with his head before walking back toward his office.

"Hey, Sean," Stephen shouted. "Nice glasses."

The comment caused the businessman to instantly drop his held expression. He gritted his teeth and peeled off the large frames before huffing behind the glass door.

Alexander glared at his Fated Mate. "You. Out."

Stephen tucked his tail and led the Omega out of the bank and into the parking lot. "Have you lost your mind?!" The wild animal in Stephen quickly thrust up and bit Alexander's neck right in his gland. "Ow! That's attached!"

"Did you do it?"

"Do what?!" Alexander was at his wit's end. His mate had completely lost touched with reality.

Stephen's heart hurt as he gathered his nerve. "Did you terminate our pup?"

The Omega's initial response was to equally flip out. But the concern on his mate's face read that he was completely serious in his inquisition. And it scared him. "Wolf-God, no. Stephen where on earth would you get that idea from?!"

"Your Sur. He came by and dropped off a note from you. It said you were tossing the bar away and our baby along with it."

Alexander couldn't believe his ears. "My Sur did *what*?!" He held his head as he struggled to make sense of the horrific act. "What letter?"

"I don't have it," Stephen confessed. "I never want to see it again. Alex, if you felt that way, why didn't you tell me?!"

The Omega wasn't having it. "Let's go. We're not having this discussion here."

On an abandoned sidewalk near the lake's edge, two hurt souls walked hand-in-hand, trying to heal a broken past. Stephen stared down at the broken concrete, trying to study any line of patterns to keep him from completely breaking down. "And then he said not to see you or the bar anymore because you weren't worth all the drama and hurt I've caused you."

Alexander was completely the opposite. He stared off across the lake, watching the sunset kiss the water, taking in his mate's every word. "Stephen, I am so sorry he did that. I can't *believe* he did that." He sighed. "Maybe that was the problem. I should have."

"Where did all of this come from?" Stephen wanted to know.

Alexander gestured to a park bench, and both sat at the water's edge. "The scenario around it is all messed up, but what I will tell you now is that my Sur has always struggled to control every aspect of his life and that included me. It's caused him to think everything heinous act he commits is justified: abusing me—if not physically, then emotionally, cheating on my Veo, trying to start a third new life with some random Omega."

"He's doing what?"

Alexander waved the comment off. A discussion for a different time. "He's been preventing me from having heats so I would never find a mate interested in me enough to bond with. Or, at the very least, he was wanting to make sure he approved of who I was with. I'm not even sure Sean fit the bill."

"If Sean couldn't pass his test, I can only imagine what he thought of me."

"Don't say that about yourself."

"It's true, Alex," Stephen confessed. "I can't change my past. I'll always be the guy who spent ten years in lock-up. What else is there to say?"

Alexander grabbed the Alpha's hand and squeezed it tightly. "How about the Alpha that rose above it? Found his Fated Mate, started a family, and has a career."

"*Had* a career. You sold the bar." Alexander shook his head. "You *didn't* sell the bar? Then, what were you at Territory One for? You were with Sean!"

"Sean is still my banker, Stephen. Like it or not, we're going to have to play nice with him." Stephen's face snarled. "*And...* he's going to play nice with us."

"How so?"

"I made a deal with him. We're not going after him for mis-leading a bank on personal interest, and he's going to leave South Street alone, and he's going leave *us* alone. No more hits, no drugs, no more smear campaigns." Alexander stared into the Alpha's eyes, hoping to pull his wolf out of him. "It's over."

The Alpha's wolf purred as he leaned in and kissed his mate. "What's going to happen with South Street?"

"I must have talked Nick's ear off for over two hours; I'm sure he's sick of me by now. But, in that time, I completely convinced him that I wasn't going to leave South Street. That's *my* bar, and no one is taking that from me."

"If you didn't sell it to him, what did you do?"

"Oh, I sold it to him," Alexander corrected. "Thirty percent."

"Thirty percent?"

"Mhm. Eric owns 30%, Nick owns 30%, and I own 40%."

It finally clicked for Stephen. "That's what Bruce meant by selling 'part' of South Street."

"In that deal, it is understood should either Eric or Nick want to sell, I have first right of refusal, Bruce and James stay on full time with a much-deserved raise they don't know about yet, and you, of course."

"Me?" Stephen asked meekly.

"My Fated Mate? Yes, you! I'm sorry I didn't tell you. I was going to, but I didn't want you to think that I did this just because you tried to convince me. I did it for us. That's why I told my Sur to *send* a letter. I didn't know he was going to take the liberty of embellishing one himself and then hand delivering it. I'm done with that man." The Omega growled in frustration as he remembered his Sur playing him for a fool. "He just knew all the right words to say— just as he always has. He told me he'd help me, and I believed it. Instead, he was hoping you'd shun me. Maybe it was just payback." He shook the thought off. "Anyway, with Nick coming on board, I get to be there a lot less and can afford to do more than pay for groceries and my rent. Like... raise a pup. And I won't need to rely on my parents anymore."

"What about your family?" Stephen asked, treading lightly.

Alexander pondered the thought. "One day. My Veo deserves it. So does my brother. As for my Sur... he's going to have to straighten out his priorities and figure out what he really wants in life. If it's not me, then he doesn't get my family."

Stephen gawked at the inner strength of the Omega before him. "Thank you for giving me a second chance." He glanced down at his mate's stomach and gently glided his hand over it. "For giving *us* a second chance. I don't know if Ray is going to listen to Sean and stay away from South Street or not. So, whatever I can do behind the scenes for the bar I think would be the best way to go about it. That guy should be buried up to his head."

"Maybe he should be thanked."

Stephen through his head back. "*'Thanked'*?"

"Yeah. Let's face it; if he hadn't gotten ahold of my prescription, I never would have gone off my medication that long to see who you truly were. It never would have unveiled my Sur's disgusting motives or his affair, it never would have opened my eyes to who Sean really was, it never would have put either him or Sean in a position for us to be left alone, and..."

"...for us to become a family," Stephen finished. "It isn't going to be easy, babe."

Alexander agreed. "Nothing is. Nothing that's *worth it* is. So, let's just hold onto each other and do this together. How about that?"

Stephen turned his body, in the last red glow of the sunset. "Alex, will you go into a mating contract with me?"

The Omega smiled. "About time you asked!" He brought the statuesque Alpha in and sealed the promise with a kiss. "I love you, Stephen."

"I love you, Alexander."

CHAPTER 10:

RECKONING ON A DAY LIKE THIS

One Year Later...

A melodic jingle rung out at the storefront. "Be right up!" George said from the back. Footfalls slowly made their way in and instantly went to their final destination. However, it wasn't the foot traffic which made the store owner's ear perk up. It was the sound of what seemed to be light coos and babbles from what had to be someone not even old enough to walk yet. The large Beta honed in to make sure he heard it right. He tossed the wrench in his hand into his toolbox and casually made his way up to the main. "Welcome to The Garage Door."

"Thanks," Stephen said back, only looking up for a second. Quickly, he focused back on his prize: a chrome emblem in the shape of a maniacal skull with wild flames jetting out. He gently took it out of the box and held in his hand, forgetting just how heavy it was.

George had seen it right. The statuesque Alpha had a large harness fastened to his muscled chest. From behind, it appeared the wanderer could have been setting up for a backpacking trip up in the mountains ... or breaking in a new look for the underground club downtown. However, when the man turned around, neither assumption was correct. Right in front of him, it was easy to see the wolf-descendent was carrying much more precious cargo. "Whoa." The store owner grinned as the reveal caught him off-guard. "And who is this?"

Stephen turned and smiled with Daddy Alpha pride as the little one in the front harness shook a noisemaker in his hand and gazed upon the pup. "*This* little man is going to be a motorcycle enthusiast one day. Just here to start him early."

George laughed. "I guess so. I would ask if there was anything I could help you find, but it looks like you found it."

A deep sigh emanated from the Alpha. "Yes, I did." Holding Crusher's logo in his hand again already was a victory, and he didn't even own it yet. Last time he was in this position, life was so very different.

A sudden memory flashed into George's mind as his quiet inner wolf cocked his head. "Wait. I remember you." Wheels turned until the right name came up. "Stephen?"

"That's right," the Alpha affirmed. "I applied for a job here last year. Tried to anyway." It was easy to see why both men found the conversation awkward. One year ago, Stephen was a lost wolf trying to find his way into a world which didn't accept him and didn't want him. Unfortunately, the interview with George at The Garage Door was the perfect anecdote for how everyone thought the Alpha's life was going to turn out. And now, here he was, proving everyone wrong.

George ran his fingers through his curly hair as he tried to navigate the conversation. "How are things?"

Stephen's pheromones rushed through the air, assuring the store owner there was no animosity on how things had turned out since. As far as Stephen was concerned, it happened exactly how it was supposed to. "Things are great. I'm the owner and a bartender at South Street Tavern. And when I'm not there, my Fated Mate and I have our hands full." He looked down on his content offspring. "As you can see."

"That I can!" George marveled at the sight. To think last year when he first saw Stephen, he was grateful for who he was and what he had become. Now, he had to consider whether he was jealous of the Alpha before him. He pointed to the shining plate in Stephen's hand. "You know, I remember you looking at that when you first came in."

"I made myself a promise that day: when the time was right, I was going to come back and claim it," Stephen reiterated.

"Is now the time?" George asked, already knowing the answer.

"Now is the time." Stephen smiled back. The Beta store owner led him to the register. The Alpha felt like he was on a mini procession to the prize ceremony of a street race.

"How is the Gunnolf bike treatin' ya? Still have it?" George asked as he logged into the register.

"I do. Had to retire it awhile as I saved up enough funds to get things replaced and refurbished as needed. Tonight, when I get off work, I'm going to add this baby to my bike, and then tomorrow, I'm going to drive up to Mountain Sound for the first time in over a decade." Excitement spilled over as the Alpha imagined himself back up there in the wilderness. Once upon a time, he used it as an escape. Now, he was using it for everything but.

"I'm excited for you!" George exclaimed as he punched in the numbers. "Cash or card?"

"Cash," Stephen replied as he pulled out his wallet.

"Spoken like a bartender."

"I get that comment a lot," the Alpha confirmed.

"Where's the little one going while you're off adventuring on your bike?"

"It's 'Grandpa Day' tomorrow. My Sur is already teaching him about being a police officer every time they play 'Cops and Robbers' with his patrol car and bank heist van. And Oliver here *loves* putting the front wheel of the heist van in his mouth or, as my Sur calls it, 'eating the bad guys.'" Stephen glanced down at his pup. "Isn't that right, little man?" Oliver cooed back which radiated a joyful laughter from both men.

"Well, damn. Sounds like everything is going right," George surmised as he wrapped up the emblem in a box and carefully placed it in a bag.

"Couldn't ask for more," Stephen replied. "Wish I could chat longer but we have a date with Omega Daddy at the bar so Oliver can go home and take a nap."

"You enjoy the rest of your day. And make sure you come back and visit me. Bring the future road warrior back with you!" George directed.

"Yes, sir!" Stephen replied as he headed out the door, ready for their daily walk.

The sun was on full display this early autumn day, giving everyone in Tauris City the benefit of its warmth and light as they hustled and bustled to every corner of the square. Most didn't even take notice of the proud Sur and his pup. But every so often, a stranger would come up and compliment the pair, most transfixed on the infant with streaks of brown hair and even darker eyes. While one of these admirers was busy doting on the pair, another from across the street caught Stephen's attention: a rogue Beta with a complimentary attire to the creatures of the night, holding a phone to his ear, but seemingly lost in a trance while staring back in a lost haze.

The Alpha himself didn't know what to say or do either. Finally, all Stephen mustered was a nod in respect and then, a subtle wave. The Beta chose to finally speak into his phone and continue his walk like nothing happened. Stephen didn't know if it was a good thing or bad thing. But, at last, right before the street rat turned the corner, disappearing into the alley he knew all too well, he caught a glimpse again and smiled in return.

***

"There you two are!" Alexander exclaimed as he saw his two favorite people walk into South Street. "I was beginning to think you two got lost."

"Nah, just enjoying the sunny day," Stephen happily said back.

"Enjoy them while they're still here. The trees are telling me those days are numbered," the Omega warned. Looking outside, he confirmed his suspicion as he noticed several green leaves painted red, orange, and yellow.

"Shh! Don't say that!" Stephen scolded. "I don't want the first brisk day to happen on my ride tomorrow."

Alexander hummed. "Already checked the forecast. It's going to be cloudy. Bring a jacket."

"Damn it," Stephen cursed under his breath.

"Hey!" Alexander shamed. He rolled his eyes, thoroughly convinced his mate was never going to curb his mouth.

"It's fine!" the Alpha waved off. "He doesn't know what we're saying."

"You keep up like that, and 'Damn it' are going to be his first words."

"You're both wrong," Eric declared as he walked by. "His first word is going to be 'Eric.'" The Alpha grinned his pearly white smile.

"And this is why we don't let you babysit." Alexander flung a bar towel over his shoulder and held his arms out. "Here."

Stephen unfastened the harness and set Oliver free from his confines. "You want the harness?"

"No, I'm good. I'm only staying for another minute and then it's straight to the car seat. With any luck, he'll be asleep by the time we get home." Alexander grunted as their "little guy" seemed to be gaining a pound a day.

"How was it, Eric?" Stephen cracked back his back—happy he could now move freely.

"Kind of slow, even for a Sunday if I'm honest. I'm heading out with Alex, if you don't mind?" the Alpha replied as he finished up a lone order.

Stephen nodded. "I'm good. What time do Bruce and James get here?"

"They should be here in an hour," Eric replied.

"Works for me." Stephen smiled at his mate.

"Are you sure you don't want me to stay?" Alexander asked, feeling guilty he was leaving his other half alone so abruptly.

"As long as no biker gang comes in to destroy the place, I think I can handle a dozen customers before Bruce and James make it in an hour," he teased.

"Very funny," Alexander replied sarcastically.

Stephen smirked as he ran his finger through his mate's soft brown hair, now free of any dyes, bleaches, or discolorations. Then, he gave him a firm kiss. "Make it home safely. Text me when you get there."

"Will do. Love you." Alexander leaned Oliver in and his Alpha daddy gave him a kiss. Afterward, the pup nuzzled into his Veo's neck, a sign he already knew it was "sleepy time."

"You know…" Eric interjected, "Oliver Warren would love to come my place and see the new saltwater fish tank I just got."

Alexander took in the not-so-subtle hint. "I promise you—next week, we will stop by."

"You better!" Eric scolded. "If I find out Nick gets ahold of him before I do…"

"I promise, Eric, you are the first in line."

"That's right!" Eric joked as he enjoyed the entitlement.

"Oh, hey!" Stephen hoisted up the small bag. "Can you bring this home for me?"

"What's that?" Alexander scanned the bag with pure curiosity.

"A promise I made over ten years ago. I'll tell you about it tomorrow," the Alpha played off.

"Sure. See you tonight."

"Bye."

Several minutes later, bar patrons found themselves glued to a new customer walking in who didn't fit. Did he not belong? No one would make that conclusion. It wasn't theirs to say. In fact, if the stately businessman wanted, he could have said everyone else didn't belong and banish them all from the premises. But that wasn't his goal. Not in the least. Tonight, he wanted to be there like any other customer, looking to connect to a soul over spirits to help make him sing. How loud he wanted to sing, he wasn't sure yet. "Is Alexander here?" the Alpha asked as he approached the bar.

"It's his night off. Something I can help you with?" Stephen asked, welcoming the patron in.

"No. Just wanted to say 'hi' is all." The elite businessman sat in front of the Alpha and contemplated his choices. "What do you recommend?"

The first thought which popped into Stephen's mind wasn't the most complimentary. "Every time I recommend Trailblazer #4, some bastard comes into my bar and tries to make my life a living hell. So tonight, I'm going to suggest Mountain Sound Whiskey on the rocks."

The suit flexed his eyebrows in response. "That was prophetic. Interesting recommendation. Let's do that." Stephen hummed in return. "Could be worse. You could be Trailblazer #1, #2, or #3. How bad do you suppose those were for them to name a fourth one?"

"Good point." The bartender tossed up a shiny glass, placed two large rocks it and filled it.

"Make one for yourself," the patron insisted.

"I appreciate it," Stephen said as he pulled out a second glass and repeated the act once again. Out of the corner of his eye, he noticed the suit fidgeting, stressing, worrying. "Rough day?"

"Actually, it's my night I'm more worried about," the Alpha confessed.

The bartender slid over one of the two glasses. Both lifted their tumblers in a salute and enjoyed their first sip. Stephen gave a loud satisfying sigh. "That hits the spot."

"It sure does."

"You ever had Mountain Sound before?"

The businessman nodded. "I've enjoyed their selections on many occasions. Been awhile on their whiskey though."

"You ever been up to their brewery in the mountains? The one right there on the lake?" Stephen asked.

The bar patron locked eyes onto his glass and swirled the liquid gold. "Many years ago."

Another customer walked up and listed off an order. Stephen went on it right away, grabbing two glasses and mixing up the cocktails. While he waited, the man became restless and finally turned to the businessman sitting there alone. "Mr. Whitmore, I just want to say that it's been amazing having you here as an advocate for Omegas and Low Types. I was at the fundraiser you had here for Jesse Minh—you were inspiring. Damn near stole the show in my opinion."

Matthew gestured with his glass. "Thank you for your support. It's because of people like you that I continue to do what I do."

The young wolf melted at the words. "Are you here alone or...?"

An awkward expression told the experienced Alpha exactly where this was going. "I was just here visiting my friend..." he glanced at the name embroidered in the bar shirt, "Stephen before heading out shortly. Hopefully, we will run into each other again sometime."

"Oh, I hope so," the sprite said enthusiastically. He wanted to stay and converse, but the bartender was way too efficient and finished the order faster than he wanted. Thus, he surrendered, said goodbye to the celebrity, and let him be.

After he left, Stephen now realized who was sitting in front of him. "Now I recognize you. You're the one who hosted that event. It's nice to finally put a name to a face."

"You were here, I take it?" Matthew surmised as he took another drink.

"Yeah. That was when I just started. I was only barbacking then. Alex speaks the world of you," Stephen said as he pushed a few bills into the tip jar.

"And you are?" Matthew placed his elbows on the table and studied the man.

"His Fated Mate."

The older Alpha's shoulders sank. "Huh. Uncanny."

"Why so?"

Matthew finally decided to bite the bullet. "Tonight, I'm sending my son off on a new journey. He meets his mate tonight."

Stephen furrowed his brows. "'Meets'? He doesn't know him already?"

"He does..." the older Alpha bounced his head back and forth in thought, "it's a contractual mate." The words didn't appear to make it any clearer to Stephen. Matthew set down the tumbler and focused. "My family has a lot of expectations. I've had them ever since I was a kid. My parents always wanted me to be in the best position to make sure I had everything. Now that I do... I guess I'm doing the same to my own son." The Alpha reflected on his own words, refusing to let any personal guilt set in. "When you're a Whitmore, that means you get things done to the best that you know how. Peyton is getting the best mating contract the world has to offer."

"Are you mating him off to a baron or something?" Stephen half-teased.

"A Type 6 Alpha," Matthew stated proudly.

Stephen dribbled his drink. "Type 6? They actually exist?"

"You've never heard of them?"

The bartender cleared his throat. "'Heard'? Yes. Know any? No."

"They are rare," Matthew confirmed. "So rare that we don't know what abilities and strengths they possess. They could be the secret to unlocking a new type of Alpha never seen on this planet before!"

"Like what?"

The older Alpha held his breath as he thought about the right answer. Then, he slumped back down when he realized. "I have no clue."

"What about Omegas?"

"There is no such thing as a Type 6 Omega." Matthew smirked, entertained by the thought.

Stephen decided to be brave. "You walked in here with a look that said you were anything but excited. Is that about your son's upcoming contract?"

The businessman bit his lip and slowly confirmed the observation. "It's related." Music from the corner speakers seeped into Mathew's ear as he reflected on so many things which happened up until now. A childhood full of expectation, a career full of expectation, and now his son, taking on his burdens. "It's a cruel joke, you know."

"What is?" Stephen leaned in, captured by the moment.

"Wolf-God gave us the ability to find Fated Mates—the instinctual pull that is the ultimate spotlight pointing out who we are supposed to be with in the world. And yet, so many out there don't get to experience it."

Stephen stood proudly. "I've been lucky enough to find mine."

"Me too." Matthew glanced away, barely believing the statement. "We as a species put so much value into finding the special wolf in the wild that we've created a society which says, 'Fake it if you can't make it.' Thus, the idea of a contracted mate was born." Matthew shook his head. "And to think there are people out there who choose to turn away their Fated Mate and deny the gift given to us."

For the Alpha bartender, the comment hit home. "Who is out there denying their Fated Mate?"

Mathew shook himself free of the spell he was under and remembered himself. "Damn, look at the time! I have to find my driver, get my family ready, and then head all the way back down here to be at The Howler Steakhouse." He cursed himself again as he threw several bills onto the bar. "Never going to make it in time. It was nice talking to you! Give my regards to Alex when you see him."

"Of course!"

Matthew straightened himself and then aimed for the door. Before he left, he turned to the Alpha bartender once more. "And congratulations to you both!"

"And to you, your son, and his mate!" Stephen yelled back.

The older Alpha's smile waned as his wolf struggled to find the same enthusiasm. But now wasn't the time for feelings. Now was the time for success.

A long winding road served as the portal which led to a whole different world. The asphalt was black and wet with the remnants of a quiet storm. Soon, the unsuspecting valley was going to be the same. Mountain Sound needed no explanation on what it was. It was everything Tauris City was not: desolate, quiet, simplistic, and void of everything Stephen knew. One year ago, the Alpha could have described Brooks Haven Penitentiary in the exact same way. But the mountain town was also different in the most important way: it was freedom. He was no longer a prisoner of the system, and he was no longer a prisoner of himself.

As he drove to higher elevation, nerves started rising in his stomach. What did he do once he got there? What did he do once he left? Everything was different now. For most of his life, he knew exactly what was coming ahead: arguments, disappointment, near-misses, and obstacles which became harder and harder to face. Then, for a decade, everything was decided for him. Now, he had the ability to do what he wanted when he wanted. The best part of it all—he didn't have to do it alone. Stephen had a Fated Mate at home. Together, they were raising a Type 4 Alpha pup who represented the one thing he never thought he'd have again: hope. The pup had his entire life ahead of him and Stephen couldn't wait.

Finally, the long grasses cleared, and some form of civilization came through. A large building complete with holding vessels sat near the water's edge. Stephen had heard a small resort town existed behind the brewery itself, but it wasn't visible from his location. Perhaps a different day, he'd venture in and see what was there, but that wasn't the reason for today's long trek up the mountain. Today was for one person and one person only. It wasn't for Oliver, it wasn't for Alexander, it wasn't for his parents, and it wasn't for himself:

"Okay. Let's say after you get your precious emblem on your bike, you got enough cash in your pocket to start over, your bag packed, and no worries left to follow you. Where do you go?" Warren laid on his bed and held his head up with his arms. Across the room, he eyed his brother who was indeed packing for his farewell journey out of his parents' grasp.

A teenage Stephen stood there and shrugged his shoulders. "I don't know where I'll end up. That's why they call it in an adventure." He roamed through several drawers, picking out his favorite shirts. It was beginning to dawn on him just how much he couldn't pack. His bag and his bike would only hold so much. He bit his thumbnail as he stood there contemplating.

Warren rolled his eyes. "I didn't ask you where you'd end up or what your final goal was. I asked you: once you get on your bike, where will you go? Gray City?"

Stephen raspberried. "Ain't no way I'm going to another large city which is just as pompous and arrogant as this one. I need a place where people take it slow and don't worry about racing to the next big thing and barreling over the person next to them to get it."

The young Omega shook his head. "I know this will sound hard to believe, but if you were to slow down yourself and actually look at the world around you, you'd find there are people here who do that too. You don't need to escape to a mountain town forever to get it."

The Alpha looked back at his brother. His face said it all: he didn't want him to leave. The thought of never coming home to see his brother didn't sit well. Before it became too heavy, he switched thoughts. "How about a visit then?"

Warren brightened up. "And not forever?"

"Yes, not forever."

The young Omega sat up with a new optimistic view. Maybe his brother wasn't going to be gone forever. Maybe time just had to pass a little longer. Maybe life just had to happen a little more before he realized what was there. After all, nothing ends. It all transforms. "A visit is good. But you still didn't answer me."

"You just cannot let this go, can you?" Stephen stared back in disbelief. His younger brother's face dimmed at the light-hearted criticism. Thus, the Alpha's wolf finally relented and removed his teeth. He exhaled as he walked over and sat on the bed next to him. "Okay..." he rubbed his chin as he organized his thoughts, "if I was to go anywhere, I'd go to ... Mountain Sound."

The Omega searched his brain for a logical reasoning. "You'd run away ... to a brewery?"

Stephen rubbed his head. "No, it's not 'running away.' It's a ... homecoming or rebirth. The opportunity to do it all again the right way. And no, I'm not talking about going to the brewery. I'm not defining my life's success based on going on their guided tour." The Alpha stuck out his tongue which made his younger brother laugh.

"Why Mountain Sound then? There's nothing up there. When you're standing on the edge of a cliff looking down into the valley and the city, how do you know you've 'made it'?"

That allowed Stephen to really consider what he was trying to sell to Warren. Now, he understood the words held water and really meant something. And not just to his brother but also for himself. The haze was thick as he begged for the right words to say. And then, finally, the gray skies cleared, and he knew exactly what the answer was. He snapped his fingers. "You wanna know how you know you've 'made it'? Here's how: When you go to Mountain Sound, find the lake. The lake stands on the edge of a cliff that peers over the valley. You can see everything from there—the entire city of Tauris. Look back down and see just how small it is. When you can look at it and say 'It's not the biggest place in the world but it's the most important place in the world to me'? That's when you've made it. When you can say 'I can't wait to be there with the people I want to be there with and there's no place I'd rather be.' That's when you've made it. And when you're up there looking down and feel like you already miss it and know you can go back whenever you want—that's when you've made it."

Warren looked into his brother's eyes and saw the passion in them. For a brief single moment, he saw Stephen as the wolf-descendent free of all the stress and worry he possessed now. It was the brother he remembered when he was a lot younger. It comforted him that, even though it was brief, it meant his true wolf was still there, and it wasn't gone. The hate, the hurt, the criticism and sarcasm, it was all just a front. His brother was still in there. But, right now, it was here to stay. Warren understood that. "I guess that means this won't happen tomorrow?" he muttered.

Stephen groaned. "Unfortunately, no. But I'm telling you, Warren. When I make it, you'll be the first one to know. I promise."

Carved into the side of the mountain was a small lake. It gave no indication just how deep it was. The crystal-clear water at the edge faded into a dark gray blue, matching the hue in the sky as the clouds casted over every inch of the horizon it could find. In the distance, thunder rolled down the mountain and into the valley, kicking up a light breeze to go with it. The wind rustled through the trees which caused Stephen to look up and locate a traveled path to the edge of the cliff.

Once he felt himself getting close to the edge, he closed his eyes and took a deep breath. His mind told him to open his eyes, but his body refused to listen. The thought of his own prophecy he once uttered to Warren being nothing but a desperate grasp at happiness frightened him. He didn't know what his reaction would be if it was nothing than a foolish fantasy—didn't want to know. The Alpha clenched his fists and gave a guttural roar down the valley as he began to regret ever venturing up the mountain in the first place. Stephen prayed to Wolf-God for the agony deep inside to just be over with—to end its relentless onslaught. But still, he refused to open his eyes.

Deep inside his soul, the inner wolf nudged him with his snout and clawed at him with its large paw. The Alpha whimpered as he dared to think he could do this moment alone. And then, a new sensation. He thought about South Street with Bruce, James, and Eric, the famous trio sweating out the night and conquering it one patron at a time with a cold drink a sharp wit. Next, his Veo Marlon and his Sur Kane grateful every time he showed up at his childhood home to tell him all the new stories and updates on his life. And finally, he remembered Alexander, his Fated Mate and Oliver, his precious pup waiting for him in their home. Every thought was a reminder he wasn't alone.

Slowly, he opened his eyes and saw the valley and the city below. The vast horizon made them both look small and frozen in time. Nothing moved; nothing made a sound. All the fanfare and all the focus of what Tauris was and what it represented was gone. There was no Rank, there was no Status, and there were no mistakes—not from here. All he had left were the people in his life who made the city exactly what he wanted. *That* was the perfection. *That* was exactly what he waited for all his life.

"I did it, Warren. I made it."

I hope you enjoyed the story of Stephen and Alexander. If you are reading this in chronological order, Roman's Reckoning is an immediate continuation. And for those who have been patiently waiting, the finale to Roman and Mikael's story is coming soon in "Aria's Arrival."

BOOK CLUB QUESTIONS

1. How do you feel about Alexander's conviction that Stephen is not his Fated Mate? Based on the events which unfolded in *Stephen's Second Chance: Part I*, do you feel Alexander's continued support of Stephen's presence is due to a possible Fated Mate connection or just the courteous actions of a good friend?

2. Zayne Desarae is first introduced in *Mikael's Moment* as Roman's future colleague during their clinicals. In this prequel, Zayne is featured as a young medical student who is among the members of the research laboratory's tour group. What do you think could be reasoning behind his very direct criticism of Dr. Birowack's work?

3. Warren Matheson, Stephen's younger brother, makes his first appearance here in a memory flashback. Describe the Matheson family dynamic with all four family members present.

4. There is a minor standoff between Alexander and Stephen regarding the Alpha's condition and return-to-work status. How do you feel about the outcome of that event? What role do you feel Rank played in who won?

5. Raymond puts Stephen in what appears to be a no-win situation which has the potential to destroy his efforts to become a new person since getting out of prison. How much responsibility does Stephen have for his actions, considering he is coerced into the actions he commits soon after?

6. In a memory flashback, we get a glimpse into Stephen's connection to Raymond before Warren died. The discussion includes commentary regarding the downfall of the Rank of Alpha. Considering the benefits, dominance, and power which naturally go with the rank of Alpha, do you feel Stephen's opinions on these negatives are warranted?

7. The same standoff in Chapter 02 between Alexander and Stephen regarding the Alpha's condition and return-to-work status comes into play again, but this time with Sean advocating on Alexander's behalf. Discuss the professional and personal reasons Sean has to stop Stephen from working at South Street Tavern. What role do you think Sean has played thus far in their relationship? What do you think he will do in the future?

8. Sean explicitly tells Alexander why he doesn't want Stephen to continue working at the bar. What do you think of Alexander's response, and what reasons do you think Alexander has when it comes to Stephen's future employment status? What do you think of Alexander's character because of it—especially when it comes to his personal relationship with Sean?

9. When Daniel visits Stephen at his home, Stephen has several poignant moments of self-reflection. Which of the reflections do you find most important? How do you think it will play out in the future?

10. Sean is very territorial over Alexander and their relationship in a heated discussion right before a major secret is revealed. Is Sean's reaction to Alexander's lack of interest in him justified? Does your initial answer change after Sean reveals his secret?

11. After Alexander comes to terms that he is indeed going through a heat, his attitude and interest toward Stephen conveniently grows. How do you judge Alexander regarding his heat and its influence to give in to the convictions Stephen has had since moment one? If Alexander's heat hadn't triggered, do you think the same outcome would have happened?

12. What modern, real-world connections can you make when it comes to Stephen being an Alpha who has sexually claimed multiple Omegas, but no Omega has ever claimed him? Discuss the possible reasons why Stephen has operated this way, not only on a personal level, but also a societal level.

13. In a very dominating Alpha move, Stephen forces Alexander to finally reveal what his true thoughts are on being his Fated Mate while Alexander is suffering due to his heat. Is Stephen warranted in using this strategy against someone he claims means so much to him? With Alexander being so closed off with his emotions up to this point, does Stephen have any other choice?

14. Eric berates and criticizes Alexander for several unilateral decisions he made at the bar in what is supposed to be a business partnership between the two of them. Eric uses those criticisms as his driving force to make a business deal behind Alexander's back. Were you surprised with all the examples Eric came up with for how Alexander wasn't being a team player when Alexander himself has claimed many times it has been

everyone else working against him as an Omega bar owner? Why or why not?

15. After Stephen lists several examples of how selling the bar could be beneficial, Alexander becomes irate and reverts to his rhetoric on the disparagement between the rank of Alpha and Omega. What approach, if any, do you think Stephen could have taken for Alexander to not fall back into his safety of becoming so defensive?

16. During the conversation with his brother Jin, Alexander concludes his lack of self-worth has contributed to how he's acted professionally when it comes to his business. How do you think that's played out in his romantic relationships?

17. What responsibility does Alexander have to tell Stephen he is the father of his unborn pup? Should it have taken the scheme for him to finally say it?

18. In *Stephen's Second Chance: Part I*, it is revealed Robert, Alexander's Alpha father, is having an affair with a younger man named Carey. Now, in Part II of the story, it is revealed that Nathan, Alexander's Omega father, is very aware of the infidelity. What are your thoughts on Nathan not giving his mate Robert an ultimatum to stop his infidelity in order for them to stay together? How do you think that decision has played out in how Robert treats his sons?

19. All wolf descendants in this Omegaverse have one ideal in common: to survive and preserve the pack. Do you think this has any influence on Robert, an Alpha father, trying to control so many aspects of Alexander's life since he is an Omega?

20. What are your thoughts on Stephen's Alpha father, Kane, regarding his overall strict philosophies in law, rules, and guidelines, considering the lengths he's gone to help Stephen evade legal consequences?

21. Do you believe Sean's sincerity when he says he once had genuine feelings for Alexander considering the conspiracy he revealed about himself in Chapter 04? Why or why not?

22. Stephen thanks Alexander for giving him a "second chance" to be together. Do you think Alexander should be equally thankful that Stephen is doing the same for him? Why or Why not?

23. In *Stephen's Second Chance: Part I*, Stephen is denied the opportunity to work at the auto shop. Do you think Stephen had to lose that opportunity in order for him to meet Alexander in the first place? Or do you believe that because they are Fated Mates, their meeting was destined regardless of where Stephen gained employment after his incarceration?

24. The death of Stephen's younger brother Warren is never fleshed out in a complete scene. Would you have preferred this event to be fully described in a flashback scene, or do you think the story benefits from it being left out? How do you think it would have changed the dynamic or tone of the story if it was included?

25. The final scene includes a moment in which Stephen gives himself a second chance to go to Mountain Sound—a promise he made to Warren right before his tragic death. Up to this point, Stephen experiences several second chances with himself and with other characters throughout the book. Which second chance do you feel is the most significant to the story and why?

AUTHOR BIO:

Lucas LaMont lives near the mountains of Colorado and has been a storyteller since childhood. Throughout the years, he has dabbled in fiction and poetry, and in his adult writing, most of his focus has been in gay fiction. Recently, he discovered the Omegaverse genre and is obsessed with it! During the Covid pandemic, he found his favorite series to read: *The Adrien English Mysteries* by Josh Lanyon (But he is very much a fan of several noteworthy Omegaverse authors). When he's not writing and reading, Lucas loves traveling to fabulous Las Vegas to gamble or staying near the rustic lakes of Minnesota to go fishing. The goal of his writing has always been to focus on the power of relationships and the journey they take. You can find Lucas Lamont on Facebook, Twitter, Instagram, and Wix.

THE CHRONICLES OF FATE:

(IN ORDER OF RELEASE)
Book #1: Roman's Reckoning (Fated Type 6: Part I)
Book #2: Mikael's Moment (Fated Type 6: Part II)
Book #3: Stephen's Second Chance – Part I (Renaissance: Part I)
Book #4: Stephen's Second Chance – Part II (Renaissance: Part II)
Book #5: Aria's Arrival (Fated Type 6: Part III) [Coming Soon!]

(IN ORDER OF CHRONOLOGY)
Book #3: Stephen's Second Chance – Part I (Renaissance: Part I)
Book #4: Stephen's Second Chance – Part II (Renaissance: Part II)
Book #1: Roman's Reckoning (Fated Type 6: Part I)
Book #2: Mikael's Moment (Fated Type 6: Part II)
Book #5: Aria's Arrival (Fated Type 6: Part III) [Coming Soon!]

Discover more at
4HorsemenPublications.com

10% off using HORSEMEN10